Boudica's Daughter

Dear Jillian,

Enjoy the read.

All the best,

Sam Hutchins

Boudica's Daughter

Sam F. Hutchins

Matador
9 Priory Business Park,
Wistow Road, Kibworth Beauchamp,
Leicestershire, LE8 0RX
Tel: 0116 279 2299
Email: books@troubador.co.uk
Web: www.troubador.co.uk/matador
Twitter: @matadorbooks

ISBN 978 183859 358 2

British Library Cataloguing in Publication Data.
A catalogue record for this book is available from the British Library.

Maps©Eric Frénée
Book cover design Chelsea Taylor

Printed and bound in Great Britain by 4edge Limited
Typeset in 12pt Adobe Garamond Pro by Troubador Publishing Ltd, Leicester, UK

Matador is an imprint of Troubador Publishing Ltd

For my mother

In memory of
Pam, Carol, Heather

Extent of the Roman Empire in 60 AD

Roman Britannia – 60 AD

Caledonia

Tribal boundaries of
early Roman Britain
AD 60-1

Carveti

Mare germanicum

Brigantes   Parisi

The Morimaru Sea

Ynis Môn   Decangli

Hibernia

Hibernicus
Sea

Lindum
Coritani

Venta Icenorum

Ordovices

Mandvessedum

Iceni

Cornovii

Clac-nyn   Saham Toney

Catuvellauni   Fison Way

Demetae   Dobunni

Verulamium

Trinovantes

Silures

Londinium   Camulodunum

Atrebates   Cantiaci

Belgae

Dumnonii   Isca

Durotriges   Regnenses

Oceanus
Britannicus

Oceanus
Atlanticus

Historical Note

Truly there is nothing more obscure, more uncertain, or unknown than the affairs of the Brittons from the beginning; partly because the Chronicles, if there were any, were clean destroyed.

Polydore Vergil's English History, *1534.*

W E HAVE NO BRITISH SOURCES FOR BOUDICA'S revolt against Rome. Our information comes from two Roman writers, Tacitus and Dio Cassius, and from archaeological sources. We know that south-west Britain was conquered by the Roman Emperor, Claudius in AD 43, and that he established his provincial capital at Camulodonum (Colchester), land which had traditionally belonged to the Trinovante tribe. A number of tribes immediately entered into a treaty relationship with Rome in which their king, or queen, became a 'client' sovereign of the Roman emperor. This meant that they retained their own council without a Roman military presence. However, it also meant the end of their dynastic rule in as much as their tribal territories would be integrated into the Roman Empire when they died. The Iceni tribe in East Anglia became such a client kingdom of Rome.

In 47 AD the Roman governor of the province tightened control over Britannia by disarming all the tribes, including those friendly to Rome. Part of the Iceni tribe did revolt against such measures, and this was due, in part, to hatred of Britannia's collaboration with an occupying force, but their king, Prasutagus retained control of the Iceni, and the client agreement with Rome remained in place. Two years after this, Camulodonum also became a colony for retired legionaries which led to a lot of land seizures. Many Trinovante tribesmen were turned out of their land and holdings. In 50 AD a Roman commercial town was established at Londinium (London) by merchants, financiers, tradesmen. Because of its estuary and deep tidal reach, it was also important to the Roman army as a military trading station and supply base.

Nero became Emperor of Rome in 54 AD. When Prasutagus died in 60 AD his wife, Boudica and daughters were brutally treated when their territory was taken over by Rome. At the same time, on the other side of Britannia, the Roman governor and his forces had invaded Ynis Môn (Anglesey) which was an island base for refugees and the Druid priesthood. There were a lot of discontented tribes who were ready to join Boudica in her uprising against the Roman occupation of their lands. Boudica's rebellion against colonial occupation is famous now because it was led by a warrior queen, one of only a few women in British history to lead an army into battle. This achievement is celebrated by the English and the Welsh with a statue of her and her two daughters outside the Houses of Parliament in London and in the Civic Hall of Cardiff. Whilst the former ironically celebrates Britain's replacement of the Roman Empire on the world stage, the latter testifies to a mother's instinct to protect her daughters from the menaces of imperial occupation.

Due to a difference in spellings in the ancient texts, Boudica has had many names in the past, such as Boadicea in English, Buddug in Welsh and Boudain in Celtic; a word which signifies victory. She has also been known as Voadicea, Bonduca, Bunduca and Voada. I have chosen to call her Voada although Boudica has now been accepted as the correct naming of the woman who defied the power of Rome. Over the centuries, many writers have chosen to write of Boudica's story, each claiming the veracity of their work. My story is a historical fiction; I claim nothing more. Having read all the known chronicles myself, I can only repeat Raphael Holinshed's own apology for his work:

I have collected (the history) out of many and sundry authors, in whom what contrarieties, negligence, and rashness sometimes is found in their reports, I leave to the discretion of those that have perused their works: for my part, I have in things doubtful rather chosen to show the diversities of their writings, than by overruling them, and using a peremptory censure, to frame them to agree to my liking: leaving it nevertheless to each man's judgement, to control them as he see cause.

Holinshed's Chronicles, 1587

But long ere this Bunduca Britonnesse
Her mighty host against my bulwarks brought,
Bunduca, that victorious conqueress,
That lifting up her brave heroic thought
Above women's weakness, with the Romans fought,
Fought, and in field against them thrice prevailed:
Yet was she foiled, when as she me assailed.

Edmund Spenser, The Ruines of Time, 1591, Lines 106-112

Tribal characters

Voada – Queen of the Iceni. Later called The Boudica, military leader of the tribes.

Prasutagus – King of the Iceni

Caitlyn – eldest daughter to Voada and Prasutagus

Keara – youngest daughter to Voada and Prasutagus

Galdus – cousin to Caitlyn and Keara, and heir to the Caledonian throne

Greer – head druid of the Iceni

Rory – Iceni military commander and bodyguard to the Iceni household

Corbreid – King of Caledonia and brother to Voada

Cartimandua – Queen of Brigantia

Vellocatus – Cartimandua's husband

Venutius – King of the Carvetii, and Cartimandua's first husband

Dubnov – leader of the Trinovantes

Blair – son of an Iceni saddle maker at Saham Toney

Diodorus – Greek tutor in the Iceni royal family

Rhonda – Iceni druidess

Sacrovar – Head druid on Ynys Môn

Taran – a bardic druid from Ynys Môn

Tremayn – a prince of the Dumnonii

Zethar – Tremayn's brother

Cogidubnus – King of the Regni

Amena – Caitlyn's serving woman

Roman characters

Suetonius – Governor of Britannia (58 – 62 AD), Commander-in-Chief of the Roman army in Britannia, and legate of legion XIV

Catus Decianus – Procurator of Britannia

Vettius – chief Roman law officer in Britannia

Crassus – older brother to Vettius, magistrate in Volubilis, Mauretania in North Africa

Marius – tribune, based in London. From a rich, senatorial family in Rome

Flavius – senior tribune of legion XIV

Cassius – prefect of legion XIV

Bolanus – legate of legion XX

Trajanus – senior tribune of legion XX

Mark Anthony – prefect of legion XX

Cerialis – legate of legion IX

Petro – prefect of legion IX

Gaius Marius – legate of legion II

Agricola – senior tribune of legion II

Poenius Postumus – prefect of legion II

Spurius – soldier based at Camulodonum, the Roman colony of veterans

Titus – decurion cavalry officer, a Baquates tribesman from Mauretania

Zia – Titus's slave

Aelius – a cavalryman in Titus's auxiliary

Junius – a businessman in Mauretania

Polyclitus – a freedman and one of the chief advisors to the Roman Emperor, Nero

Prologue

Venta Icenorum – 52 AD

THE EAST WIND SWEPT ACROSS THE FENLANDS, bending the reeds so harshly that it would break their music and drown them in the marshes. Overnight, the dull autumn weather had changed so that a granite sky now pressed heavily over the flat lands, and the cold, wet blasts of rain had driven the farm animals into their sheds and stables. The people were all indoors, and here and there wisps of smoke threaded themselves through the thatched roofs and were instantly sucked away by the hungry wind. Inside one roundhouse Keara was sitting cross-legged on a fleece of fur looking intently at the board game on the floor. A warm peat fire kept the damp air at bay, but not all the rain could be kept out. Her game player, a rugged old man, whose hut it was, had placed one or two pots on the floor to catch the dripping water.

'You must bring all your stones into your corner of the board,' the old man was telling her, 'and then bear them off before I am able to remove my own counters. It is a game of both strategy and luck, but more strategy than luck.'

Keara threw the dice, but still could not move her counter. The old man's counters occupied all the columns in his corner of the board so that Keara was blocked. Her dark jet stone sat on the bar in the middle of the board. Its polished surface flickered with tiny waves of light from the fire and drew them in. Greer frowned and pressed both his index fingers against his lips as though in thought. Howls of sound without and crackling flames within embraced images of Keara's face on the surface of the stone. Her head and hair seemed to roll in folds of light and darkness, and seconds passed before the child broke into Greer's silence, suddenly afraid of the game, 'What must I do?'

'What can she do?' It was a rhetorical question, barely uttered aloud. The man stirred himself. 'Yes, I have blocked my opponent's every move.' He tapped his fingers together slowly contemplating the small girl on the floor. Her hair had come loose and so she had tucked a few strands of it behind her ears in order to concentrate on the game; her concentration was intense, almost carved onto her forehead with her eyebrows pushed together and her mouth closed tight. Greer spoke again, 'Keara, you must now wait until I take my counters off the board, or until I make a false move.'

'I see, I see how it works,' the child cried in her excitement, not taking her eyes from the board, 'I have to wait until you move a counter and then I can move onto a column with only one of your stones on it.'

'But only if the dice let you.'

Keara's lips puckered as she focussed on the game. Greer had learnt to play it many, many years before on his travels in the East, and was now teaching it to the child in front of him: a dark-haired and thick-browed girl of nine. Muffled in his great cloak he threw his own dice and moved two counters. His white stones clicked on the wooden board making the others tremor. Outside a horse could be heard cantering into the muddied homestead. Greer shivered and threw a brick of peat onto the fire. In the failing light of the late afternoon, it seemed madness to be out in this rattling wind.

Some time later, the door was pulled open making the flames dance and buckle from the draught. Someone was holding the door open for another to enter. It closed behind him. On sight of the man, Keara immediately jumped up and grasped his arm, pulling him towards the fire. 'Father, Father, Greer has been teaching me how to play backgammon. Look, look at the board. There are so many pieces, but it is not that difficult. I can teach you afterwards and we can play.' There was no response from her father. He half-staggered towards the fire and then crumpled onto the rugs. Water trickled off his thighs and clothing forming small pools of dark patches around him.

'Light the lamps,' Greer said, turning sharply to Keara, and then he gripped the man's shoulders. 'My lord, Prasutagus. Tell me. What news did the horseman bring you?'

Keara obeyed Greer. She lit a taper from the fire and began to light the ceramic oil lamps in the room. The new light made the shadows cringe back against the wattle and daub walls and then settle along the skirting as though waiting to pounce. She sat down next to her father and looked at his anguished face which made her nervous. The corner of his mouth twitched. Then he rubbed his forehead with one hand before beginning, 'He is dead.' He stopped and looked at the ground.

Keara felt frightened by the immediate tension in the hut. Her father then repeated the same news in a flat, expressionless voice, 'He is dead. Taranis is dead.'

'It's not true,' Keara cried out contesting her father's ugly words, but the expression on his face told her that it was. She felt suddenly distressed by the look of pain on her father's face. 'Daddy, no, no. It's not true. I don't believe you.'

She thought back to the last image she would ever have of her brother and could remember her father's pride and her mother's fear the day he had left for Rome just the summer before. Taranis had felt no fear, just the joy and hubris of having been chosen by the Emperor himself for his schooling in Rome at the age of twelve. On the day of his departure, he had dressed as a Roman cavalryman and had cantered off with his Roman escort towards the coast where a galley had carried him away to Rome. She had felt resentful that day - resentful that he, as the son and heir to her father's crown, was to be educated in the great Roman capital and would learn to read like a scholar and fight like a legionary whilst she and her sister were left behind in the flat mud lands of Iceni. Yet, she had missed him. She had missed his teasing her, his playing with her, racing her on horseback, and even his fighting with her. She could not comprehend his death far away and alone in another land. His definitive loss was almost beyond her comprehension and she felt a chasm open up in front of her, a black hole of grief, fear and even anger. Her breath came in short, violent bites of air, 'I don't...'

Prasutagus grasped her flaying wrists before hissing into her face, 'It is true. It is true. Your brother is dead.'

'I... It...' She could not find the words and could not control the thick uneven sobs that stopped her breath. Her father took her shoulders and held her still. Even as she tried to pull away, he held her to him.

'Keara, it's true.' In a broken voice he added, 'Be still now. Cry my child, cry.' Holding her tightly to him, he seemed to pull strength from her. He found enough voice to turn to his Wise Man and ask, 'Greer, what does this mean for our tribe?'

'Are you sure of this news, my lord?'

'Yes, yes. The man carried a sealed message from the Emperor in Rome.'

'How did Taranis die?'

'Of the sweating fever this summer, along with thousands more.' There was a moment of pained silence before the king resumed, 'My poor child. I never should have agreed to this friendship with Rome. I never should have accepted that my child, my only son, should be educated in Rome.' He fell into a brooding silence.

Greer tried to rouse the king from his stupor. 'The world has changed Prasutagus. We had no choice but to become allies with Rome. Your son had to be sent to Rome in order to be educated in Roman ways, and it was in the best interests of your family and of the Emperor himself. One day Taranis would have returned to govern the Iceni Kingdom.'

'Yes, in the name of Rome,' Prasutagus cried.

'That was the peace agreement, and it is the Roman policy everywhere across the Empire. Please do not blame yourself. No one can read the future.'

'But I do blame myself. Taranis, Taranis, forgive me.' The king was speaking to both Greer and to his dead son. 'What does this mean... for my people? ... Taranis was my heir.'

Greer hesitated. 'Sire, I know your pain. I have known Taranis since he was a young child. We will mourn his loss. But look at your child, Keara. She suffers too, as does your daughter, Caitlyn, as must Voada. Where are they now?'

'The Queen is in the great hall with Caitlyn. They heard the news with me. But I need to know from you what I must do before I face my people.' His eyes pleaded for help.

Greer held his coarse greying beard in his fingers as he tried to grasp the full implications of this sad news. 'Caitlyn is your eldest daughter. She is now your heir and must become Queen of the Iceni after you.'

'But she is a girl. Roman law, and our client agreement, will not allow her to govern,' Prasutagus protested. He suddenly coughed and held his fist to his chest, rubbing it for relief.

Greer frowned. 'You may have other sons still. If you don't, you do have Caitlyn. She will be a good leader for your people despite Roman law.'

Prasutagus shook his head in dull protest and groaned, 'You are right: you do not know the future. Even a druid such as yourself cannot read the future. But I see it: a place of desolation and loss. A place of madness. Oh, what have I done? What have I done? What have I done?'

I

A comet was seen in the sky that summer, appearing in the north and then travelling westwards over several months before curving south and disappearing. It was no ordinary fire in the sky for it looked like two moons joined together and had surely come to announce the passing of a king or the death of an emperor. Whatever its portent it could only mean one thing – a storm was coming.

LONDINIUM – 60 AD

VETTIUS, THE GOVERNOR'S LAW OFFICER IN Britannia, had been sent over from Rome to represent the Emperor's juristic matters in the province. He was a thickset man with dark, oiled hair and a heavy ring on one hand. That ring now clinked against the bronze beaker as he replaced it on the Procurator's desk before speaking, 'Catus, why have you called me into your office?'

The Procurator laid down the writing tablet he had been reading and leant back comfortably against the warm furs of his chair. 'As you administer the Governor's legal and administrative duties in his absence you need to know what actions I will soon have to take, and what consequences there may be.' Catus pushed his large lips out and raised his eyebrows, waiting for a response, an exclamation of curiosity from his colleague. Vettius surveyed the ample figure of the man across the desk from him, a man already past his prime with greying hair and crow's feet around his eyes: an unseductive but sedulous pen pusher.

'So?' Vettius opened his hand and waved it towards Catus inviting him to continue. 'What is going on?'

'I have heard that King Prasutagus is dying.'

'Dying?'

'Yes. He has the wasting disease and is constantly spitting blood. From all accounts he can hardly breathe now.'

'Well, I don't need to know all the details, but you would like to discuss his will and the client agreement between the Iceni and Rome, I imagine?'

'Yes. Of course I understand the client agreement, the political and legal document signed by the two sovereign powers. My job is only to determine the taxes, call in loans, and pay wages, but soon I shall have to do the paperwork when the political status of the Iceni kingdom changes. And Suetonius is now in his winter quarters on the borderlands. However, Prasutagus's will poses a dilemma. In his will he leaves only half of his lands to the emperor and the other half to his wife and daughters...'

'That's enough,' Vettius interrupted. 'Prasutagus's will has no legal standing under Roman law. He may think to protect his family's wealth under Celtic law, but the client agreement has more political power. When the King of the Iceni dies, his kingdom and his lands will be incorporated into the Roman Empire as was originally agreed to, and signed, by King Prasutagus. So, if the king's wife tries to keep control of all, or part of, the kingdom then the law is very clear: she may risk flogging, even execution, but, if it does come to conflict and rebellion there is the military recourse.'

'But Suetonius and most of our army are in Cymru and, though I am not expecting any trouble, there was a small uprising a number of years ago when Prasutagus was named King.'

'There is another legal sanction then, one that could be applied at the first sign of trouble and which would stop any royal uprising from getting started.'

'And what is that?'

Vettius inhaled a short breath before replying, 'There is a precedent for such a sanction. If an uprising were to involve female subjects, as might be the case here, then the two maids could be unmade. Little matter who does it since it is a symbolic move. Personally, women are not in my line of interest, but the significance of rape is clear: it ends their dynastic rule. It also means that if, at a later date, their resistance continues these women could be executed. Under Roman law you cannot execute a virgin.'

Catus crossed his hands on his stomach, contemplating the past agitations of the Iceni tribe, before looking up at Vettius again. 'They were given Roman citizenship when the client agreement was signed and have since been introduced to Roman civilisation and education. Let us hope they understand the rudiments of our laws enough to see the precedence of the client agreement over the king's will.' He paused a moment, agitated by the implications of such a conflict of interest. 'You see the Iceni kingdom is one of the richest in Britannia. It brings a lot of money into Nero's coffers, and it needs to stay that way. It's not just a question of integrating the Iceni lands into the Empire, but of ensuring a smooth political and economic transition. I have to make sure of that and, with the Governor absent, I also have to keep the peace.'

He might look like a bureaucrat, Vettius was thinking, but the man facing him was also known for his economic shrewdness.

'Why has Rome invested so much in Iceni territory over the years? I know a number of senators have funded joint ventures, but the land there is so flat and wet. What could it possibly have?'

The Procurator poured some more wine into his glass. 'Would you like some, Vettius?'

'No, thank you; I am happy with my hot brew.'

'Have a date then?' Here, Catus picked up a small bowl of stuffed dates and offered them to him. Vettius felt obliged to take one. He held it up to the light and then bit into it. The soft, and still warm, almond and pepper stuffing was a fine complement to the sweet and salty coating of the date.

'Mmm,' he conceded, 'This is quite delectable.' He reached for another. 'Where did you find this recipe?'

'The chefs here use Apicius's recipe book. But the salt comes from the Iceni lands. That's what the Iceni have: salt; the means of preserving food and a primary necessity.'

'Just salt?'

'No. Their wetlands are also excellent for transport, which reduces the costs of imports and exports between the hinterland and the continent. They also have cattle and pigs for meat, and sheep for their wool. The Iceni are a chief exporter of cloth, leather, ponies and hunting dogs. They also produce a lot of bronze goods, such as the beaker you are drinking from, as well as a fine range of jewellery much admired in Rome. Shall I go on?'

'No,' Vettius laughed. 'I am convinced, but we also have the huge salt industries in Mauretania and Numidia you know.'

'African salt supplies the southern parts of the Empire. The white gold of the Iceni supplies the needs in the north. As you can understand, there is a lot of money in play here. The Iceni contribute to Rome's stable economy, but they are still a barbaric and wild people. I much prefer the cosmopolitan life of Londinium.'

'Is that why you have your offices here?' Vettius enquired.

'It may only be a trading post, but it is better placed for communication and is far more attractive to financial backers than Iceni lands ever will be, especially since I have a garrison troop here. Already the city is full of merchants, following in the steps of the army. This is where all the luxuries of the Empire are to be found. And my home comforts.' Catus put his feet up on a small footstool and helped himself to a date. For a moment they both listened to the sounds of building works in the basilica. Some tiling was being finished in the forum, and the fresh smell of paint was in the air. Outside they could also hear the dull thud of carts on the streets and the call of street vendors in the cold, winter air.

'This is my last posting,' Catus mused aloud, 'and I don't want any trouble. I only hope that there will be no conflict in the province when the moment of Prasutagus's death finally arrives and I have to collect Rome's due.'

VENTA ICENORUM

Death.

Death clung to him in a fine veil of glistening moisture. It clung to his skin and to his hair. It clung to his clothes and to his bones. But it was in his eyes that death glared back out at the king's family. Voada and her two daughters sat by the king's bed, grieving, holding hands, and anxious. Prasutagus lay on soft fur coverings with colourful embroidered cushions at his head. His youngest daughter, Keara looked up at the wattle screen around his bed and at the rich wall hangings that decorated the large roundhouse. She found it difficult to bring her eyes back to the body of her father until the central fire crackled suddenly and one of the burnt logs crumbled into ashes.

Her mother began to recite a poem of departure to aid her husband's soul on its journey back to the earth,

Death is but a time of waiting between waves
A time of rest and peace before a new journey begins
It is a moment of reflection, of clarity and stillness
But it is also a moment of loss and withdrawal
From family, friends, places known and loved
Until the land returns and we are reawakened on the
beach of life.

Voada closed her husband's eyes, placing a golden aureus on each eyelid. One coin showed her husband's head as king of the Iceni tribe whilst the other showed a rearing horse, symbol of the Iceni's power. Then she squeezed her daughters' hands and smiled faintly. 'Your father is at peace now. We must reassure our people and make arrangements for his funeral.'

As they stood up, Keara wrapped her arms around her mother's shoulders, casting a sideways look at her father's body. It lay straight and empty on the fur-lined bed. It was no longer her father; he was gone, but she felt a fleeting presence of him still in the room, just a moment before he took wing for the Otherworld.

'*Slán abhaile dadaidh,*' she whispered.

'Your father will travel home safely.' Voada smiled, stroking Keara's long, dark hair.

'What will happen to Caitlyn now?' Keara asked, worried about her sister's future, and her own.

Her mother pushed her gently away, holding her at arm's length so that her two daughters stood side by side and she could speak to them both. They were of similar heights, with the same build, yet they were very different, Voada thought. Caitlyn was the *pure beauty* her Celtic name signified, with fair, soft features, whilst Keara's looks were heavier and darker. This was possibly due to her thicker brows and the brooding frown she often wore.

'You heard what your father said before… before he died,' Voada began. 'He sent the legal documents to Londinium a few days ago. We must now send a rider to the Procurator, Catus Decianus in Londinium, announcing his death.'

'But what about our people, our lands and Caitlyn? She can't be queen over half of everything. And who decides which half she will rule?'

Voada held her hands to her head a moment. 'I know, I know, but your father thought it was best, and the only way to protect the Iceni clan from Nero's greed. As a client king of the Emperor Nero, our lands and tribe would normally be integrated into the Roman Empire upon his death. That is the Roman arrangement with all the client kings in the Empire. Your father thought that by leaving half of everything to Nero in his will, it would be enough to pay the death duties and satisfy Nero's greed. Hopefully, Nero will let Caitlyn become queen in her own right and keep peace in the kingdom.'

'But they would have to name a Roman administrator for Nero's half of our lands,' Keara interrupted. 'Our people would never accept that.'

'They would if Nero allowed me to rule.' Caitlyn, only a little older than Keara, spoke for the first time. Her face was as pale as her father's in the dim candlelight of the richly decorated chamber.

'And the Romans would never accept that,' Keara scoffed. 'Why not? Because of Roman law: women cannot hold public office.'

'But I am inheriting rule over the Iceni. Look at Cartimandua: she is High Queen of the Brigantes in the North.'

'Yes, but she is a client queen. Once she dies, the Brigantes are integrated into the Roman Empire. There will be no king or queen after her. It's a good thing she has no children, but her people will rebel against the Roman occupation of their territory.'

Voada frowned suddenly. 'Stop this at once. This is no time for politics or disputes. We must wait for an answer from Londinium. For now, we have to make arrangements for the funeral and send out messengers to all the clans and Roman officials to attend the funeral rites. At least your father had a good life and, despite the final pains of illness, he died in his own bed, with his family by his side.'

The two sisters looked down on their father's face: rugged and worn by the winds that blew harshly across their flat-water lands on the eastern coast of Britannia, but it was a face that was seemingly at peace. Keara thought back to those rare, but precious moments with her father, many years before he fell ill, when he had taken her, Caitlyn and their brother, Taranis on hunting expeditions with the other Iceni warriors. She and Taranis had loved hunting the wild boar with him, something that Caitlyn had always hated because it was dangerous. And whilst Caitlyn had enjoyed fishing with their father, Keara had hated it because it was so long, boring and malodorous. Yet it was then, she remembered now, that Prasutagus had taught her all the names and habits of the birds living in the wetlands, such as the long-legged black and white stork and the rather thickset and secretive bittern. But her favourite wader had always been the black-tailed godwit with its long, pink bill and white rump, perhaps because the female, though lacking its partner's colours, was the larger of the two. She felt something being pushed into her fist: it was a linen kerchief from Caitlyn. She wiped her eyes quickly, but couldn't bring herself to look at her sister. A sudden feeling of resentment crossed her heart:

Caitlyn had now risen above her. Henceforth, she would be dependent on her sister's handouts. She did not know then that Caitlyn's queenship was a poisoned chalice.

Outside the roundhouse, Rory and Greer waited patiently under the eaves for Voada to appear. Cold in the December frost they stood still, with only their breaths floating in frozen clouds around them. They made a strange contrast, side by side, in front of the closed entrance. The former, a burly Iceni warrior, was well wrapped in his dark tunic and fur cloak. He held his arms crossed on his chest as he stared out across the village and the low lands beyond; uncommunicative at the best of times, he was now preoccupied with the unknown future, and did not speak to Greer. The druid was a little taller than Rory, but was thin and grey: grey hair, tied at the back with dark ribbon, grey eyes and skin. He held his hands behind his back and was staring down at the hem of his woollen gown in the sodden earth. He, too, was lost in his thoughts and knew that he would have to advise Voada well in the coming days and weeks, although she would probably listen more to Rory's demands for action. Rory and his men had hated being disarmed by the Romans more than ten years before when the new Governor of the Province had wanted to tighten control over the Britons, even over its allies, the Iceni; he still hated it.

A young man was walking towards them: Galdus, by the looks of him, Greer surmised. He still walked and dressed like a Caledonian prince, despite the Roman education he had received with his cousins in Prasutagus's household. The young man nodded at Rory, but smiled at Greer with his clear blue eyes framed by a head of fair hair. 'Can I go in now?' he asked the druid.

'No, you still have to wait. The Queen and your cousins are laying out the body of the King. They have not called anyone yet.' However, at that moment the wooden door opened inwards and in a low tone Keara called to her cousin. 'Galdus, come in. We have finished now, and you too, Rory and Greer.'

Rory called to another man to replace him before he stooped to enter the low doorway behind the other two men. Keara's knuckles clenched tightly on the dark hazel planks of the door as she pushed it closed after them, and then went to stand by her cousin's side. It was dim in here after the brightness of the winter sunlight, but warmer too, and sweeter. A huge fire now burned sluggishly in the middle of the hut, along with several beeswax candles which added a light scent of honey to the room. Keara took Galdus's cold hand and led him to the royal bed against the wall. He knelt down respectfully by the king's body. Rory joined him, but Greer remained standing at the foot of the bed. He glanced briefly at Voada who nodded to him to join her by the fire.

'We must have a meeting of the Council,' Voada began, 'and name Caitlyn Queen as quickly as possible.'

'The Romans will not accept her as such: it was never part of the client agreement.'

'But my husband made a will, a Roman will.'

'I know.' Greer smiled grimly, looking into the dancing flames before them as though trying to read the augurs. 'But Nero is greedy, as is his Procurator, Catus. These are troubled times and I do not know what is in the future for us. If I seek advice from the Druid Council on Ynys Môn, they will tell you to rebel against the Roman occupation of your lands which is what all the young warriors of the clans want to do. Even Galdus's father, your brother and King of the Caledonian clans calls for the southern tribes to rebel. He is only blocked by Cartimandua's confederation, which holds the lands between the Northern and Hibernicus Seas, between us and those who want to remain with Rome.'

'Not all of them,' Voada interrupted.

'Venutius and his small Carvetii tribe have loyal sympathies to Britannia, but very little power, even if he is married, was married,' Greer corrected himself, 'to Cartimandua. Invite him to the funeral. Perhaps he will offer safe passage for the Caledonians to travel south through his lands or help them pass along the coast.'

'We must draw up the guest list at the council, today if possible, and send out riders tomorrow, but Venutius cannot come. He is virtually an outlaw since his tribe rebelled against Cartimandua's rule and she cast him off in favour of that sycophant, Vellocatus – his armour-bearer of all men!' There was suddenly a cold draught from the door as Rory left the hut.

'He's gone to call the Council,' Voada said. 'My husband died too soon. Keara and Caitlyn are still young girls.'

'You were the same age as Caitlyn when you left Caledonia to marry Prasutagus.'

'Yes,' Voada sighed, 'but that was before the Roman invasion seventeen years ago. And to think that Keara was born that sad year.'

'Come,' Greer said, 'you must eat something now, so must the young ones and then you should rest before the Council. We have a king to bury.'

'I must see the riders,' Keara said, turning to her cousin who stood on a narrow strip of meadow land beside her, not far from the road. 'It's the Procurator, I am sure. I want to see his face.' She drew back her hair from her face and tied it in a knot. Pressing her lips together, she climbed the slope to the Roman road to Camulodunum and called back to Galdus, 'Come up here. Let's see the face of the man who has stripped our land.'

The sound of horses' hooves could be heard clearer now, crunching on the lightly frosted ground, and approaching on the road from the south. There were a great number of horses in the Procurator's retinue, all well-equipped and eye-piercing in their shining armour and weaponry. The leading cavalryman held up one hand to call for a halt, and then spoke to his companion, an older man who appeared to know the roads well, but hesitated. Keara and Galdus could not hear what was said, but lying low on the ground they watched as the riders dismounted in order to rest their mounts and lead them to drink from the slow-flowing river. Keara's pale fingers clutched the frozen blades of grass in front of her. She bent her head to one side and whispered, 'Will they see us from here do you think?'

Galdus did not hesitate as he smiled into her dark, beguiling eyes. 'No, our ponies and Sapho are back in those willows and we are hidden by the bend in the river, but why don't we show ourselves? They are on Iceni land now and pissing on it too.' He had raised his voice a little more as he pointed at the soldiers relieving themselves in the reedy water. Galdus was never very discreet, even at the worst of times such as now, her father's funeral. He was ready to stride down to the Roman soldiers just to stand and stare at them. Proud and impetuous, Galdus would much rather swear and glare at them, trespassers on his clan's lands. But then he did look more Celtic than her, Keara reflected. He had short, blond hair with a long, thin plait of hair to one side, and he still clung on to his Caledonian accent despite his life with them in the South.

Keara thought of her father lying in state in the tribal centre of Venta Icenorum just waiting for his last public appearance at his burial and funeral feast. Guests were arriving from all over the land, although fewer than invited. As had been expected, Venutius could not come, or would not come, since Cartimandua was to be there with her consort, Vellocatus. Corbreid, Galdus's father and brother to Voada, could not come either. He would not leave the Caledonian lands and did not trust the Roman occupiers in the South. The tribal leaders from the free lands in the West would not come either because, to them, Prasutagus had sold out to the Romans whilst they, still under siege, were fighting a war of resistance against the Roman Governor and his legions. Few druids would be able to leave the Island of Ynys Môn to travel to Icenorum since they were hemmed in by the Roman legions, and travel by sea would take too long. It was probably just as well since the last two harvests of wheat and barley had been weak, and with part of the tribute to Rome being paid in cereal grains and other foods their own larders were bare. How would they be able to feed the guests who *were* coming?

Keara turned her thoughts back to the Roman men below. Their equipment sparkled in the cold sun. It all looked so rich and splendid, but there was one man with no armour or weaponry; he rode a horse in the centre of the cavalry and was wearing a warm sheepskin travelling cloak over a dark toga. He seemed to be in charge for he shouted to one of the men to help him off the horse. He couldn't ride very well, and walked stiffly and heavily round his horse telling his man to take the animal off to the water.

'At least he kept me warm,' he muttered to a young officer who had climbed off his own horse to join him. 'How much further is it anyway?'

'Another two hours,' the man answered, speaking with the distinct accent of the Roman elite.

Catus stared at him, uncomprehending. 'You said that two hours ago. Won't we be late for some funeral or other?'

'No, sir. The funeral will be held tomorrow morning.'

'You mean we are actually staying overnight in some barbarian shack?' he gasped, raising one eyebrow.

'Sir, the Iceni centre is actually quite comfortable, and they have begun building in the Roman style. We also have a small auxiliary fort close by.'

Catus rolled his eyes at the man and puffed, 'They say they don't have enough money to pay all the tribute on time – one of the richest tribes in Britain – yet they find the money to start rebuilding their tribal centre. You astonish me, Marius. I just want this to be over, so I can get back to Londinium as soon as possible. I have other things of more importance to do and it is the Governor, your general, who should be here, not me.' He pushed his fat lips out as another man ran past him from the pack animals at the back of the train. He had a slight limp and looked a little dishevelled from the journey; his blond, greying hair fell across his face hiding the lines of middle age.

'Another barbarian,' Catus muttered.

'He's Titus's man, sir, from Dacia. He's the slave who looks after his horses and equipment.'

'Well, he must do a good job: Titus has the best-kept horses in the unit.'

The slave ran forward to the decurion who had been leading the Roman riders and took his black war stallion. Titus came to join Catus and the young tribune standing beside him.

'Sir.' He nodded at them both. 'We have a few more hours before it gets dark.' Then he lowered his voice so Keara and Galdus could not hear them.

Keara and Galdus stared down at the small group. As a tribune, Marius was of the senatorial order and looked like one, despite his legionary uniform and his show of respect to the Procurator. He was the son of a rich Roman senator, sent to Britain for one year as part of his military service and training for political life. Thin lips and thick eyebrows could not hide the constant look of calculation in his eyes. The three men were roughly of the same height, though Titus was a little taller. They were not of the same age either. Catus was near retirement and after his administrative services in Britain had plans to move to a comfortable and rich estate in the south of Gaul. Marius was in his early twenties. Titus's age was difficult to guess: he may have been only a little older than Marius but he carried more seasons on him. He dominated the group of men with his physical presence and lithe movements; he was well-built with short black hair and a close-shaven beard. Keen, dark eyes and a heavy brow suggested something hard about him. Even his voice was stern. Keara looked at his uniform: the scaled shirt covered a long-sleeved woollen tunic and trousers fit for the British winter. On his head he wore a light iron helmet with no protection for the ears and he wore comfortable leather boots. A sword was attached to his left hip and a small, round shield hung on his back. He had left his other weapons with his slave.

Keara rolled onto her back. 'He doesn't look very Roman.'

Galdus turned onto his side and gazed at his cousin. His eyes were a little dilated as he smiled at her. 'Which one doesn't?'

'The decurion.'

'That's Titus. It's because he's not Roman. He's a *barbarian* like us. They say he's from the Middle Atlas Mountains and part of the wild Baquates tribe, but was given to Rome as a hostage, as tribute to keep the peace between the Baquates and the Roman occupied lands of Mauretania on the North African Coast.'

'Like my brother you mean?'

'Yes.' Both thought of the child, Taranis who had been sent to Rome to be educated in the Roman ways and to do his military service in the legions. He would have returned home as a Romanised adult to take over the administrative rule from his father, had he not died before of the fever. Galdus thought of his own position and spoke aloud, 'But your brother, you and your parents were given Roman citizenship. Titus doesn't have it. He will receive it when he finishes his service in the army. I am not a Roman citizen.'

'You are not a political hostage either,' Keara smiled; 'We are your foster family. We are meant to educate you. Not much success there though!' she laughed.

Galdus pulled Keara's hair slowly out of its knot and gave her a broad grin. 'But you have educated me in the ways of our enemy; that was always my father's plan.' He pushed a lock of her hair behind her ear.

There was the sound of a twig snapping and Galdus was immediately on his feet. Keara rose more slowly and looked in the direction of the river. Titus stood there, a broken twig in his hand. How long he had been standing there neither of them knew. The sun lay behind him so that his face was in shadow. He was shortly joined by Marius who gave Keara an appreciative smile. 'So you have found us some Iceni spies,' he drawled.

'We're no spies,' Keara cried and was about to add more when Galdus stopped her. He had no weapon on him but a hunting knife beneath his shirt. Even so, he knew they were no match for a cavalry detachment.

'Say no more.' He spoke in Caledonian. 'We just say we are going to King Prasutagus's funeral.' He repeated this in Latin.

'Must be true,' Marius said; 'This one is too beautiful to be a peasant girl and they both speak Latin despite the boy's bad accent. They wouldn't be travelling on their own though.' He looked at them both. 'Where are your companions and your mounts?'

'We are Icenian and don't have far to go. We are on our own and our ponies are behind those trees,' Galdus replied. Both men turned in the direction of the trees and saw two ponies tethered beneath the hanging branches of a willow. They also saw a huge, golden fawn dog standing to one side, alert and watchful. Keara raised one hand flat towards her dog and called, 'Stay, Sapho, stay.' The dog lay back on its haunches relaxing once again.

'What is it?' There was a cry from the Roman road. It was Catus who was trying to remount his horse and had to stand on a stool that a slave had placed on the ground for him. 'We must get on.' He saw the two Icenians standing between Marius and Titus and called out, 'What are you doing with those peasant children? Leave them now. Marius, come by me. Titus….' But one look at the frown on Titus's face and he stopped. He muttered instead and gathered up his reins. 'When you're ready then, Titus.'

'I want your names,' Titus said in a low, cold voice that carried sharply on the air.

Keara stepped forward, speaking firmly, almost defiantly, as she responded to the command of the Roman soldier, 'I am the Princess Keara, second daughter to King Prasutagus of the Great Iceni. And this is Prince Galdus, first son to King Corbreid of the Caledonian Confederation. You are travelling to my father's funeral and are now in Iceni territory. As such, you are our guests and we will be there to welcome you when you arrive in your two hours.' She turned and walked swiftly to her pony with Galdus on her heels.

'Are you mad?' he cried. 'Do you want to provoke them?'

'He asked for our names; I told him. These Romans will do nothing against us on our land. We are *allies* after all, and they are going to Venta Icenorum for my father's funeral. I want to be home before they arrive.' She leapt into the saddle and, calling her large mastiff to her side, she was off. She didn't even look back to see the dark look on Titus's face as he contemplated, not only the horsemanship of the two departing youngsters, but also the size of Keara's four-legged companion which was almost as big as her pony.

The following morning dawned dark and wet. Keara and Caitlyn had woken beside their mother in the large roundhouse, but they had hardly slept. They rose together and ate a small breakfast of oats and milk. Voada had sent the serving women away so that she and her daughters could help each other to dress. It was nice to be just the three of them; a quiet moment together was rare indeed. Voada brushed their hair, first Caitlyn's, then Keara's, speaking to them both all the time.

'It will be a hard day for you. I remember when my mother died when I was a child.' She paused and held the brush in midair above Keara's head before continuing, 'My brother and I were told by our father, the King that we were not allowed to cry in public. It was a difficult day. She was buried in the High Lands with all those who had gone before. Many of the clans came to pay their respects and make offerings to the gods.'

Keara and Caitlyn turned on their stools to look at their mother as though seeing her in a new light; she rarely spoke about her family and all that she had left behind when she came to Iceni to marry their father. Since that day, she had only returned once: for the burial of her father and the crowning of her brother as High King of Caledonia. She had news, but it was not the same thing. And she had Galdus, her brother's son, who would one day return to Caledonia. She knew now that she would never return.

'My brother and I were very close ... as you and Caitlyn are.' She nodded at the two girls. 'We fought together, of course, as all brothers and sisters do, but we would not let anyone else fight with the other.' She smiled fondly at her daughters. 'You must always be there for the other.' She put the brush down and picked up a comb. She parted Keara's hair and began braiding it. 'I learnt to fight first against my brother, and then with him.' She stopped speaking, musing over her childhood. Eager for their mother to continue, Caitlyn prodded Keara so that she would ask, 'Did you have lessons?'

'Err, yes, we did.' She shook her head as though trying to wake herself. 'We were trained first by the female warriors of the royal house. Then, when we were older, we were taken on raiding parties and would fight against the neighbouring clans.'

'Mother!' Caitlyn cried, looking at Keara in secret complicity. 'You have never told us this! Your guardsmen train us, but we are never taken on raiding missions.'

Voada flashed a sudden smile at her daughters. 'That is because we now live in a Roman zone of Britannia and we don't have any quarrelsome neighbours. That's enough talk for now. We need to finish dressing.' She helped Keara and Caitlyn on with their cloaks and attached their brooches to each shoulder. 'We must join your father's funeral bier outside.' She hugged each girl to her and then pulled on her own cloak.

By midmorning they were following their father's bier to the ancestral mound of their family. It lay just a mile from the Iceni town. Although a Roman citizen Prasutagus had chosen to follow his ancestors in their beliefs and customs. He lay washed and anointed on the four-wheeled chariot that led him to his final resting place, and was followed by his family, his kinsmen, other tribal leaders and Roman officials. Some were on foot, some on ponies or chariots as they followed the retinue of mourners along the wooden causeway across the fens. Many carried gifts to be placed in the tomb for the king's afterlife, and also offerings to the goddess of the fens.

The walk was slow and long but a musician was playing a flute at the front of the procession which softened the dullness of the morning and pushed back the banks of ashen mist across the treacherous fenland. Every few yards, someone in the procession would stop and make an offering to the goddess Breckia, by pushing a brooch, a bracelet or other item of value between the planks of wood of the trackway where it would sink into the murky waters of the Underworld.

Once arrived at the site, a green knoll in the mire of marshland, the chariot, bearing the king's body, stopped in front of the entrance to the mound. The people assembled before the chariot, where a raised platform had been constructed for the great number of people who were expected to speak. Amongst the mourners, Keara saw Queen Cartimandua with her consort, Vellocatus and a number of their followers. Cartimandua looked splendidly well-groomed for the occasion; she obviously followed the latest Roman beauty tips, Keara thought. Her eyebrows were plucked thin as they arched above dark, brown eyes. She also wore a lot of make-up to give some colour to an otherwise ivory face which was framed by the curled and thick velvet hair of her head. Vellocatus clearly lived in the shadow of this lustrous woman, but it was obvious why she had chosen him: the man was handsome and sensual, even if he had no moral values, Keara concluded.

It was also interesting to look at the guests' clothes; a great number of them wore the formal black togas of the Romans, but an equal number had chosen to wear the traditional clothes of the Britons. Dubnov, the chief of the Trinovantes, neighbours to the Iceni, wore the costume of his tribesmen: the long, striped trousers and fur belt with a thick woollen tunic. He had braided his long hair with beads and wore golden armbands over each sleeve. He had come with a number of men who each wore their hair in the same manner.

Tribal leaders from other clans were dressed in a similar fashion, although some had also chosen to wear the blue woad tattoos on their hands and wrists for the funeral. Present, too, was the wealthy king, Cogidubnus of the Regni tribe whose lands lay south of the Tamesis river beyond Londinium. He was another client king of the Romans, from whom he derived most of his wealth. He was a valuable ally as he assured the protection of the south coast for the Romans – and so the Romans paid heavily for his loyalty. Cogidubnus had travelled to the funeral by ship and was wearing a black Roman toga, but he would soon be attending his own funeral, Keara mused wryly, judging by his age.

On the Roman side there was Cerialis, the legate of Legion Nine whose legion held two forts at Lindum in the North and at Clac-nyn just over forty miles to the northeast. He had a reputation for being young and impetuous, and was the only Roman general present. The other generals could not come: Suetonius, commander of the Roman forces in Britain, was busy fighting in Cymru and he had the other two generals and some of their forces with him.

As the assembly settled in the open space before the knoll, a young bard began singing a lament of departure for the dead king. His voice floated on the wind and then melted away into the waters of the earth. High in the sky Keara noticed a hawk circling above them: messenger of the gods, was it blessing Prasutagus's passage into the world of the dead or warning the living of what lay ahead? she wondered. She heard the sound of a carnyx being blown and turned her head back to the mound where Greer was now emerging. The huge bronze trumpet was used on ceremonial occasions, but Keara hated the sound: it blared out so loudly; it was enough to wake the dead not inter them, she thought, but perhaps that was the purpose as the ceremonial ritual opened the doors between the worlds. Slowly the people fell into silence as they waited for their religious leader to climb the steps. After a few dull thuds on the wooden boards Greer, the Holy Man, Archdruid of the Iceni members stood alone before them and looked into their faces below.

Before addressing the mourners, he made the sign of the crescent moon on his forehead and then began. 'Today is a day of mourning and a day of joy: we mourn the loss of our king, Prasutagus, who was a great leader, warrior and father to his people, but we also praise his life and celebrate the passage of his soul into the next world where the gods welcome him home.' Greer had a soothing voice which caressed the air and the assembly. He spoke for a few minutes and then signalled to Rory to make the sacrifice. A wild boar was dragged from its strong wicker cage and pegged down into the earth with ropes. A number of warriors helped Rory to hold the animal in place so that he could cut its throat. The beast squealed and kicked violently as Rory held a sharpened knife of iron above his head, then brought it down, thrusting the blade deeply into the boar's throat. Then he slit it open. Sprayed with the blood of the dying animal, he quickly dropped the knife and held a bronze cup beneath its throat in order to collect the hot, red liquid which he passed to another man for Greer to hold. Greer held the cup up to the people before descending the steps and emptying it into the fen waters with a blessing from the gods. It was then the role of Voada to speak. She welcomed the visitors and thanked them for their gifts to the king. She also said that Prasutagus's household slaves were now freed from bondage and could live with the tribe in freedom or return to their homelands. She remained on the platform as the other speakers came and went.

One of the most surprising speakers was Titus, the Roman decurion. His speech was short and brusque, but, reading the words that Catus had given him, he spoke on behalf of the absent Governor who hoped that the friendship between their peoples would continue. Keara really didn't understand why Catus had delegated this duty to a subordinate as it was Catus who was meant to represent Suetonius and the Roman emperor but, when Titus turned from Latin into Celtic, she understood why: he was an excellent linguist. He even gave the speech in Caledonian and she was sure he was looking at Galdus when he spoke.

As the body of Prasutagus was carried into the mound, Voada descended the platform and her two daughters joined her to follow their father's body into the tomb and place the first gifts on his body. Keara tripped on the step as she entered the dimly lit chamber and had to grasp the wooden doorframe to stop herself from falling. Voada gave her a critical stare at this inauspicious sign. 'Do not stumble as you cross the threshold into the Underworld. The Iceni royal family is not falling yet.' She gave a hollow laugh and pulled Keara into the chamber along with her sister. The king's bier was placed on a low wicker frame on the ground by his household slaves who then left the grave to the three women. Voada and her daughters knelt by the king's side in order to place their gifts on his body: his ceremonial silver sword, his bronze armbands and golden torc.

Keara's eyes had grown accustomed to the dark room and she looked around its walls and floor. The chamber was furnished with some of her father's most cherished possessions and richest furnishings: couches, stools, cushions and chests lined the walls and were loaded with foods and decorated with wall hangings. Warm fur rugs lay on the floor, as did some finely carved iron firedogs carrying a spit of pork. Her mother stood up to kiss Prasutagus's forehead one last time, then left the burial mound. Keara and Caitlyn did the same. One by one the other guests entered the burial circle to place their offerings with the king. Some brought him food and wine, others plaids and cushions. When the mound was finally empty, the slaves placed more food and water within and then the Iceni warriors closed the entrance and sealed it with stones and peat. Everyone was to return to the royal estate for the funeral feast.

During the feast of mussels, winkles, roasted venison and pork, a bard recited a number of poetic elegies praising the life of the king and his ancestors and, despite the formality of the occasion, there was music and heavy drinking late into the night. From time to time, drunken laughter could be heard as friends and neighbours exchanged news and discussed past stories. In the great hall, the royal family sat at the head table, along with Catus and the tribal leaders from the Britannic kingdoms. Snatches of conversation could be heard around the hall as voices were raised then lulled. Keara felt lulled herself by the length of the day and the warmth from the great fire in the centre of the hall. To her right sat Galdus, and he was talking with Cartimandua; she was giving him news of his father and brothers in Caledonia, and Keara felt sad for her cousin's sake that his family could not be here.

'They are well,' Cartimandua was saying, 'but I still have trouble with my ex-husband, Venutius, and his Carvetii men. They are constantly trying to foment rebellion along our frontiers whilst smiling back as though we were friends.'

'Are you still holding his brother and cousins?' Galdus was quite blunt in this question, but Cartimandua didn't seem to mind.

'Yes: they are my guarantors of Venutius's behaviour. He daren't attack me openly because I would have his family executed.'

'Isn't that a bit harsh? I mean, since the failure of his rebellion three years ago his position is now very weak, and you do have the support of your new husband, Vellocatus and his tribe.'

At the sound of his name, Vellocatus, sitting next to Cartimandua, turned his head and spoke, 'My wife can always count on my love and devotion. And where I follow, my men will follow.'

Cartimandua smiled back. 'Sentiments aside, the political reality is more complicated than that. A friend one day is an enemy the next.' She gave Galdus a grim smile. 'Catus has invited Voada and her daughters to Londinium next month for the reading of the will. We shall see what happens then. Fortunately, I shall be safely back home.'

There was the sound of shouting further down the hall and then a brief scuffle. All heads turned to look, but with many now standing it was difficult to know what was happening. Some words could be made out such as 'Celtic virtue,' 'Caitlyn' and 'bastard'. It sounded like the voices of Marius and Rory, but even sober, which he was not, Marius was no match for the Iceni warrior. Rory would not have his new queen's virtue insulted by the Roman occupiers. Guest, he might be, but, by calling into question Caitlyn's virgin status, Marius had broken all the rules of social etiquette. Rory, drunk too, knocked over his bench and rushed at Marius, headbutting the Roman and punching his body before the man could even raise his arms. Rory had to be dragged off Marius by his own men. Marius lay slumped on the ground splattered in globules of blood. Visibly he had a broken nose, a split lip and a long, dark slash marked his arm. Rory must have used a knife on him.

The crowd parted to let Voada and Catus enter the empty circle around Marius. Keara had also joined them, along with her sister and Galdus. Catus had to tell Titus to help Marius: the man was losing too much blood. In slow, measured movements Titus bent down next to the fallen man. His slave, Zia came running towards his master with a small chest from which Titus pulled out some medical material.

Voada offered the help of her druid. 'I can call Greer if you like. He knows about medicine.'

'No, that won't be necessary,' Catus replied. 'This man knows what he's doing.'

Titus had already bound the arm with a ligament to stop the blood flow and was cleaning the arm and lip with alcohol. Marius had come to and was screaming out in pain, clutching his nose with his other arm and cursing Titus for hurting him further until Titus slapped his hand off his face and gave his nose a deft tweak.

'Well, that's put his nose back into place; the same can be said of the man.' It was the slave, Zia who spoke. He had already threaded a needle and held it out to Titus. He might have been punished for such outspoken words, but they were said in Celtic and by then Marius had passed out again. Titus began stitching the skin on the arm together. He was very methodical in his work, but it was clear that the cuts to his arm and upper lip would leave scars. When he had finished, he told Zia and some other slaves to carry Marius to his bed. Then he stood up and saw Keara looking at him with curiosity. He stared back at her for a long moment, but his face was closed. Speaking to Voada, and then to Catus he said, 'With your permission I shall retire for the night.'

Without waiting for permission, he turned and walked out of the hall. Catus presented Voada with his excuses for the behaviour of his tribune and then he signalled for his men to withdraw for the night. Slowly the Britons, including Rory, returned to their seats and the drinking resumed.

II

LONDINIUM

THEY HAD SAILED ALONG THE EAST COAST FROM the Iceni kingdom, along the Trinovante coast to the Thamesis Estuary in Catevallauni territory and were now following the river up to Londinium. Curious to see the commercial heart of Britannia Caitlyn, Keara and Galdus were on deck with Voada and Greer, staring at the warehouses and workshops on the waterfront. The river itself was busy with boats and traders from different ethnic backgrounds and cultural origins from all over the Roman Empire: Europe, Africa, the East. A lot of the traders had to speak Latin in order to be understood. Keara also recognised Greek and Celtic but couldn't identify other languages. Further up ahead, they were approaching a timber bridge that connected the two sides of Londinium. It had a drawbridge to allow ships through – and so through it they passed, keeping to the north bank. In places the water was dirty with sewage, dyes and other waste material as drainage from the city flowed into the river.

'Anything but inspiring,' Voada grimaced, as she leant over the gunnel.

'It's only a trading station for the moment,' Greer responded, 'but it has been laid out in the Roman fashion – and the Procurator has his offices here. It's from here that the wealth of Britannia is exported to feed the whims of Rome.'

One of the city's pilots nudged his boat alongside their ship and grasped the rope ladder that one of Rory's men threw down to him. Rory came to stand next to the pilot when he boarded the ship. After inspecting their papers, he directed them towards some stone buildings up ahead: it looked like a Roman-style villa. When they nudged against the wharf, the pilot jumped out and sent a boy off to the basilica to inform the Procurator that the Iceni royal household had arrived. He then walked up to the villa, telling the slaves to open it up for their visitors before returning to his own small boat which had been following. Taking his leave, he returned back down the river with his mate. From the villa there was a sudden noise as doors were opened and a number of slaves came tripping down the embankment to the Iceni ship in order to help the visitors with their baggage. Rory and his men held on to their bags, but the others were glad to have help. They were guided inside by the slaves and served warm wine and spicy almond biscuits before the slave boy came running back from the basilica and said the Procurator would see them in the morning. He gave a letter to the head slave who paid the boy and then opened the letter for further instructions.

'It seems to be pretty organised,' Caitlyn spoke. 'We even have heating in the floors.'

'Well, they were expecting us,' Voada said. 'We'll see how organised they are tomorrow when the will is read.'

Keara started to follow her sister to the room they were

sharing, then turned to ask, 'Can we go out this evening, Mother, and visit Londinium?'

Voada looked at Keara's eager and expectant face. Both her daughters and her nephew looked keen to discover this new metropolis, but it was not the moment for such explorations. 'This is a new Roman city,' Voada addressed them all. 'It is chaotic and unsafe. You will see it in the morning when Rory and his men accompany us through the busy streets.'

'But we can take care of ourselves,' Keara protested.

'No, that is not the point. It is late. We are tired. And we are here for more serious matters than sightseeing.' Voada sounded tired as she signalled to the slaves to light the lamps and close the shutters for the night. 'We will eat together and then listen to some music before going to bed. At least that way you'll sleep well.'

The youngsters exchanged looks, not that convinced by Voada's prescription of night music, as they gazed upon a large hydraulic pipe organ at one end of the dining room. Two slaves had already entered the room and approached the organ. One knelt on the floor in order to operate the hydraulic handle. The other sat at the keyboard and began to strum some of the keys. 'Very pleasant, I'm sure,' Keara responded with one eyebrow raised, 'but I think I'll have an early night.' She went off to her room to unpack her bags.

'And don't think of climbing out for a night visit when I am asleep,' Voada called after her; 'Rory's men are watching the grounds.'

Keara slammed the door shut.

'Would you stop moving and sighing,' Caitlyn complained; 'You're keeping me awake.'

Keara kicked the blankets off her. 'I'm too hot.' She blew her cheeks out; 'I'm not used to the heating.'

'Then open the window.'

Keara padded over to the encasement and pulled the window open. Holding the frame, she breathed in the rush of cold air, then turned and leapt back into the bed next to her sister. A garden lantern cast some light into their room and onto their bed. Both girls were awake now, listening to the dull creak of the lantern swinging on its chain.

'I wonder what the basilica looks like,' Caitlyn spoke.

'Red,' Keara said, stressing the syllable; 'We saw it from the ship yesterday. It's big and red.'

'I know that,' Caitlyn whispered, 'but it's the seat of the Roman Procurator in Britannia.'

'It's only a trading station, Caitlyn. It's nothing like Rome.'

'How would you know? You've never been to Rome.'

'No, but I listened to Diodorus's lessons, and to Greer. He's been to Rome.'

'Greer has been everywhere.' Caitlyn paused. 'Would you like to visit Rome?'

'I don't know. I would like to travel. Galdus has asked me to return to Caledonia with him and visit the tribes.'

Caitlyn's eyes sparkled. 'What did you say?'

'I said that I might. As Corbreid's heir, he'll have to tour his lands. And if the Romans let you rule our tribe here, then I'll feel... Oh, I don't know, out of place. I think I'd like to travel, but I would like to go with Greer on his pilgrimage around Britannia and the isles. He said I could travel as his apprentice and bard.'

'Oh.' Caitlyn sounded a little disappointed.

'And what are you going to do?' Keara asked.

Caitlyn mused over this question for a moment. 'As Queen of the Iceni I will try and keep the tribes together. But the taxes are so high that I don't know if I can.'

'You'll have mum's wise guidance there,' Keara retorted.

And then Caitlyn poked her in the side, where she was most ticklish, and giggled, 'Oh, because Mum wouldn't let us visit the city at night!'

'Yes, exactly.'

The morning came, crisp and sharp. The pale, blue sky and the frost-laden air threw schisms of light over the villa as the Iceni royal family followed their Roman escort out of the gates and into the busy streets of Londinium. Titus had been sent to lead them to the Procurator's offices in the basilica and had addressed himself to Voada and Rory in the small courtyard of the villa, hardly acknowledging the presence of Caitlyn, the new queen of the Iceni.

Keara stared curiously at his square back as he and his men furrowed a passageway for them through the busy streets of Londinium, but she was quickly diverted by the throbbing life of this new Roman town. She watched the different merchants, the shopkeepers and tradesmen who were hurrying to and fro opening up their stalls, shops, warehouses and workshops along the riverside and the streets running into the city. The roads were already blocked with carts, carriers and donkeys laden with cloth, foods and amphorae from all over the Roman Empire. The noises and smells were almost unbearable and not something Keara was used to: a strange mixture of cries, movement, crates, coins and running water as they passed the public baths, not to mention the distinctive odour of pungent urine emanating from the huge street urns that had not yet been emptied of their night's contents. Some houses were still pouring their chamber pots into the urns hoping they had not missed the morning's waste disposal cart. Further on, Voada's group passed a small temple to Mithras before joining a wider road leading to the forum and basilica.

As city hall and court of justice, the basilica was a rich and imposing building; it faced them now as they entered the forum. Other military guards came forward and led them across the courtyard to the public building. They crossed the great hall with the judges' tribune at one end and government offices on either side. Outside the Procurator's offices Titus told one of his men, a man he called Aelius, to stay with the Iceni men whilst he led Voada, Greer and the two girls inside, telling them to be seated on the low couches before the Procurator's desk. Some slaves came forward with trays of sweet cakes and mint tea, but Voada waved them away. They were left to wait for a long time, which seemed very unnerving, Keara thought, with Titus frowning down on them and the slaves standing in silence by the walls. Catus and the Roman jurist for Britannia finally made an appearance, accompanied by Marius, whose scarred face still shone purple. Two other officers accompanied them.

Catus introduced Vettius Valens as the Governor's law officer in Britannia. 'I am sorry for the delay,' Catus began. 'I needed Vettius here,' he indicated the alluring, well-kept man who bowed slightly at the Iceni family, 'to clarify one or two legal points for us because we have two documents which are important: the client agreement, signed by King Prasutagus for the Iceni kingdom, and his will, which contradicts the original agreement he made.'

'Which one has more power?' Voada interrupted, already out of patience with the Roman administration after her long wait.

'It is the client agreement, naturally,' Vettius answered, seating himself next to Catus at the wide desk. 'Prasutagus's will can be respected as far as his personal wealth is concerned, but, as for Iceni lands and the kingdom, they must be incorporated into the Roman Empire as was originally agreed to by the king.'

There was a slight pause as everyone in the room seemed to reflect on this. A little agitated, Voada spoke rapidly, 'What does this mean exactly? That our daughter, Caitlyn cannot be queen? That the Iceni royal family comes to a stop? Caitlyn has already been declared queen. And what does this mean for our people? They will never follow a Roman regional governor?'

'It means,' Vettius answered, 'that your daughter, Caitlyn cannot be queen.' Here, Voada sprang up to protest, but, quite unperturbed, Vettius continued, 'and that the Iceni kingdom and people are now an integral part of the Roman Empire. They must obey the Emperor Nero. Their first loyalty is now to him. You must also pay the death duties: gold, silver, grain, lands, horses, dogs, and, of course, men and slaves for service in the military forces and government administration.'

Greer, Caitlyn and Keara rose, too, at this damning sentence. Keara noted that the other Romans in the room were suddenly tense, more alert and still, all, save Marius, who seemed to be enjoying the Iceni's discomfort and found it difficult to hide his amusement. Keara also noted Titus's creased brow, but felt that his frown was not directed at the Iceni group.

Voada could barely restrain her anger. 'This is not possible,' she cried. 'We have always shown the greatest respect for Rome, and friendship with its emperors. We have kept Eastern Britannia at peace with Rome and have helped develop commerce with the Empire. Nero cannot now step on us underfoot. He still needs the cooperation of my family and the friendship of our people.'

At Voada's high voice Catus raised his hands. 'Ssh, Ssh. You must remember that your people have enjoyed years of prosperity thanks to the generosity of Rome. Many members of the Senate have lent your people money over the years in order to develop your trade links with Europe and to invest in your roads and building projects.'

'What do you mean by *loans?*' she suddenly asked in a dangerously low voice.

'I mean the money that was lent to you originally when you signed the client agreement.'

Voada took in a deep breath. 'The money that we originally received from Rome was given to us as gifts of friendship. Tell them Greer, was this not so?'

'Yes, it was, to my understanding.' Greer looked from Catus to Vettius.

'No,' Catus answered, gathering some papers together. 'These are the original loan certificates. Not only must they be repaid, but, following the death of Prasutagus, a number of senate members, including Seneca, close councillor to the Emperor, have called in their loans which means you must pay them back within a short period of time.'

'How short?' Voada asked, glaring at Vettius and Catus.

'You have two months,' Vettius answered, 'according to the legal terms.'

'Two months!' Turning to Greer and her daughters, Voada added, 'We must leave, now.' Her voice seemed heavy as she also thanked Catus for his hospitality. 'If it is hospitality?' she cried; 'Perhaps we will receive the bill for our overnight stay in Londinium. As we cannot now afford a second night, we must return to our ship and leave for our homeland this afternoon.' With this she left the room, passed her men outside the door and strode down the hall and out into the light of the forum, with her daughters trying to keep up. As Greer left more slowly, Catus repeated to him, 'The Iceni have just two months. They must pay. They are no longer an independent kingdom.'

Greer gave him one keen glance before he retorted, 'What do you know of independence? You have been in service all your life.'

Venta Icenorum

Galdus blew out his cheeks again and crossed his arms. 'I don't really understand Greek theatre and don't see the point.'

'The point,' Greer spoke, 'is that Greek drama has a lot of political lessons to teach, lessons you need to learn as you will be King of Caledonia one day. I hope Caitlyn and Keara understand that too, although their political futures are not so sure. Now, answer Diodorus's question.'

Their Greek tutor repeated his question, 'What is the message of Aeschylus's play, *The Persians?*'

Keara had been staring out the window of Diodorus's school room and was only half-listening to the lesson. The winter sky was clear and blue; a few blackbirds were soaring high above some trees in the distance and the wind was picking up. She was running her hand slowly through Sapho's warm fur. The dog's chest rose heavily as the young, female hound breathed deeply and snored through her flabby lips. This afternoon's lesson was in Greek, and Greer had asked to sit in too, as he liked Greek drama, particularly tragedy. Keara heard her sister answer the question, 'It is a celebration of Greek victory.'

She looked at the brooch on her tunic: an ivory amulet of a white owl, and her thoughts returned to a morning when she was a very young child. She had woken quite early to discover that an owl had been watching over her all night. A beautiful white-plumed owl had been sitting on the headboard above her face and when she opened her eyes, there it was, staring at her. They had regarded each other for a fractured moment in time. Keara had smiled. The owl, with its heart-shaped face and dark eyes, had calmly maintained its study of her, wanting to speak, but then the spell was broken. Her mother had opened the door of the roundhouse and, startled by the noise and the light, the owl had instantaneously spread its wings and dived low, brushing Keara's face as though kissing her on its way out into the early mists of that new day. Associated with the Greek goddess, Athena, Diodorus had told her mother that the owl meant that Keara would be blessed with wisdom, courage and skill, but as the owl was also associated with the Iceni symbol of the prophetic moon, Greer had told Voada and Prasutagus that she would be a seer. Years after that, when Galdus had come to stay with her family, he had told her that in his tribe the owl was an ill omen, a sign of death but its eggs were good for a hangover. Since his interpretation of this sign, she had always worn her brooch as a talisman.

Suddenly her name was being called. 'Keara, do you agree with this?' Diodorus was an intelligent man and she had always enjoyed his lessons in Greek and Latin. She smiled at him, trying to recall his question: *What is the message of Aeschylus's play, The Persians?* She reddened a little before answering, 'Aeschylus was a soldier and a playwright. He wrote *The Persians* after the Greek victory over the Persians at Salamis in order to show that great empires such as Persia could fall. It was a Greek celebration of victory, but it was also a warning to the Athenian democracy that pride comes before a fall. It was because of Persian *hubris* and their neglect of the gods that they lost the battle against Athens.' She breathed out quite deeply and wondered if she had actually answered his question. She furrowed her brow, looking uncertainly at her tutor.

Diodorus smiled. 'That is right. It shows how great empires rise, and fall.'

'You always have to outdo me, don't you,' Caitlyn complained, turning on her sister. 'I was right: it was a celebration of victory.' She had been on edge since their return from Londinium. Implicated in negotiating a settlement with

Rome, but inexperienced as a ruler, she was still burdened by all her responsibilities and was heavily dependent on the leadership of her mother and the advice of Greer and of Rory, which were not always compatible.

'You don't have to come to our lessons, you know,' Keara scowled; 'As Queen I'm sure you have other things to do.' But she knew that her sister still needed this space, this time apart with her and Galdus, away from the Great Hall and its council.

'Never mind that now,' Voada cried, pushing back the door curtain as she entered the room. 'Greer, a messenger has arrived from Ynys Môn. Diodorus can you leave us now.'

Diodorus bowed to his queen regent and left the building. Greer looked suddenly older and very tired. 'Who has braved the winter roads to bring us news from the Holy Isle at this time of year?' he asked.

'It is Taran, one of the bardic druids, who is travelling the roads to give news to all the tribes. Rory, you can bring the messenger in.'

The curtain was drawn back again, and Rory led a tall, redheaded man into the low-ceilinged house. He had to bend down in order to enter the doorway. He gave a sombre smile to Greer when he saw him, which Greer returned with a clasp to his arm. Greer returned to his seat by the fire and indicated for the man to sit down.

'What news from Ynys Môn?' Greer opened.

'Not good,' responded Taran. 'I am travelling across the lands to give news of Roman movements. Suetonius Paulinus has been in his winter quarters in the West but has now begun his new campaign season and is harrying the western clans again: the Ordovices and the Deceangli. He is leading Legions Fourteen and Twenty with him and has broken through the tribes to the Hibernicus Ocean and is planning to invade Ynys Môn.' Weak with fatigue, Taran almost collapsed here, but

Greer held him up whilst Voada poured him a cup of warm mead.

'This is bad news indeed.' Greer seemed to say this to himself, then raised his head to Taran. 'What other news do you have?'

'He has left Legion Two in the Southwest, and Legion Nine at Lindum and Clac-nyn to guard his rear but he has most of the commanders with him. He will destroy our centre of worship on Ynys Môn and destroy our gods unless ... unless he is distracted.'

There was a moment's silence before Voada spoke, 'Are you suggesting rebellion?'

'It is the only way,' Taran pleaded, clutching Voada's cloak. 'If the tribes rebel in the East then Suetonius will be forced to stabilise the situation in Britannia before trying to conquer Ynys Môn. Ynys Môn is our Sacred Island. It must be protected.'

Both Caitlyn and Keara were shocked into silence, a silence which was broken by Galdus's question, 'We must protect Ynys Môn, but how?'

'We have no weapons,' Rory added, 'but we must fight.'

Greer raised a hand to indicate that, as the druid of the Iceni, he had made a decision. 'I will travel to Ynys Môn myself to see what is happening. The Romans may be making plans, but their progress will be slow, and they will not attack Ynys Môn before the winter is out. The western tribes can continue to harry them and maybe the tribesmen from Hibernia, across the sea, will come and fight the Romans too. First, Taran, you must rest.'

Caitlyn touched Greer's arm. 'Why are the Romans so interested in Ynys Môn? They are normally tolerant of religious differences in the Empire. I don't understand.'

'My dear child, my Queen,' he corrected himself, 'it is

because our Sacred Isle is a place of political refuge, a place that protects our lands and peoples from Roman oppression, and it foments rebellion. Pilgrims may go there for worship and for study, but warriors also go there to consult the stars and to organise defence and retaliation.'

'Don't forget the gold,' Taran interrupted; 'It is not called the Golden Isle for nothing. Nero wants our wealth.'

'Yes,' sighed Greer, 'Roman greed. Ynys Môn controls the Hibernian gold route into Britannia and is an important trade centre for Britannia, especially as it is also rich in copper. If the Romans can destroy Ynys Môn, then they can control the western tribes which will give them unlimited access to our land. The lands in the West are particularly rich in minerals, and the Romans have already started mining. Very often everything comes down to economic power.'

'I will return with you,' Taran said. 'I have reached the last tribe on the eastern shores, so can now return home.'

'Thank you, yes. I would appreciate your company, Taran. I need to go to my rooms for the moment and prepare for the journey.' Turning to Voada he asked, 'Can you ask Rhonda to come to me?'

'Yes.' Voada indicated for Rory to send someone to find the Iceni druidess. 'Why do you need to speak to Rhonda?'

'It is only to oversee my duties whilst I am away.'

'And how long will you be away for?' asked Voada.

'The roads are slow in the winter, and sometimes dangerous. The wolves are hungry at this time of the year, so Taran and I shall only travel in the daylight, and shall travel with care.'

'Would you like Rory to provide you with an escort?'

'Certainly not,' Greer almost laughed; 'We do not want to attract attention. Two druids travelling on a pilgrimage to the Holy Isle is nothing unusual, despite the Roman ban on druidic practices, and we both know how to take care of ourselves.' He bowed to the small group. 'Taran needs to sleep now and I need to pack. Goodnight to you all.' He gave them a small smile of reassurance and left the hut.

Londinium

Catus sat at his desk reading the letter from the Emperor again.

> *The Kingdom and territory of the Iceni are to be formally integrated into the Empire. With the death of King Prasutagus, the client agreement comes to an end. There will be no negotiations. No sedition will be tolerated. As Roman citizens the King's widow, Voada and his two daughters will be provided for, but if they question their new status, then Roman law must be applied in order to demonstrate the end of their dynasty.*

Catus scratched his nose, then called to a slave at the door to fetch Vettius Valens. Grateful for the hot wine, he added more honey and stirred it slowly before drinking greedily, dreaming of the Iceni wealth that was about to drop into his coffers, but equally anxious about the future possibility of a disturbed peace. What if Voada refused to pay the inheritance tax and hand over Iceni lands to the imperial estates? They were a powerful tribe, Catus reflected, proud and fierce, but unarmed, and a number of their men had already been conscripted into the Roman army and sent for service abroad. It would be good to get his hands on their gold and to have complete control of their salt trade and sea routes. He was interrupted by the entrance of Vettius, as well-groomed as ever, who gave Catus's slave an appraising smile as he threw him his thick woollen cloak and sat down in one of Catus's basket chairs. He made himself comfortable before offering the Procurator a dried olive from a leather pouch in his hand. Catus looked at the black, velvet berries and could not resist. He helped himself to two, chewed on them for a moment, and then spat the stones out into his hand.

'Your olives are always so delicious. I cannot find any as good as those here. Where do you find them?' he asked.

'They come from my brother's olive estate and are the finest in the Empire.' He smiled his vellum smile. 'They remind me of the heat of the sun, the dry earth and warm winds. But by Jupiter,' Vettius suddenly complained, 'it's hot in your office Catus. You must have the hypocaust on overdrive.' He shook his head, and then, turning to work matters, he asked, 'So, what do you need my advice on?'

'I have the letter from the Emperor about the transferral of the Iceni kingdom to Roman control. I would like you to read it and outline all the legal implications and problems as you understand them.' Catus passed him the scroll. He let Vettius read the letter, glad for a moment's respite to enjoy the warmth and comfort of his room. He lay back in his chair with his feet up on a stool, as was his manner, and stared vacantly at the wall paintings behind Vettius. The central panel showed Bellerophon riding Pegasus and killing the Chimera, a monster with a goat's head, a lion's body and a dragon's tail. If only it was as simple as that in Britannia, he thought. This Chimera of Britannia was all too much for him. The savages were a simple people, he felt, but too ignorant and vulgar for him.

Vettius interrupted his thoughts. 'Nero's orders are very clear. You need to send soldiers into the Iceni kingdom and officially take it over. You must nominate a council of Iceni members and Roman officials to help with the running of the new territory. You know the protocol for that since we have already discussed it. You must now take over direct control of the land and road taxes, the mines, the military enrolments and grain supply.'

'I know my job, Vettius, but these are uncertain times and after seeing Voada's anger when she came to hear the reading of the will I am not sure that she will be so docile.'

'What have you to fear from a single woman and her two daughters?'

'She has a lot of support behind her; she is a powerful woman and inspires men!'

'Yes, but the Iceni tribe has been at peace for a number of years. The people have enjoyed Roman advantages and investment. They don't want to lose that.'

'Talking of investment,' Catus's voice rose, 'have you read the last part of the letter? There is a postscript about the Roman loans again.'

'I am only a legal officer. You are our finance expert. You tell me.'

'Under the Emperor Claudius a lot of money *was* given to the Iceni royal family and other leaders. However, Nero is now saying such investments were only loans, so Roman senators are calling in their money. I know the Iceni are a rich people and I am looking forward to getting my hands on their wealth, but they don't want to lose that. Our Roman officers may well meet with some resistance when I send them in. Don't forget that Prasutagus tried to leave half of his kingdom to his daughters.'

Vettius stood up. 'I must write a report for the Governor who will probably want me to send a report to his general, Quintus Cerialis just north of the Iceni kingdom. That will put Legion Nine *Hispana* on alert if you need their support.'

'Thank you Vettius, you might need their support too, since I am sending you out with my officers in the next few days. You are representing the Governor whilst he is away in the West, and you must do what needs to be done in order to apply Roman law.'

Vettius gulped and turned a shade darker, but said nothing. He didn't need to; the glower in his face was enough to warn Catus.

'I am not going back to that barbarian rookery,' Catus stormed, throwing the two olive stones onto the floor in his frustration. 'I may be Britannia's finance officer, but you are its legal officer, and you represent the General – and the Emperor, so you *will* go.' Vettius did not reply. He gave Catus a cold stare. Then he spat an olive stone out into his hand and placed it on Catus's desk. He turned and left the office, collecting his cloak from the slave on his way out. He was fuming with Catus because he really had no choice in the matter. He had hoped that because of their good working relationship Catus would not send him to Iceni, but Catus was right: he *did* represent the Governor and so he did have to go to Venta Icenorum in order to impose Roman law.

VENTA ICENORUM

The Roman cavalry soldiers rode for several days before reaching Iceni territory, and had only briefly broken their journey in the town of Camulodunum in Trinovante lands which served as both the capital of Britannia and as a Roman colony of veterans. At the colony, Vettius had sent a dispatch rider along the main Roman road to the Ninth Legion at Clac-nyn and again onto Lindum in the mid northeast of Britannia. From the Roman fort of Clac-nyn, south of Lindum, Quintus Cerialis controlled the Fen Causeway, a system of roads, tracks and canals across the fens and through Iceni lands. Satisfied with these precautions, Vettius rode across the brecklands, a dry, gorse-covered landscape before Venta Icenorum.

He had a large detachment of men with him, many of whom were Roman slaves from Catus's offices, but he also had a Roman medical aid, and the cavalry officer, Titus, his men, and the tribune, Marius. Marius had been assigned the direct protection of Vettius whilst Titus and his men were to take a great number of the Iceni ponies and horses needed for the Roman cavalry. Titus had an eye for a good horse; his own were amongst the most impressive. His black Arabian stallion was wide-nostrilled, with strong, straight legs and a broad chest. He had chosen it for its endurance, and for its bite, Zia always thought, when having to dress the animal. Titus's second horse was equally unnerving. Only Titus's dappled packhorse was calm and gentle, which was a good thing for Zia as she was his constant companion on campaigns.

They reached the final stretch of road which followed the river Tas leading into the south gate of Venta Icenorum in the late afternoon. It was now the end of winter, and yellow primroses were beginning to appear along the roadside.

'Flowers of courage and young love,' Zia had murmured as his packhorse lowered her head to sniff the grass.

'Good for your old joints,' Titus had muttered, as his horse trampled them, overtaking the baggage animals on his way to see Vettius at the front. Zia had frowned at this provocation, fully aware of his master's irritable mood swings over the last few days, since leaving Londinium in fact. Their stop in Camulodonum had not helped things as he and his men had been made to feel their place in the world: not slaves, not freedmen, and not Roman citizens either. Marius had enjoyed pulling rank on Titus, but only in the presence of Vettius. Any other time Titus's own presence was enough to put Marius back into his place.

In Camulodonum there had been an incident in which

Marius had drunk too much good wine at one of the taverns. As the tavern had been built into a small part of the very substantial, reconverted military hospital, Marius had got lost on his way to the latrines. A number of fellow drinkers, war veterans from the Britannic wars, had eventually found him singing in the hospital stables and had dragged him back to the tavern for rich pickings. When reprimanded by Vettius the following day for a lapse in his personal protection, Marius had defended himself by saying that he had had to spend the night in the military hospital after being thrown by a horse that Titus had trained for him. Not wanting to hear anything more of such a story Vettius had docked money out of Titus's pay as a fine. Titus was still fuming; Marius was still nursing his sore head.

They marched into the Celtic town of Icenorum which did show some signs of Roman construction, much to Vettius's relief. There was an empty garrison and a stone building where a few Roman soldiers were employed in civic duties. Some baths were being constructed down by the river. One or two villas lay outside the town and that was it. Vettius went first to the Roman buildings to call for the service officer and then sent him off to find Voada. He settled himself before a burning brazier in the small square building and sent his own men out to start an inventory of Iceni possessions: animals, lands, goods, dogs and slaves. He didn't have long to wait before Voada was brought in to see him. He had Titus and Marius on either side of him though neither was talking to the other, which was a relief to both men.

'What are your men doing on our lands?' Voada asked, glaring at the Roman law officer.

'The Governor's men are following Roman law and the instructions of the Emperor. As you have already been informed, this territory is now part of the Empire which is what King Prasutagus agreed to when he first signed the client agreement with the old emperor, Claudius. The Procurator, Catus, has remained in Londinium and has sent me to impose the law.' Vettius spoke in a dry, formal voice.

'But Catus should be here himself.'

'I agree, madam.' Vettius grimaced in a look of mock horror. 'This is not to my taste at all, yet, as I am the law officer in Britannia, I must do my duty which means that we shall be here for the next day or so, and you must pay up. You have the inheritance taxes to pay in full, and the loans to reimburse to investors in Rome.'

'How will your presence in my daughter's kingdom help the friendship between our people and Rome? How can we pay? We have nothing more to give.'

'First, this kingdom does not belong to your daughter, or to you. Secondly, the Iceni have lands which will become part of the imperial estates, and your tribe has many other valuables such as its hunting and fighting dogs that are almost priceless in Rome.'

Voada winced before retorting, 'You cannot do this. We have always been a loyal people. We also have a royal family who have been chosen by the gods and followed by the people. We cannot pay now, at this moment; we would have nothing left to survive. What will become of my family?'

'I see you are refusing to cooperate.' Vettius stood up, noting Voada's hard, set eyes. He signalled to Marius. 'I know exactly what will become of your family. Where are your daughters?'

Keara and Caitlyn were in one of the roundhouses. Despite the dull grey of the late afternoon, Caitlyn was working on her loom. The central fire gave off enough light, and there was still some daylight through the door. Keara was making a harness for one of her horses and was lacing brightly coloured beads onto the shoulder straps. Both had been curious to see the

Roman cavalry and officials arriving from Londinium, but had been told to stay in their roundhouse. There was a heavy foot outside the doorframe and then the hut turned a deeper shade of crimson as a man entered. In the dim light from the fire, Keara recognised him as a Roman legionary, one who had come to her father's funeral.

'You must leave,' the man said, addressing Keara; 'I must stay with your elder sister.' Keara recognised him as Marius, the Roman tribune and a shudder went through her as she saw the carnal look of greed on his scarred face. Even Caitlyn turned pale, twining her fingers around the threads of wool as though attaching herself to a disintegrating anchor.

'Amena,' she called, looking desperately at the door. 'Amena.'

'Your serving woman will not answer you, and neither will your mother, nor your men, or your dogs,' Marius laughed, 'but they will hear you. Now, little sister, you must leave.'

'No, I am not leaving you alone with my sister.' The two girls looked at each other: a moment of such intensity and fear, an exchange that recognised this time, this here and now, as one of irrevocable threat.

Two other soldiers had entered the roundhouse and seized Keara by her arms and shoulders, dragging her towards the door. Instantly, she began kicking and shouting, 'Don't touch me. Get your hands off me. Let me go.'

She could hear her sister beginning to panic and scream as Marius lurched towards her, knocking over the standing loom and the stool beside it. The last glimpse Keara had of her sister was of her being thrown down onto the woollen rugs that littered the floor, her shoulder bare where the sleeve had ripped. The door closed. Outside, she saw her mother running towards her shouting for her to run, but then her mother was caught and held by other soldiers and dragged towards a post whose sole purpose was for the raising of Roman standards in front of the barracks.

'Do not touch my daughters. I am warning you,' Voada screamed. 'Do not touch them or you will pay with your lives. Every one of you here today will be cursed and the gods will not spare you.'

By this time, Vettius had arrived in the cleared space and was giving orders for the tribe's people to be held back in order for them to witness the justice of Rome. He read Nero's proclamation for the integration of the Iceni territory into the Roman Empire and for the destruction of any resistance. 'Clearly,' he began, addressing Voada, 'your family represents a menace to Roman stability since you refuse to take your lawful positions as Roman citizens in our new territory. Not only have you refused to pay your taxes and reimburse your debts, but you continue to play the dynastic card in order to retain rulership over the Iceni. Under Roman law you must be condemned, and I have to make an example of you. Your people will see the might of Rome in the clear light of day. If you were men, I would execute you. As you are women, you shall be flogged, Voada, and your two daughters must be violated.'

'No, no...,' Voada cried, contesting this sentence in disbelief. 'This is not possible.' Doubt could now be heard in her voice, and then an edge of panic, as she added, 'I beg you, please do not touch my daughters.' Yet the sight of Vettius's determined face, the silence of the crowd, finally convinced her that their sentence had been dealt; Voada gasped a final, broken plea, 'Kill me if you will, me, kill me, but do not touch them.'

'Roman law must be applied. I have been ordered to take these steps because of your resistance. However, if your resistance continues, then I, or rather the Governor's men, will execute you and your daughters. Remember that, as they will no longer be children, we will be able to execute them under Roman law.'

He gave orders for Voada to be tied to the post and whipped. A squat man, no taller than Voada, came forward and began to drag her the remaining yard to the post. With Voada's resistance the man was panting through his broken, yellow teeth, and his pockmarked skin turned crimson. In the end he was helped by other soldiers. Vettius looked with disdain at the ugly man and turned away from the scene. He told Titus's men to take Keara off to another roundhouse.

'You see to her,' he said to Titus, pointing his chin at the young girl who was imploring him to make all of this stop. There was a moment of pause in Titus's movements before he stepped backwards and asked, 'And, why me?'

'Oh, because I prefer other things,' Vettius cried impatiently, clearly finding the whole episode distasteful. 'And I don't like to witness any suffering. I shall be in the bathhouse. However, if you don't like it send in another man. It only has to be done once, but if they have already lost their virginity, it doesn't have to be done at all. It is only a legal technicality. But where are the Iceni men, the old queen's guardsman and his warriors?'

'They are transporting money from the royal mint here to the coast and will be back in two days. They have the queen mother's nephew with them too.'

'Why are they taking money to the port when they should be paying Rome?'

'Apparently, it's to buy more grain from abroad as it was a bad harvest here and the people are hungry.'

'Never mind that now, get on with your job.' Vettius turned and left.

My job! Titus cursed as he raised his head and looked at the roundhouse where Keara had been locked in. He looked too, at the man who was about to whip Voada: a rough, unshaven man from the Roman garrison at Camulodunum, and then he strode off to the roundhouse, listening to the cries and protests from the people. A skirmish had broken out as some of the Iceni men tried to break through the ring of Roman soldiers and rescue Voada and her daughters, but they were quickly overpowered as they had no other weapons but their fists. These men were tied up and dragged away, leaving only the dogs to bark in outrage. Wild with fear the dogs were being rounded up in order to be transported to Londinium and sold on the continent, along with the Iceni men; Britannia's men were often bought as exotic curiosities to furnish the homes of the wealthiest Roman families in the eastern and southern parts of the Empire, but Britannia also provided the finest hunting dogs in the known world. A group of Roman slaves was having a lot of trouble harnessing a rather large mastiff which was creating havoc among some baskets of food. At last they succeeded in encircling it, then tying it down and muzzling the animal, despite the snarls and bites they received. Titus recognised it in passing as Keara's mastiff and furiously kicked a broken pail out of his way.

Caitlyn could still be heard screaming, or rather crying, until only a faint keening whimper could be heard. Marius took his time. He pulled off his tunic and withdrew the belt from his breeches wrapping the wide soft leather around his knuckles. He could not help smiling with appetite, savouring the sight of such fearful beauty. But he would see more and have it all, he thought. He must bend her and break her in. Only force would do for such a barbaric people. He straddled her body, with a knee on either side of her hips to keep her down. Slowly he held his clenched fist under her chin until the buckle of his belt grated her skin and drew blood. Leaning forward, he held her arms down with his elbows. He was enjoying this play of strength, and he waited for her to stop resisting. Then, he pressed his body heavily against her own. Caitlyn whimpered some more but could hardly breathe. Eventually, she stopped moving and Marius drew up her skirt and kneed her violently in the groin until her thighs split open. 'You'll like this tickling,' he whispered sweetly in her ear. His manhood was swollen hard between them and the excitement he felt was difficult to control. He rubbed his penis between Caitlyn's thighs before feeding it into her and thrusting hard and deep into her flesh. The rhythmic moves of Marius began to push Caitlyn down into a place of darkness and horror, a world in which her distress allowed her no vision and where the self ceased to be. She became detached from her body, floating above an unfamiliar world of stillness and shadows, waiting for it to end. The man continued shafting her and drops of sweat peeled off his straining shoulders until the final shudders, and then he collapsed on top of her.

'The first time is always the best,' he sighed at last, stroking her wet cheek with his forefinger.

Voada was utterly silent as the strokes and the blood began to fall. She counted them: one, two, three, twenty-one, two, three …, concentrating on the pattern of sound rather than the pain she felt. That pain was real and physical, but the other pain could not be measured. She could not save her daughters from the violation of their bodies. She had seen Keara's face, heard Caitlyn's cries, the calls of her innocent daughters. She gave a convulsive pull as she tried to tear away from the ropes holding her arms up. The man with the whip, whom the others called Spurius, laughed at her display of anger and humiliation, enjoying the spectacle of the captured animal.

'Nothing you can do for them now. Too late for your bitches. And if they're in heat, they're probably enjoying it.'

She closed her eyes, but could not block out the sounds or her thoughts. 'You will pay for this she screamed at the man striking her. 'You will all pay for this. I swear on the blood of my ancestors that I will have revenge. My people are witness to this. You had better kill me now for if you leave me alive you will regret it later.'

Spurius only laughed, but this time with less ardour: the effort of raising the whip was beginning to show. He continued his job trying to extinguish her threats with his lashes until only the reflex shudders of Voada's body told him that the woman lived still.

Titus told his men to leave the hut as he entered, then closed the door, shutting himself in alone with Keara. This was not for the world to see, he thought. There were some muffled snarls and curses, even a cry of pain from Titus himself. A wooden stool suddenly hit a wall and splintered into shards. One of the men outside the door sniggered and called out, 'Do you need a hand sir?'

'No,' Titus yelled. 'You keep to your post or this fiend will kill the both of us. I will deal with her. She's all mine.'

'Yes, sir.' Evidently, the man and his fellow guards were finding the incident very entertaining. They listened to more furniture flying, pots breaking and glass smashing, and to what even sounded like a knife being embedded in the door's planking; a point could just be seen next to the guardsman's ear. He stepped further away from the door. The fight continued, noisy and messy, until finally there was a lull in the storm, and a silence set in, a silence that dragged on, but which could not be measured against the cries from the crowd and the strokes of the rod. When Titus came out, some little time later his jaw was clenched tight as he stared at the dirty earth before his feet. Then he raised his head and held up a bloodied cloth for the people to see.

'Justice has been done,' he frowned. 'She can be examined.' He caught Zia's condemning eye from behind the Roman soldiers and his expression hardened, but it was Titus who looked away first. He signalled for his men to let some of the serving women through to help Voada and her daughters. The queen regent lay slouched at the bottom of the post, her back a criss-cross of bloody streaks. The soldier who had whipped her was cleaning the blood off his whip and grinning broadly at his fellow soldiers. 'Yes, justice has been done. Some men have all the luck.' And he thrust his pelvis out with one hand on his crotch which made the others laugh. Titus's mouth twitched. Then he walked towards Zia.

Several women were moving around the hut carrying bowls of warm water, herbs and cloths. The people had carried Voada and her daughters into the roundhouse of Una, their medicine woman, where they could be cared for on soft fur mats around the fire. Voada had lost consciousness and had been placed on her front so that the women could clean her back and dress her wounds. Caitlyn lay in a stupor staring empty-eyed at the ceiling, watching the wisps of smoke rise from the fire in soft, concentric circles and disappear through the straw thatching of the roof. She said absolutely nothing now and showed no resistance to anyone, not even to Rhonda, the Iceni druidess who lifted her legs whilst Una examined her hymen.

'She's no virgin now.' The Iceni medicine woman soothed Caitlyn with soft words and stroked her forehead. 'It's over though. I shall clean you up and give you something so that you can sleep.' She turned to Rhonda and added, 'I'll have to give our Queen a few stitches too, so you'll need to pass me some of that comfrey over there.' She pointed to a shelf on one side of the room. 'You can make up a paste of it. And find me some fresh sphagnum moss too: I need more than cloth to staunch the bleeding.'

Keara had stood up and despite the blood stains on her thighs, she walked over to her sister and, kneeling down, she took her hand. 'I'll hold her whilst you put the stitches in,' she said to Una, and she stroked Caitlyn's hair with her other hand. There was a lull for a few minutes as the women tidied up Caitlyn and applied a poultice of comfrey onto the stitches to stop any infection. Keara could hear some of the other women whispering at the back of the hut, 'What will this mean now?' It sounded like Amena, Caitlyn's maid servant.

'It means war.'

'Voada will kill Catus for this order.'

'I hope they didn't have any diseases.'

'Be quiet all of you,' Una spat between her gap-toothed lips. 'I don't need your help now, so go and get clean water, and some soup. It's very late, but I need one of you to stay with our lady Voada.' She lay Caitlyn's legs out straight and then told Keara to lie down again so she and Rhonda could examine her next.

'How is my mother?'

'She has fainted from the pain, but she will recover,' Una reassured Keara.

'Thank you, Una. I can clean myself, you know.'

'I know you can, but it also has to be an official examination for the Roman law officer, and your mother. I am sorry my child.' Again, Una's voice was gentle as she placed her hand against Keara's shoulder, pushing her down onto her narrow bed. 'Let me have a look.' But Keara resisted as Una pulled her knees apart. 'Don't be timid with me, child. As your medicine woman, I used to nurse you when you were a small baby and have seen it all before. I promise I won't hurt you.'

At last, Keara relaxed a little and let Una wipe the blood

away with a warm sea sponge whilst Rhonda held her hand and recited a prayer to Sirona, the goddess of healing. Rhonda, as a plump, breezy woman, was reassuring and calming, whilst Una's swabs were firm and gentle.

Una turned to another woman standing behind them and said, 'Keara's hymen has been broken. Neither girl is a virgin. Go tell the Roman doctor he can examine them now to confirm this, and tell their law officer too. He has what he wanted.' The woman bowed and left the hut.

Una looked at Rhonda fearfully, and whispered, 'What do we do now?'

'We must obey the gods; they will surely ask for war. And their mother will demand revenge.'

On her mat Keara turned her head to look at the prone body of her mother with its welts and smarts; they stood out like sparring flames in the firelight, and Keara shivered.

III

Iceni wetlands

GALDUS WAS HELPING TO ROW ONE OF THE TWO boats carrying the grain, along the river. The long planked boats lay heavy in the water with enough wheat to finish the winter. Rory had bought the grain from a Frisii merchant galley which had just crossed the ocean from the low-lying delta lands on the continent and had met them in the port of Yare. The Frisii merchant may have been eager to help them, but he had also been pleased to make a profit, knowing they had no choice but to pay his price in ingots of silver. He had refused to take any of their Roman coins, saying he didn't want to be accused of trading with Rome or its allies, and what was more, he insisted, the Iceni royal mints debased the silver content of their coins for the Roman Empire – this was true *and* was well-known, so Rory had paid in silver.

Galdus was tired of pulling on the oar and more used to riding a horse than rowing a boat, but it did keep him warm in such cold, damp weather and, furthermore, he reflected, the great swathes of water reeds did protect him from the fierce

winds that swept across the fenlands. He looked sideways at
Rory who seemed to find the rowing easy. From up ahead,
Galdus could make out another boat flowing down the river
towards them. It was much smaller and carried only one
man. It was Celtic like their own boats and Galdus could just
discern the Iceni symbol on the side: two crescent moons,
back-to-back. As they came closer, Galdus recognised the man
from Venta Icenorum: he was one of Voada's messengers. He
pulled up by the side of their boat and held on to the gunwale
with one hand.

Addressing Rory, he breathed out heavily, 'My lord, Voada
and the royal household have moved to Saham Toney. She has
asked me to tell you not to stop at Venta Icenorum but to
continue on the river at night.' Both Galdus and Rory were
startled.

'What has happened?' Rory asked.

'Catus Decianus sent men from Londinium to impose
Roman law and confiscate much of our lands and homes.
They have left our settlement and taken most of our horses,
dogs and hides. They have even emptied the royal mint. There
is more news, but I am sworn to secrecy. Voada will tell you
herself. However, as there is a Roman garrison at Venta
Icenorum you are to row the boats past them at night without
them seeing you.'

'Aren't the Romans suspicious at Voada's sudden move?'
Rory asked.

'She has told them it is for a religious pilgrimage to our
sacred well, for a cleansing ceremony.'

Here, Galdus interrupted the messenger, 'A cleansing
ceremony?'

But Rory was also posing another question, so the
messenger turned to him instead. 'Why has she chosen Saham
Toney?' Rory was asking.

'Because the Roman garrison is no longer occupied there. The Roman Governor, Suetonius, called the soldiers up to join him on his campaign in the West. The fort has been closed for several months now as Suetonius does not expect any trouble from our tribes in the East. For him the East is stable under Roman control.' Here, he let go of their boat and began paddling to the second boat before following them back up the river.

Rory told Galdus to keep rowing. 'Further up, we'll continue on the Yare River and miss the Tas subsidiary. We should be far enough away from the Roman garrison not to wake the dogs. We'll have to stop first and rest. We can continue in mid-night.' He shook his head before continuing, 'I don't like this.'

'Neither do I,' Galdus nodded, staring at the silent waters ahead.

SAHAM TONEY

Rory was mad with fury when Voada gave him the full story. They had arrived at Saham Toney the following evening, for it had taken many hours to row the boats up the river Yare, and then drag them across the marshes to meet the river Wissey, and then to continue rowing to the Great Lake on which the Saham settlement lay. They had managed to avoid Roman eyes for they knew the land well with its many rivulets, streams and marshes. Arriving at the Iceni village, they had brought the boats up onto the shore within the palisaded walls and left them to be unloaded by other hands. Rory had stridden up the bank onto the higher ground and told Galdus to follow him to Voada's hall in the centre of Saham. There, they had found Voada sitting at a desk with many papers, wax tablets and seals on it. There were no women with her, just a few armed warriors which was an unusual sight. A serving man was lighting more lamps, but then withdrew. A grim silence had filled the hall when Rory and Galdus entered. The warriors present had given them a curt nod, but many could not meet their eyes. Voada had not smiled at them, and she had not stood either.

'I am glad to see you both. Thank you for the grain, which is much needed as we have a campaign to feed.' When she saw the look of eager surprise on their faces she leant forward slightly and added, 'There are things we must discuss and organise. You were gone just a few days, but a terrible tragedy has befallen my family and our great tribe since then.' She turned to the men standing before her and dismissed them, 'You can leave me now with Rory and Galdus but prepare your horses.'

'Are we to leave tonight?' one of the men asked anxiously.

'Do not fear the wolves,' Voada answered, 'for we are the wolves and the only dogs we have to fear are the Roman imposters.' She turned a searching gaze on Rory and Galdus and began to tell them what had happened to her and her daughters. It was a difficult story to tell – harder still for the two men to hear. Rory interrupted her several times, storming at the 'bastard Romans' and vowing by all the gods to cut down every last Roman in Britannia. Galdus was white, shocked and dismayed. When Voada finally finished speaking, she looked at the expressions of fierce loathing on their faces. She told them to stay calm for the moment, which, at first, Rory refused to do.

'I will have their heads for this,' he cried out. 'I will not be calm and do nothing whilst they feast on our flesh and spit on our honour. They march on our land and take the very earth that our ancestors fought for and died on. We will have revenge, my lady. We should never have laid down our arms for them and offered them the hand of friendship.'

She nodded at her military commander and then rested her elbows on the table before her so that she could lean forward even further and speak, 'You are right, Rory: we cannot do nothing. I am sending your warriors out tonight as messengers to the other clans in Britannia. We can no longer run with the hare and hunt with the hounds. The tribes who are friendly to us and against the occupiers will answer my call and join us at Fison Way within the month. I am calling on the Trinovantes in the South, the Corieltauvi, west of the Wash, the Carvetti in the North, and all the tribes in Cymru who are already fighting against Suetonius's army in the West.' With narrowed eyes she gripped the sides of the table and cried, 'Yes, this is rebellion. I want revenge. I want destruction. I want war! The Romans must pay for what they have done to my daughters, and they will pay with their lives!'

Rory's shadow seemed to shake on the walls, like a bear stretching its back after a long winter of hibernation. He said, 'We were a free people before the Romans came. We must take back our lands, our territory. We shall drink their blood, and our dogs will feed on their bones. I vow to you Voada, I will give you retribution, or die.'

Voada smiled at Rory. She knew no other man more loyal than him, nor any warrior more formidable. 'I know I can count on you.'

Galdus was still trembling. He had turned so pale that he could hardly speak. 'Where are Keara and Caitlyn?' he murmured at last.

'They were at the shrine of Sirona today with Rhonda, asking for healing, and should be back soon.'

'Then I have to go and meet them on the road.' He had

already turned to leave, but Voada called him back. She still found it difficult to move, and her standing was evidently painful. 'Galdus, I have a mission for you.' She held out a letter, sealed with the two crescent moons of the Iceni. 'Take this to my brother, your father in Caledonia. As king of the North of Britannia, I want him to raise an army and come south to our aid. The whole of Britannia must stand united against the Romans this time for, if we do not, then the Romans will pick us off one by one like the acorn from the oak, and stamp us out forever.'

Galdus shook his head, refusing. 'I cannot leave my cousins. I will fight with you and send one of my men instead. I must stand by my cousins here.'

Voada searched his face for a moment. 'I must keep you safe for your father and for the Caledonians. You must return to your home and lands.'

Her nephew refused again. 'No. My place is to stay and fight with you. My father will join us.'

Finally, Voada acquiesced. 'You can stay with us then, but I want your man to leave in the morning. He must go downriver to the Wash and from there, sail north to Caledonia. But he must not stop on the Brigantian coast for Cartimandua is not to know of this visit in the North. Is that clear?'

Galdus nodded a *yes*, taking the letter for his father. 'I will add my own letter too, for my people will fight with the Iceni.' He turned quickly and walked out into the thickening dusk.

Keara saw him as she came cantering into the open square before the great hall. She pulled in the reins tightly, so she could pull up by her cousin, scattering earth onto his shins. Then she slid off the animal's back and looked at Galdus's troubled eyes: he seemed relieved to see her, but his stare was also one of discomfiture. There was an awkward silence between them broken suddenly by Keara's faint smile. 'It's alright you know: I'm still the same person as before.'

'It's not that, you know it isn't,' Galdus cried suddenly. 'If only I had been there. I would have stopped those Romans. I …' There was a moment of hesitation before he added, 'I would have stopped that Roman.'

Keara hung her head as though trying to stop herself from crying out *There's nothing you could have done. There's nothing anyone could have done.* Stepping forward, she placed her hands on Galdus's chest and looked into his face. 'There were too many of them. If it hadn't been him, it would have been another soldier. And if you had resisted, you would have been whipped like our mother, or dead. It's enough that we are alive.'

'And that we are going to fight back – at last! If only our peoples had stood by the Iceni faction that rebelled fourteen years ago.'

'But we were only children then and, although my mother supported the rebellion, my father was against it. He said our future lay with the Romans. If it hadn't been for his loyalty to the Romans, he wouldn't have been given the kingship of all the Iceni factions which is what united us.'

'Yes, but the Iceni should have united then as a federal union. Look at Cartimandua's federation of Brigantian tribes in the North. They are held together by Cartimandua's leadership and we must try and break that or bring the whole federation onto our side which we will never do. I have a man leaving in the morning for Caledonia to give news to my father and I want him to contact Venutius on his way. Venutius's Carvetii tribe is the only one in Brigantia that is openly against Cartimandua and Rome. He will join us, I know, and so will my father. My father will fight for the honour of his sister and of you, his nieces.' Here, he reddened a little and took her hand. 'As I will.'

Made uncomfortable by the warmth of Galdus's declaration, Keara patted his hand with her free hand so that she could withdraw the one he held. Noting her discomfort and the absence of Caitlyn, Galdus asked where she was.

'She had to travel by wagon and has gone directly to her room. Our druidess is with her. She will hardly speak. Her maid, Amena forces her to drink and to eat a little.'

'Good. She must eat. What did you do at Sirona's shrine?'

'We threw curse tablets into the well. I wrote Caitlyn's out for her and held her hand until she dropped it into the waters.'

'What did you wish for?'

'Revenge, and freedom.' Then her voice dropped. 'And for Sapho.'

'Sapho? Where is she?'

'She was taken, along with our other hunting dogs and many of our ponies, down to Londinium as payment-in-kind, for our taxes. I will get her back.'

'If we don't find her, for she may have been transported to the Continent by now, I will get you another one.'

'Galdus!' Keara half-cried in reproach, dropping her arms. 'I raised Sapho as a puppy and she will be lost without me. I will find her.'

'I know. I'm sorry.' He didn't know what else to add, so asked if he could see Caitlyn.

'Wait until tomorrow. It's late and dark; she'll be trying to sleep, but has mostly nightmares. I'll tell her you will see her in the morning.'

'Yes, thank you, Keara,' Galdus responded, 'but let me take your pony for you. Go and be with her now.' He didn't wait for an answer, but took the reins from her hands and led her pony off to the stables where Blair, a young, fair-headed lad took the animal from him.

YNYS MÔN

A translucent brume gave the island of Ynys Môn a mantle of dreamlike wonder and magical horror in the dim light of early dawn. The Sacred Isle of the druids was well-known throughout Britannia as a place of pilgrimage and learning, but also as a place of sanctuary where political and military activists could claim refuge in times of need. And that is why it had to be destroyed. Continuing the work of the Roman governors before him, Suetonius Paulinus was proud to be the general who would destroy the last druidic stronghold in this land.

He had drawn up his men on the Britannic side of the Menai Straits. Flat-bottomed boats were ready on the water, waiting to take the men across to Ynys Môn. The first boats had already started to cross. The cavalry was also set to cross the fords on horseback or to swim beside their horses where the water was deeper. Yet, many of the men were trembling as they stared across the green, choppy waters at the gnarled claws of the opposing headlands where the hordes of Celtic peoples lined the shores.

A dark, armed mass of Celtic warriors stood on the island's beaches and rocky outcroppings, ready for the Roman onslaught. They came from many parts of Western Britannia and Hibernia and were already whooping their war cries. Amongst them the Carvetii tribe of Venutius stood closest to the druid priests who had all raised their arms to the skies in order to draw down curses on the Roman invaders. But the most awesome spectacle that confronted the legionaries was the host of black-robed women who stood like furies with burning torches and dishevelled hair. At this imposing sight, many Romans were half-paralysed with fear or else spellbound by the chanting of the Isle's priestesses until their general came down onto the sands to address them:

'Men,' he began, 'do not be afraid of a group of fanatical women. There are more women over there than men. Their gods will not help them for they have abandoned Britannia. Our gods are more powerful and so are you. We have given thanks to Mars Ultor and we have purified our weapons and our souls. You are better armed, better trained and better disciplined than their groups of barbarian warriors who fight almost naked with no protection. The other men are their priests who know nothing of war. Remember that this is their last stronghold. Once we have Ynys Môn we hold Britannia in our hands, and all the glory will be yours, and honour.' He moved from group to group giving the same talk.

Despite the mist-bound light of early morning, the general was clearly visible with his red, plumed helmet and crimson cloak. He was surrounded by a number of fully armed guards: tribunes and centurions who acted as advisors, bodyguards and messengers. He turned to one tribune, Agricola, who had been sent up from Legion Two now stationed on the River Exe in the South. 'Go tell your legate, Gaius Marius to speed up the crossing. We have men about to land, and the natives are already throwing their spears into the water. Our men need support, particularly the auxiliary forces who are lightly armed.'

Agricola stared intently at the chiselled features of Suetonius with its lean nose and clean-shaven jaw. The young and excited tribune felt so proud to be serving on campaign with such a military leader. 'Yes, my general,' he cried. He spun on his heels and sped off to the water's edge to find his legate.

On Ynys Môn Greer and Taran stood with another man on high ground near the shore. The man was a rugged warrior of middle years who seemed pressed to return to his men. Lean and tall he carried an aura of command around him: that of a man used to being obeyed, although not in every case. It was Venutius, King of the Carvetii tribe in the North, and the ex-king of the Brigante confederation, and ex-husband of Cartimandua.

'The Romans are crossing. I must return to the front,' Venutius had to shout over the din from the beaches.

'One last thing before you go,' Greer began: 'Can you send one of your ships around the Cymru coast to Kernow and tell the Dumnonii clan to harry the Roman Legion Two and keep them pinned down in their fort at Isca Dumnoniorum? It is a request from our Archdruid. It shouldn't be too difficult as Suetonius has brought its legate up with him and their senior tribune, leaving just the prefect in charge of the legion. If he calls for reinforcements from the South, we don't want the prefect to be able to send any.'

'Yes, I'll send a ship immediately from the other side of the Isle. If the winds hold good, it should be there by this evening.' He nodded at both men and left them.

'I shall pray for you,' Taran called after him.

'It'll take more than a prayer to save us this time,' Greer responded sourly. 'Come. Let us join our Lord Sacrovar and the Council of Elders in the Holy Grove. He wants me to return to Voada as soon as I can. No doubt it is with the same message as for the Dumnonii in the Southwest.'

'To keep the Ninth legion pinned down in the East,' Taran concluded.

'Exactly. The Iceni must foment a rebellion.'

They both walked quickly through the ancient trees of golden oak and nestled mistletoe until they reached the open space where an emergency session of the war council was being held. Messengers were passing to and fro between the shoreline and the council in the Grove. An altar had been bedecked with spring flowers and speckled with drops of fresh blood where a roe deer had been sacrificed. A young prophetess was wiping the blood off her hands and speaking to the head druid, Lord Sacrovar. After a few moments, Sacrovar addressed the members of the council.

'She has called on Cernunnus.' He raised his old hands to the council, 'And Cernunnus has spoken in the entrails of the wild deer. Resistance must continue against the Romans or all will be lost for the tribes in the West. But Britannia will never be completely conquered and one day the Romans will leave. What the Germanians achieved against the legions of Varus over fifty years ago we can achieve today.'

A member of the council, who had been seated on the floor of the forest, rose to his feet with a message. 'Our men are hard-pressed on the beaches and many are already falling. Perhaps we can keep them off for a day or two, but not for more. Without reinforcements we will have to fall back and retreat to Hibernia.'

'I will never abandon our Sacred Grove,' Sacrovar cried. 'The Romans would destroy it and all our sacred temples.'

'Then the gods must protect us,' the man rejoined.

At this point Sacrovar spied Greer through the mass of priests and quickly excused himself from the council. He had to be helped away from the assembly by two young apprentice druids. They helped him to sit down on a lichen-draped rock by their sacred pool and left him alone with Greer. Here, the noises from the battle line sounded muffled and far away. The spring air was warming up, busy with teeming life and flecks of dust that sparkled in the shafts of early sunlight. Greer sat down next to Sacrovar and waited for the other man to speak, but he was silent, contemplating the still waters of the dark pool.

'What else did the prophetess tell you?' Greer nudged at last.

'How do you know she told me something more?' Sacrovar grunted, tossing his long white hair off his bent shoulders as he turned to face Greer.

'We have known each other for over fifty years, my friend. We studied together, boarded together, and have fought together in the Britons' resistance movement since the beginning of our strife; I can read your face.'

Sacrovar sighed. 'Our ways part here, Greer. I must stay on our Holy Isle and will join our ancestors in a short while. My sacrifice is necessary, but you must travel back to Voada's kingdom and raise a rebellion in the East.'

'There is always retreat into Hibernia.'

'Not for me,' Sacrovar smiled. 'I am far too old, and proud. Our peoples need me here. Speaking of whom, I should go down to the front to inspire them in person.' Here, he tried to stand, but his weakness was evident. Greer helped him up and called over to Taran to stay with their Archdruid.

'One last thing,' Sacrovar whispered into Greer's ear: 'travel by sea to the River Dee. Then cross overland to the Iceni. With hard-riding and the gods on our side, you can be there in two days but must leave now.'

'First, I will send a message to Voada, by rock dove, and then will follow with a slower foot.' Greer clutched his friend's arm as he added in a breaking voice, 'I hope to see you in the everlasting land of our heroes.'

'You will.' Sacrovar slapped him on the back. 'Now be on your way.'

Clasping his staff with strong fingers Greer gave him a resolute nod. Then he turned and left.

SAHAM TONEY

Voada was reading the message from Greer that had been carried home by the pigeon. 'The news is not good from the Holy Isle.' She passed the small piece of paper to Rory by her side as one of her maid servants continued to twine her hair into a long braid of russet pleats.

'Ouch!' Voada cried out angrily as the woman's bone comb snagged her hair.

'I'm sorry, my lady.' The woman bowed, wary of this new mistress. 'It is finished now.'

'Good. Leave us.' The woman tucked her combs and ties away in a basket and left the room.

Still holding the fragment of paper that Voada had passed to him, Rory held out his arms in a bemused manner. 'Voada, you know I cannot read.'

'Greer has used the Ogham code system which you can read.'

Rory looked again at the lines and crosses on the note and with a slow, halting voice began to read, 'Holy Isle under attack. Must divert attention in east. Back two days.' He paused. 'It is terrible news, but it is good that Greer is to return to us and that we have the sanctity of the Great Lord on Ynys Môn to begin our rebellion. With Ynys Môn under siege, we must strike the Romans very soon.'

Voada pushed back her chair and stood up throwing a woollen cloak around her shoulders. 'Come Rory, I want to see our preparations.' Rory stepped in beside her as she left the roundhouse. Outside in the afternoon sunlight, the Iceni stronghold was in full movement: the air was filled with the smell of horses and leather, and the sound of metal working could be heard from the royal mint. Not only was the mint producing cheapened coins, it was also turning out weapons to rearm the Iceni warriors and metal work for harnessing the horses. Voada called for horses for herself and Rory and then they trotted out of the settlement down the main track to the corral, a short distance from the outer fence. Even here, the road was busy as new people were arriving at the settlement every hour of every day; many were men who had come with fathers and brothers to fight as warriors. They had left the farmsteads in the countryside to be run by their wives and sisters, but some had brought the women with them too, to fight in the same cause.

At the training ring Voada halted her horse in order to watch Keara and Caitlyn fighting on horseback. Both were well-armed with iron swords and a circular, copper shield attached to the saddle. They had two javelins apiece, each enclosed in a case on their backs. For the moment, their instructor, one of Rory's warriors, was telling them to gallop hands free in order to use their slings and to fire the stone shot at a moving target. He was a good teacher, both patient and encouraging. He stood by the fence, squinting at the horses and their riders. Keara was by far the more accomplished of the two. Caitlyn was good, but she was slower in her movements. Despite this, she had recovered a little of her spirits and held the same, single-minded hatred of the Romans as her sister.

'Varney,' Caitlyn called to the man. 'How are we doing?'

'Just fine, just fine, my Queen,' he responded with an encouraging grin, 'but you need to bend your knees a little more so that your calves slide back further along the flanks of the horse. Hug its sides with your thighs and tuck your feet a little under its belly so you can go faster. But keep your back straight and concentrate on your target.' He flicked his long, brown hair off his shoulders and told the girls to try again.

When the lesson broke up, the girls had to unsaddle their horses. Blair ran over to help them. He was the son of their saddle maker and quickly took the saddles and harnesses to his father. The man hung the saddles over a fence and began to rub the leather with a rag and goose fat. He told his son to rinse the metal bits of the harnesses. Then the boy picked up a basket of tools and came sprinting back to clean the horses' hooves and brush their coats. At last, the girls unleashed the two stallions into the nearby meadow and Voada called her daughters to join her. She handed her reins to Rory and told him to stay at the arena with Varney.

'No,' he answered. 'I will obey you in most things, but I will not leave you alone outside of our fortress. I am your closest guardsman, and bodyguard to you. We need you alive and kicking.'

Instead of anger, Voada smiled to herself and let him follow them down to the lakeside. Here, she sat on the sands and viewed the wide expanse of murky waters cut up by pikes of reeds. She didn't realise that Keara had taken her hand. 'Greer will be with us soon,' she began, looking at the expressions of relief on both girls' faces. 'He'll be here in just two days. A messenger has been sent to tell him we are now at Saham Toney. However, the meeting point for the tribes that come to our cause is at Fison Way, as it is the main ceremonial centre for the Iceni and for the Trinovantes. It is just ten miles south of us on the Icknield Track Way so is easy for us to travel to, once all the tribes have arrived.'

'It's also the crossing point going south to Londinium,' Caitlyn spoke, 'which we will burn.'

'Each thing in its time,' Voada nodded, staring at her daughter. 'The Holy Isle is being attacked by the Roman legions, so we must attack the Roman capital at Camulodunum first which, we hope, will bring the Ninth legion down from its base at Clac-nyn.'

'Will it be enough to save our Holy Isle?' Keara reflected gazing across the waters at the further shore.

'We hope so.' Voada gave a hollow laugh and shook her head.

'Haven't the Romans noticed the movements of the Britannic tribes here, in the east?'

Voada marvelled at Keara. 'Of course they have, but we have our own spies amongst the Romans who are planting different stories in order to counter the truth. Fison Way is an important religious centre preparing for the festival of Beltane and, don't forget that, thanks to the Romans, our peoples are nominally unarmed so pose no threat to the Roman occupier.'

She smiled up at Rory for both knew that the majority of their tribesmen had simply buried their weapons fourteen years before so that they would not be confiscated by the Romans. What the Romans had ignored when they had unarmed the friendly tribes in the southeast was the great ancestral value of the Britons' weapons. Many of the swords had been passed down from father to son and would not then be passed on from Briton to Roman. The people had preferred to return the weapons to the land rather than give them to the foreign occupier. And so, they were now disinterring them and polishing them up.

Voada turned again to her daughters. 'As soon as Greer arrives we must have a council of the tribesmen here in Saham Toney. You must both be there, especially since Caitlyn, you are the Iceni Queen. Greer is our druidic leader and I hope to be elected the military and prophetic leader for all the tribes that join us. We will then move to the people waiting for us at Fison Way.' She stood to leave, but Keara wanted to stay a little longer at the lake.

Voada shrugged. 'Yes, but stay close to the drove track.'

Keara watched them walk back to Saham Toney and then she wandered down to the water's edge where a small coracle lay attached to some reeds. Alongside, she saw a number of wicker baskets for eel fishing and a long wooden pole. Drawn by the water, she climbed into the coracle and, grasping the rod, she pushed the boat into the lake. For some time she navigated the grassy waters until she was far away from the shore. Keara lay back in the boat. She pulled a knife from her belt and contemplated its smooth, velvet surface against the blue depth of the sky. Stroking a lock of her hair between her fingers and thumb, she held it up to the light – then sliced it off. She continued, working faster, dropping the long shocks of hair into the water, like offerings to the gods. She watched them float away. In the late afternoon light, she stopped her work and gazed up at the vault above. She began to read the clouds that skittered across her cropped head like startled bats fleeing the night owl. Rocking softly on the water Keara felt half mesmerised by Nuada's oracle of war and flight, of fear and darkness. God of the winds, the sky and of war, Nuada was telling her that the Romans must flee the fury of the Britons and the wisdom of the druids – or was it her?

She could not understand the signs of the gods anymore: they were no longer protecting this earth of hers, her family and people. Confused, alone, she felt startled by the darkness around her. She had fallen asleep and wasn't sure where she was anymore. Surrounded by water she could not see the shore. Frightened by her isolation she tried to keep the panic at bay but could not find the pole: it must have floated away whilst she was asleep. She suddenly felt that she was being sanctioned by the gods for her doubts and started to pray, but even then, she felt that her words would serve no purpose. Rowing frantically with her hands, she eventually touched the stiff reeds of shallower waters. She grasped them violently, pulling the coracle towards firm ground, but the sudden outline of large, dark beasts standing between her and land frightened her again. It was only the echo of her name along the shore that brought her to her senses. Calling back in such relief, she recognised the voice of Galdus as he came running towards her splashing through the squelching waters. He pulled up short on sight of her head. 'What have you done?

And where in the name of all the gods, have you been?' he cried, both alarmed and relieved. 'We have been looking everywhere for you.'

'I just, I just went out in the boat and must have fallen asleep... I'm sorry,' she said, half-crying, as she leapt out of the boat and threw her arms around her cousin. 'I didn't realise it was so late, and I lost the pole and got lost.' She was laughing now as she recognised the stupidity of her fear and mooed back at the *large dark beasts* munching the grass.

'Others are out looking for you,' Galdus frowned, hugging her to him and brushing strands of hair off her shoulders. 'I was so worried. You need a guardsman to look out for you and... someone to do your hair; I'll not leave your side again.' He breathed into her short, uneven hair, savouring the damp scent of grass and wild flowers in it, the warmth of her skin. He pressed her head to him, thankful that she was there with him, his for this moment.

Keara drew back, a little abashed, thinking only of the trouble she was in. 'My mother will kill me for this.' She indicated the lake and then pointed at her hair.

'I'll protect you from your mother,' Galdus laughed softly, 'but only if you promise not to do that to me again.' Reluctantly, he let Keara go and said, 'Come on, we better get back to the settlement before your mother sends out the whole company of warriors for you. She already has Rory out with his men.'

They walked up the slope and into the cow field.

'I won't do that again, Galdus, but I will tell my mother that I had a message from Nuada.'

A few days had passed, and despite the initial anger, and acrid invectives of her mother, Keara had been forgiven, though she had been confined inside the boundaries of the settlement until the day of departure. Greer had been to see her and her sister

a little every day since his return, but they had found it hard
to talk so, often, Greer would sit down outside on the grass
with just Keara, and they would play a game of backgammon.
He tried to hide his anxiety from her, but traces of it were
always visible in the lines of his face. Neither knew what to
say. Concentrating on the game seemed to help both of them
focus on the strategies of the opponent and to anticipate future
moves. They helped each other, exchanging advice, warnings,
false information, opportunities, until one of them had won the
game, though neither had lost since they had worked as one.

'One day you will surpass the master,' Greer recognised,
one afternoon.

With her elbows on her knees, Keara looked up at the old
druid. 'If I do, it is only because I have had the best of teachers.'

'If I were the best, I would have anticipated every move
that has recently been made.' He scowled at himself, at his
own stupidity. 'And I would have seen the Romans' coming.'

Keara felt suddenly more tense and wary. She drew herself
up and, feigning misunderstanding, she replied, 'You could not
have saved Ynys Môn.'

'No, I know, but I could have saved you.' Abruptly, he
stood up and gazed around at the bustling preparations for
the coming campaign. Then, he looked towards the sluggish
lake lying sleepily under the warm sky. He felt the soft rays of
sunshine on his face and in his hair, and seemed to meditate
for a brief moment before placing a hand on Keara's head. 'I
will do what I can to save you now.'

FISON WAY

Keara rode side by side with Galdus, a little behind her mother
and elder sister. She looked at the sloping back of Greer as he

rode beside Voada and Caitlyn. He had aged in just a few days, unable to bear the weight of loss, it seemed to her. But what loss? The loss of peace? The loss of freedom and their way of life? They had already lost everything. The tribal chieftains present at the war council the night before had all agreed upon that. They had even agreed to elect Voada as their war leader. This was a fragile decision, Greer had told her, because of Voada's sex, but a necessary one because only she could command enough support and the requisite courage in the field, and one which avoided the rivalry between the other clan leaders.

Galdus woke her from her reflections. 'We are nearly at Fison Way. We will only rest for one night. That's what was decided at the war council, but I could continue to ride on right now to Camulodunum and kill those Roman bastards. Every Iceni is ready and impatient to attack.'

'Yes, but my mother must address the other clans and invoke the gods for their blessing. If the signs are right, only then can we move on to the Roman colony.'

'We have already had plenty of signs, so have you.' Keara knew that he was referring to the signs that the god had sent her on the lake, but she had her own doubts about that. 'So have the people in Camulodunum,' Galdus continued, and here he chuckled to himself. 'We have sympathisers within the colony who have heard shrieks and yells coming from the senate house and from the theatre announcing the fall of Rome. We have also been helped by the blood-red water along the coast, spreading as far down as the Tamesis estuary. Obviously, the foreign colonisers don't know that it is caused by red algae. They think it is a sign from the gods of their blood being spilled, especially since others have also seen the shapes of human corpses left in the sand by the ebbing tides, along with a great number of empty houses under the water. But our *magnum opus* has to be the statue of Claudius.'

Even Keara smiled here and had to ask, 'Do we know who did it?'

'Of course,' Galdus raised an eyebrow. 'Some of Dubnov's men from the Trinovantes. They pulled the statue down in the dead of night before the Temple of Claudius. It now has its face in the dirt and its head facing Rome.'

'As though it were fleeing from the enemy, back to Rome,' Keara reflected.

'Exactly,' concluded Galdus. 'At least that is how it was interpreted in the morning when the people of Camulodunum found it. So, they have probably already sent to Cerialis asking for aid from his legion at Clac-nyn.'

'Cerialis won't send men to Camulodunum on the basis of a few bad omens.' Keara was quite sceptical about any help being sent to the colony. 'For one thing, there is, as yet, no real cause for alarm. And another thing is that all the men of the colony are ex-legionaries and quite capable of defending their settlement.'

'You think so? They are old and infirm. There are only a few active legionaries still based there, and it is a settlement with no defences. They filled in the ditches many years ago in order to claim more building space and make more filthy money. And you know that no help can be sent from Londinium as most of the fighting men are with the Governor in Cymru.' There was a moment's silence before Galdus added, 'And Cerialis will be taken care of.'

'I wish Catus would be taken care of too,' flushed Keara.

'He will, I promise you Keara. I will do it for you myself, when we get to Londinium.' He reached across and gripped her arm a moment as though making real on his promise. 'I would do anything for you.'

They were approaching the defences of Fison Way: a series of outer ditches and ramparts enclosed the ceremonial and religious centre of the Iceni. Many of the tribes were already encamped outside and gave a roar of salute to the approaching Iceni band. Many gave a short bow to Caitlyn and Voada as they passed between them, and the mother and daughter nodded back. Greer had dropped behind by then in order to join Keara and Galdus as they entered the only access into the stronghold: a central path into the eastern wall. The group rode along a straight corridor between a fencing of high, thick posts of oak up to a timber gateway which lay open onto a square enclosure. Without stopping they continued on the path to the opposite side of the wide grounds where a two-storied building stood flanked by a number of roundhouses, huts and workshops. Servants from the central building already stood aligned outside and immediately came forward to take the reins of the Iceni horses and lead the royal household inside so that they could make their final plans with the other leaders.

Around fifty clan leaders, high-ranking warriors and druids packed into the large roundhouse that evening, but it was no easy task calling a count. Apart from the Iceni and the Trinovante leaders the other groups represented smaller disaffected factions of other tribes such as the Cornovii, the Corielatavi, the Dobunni and the Atrebates, tribes which dominated the inner swathes of Britannic lands and who had already succumbed to Roman control. All of the tribes on the western coast were anti-Roman but were still busy fighting the Romans in their homelands in the west.

The council was held in the great hall with many sitting on the long, carved trunks of wood that served as benches. Keara sat in the second row, behind her mother and sister. Rory and another of his guards, Varney, it was, sat beside her keeping a watchful eye on proceedings. She looked at the lime-washed walls and the Iceni motifs that decorated them: the horse, the dog and crescent moons. She saw that the curtains had been drawn between the woven screens that enclosed their bed chambers. A gallery trimmed the hall under the eaves and a lot of provisions had been stocked there in wooden crates, baskets and clay jars. There were also great slabs of meat hanging from the rafters as it was dried and smoked there. *Would it be enough to feed them all?* she wondered.

It was getting hot in the hall with all the sweating bodies around her. The great fire had been banked down with slabs of peat, but braziers had been brought in and were burning at either end of the building in order to keep the central space clear for the different speakers. Voada stood first in order to welcome them all.

'I will keep this brief because I know you are all tired after the long journeys that you have made, and I thank you for answering my call. You all recognise the justice of this call or you would not be here, and you have all heard of how the Romans have treated my family and my people who were once loyal to Rome. It has been the same for you.

'You all know that in this fight we must triumph or die. This time there will be no middle ground for the weak or undecided. And this time we will overcome our enemy because we now stand united against injustice, tyranny and oppression. Tomorrow we will rise early so that our men can gather in the open air before this hall and be addressed by me and blessed by the gods.'

Voada sat down and was replaced by Dubnov of the Trinovantes. He was not an orator like Voada. His language was quite brutish, but the message was clear, even poignant, which was surprising, coming from such a loud and imperious man.

'The Trinovantes will take back our lands from the Catuvellauni, who have held them for over fifty years and who handed them on a plate to the Romans when I was a child. I was born into slavery, but I will not die a slave. My people all stand behind me in this for we have lost much over the years and have nothing else to lose. Our victory will be easy and swift, for the gods of vengeance are on our side. When we have won, we will feast on the flesh of our enemy. Not even their brats will be spared.'

Every tribe was given time to speak, and they each gave their name, their numbers and skills, but before they broke up for the night Voada told Caitlyn to address the council. Young and troubled as she was, she found the courage to stand and face the assembly. Looking at such delicate beauty the hall fell silent as the Britons listened to the few words she spoke, 'My people have declared me Queen of the Iceni though Rome does not recognise me as such. When this war is finished, and we have driven out the Romans from our island land I will remember my friends and allies, and I will always be loyal to those who stand by me today. Thank you everyone.' Every man in the hall stood as one and whooped in the air, shouting their support for such a courageous leader.

Standing beside Keara, Rory raised his cup to his young queen. He was followed by every man present, who raised their cup to toast the new queen's reign and their victory over the Romans.

In the early sunrise of that spring morning all the clans gathered in the huge enclosure, awaiting the ceremonial assembly and official blessing of the gods. The Beltane fires had been burning from the early hours on either side of the gateway, and would protect the lives of those who passed between them. Greer had stood next to the fires since he had first lit them. Rhonda was by his side and she was feeding the flames with pine cones so that they gave off a sweet odour of incense. When it was time for Greer to join Voada and her daughters, he left Rhonda to tend the fire by herself. The Iceni royal family was splendidly clothed in bright colours, rich fabric and golden jewels, fit for a crowning. A sea of warriors filled the enclosure, and many more lay without the walls. So many had answered Voada's call that it was impossible to count them. In later stories, some said more than a hundred thousand men had answered Voada's call-to-arms. They clapped their weapons and shields together and howled for action, the sanction of the gods, victory and freedom.

Slowly Voada ascended a tribunal, fashioned out of earth, and the men became calmer and quiet. Tall as she was, she appeared terrifying with her woad-painted arms and face, her fierce eyes, and mass of dark red hair that fell to her hips. She wore a long tunic of diverse colours, over which a thick mantle had been fastened with an Iceni brooch in the form of opposing crescent moons. Around her neck she wore a heavy gold torque and in her hand she held a spear.

'You have learnt by actual experience how different freedom is from slavery,' she began, sweeping her eyes slowly across the vast swathe of warriors before her. 'And though some of you may have been deceived by alluring promises of a better life in the Roman way you have learnt the truth. Now that we have tried both we have learnt how great a mistake we made in preferring an imported despotism to our ancestral mode of life, and we have come to realise how much better is poverty with no master than wealth with slavery. What have we not suffered, of the most humiliating sort, since these men first made their appearance in Britannia? Have we not been robbed entirely of most of our possessions? And what we have left, we must pay taxes on. Besides pasturing and working the earth for them, do we not pay a yearly tribute with our bodies, giving up our young men for service overseas in their military forces? How much better it would have been if we had been taken into slavery once and for all rather than possessing empty titles of freedom. How much better to have been slain and to have perished than to go about with a tax on our heads. Yet why do I mention death for even death is not free of taxes with them. And why is it that, though none of us has any money, we are still stripped and despoiled like a murderer's victims?

'But, to speak the plain truth, it is us who are responsible for our own fate in that we allowed them to set foot on this island in the first place instead of expelling them at once as we did their famous Julius Caesar. As a consequence, although we inhabit so large an island that is encircled by the sea, and although we possess a veritable world of our own separated by the oceans from all the rest of mankind, we have been despised and trampled underfoot by men who know nothing other than how to secure slaves, grain and gold. However, even at this late hour, let us, my countrymen, do our duty while we still remember what freedom is, so that we may leave to our children their freedom.

'All this I say to you, not to inspire you with hatred of the Romans or fear for the future, for those you already have, but to commend you for being here of your own free will, and to thank you for uniting with me and with each other against the common enemy. The Romans are not superior to us in numbers or in bravery. We know the land, its forests, its lakes and hills, and we have the gods on our side. Let us show the Romans that we are the bears and the wolves. They are the rats that eat our grain and the foxes that run away.'

When Voada had finished speaking to the tribesmen before her, she performed an act of divination. As military leader and as prophetess for her people, she needed the gods to show their favour of her enterprise. As Keara well knew, watching her mother bend down, there was a hare hidden in the folds of her underskirt. Deftly, and unseen, Voada pulled loose a ribbon and released the young hare, which immediately sprinted off the tribune to the south and, since this was interpreted as an auspicious sign by Greer, the whole multitude shouted with pleasure. Voada then raised her hands to the sky, pointing the spear at the sun.

'I thank you, Andraste, goddess of war and of victory, for blessing our fight. The men and the women whom I lead into battle know the art of war and have the hearts of courage. I supplicate and pray for victory, protection of life and liberty against the Romans, men who are insolent, unjust, insatiable and impious. They are men who take our boys, violate our women and rape our lands. We will now join together and march on Camulodunum.'

Many gave a yell of delight, impatient to leave, to face the Roman enemy and take back their lands and wealth, but first, they had to pass through the Beltane fires onto the roads of war. Caitlyn was the first to leap across the flames on her startled mare, closely followed by Voada and then Rory and Galdus before they trotted through the gates and along the enclosed lane to the open road. Many horses hesitated before the fires, but if the horse refused to jump this was interpreted as a bad sign for the rider. Keara took her place beside Greer, who gave his blessing to every Iceni warrior as they passed through the fire. Those who were on foot, or who were to travel on wagons outside, walked between the two great fires. The warriors from the other clans were blessed by their own priests. At last, Keara leapt onto her horse, and she, too, jumped across one fire as Greer passed through the other. As he did so he signalled goodbye to Rhonda.

'Look after our people,' he cried.

IV

Camulodunum

Spurius was anxious. He was trying not to be, and was oiling the attachments on his segmented plate armour and polishing the strips with an intensity that was unfamiliar to him. Sitting on a bench in the armour room, he needed a drink – another one in fact. He wasn't meant to drink whilst on duty, but, based in the small garrison in the Roman colony, life had become less arduous than elsewhere in the Province. He was due to retire soon and had already reserved the land he wanted for his older days. In fact, he had already begun building on it – well, rather, his slaves had, and he was charging a high rent to the small Trinovante family who was farming the land. He put his armour back on its rack and placed his cleaning tools in their box. That drink was calling to him, and he needed to speak to others and find out what was happening.

He hurried from the garrison which was always open; its main role nowadays was to help the retired soldiers with their pensions and administration. Camulodunum's garrison also collected the taxes, grain and land from the Trinovante tribesmen, and oversaw the building of the Temple of Claudius. He hurried past the Temple, which was almost finished, but he cast a fearful eye at the statue of the dead emperor, Claudius which still lay in the dirt where it had fallen. As soon as he saw the tavern, just before the theatre, he broke into a small trot and raced into the open door. He ordered an ale and threw himself down at a table. An old man sat opposite him. Spurius knew him from the colony; the man had lands next to his.

'Any news yet from the Governor and from the Procurator?' the man asked.

'Suetonius will only send the Ninth legion down to us from Clac-nyn. He's too busy on Ynys Môn,' Spurious responded, taking a gulp of his sour ale.

'That should be a match for the tribesmen. And what about the Procurator? Has Catus sent us any men from Londinium yet?'

'Yes.' Spurius shook his head and gave the man a disabused look. 'Just two hundred soldiers. That's not enough.'

'Where are they then?'

'At the main gates north; they're looking over the river and trying to build up some fortifications.'

'And what are you doing here? Shouldn't you be with them?' The old man put his cup down as he spoke, and a small dribble of wine ran down his chin.

Spurius felt uncomfortable under the man's gaze but drank deeply before answering, 'I have been cleaning equipment in the garrison and needed a drink before going back on duty. And what about you? We know there is trouble brewing. Shouldn't you be helping too?'

'No, I don't think there'll be any trouble,' the man smirked, showing his toothless gums. 'And we've got Cerialis's Ninth on its way. This rebellion will be over in no time, just like the last one, and the one before that. And you have no need to worry: after all it's just a horde of women and you've dominated them before.' Here, he chuckled, and Spurius knew he was alluding to his whipping of the Iceni queen mother. His back stiffened.

Suddenly, there was the sound of an alarm: a horn was blowing, signalling an attack. Spurius stood up abruptly, and then sat down again. He needed another drink.

'Get off,' the retired soldier said to him. 'Get back onto duty and do your job for once.'

Spurius stood up again and decided to hurry back to the garrison.

At the garrison Spurius could see a great deal of movement. Soldiers were running in and out of the building, collecting armour and weapons. An auxiliary cavalryman was there on horseback. His hands held the pommel of his saddle as he bawled out orders to the men to work faster. Spurius recognised him as the decurion who had violated the Iceni princess, and felt reassured to find someone in the same delicate position as himself.

'Get yourself armed,' Titus shouted at him fiercely, 'and join the North Gate.' Then he turned his black stallion round and began galloping back to the North Gate himself. From his saddle Titus could see over the low land, across the river to the north. The plain was a flood of Celtic tribesmen moving slowly towards the river from every angle. Marius was at the gate too; as a Roman tribune, he had command of the forces until Cerialis arrived.

'Have you told the women and children to leave yet?' Titus almost shouted.

'It's too late,' Marius answered, half-paralysed with fear. 'Whilst you were at the garrison we have had news that the whole colony has been surrounded.'

'You know that we do not have enough men, even with the veterans, to defend a whole colony that has no defences. We must pull in and hold out until reinforcements arrive. Send the women and children into the Temple Square and barricade it closed. It is the surest place until Legion Nine gets here.'

Marius rubbed his head angrily for a moment, and then called to another soldier, 'Send the women and children into the Temple and tell the men to pull in from the outer walls. We will defend the Temple Precinct.'

Titus jumped off his horse and told the other cavalrymen to do the same. Then he indicated for them all to let their mounts go. He slapped his stallion's flank and the horse galloped off outside the gate and along the river.

'What are you doing?' Marius cried.

'They can't help us here. If we are retreating into the Temple Precinct they will only be in the way, and the Britons would kill them. If they make it out, they will probably follow the river south, away from all this noise, and Zia should find them at the farmstead where we left him with the other mounts.' He signalled to his unit of men to retreat. The first Britons were already crossing the river bridge just a short distance away.

'Why didn't you destroy the bridge?' Titus creased his eyebrows in annoyance.

'I left it for the Ninth Legion to cross!' Marius cursed.

'Well, it's now there for the Britons to cross,' Titus rejoined. 'We must fall back. Let us hope that our Roman forces *are* on their way.'

The Roman road from Clac-nyn followed the ancient trackway across the hills from the Middle Lands down onto the main supply road and through the flatter, wooded areas of the Southeast. Cerialis had almost two thousand men with him, including a unit of five hundred cavalry. With forced marches of twenty-five miles a day, Cerialis knew his men would reach Camulodunum in three days. However, the Legate's Prefect was anxious.

'Sir, the men are tired, and we are vulnerable here.'

Here was in an extended line leading through thickly wooded, and silent, terrain. It was uncannily quiet for a warm, spring afternoon. All that could be heard was the stomp of the infantrymen and the clatter of their back packs behind the vanguard of cavalry. They would have to stop soon anyway because the horses needed food, water and rest and, what was more, the baggage wagons had fallen so far behind, they were no longer visible.

'Sir, the scouts still haven't come back.'

'Petro,' Cerialis said, sounding impatient and tired himself, 'this road is a Roman road. We have two thousand men with us, all of whom are highly trained, skilled and experienced in warfare. The rebels cannot have more than a thousand men, half of whom are probably boys. They do not know we are coming and, even if they did, they are certainly no match for my legion. We must protect Britannia's hinterland for the Emperor, and we have had our orders from the Governor. We will get to Camulodunum before the tribes, so we must sometimes take risks in life and war. Am I absolutely clear?'

Petro breathed out, 'Yes, you...' He did not finish his phrase. His eyes suddenly lost their expression of annoyance and turned to one of surprise. The man looked down to stare confusedly at the arrow fixed in his larynx just above his metal cuirass. Then he looked up again at Cerialis but could not breathe. The blood was already spurting from the wound and pouring out of his mouth. He let go of his reins and slid from the horse. There was immediate shock and panic as the other soldiers understood what was happening: Legion Nine was under attack. From either side of the track Iceni warriors had suddenly appeared. Emerging from the trees, bushes and gorse that hedged the lane, they fell upon the dislocated line of Roman soldiers in one swift movement.

Cerealis had a reputation for being impetuous and rash, but he was certainly no coward. He immediately pulled up his shield from the flank of his horse and drew out his sword in order to enter the fray, shouting orders at the men to group together in their cohorts. They obeyed, pulling together for a better defence, but their movements were clumsy, hampered as they were by equipment and surprise. The legionaries were already falling, being slaughtered in their hundreds. Despite their training and discipline, they were undermined by the sheer numbers of the enemy and by the suddenness of the attack.

Cerialis recognised the Iceni fighters leading the attack on both sides: Rory and Varney, from the Iceni's royal guard on one flank and the young Prince Galdus on the other. Galdus had one of the Iceni princesses with him, Keara, who was almost unrecognisable under her woad body paint and short-cut hair. There was a ferocity in their attack which was unnerving. Enraged and fearless they stormed through the Roman flanks. The legionaries had managed to shuffle off their packs, but many did not have time to pull out a weapon or to put up a defence. They found what they could, a knife, a stick or rock, but were cut down like animals in the slaughterhouse.

Cerialis's cavalry could do nothing to relieve the legionaries on the ground. They were cut off at the front and the rear by Iceni riders. Keara was one of them. She had jumped onto a riderless horse and was fighting her way towards the vanguard where Cerialis was resisting. The long period of waiting had paid off. Rory's men had killed the Romans' Catuvellauni scouts hours before and had used their own scouts to assess the Romans' movements and calculate the most viable point of attack: the forest in late afternoon, when the Romans were tired. In this brief battle, there was no time for thought or feeling. Keara pushed forward, instinctively hacking at arms and heads in order to forge a passage towards the legate and his officers. The Roman cavalry was already drawing away.

The situation was irremediable for the foot soldiers, and the massacre was devastating. The Britons were taking no hostages and leaving no survivors. Cerialis and his cavalry could do nothing for the legionaries. They could only look out for themselves and had to fight their way back along the track and out of the woods before reforming in open land and galloping cross-country towards the lowered sun. As dusk began to fall, it seemed that they had lost the pursuing Iceni riders and they continued to ride on into the night and into seemingly friendly territory. Eventually, Cerialis turned north to rejoin any remaining cavalry on the road back to Clac-nyn. His footmen had been decimated. He could do nothing for Camulodunum. The colony was on its own.

Voada rode across the bridge with the Trinovante chief, Dubnov at her side. Caitlyn and Greer rode with them, the hooves of their horses dappled in crimson mud as they followed the road into Camulodunum and towards the Temple of Claudius. The bodies of Roman veterans could be seen strewn in fragmented limbs along the south bank of the river Colne, and on the streets lay the puzzled forms of women and children. Dubnov told his men to spare no one. The odours of blood, sweating flesh and putrid bowels hung everywhere on the air whilst maddened dogs barked at their hooves, drunk with crushed bones.

Dubnov was exultant as he and his men were able to reclaim the lands of their ancestors, and the city of his birth. There was still heavy fighting in the Temple Precinct. Dubnov joined the fray as Voada, Caitlyn and Greer watched the quick movements of the bloodied men. They came to a standstill at the line of combat. There were a lot of flames as Dubnov's men torched the buildings, stores and taverns. Through the thick smoke, the sights and sounds were muffled a little so that everything seemed unreal. Caitlyn stared with wonder at the Temple of Claudius and the numbers of people running into it. Were they laughing or crying? she thought, as they ran up the steps, passing through the giant stone columns of the portico and into the Temple itself, pulling the great portals closed behind them.

In the consuming smoke and flames Marius could see nothing before him but the slowly advancing outline of Titus, who was being pushed ever backwards onto him. He heard the hollow thuds of the temple doors being closed and barred somewhere further behind them and realised in a moment of horror that they were condemned. The noises, the cries, the clash of metal, the breaking of wood, seemed suspended on the smoke as he contemplated the heaving back of his fellow soldier and thought of the family he had left in Rome; he had only a fragment in time to fear their loss before his back thudded against a brick wall and panic engulfed him.

'Get in there. Move! Get in there and stop pissing yourself!' It was the voice of Titus, pushing him between the wall and a wooden barricade into a doorway. 'If you want to get out of this alive then do as I do.' The man had already pulled a burning cart into the doorway behind them and began to strip off his armour.

'What are you doing?' Marius managed to splutter. 'We'll choke in this smoke.'

'Chuck your weapons and armour into the cart and help me lift this stone,' Titus ordered, as he threw the last of his weapons into the flames. 'Only keep your knife.' Marius finally understood what Titus meant to do and shuddered as he looked at the dirty stone seats of the public latrines and then back at the burning barricade.

'No time for histrionics,' Titus sneered. 'We'll lift this. Then you get your arse in.' Titus quickly joined Marius in the drainage system beneath the city, and they lowered the long slab of stone back into place. 'We follow the sewage.'

'Come,' Voada spoke to her, breaking into Caitlyn's reverie. 'We must dismount here and can rest in the open theatre until the Temple falls.' They had to lead their mounts carefully across the broken glass and tiles, the shards of pottery and splintered wood that strewed the cobbled road and the walkway leading to the theatre. In the open grounds, they tied their mounts to some fencing and sat down on the fixed benches around the arena.

'How long until the Temple falls?' Voada stopped one of Dubnov's men.

'I don't know. Depends how much food and water they have inside. They hope to hang on until reinforcements arrive.'

'Then let them hope,' said Voada in a cold, hard voice. 'Let us enjoy the spectacle until the end. We will enjoy the fires and the cooking out here, and watch them starve in their dark tomb within.'

'When will we hear back from Rory?' Greer asked.

'Tonight, I should think. In the meantime, we need to make ourselves comfortable for the siege.' As she said this, some of their supply wagons began to roll into the theatre grounds; Voada gave orders to start unloading them and to set up camp.

Outside the theatre the city of Camulodunum was burning and would continue to burn for several days. The sky had turned a grey-bluish bruise through the tendrils of smoke, tendrils that stretched and swirled through the air and across the city and river. From places over the land, other columns of smoke could be seen dispersed by the wind as Roman farmsteads and abandoned watchtowers were burnt to the ground. No prisoners were taken. Such was Dubnov's rage and Voada's desire for revenge that orders had been given to spare no one. The Trinovante men spent the next few hours seeking out any survivors hiding in cellars, wells or drains. Whenever they found stragglers, they would drag them out of their hiding hole; if these captives were not killed immediately, they were made to carry timber logs along one of the many roads leaving the city, where they were then crucified and left to contemplate their vanished world and miserable ending.

That evening Galdus, Keara, Rory and his men joined the Britannic tribesmen at Camulodunum, and there were celebrations to thank the gods for such a victory. Men collected wooden beams, planks and other debris from the buildings; they piled them high in the Temple Precinct and began a huge bonfire. A number of tribesmen also laid out tables of food and drink, placing them with makeshift benches, chairs and couches that they had salvaged from the surrounding houses. There was to be an offering of gratitude to Andraste, the Iceni goddess of war and victory, and also to Cernunnus, the hunter-god. Keara sat on a bench in the front row, closest to the fire, along with her family and other members of the warrior elite. The elation and excitement of all around her were palpable and contagious. Like riding bareback on the withers of an uncracked horse, she could feel the freedom and wildness of the crowd around her. They had taken Camulodonum. They had defeated a Roman legion; its legate had turned tail and fled before them. No one could resist their force now. Mesmerised by the winking light before her, she dreamed of an island free of Rome, and of a land that belonged once again to her people.

She looked at the improvised Celtic temple her people had set out in this Roman precinct. The fallen statue of Claudius had been hacked to pieces and dragged off so that the central fire could be built up with many incense burners and torches illuminating the outskirts of the square. Sitting cross-legged on the flat paving stones a number of masked warriors formed a perimeter around the fire. Keara's eyes rested on them for a time, looking at the glistening sweat on their arms as they each pressed a short club onto one knee and held the decapitated head of an enemy on the other. Fresh blood dripped still onto the flagstones looking like the spilt drops of ink on parchment. One masked warrior struck her as different from the others: his hands were empty, and she wondered why he had nothing to hold, but then she saw a long, iron sword on the ground in front of him.

Greer stood before the people with his back to the fire. He looked nothing like the druid that Keara had known all her life. Threatening and imposing, he had dressed himself for the occasion in a huge mantle of mistletoe that Caitlyn and her women had woven for him all that afternoon and evening. His face was covered with a light bronze mask, just like the seated warriors, with only three openings for his eyes and mouth. Around his neck hung many golden chains strung with the talismans of the Iceni: crescent moons, suns and chariot wheels. And in his arms, he held a heavy wicker basket which he placed on a platform so that he could hold his oaken staff and pound it into the ground. All fell silent as he stood before them and began to chant an incantation to the goddess in the ancient Britannic tongue. With his eyes half-closed, he skipped over the rolling verses of his invocation, 'We thank thee great goddess of war and revenge for the victory you have given us this day. You have allowed us to reclaim this earth, the land that belongs to you and to your people, and to cast out the Roman invader. The Romans sought to expel us from this world and from the lives we have always known in order to impose their will, their taxes and their gods on our heads. We will not bear this weight. We are a free people, and victory is ours.' The people roared, waving weapons in the air and shaking rattles and bells in a great cacophony of sound. With his last words, he indicated for Voada to rise and come forward, and the people fell silent again. Even those in the Temple were quiet as they listened to the frightening sounds of this barbaric ritual.

'Andraste gave our leader the signs for our victory and this has been accorded.' Greer spoke in a portentous tone. 'Let Andraste now give Voada her title of Victor.' He opened the lid to the basket and pulled out a large horned helmet upon which a golden torc balanced. The people gasped when they saw the basket shake violently, for there, where the helmet had rested sat the huge, long-eared hare of Andraste. Voada immediately bent her knee in honour to the goddess before her. Greer stepped forward and placed the horned helmet on her head. 'This is from Cernunnus, the god who hunts down its enemies,' he bowed. Then he took the torc from its horns and slid it around Voada's neck. 'This is from Andraste, the goddess who names you *Boudica*,' he shouted to the people, 'meaning the Great Victor.' He pulled Voada up and turned her so that she faced the tribes.

'Boudica! Boudica!' they chanted.

'I thank you, Andraste, for your blessing and your gift of victory,' Voada spoke, raising the basket in her arms so that the people gazed in wonder at the embodiment of their goddess. 'Such a victory is priceless, and we can only repay it with the blood of our enemies.'

There was the noise of shuffling as several war prisoners were dragged forward towards the fire, gagged and cuffed.

They were pushed to their knees, writhing and jerking to be free, but to no avail. The sworded warrior rose from the ground. Then, one after the other, in rhythmic timing, he decapitated these human offerings to Andraste. With this, Voada knelt down on the blood-drenched stones and let the hare run free. It raised its ears, twitching them violently before racing off, zigzagging between its worshippers into the darkness. Moments later a Trinovante druid came running back into the precinct with a torch and, having followed the bloodied paw marks of the hare, he shouted, 'It has run to the east side, to the right of the Temple.' Such good tidings led to a sigh of thanks to the gods.

Then Voada, newly named the people's *Boudica*, threaded her fingers through a number of the severed heads, which lay gently rocking on the ground, and she walked towards the closed portals of the Temple of Claudius. Addressing the besieged Romans inside, she called into a chilling silence, 'You have seen what your foreign gods have done for you,' and here she slung the Roman heads onto the porch. 'Nothing! Britannia is the land of our gods, not any false Roman god, and your temple will not protect you from our fury, nor our justice.' Here, her men ran up throwing bales of straw and burning faggots onto the main porch of the Temple. Voada scoffed, 'We do not want you to starve as you wait for your rescuers. At least you will have something to feed on in the coming days, which is more than you gave us.' This raised a great whoop of laughter from the Britons, but from within the Temple there was no answer, only the occasional cry of a baby or young child, as their wait, or their wake, continued.

Outside, musical instruments began to sound on the night air, and the food and drink were served. Under a deep, dark sky and gibbous moon, the Britons celebrated a heroic victory: they drank and danced, they sang – and slept little.

The next day Voada had a most satisfying moment when a man was found hiding in a drain behind the Temple. He had been found by one of her Iceni men and recognised, too, as the Roman who had whipped her at Venta Icenorum. Dragged before Voada, Spurius had pleaded with her for pity, begged for mercy, promised her his lands and wealth in exchange for life, all to no avail. He made a pitiful sight as he croaked like a crab on his hands and knees praying to his gods for protection, but Voada was unmoved. Hatred bit into her like a fierce knife and she spat on him. 'Execution is too good for you, but you will be executed: a slow, gelded death for the crimes against my family.' She ordered Rory to have the man castrated in front of the Temple.

Spurius was dragged backwards, screaming and kicking, his contorted mouth drooling until someone stuffed it with a dirty cloth. There was not a single look of pity from the waiting crowd of warriors. Voada had called her daughters to her side to watch Iceni justice, and they were both impassive as the man's legs were held apart and Rory bent down to cut the man's testicles off, one after the other. Rory slung the flaccid balls to the dogs to eat. Then he pulled the cloth from the man's mouth and used it to clean his knife. There was only a little blood trickling from the wound.

'I don't want you to bleed to death, do I?' Rory sneered.

The man whimpered and cried, but now his words were incoherent streams of dribble. Voada had him strung up and crucified in the exact same place where the statue of Claudius had once stood. There, he had blubbered and moaned for two days until the final fall of the Temple and his own death claimed him.

Before its fall Greer had asked to speak to Voada in her makeshift tent in the theatre. 'You must decide what to do with those still inside the temple,' he had begun.

'They will all die.' She had shrugged her shoulders quite indifferent as she indicated for him to take a seat, but he had remained standing.

'There are women and children there too.'

'Did they consider our women and our children? Look at my scarred back. Look at my daughters.'

'Voada, this is revenge, not justice.'

'You spoke yourself of Andraste's revenge in last night's ceremony,' she had riposted.

'Aye,' Greer had replied, staring at the ground. 'I know, but those were the words of the ritual, and you, and Andraste, have had your revenge. We have won. I do not like this bloodbath. At least, let the children go.'

There had been a moment of hesitation. 'I cannot,' she had sighed, less with anger than with resignation. 'This is what the tribes want. If we are to stay united, I must appear strong and let them have their full revenge and let them retake their wealth from these Roman thieves. What is more, we do not have the food to keep prisoners or Roman slaves. They must die.'

'But you are the Boudica now. The tribes will follow you because Andraste has promised them victory through you.'

'Andraste is our Iceni goddess. The other tribes have their own gods. And whilst all the Britons follow the hunter, Cernunnus, it is only for one season, so I can't keep the tribes together for long.'

Sadly, Greer had acknowledged the truth of this, but he had held her eyes, frowning. 'And what about the pillaging in the surrounding country? We need to be faster and more structured if we are to relieve Ynys Môn from Suetonius's attack.'

'Greer, I would like nothing better than to march straight up to Ynys Môn, but the tribesmen want to go to Londinium first.'

'Is that for more pillaging, and for Catus?'

Voada had felt her anger rise at Greer's accusing tone. 'We need to take control of Londinium in order to prevent Roman reinforcements landing from Gaul. This will cut Suetonius off. But yes, Londinium is a wealthy city and holds a lot of supplies that we need in order to feed our men in the coming weeks, months even.' Voada had paused, before adding in a more tempered voice, 'I also want to find the men responsible for 'touching' my daughters, and the man who gave the orders to do so. He has dishonoured my family. I cannot repair the harm he has done to Keara and Caitlyn but when I find him I will take his life.'

At this, Greer had bent his head and given Voada a grim nod, 'You are our leader and must decide what is best for our people, but the gods will decide what is best for our land.'

Titus and Marius lay in the public latrines of the Temple Precinct for many hours. They had moved further along the sludge of shit into a wider sewage channel underground where Titus had told Marius not to speak, nor to move. Here, they waited, listening to the scuttle of rats, and the massacre above. They could see nothing, but could smell everything: the shit, the piss, the blood and burning. They could feel these things too: the itching, prickling on their skin, the searing of their eyes.

'I will kill you for this plan,' a weary and tired voice hissed at Titus. 'We must have been here for over a day now. I do not want to die like this.'

'Do you think this was planned! You're lucky to be here at all and not with those poor bastards in the Temple. When the Temple falls, they will all be massacred. And all we can do is wait here until the Britons are tired of searching the water works and pipes, and even then, we can only come out in darkness.' Marius was silent. It seemed like the following night when finally, Titus shuffled Marius's head with his boot and began drawing himself forward on his elbows. They took a right fork into a different drainage system and found themselves crawling underneath the town's water works. Although this could be opened from the outside for repairs, it could not be opened from the inside for an escape. The two men continued to crawl forward as silently as they could, and from time to time they heard muffled bawling from the chambers of the hydraulic system and water tanks. The water works were as big as the Temple itself and as they were roofed over many warriors were camping there. The two men could also hear a number of hammers falling on bricks and ceramics.

'What are they doing?' Marius whispered.

'Probably destroying the pipes to the Temple to stop the water supply.'

'They are barbarians and we will be killed when they destroy this pipe.'

'I doubt they will touch this pipeline just yet,' Titus said. 'They don't want to be flooded with Roman shit. They would have checked these channels yesterday and will now have men posted on the river Colne where the sewage comes out. Keep moving forward.'

The sounds dropped away behind them as they left the water works and reached one of the northern gates of Camulodunum. Here, the trench opened into a wider drainage ditch, leaving the city, but the line was still covered with great paving slabs. The two men continued along this until a small breeze could be felt on their faces coming in from the river. Titus waited at the opening, listening for any sounds from the river bank. An otter was swimming a few yards upstream in the cleaner water. Its long, slim body moved sleekly just underneath the surface, its head and whiskers cut the water line dispersing small ripples in its wake. Titus still hesitated to come out. He could hear a little movement on the bank: the quiet movement of earth and twigs. He peered into the darkness and by the light of a crescent moon could make out the shadow of a bulky, short-legged wading bird very close to them which was pecking the earth for worms and spiders. As Marius began squirming in the ditch the startled woodcock immediately took to flight. The Roman was already pushing Titus forward, impatient to be out at last and desperate to breathe fresh, cool air and to drink clean water.

They both slithered into the cold water, along with the grime, mud, shit and urine from the city. As they broke surface a few yards down the river, they suddenly found themselves being pursued by a pair of Britons who had broken from the undergrowth at the sound of their movement. Splashing water and breaking reeds could be heard in the darkness as legs waded into the water after Marius and Titus. One of the Britons called for aid, and a group of Trinovante warriors appeared on the bank. The silhouettes of the Roman soldiers were easy to make out on the water. A spear pierced the surface close to Titus and remained standing up in the sludge. Titus pulled it out and quickly took aim in the trees returning the spear to its owner. It seemed that he did touch someone as there was a shriek of pain but no more.

The two Britons in the water were approaching slowly through the muddy depths. They had their shields and swords out. Marius and Titus had only their knives and did their best to parry the thrusts and cuts. With the small slice of moon above the trees, it was difficult to see. At times it was easier to calculate an opponent's move by their reflection on the water, but none found it easy to fight in the river. No more spears were falling. It seemed that the Trinovantes were worried they might hit their own men, so they were beginning to wade into the water to join the fray. The first two Britons were fighting well, though their long swords were difficult to wield in the river. The smaller of the two had engaged Titus in deeper water, but was no match for the more experienced fighter. It was only when the Roman stepped backwards and tripped over a river stone that the small Briton was able to thrust his sword at Titus's chest, blocked just in time by the other's timely find of a flat rock. However, at this moment the Briton saw the Roman soldier's full face and hesitated for a second. Titus, too, saw the Briton's face, but gave no sign of recognition. His face closed: hard and angry as he plunged backwards into the depths and disappeared.

'Careful he doesn't attack you from under the water. Move away, quickly.' It was the voice of Galdus addressing Keara. Turning his own attention away from Marius for just a second, he took a slash to his sword arm and dropped his weapon. The Roman turned and fled into the middle of the river. Seeing this, Galdus picked up a rock from the riverbed and threw it with great precision after the man. It struck Marius on the side of his head and he lost consciousness, sinking into the water. The body came up again further down the river where it floated just beneath the surface before being swept away by the current. The two Iceni warriors were quickly joined by the Trinovante tribesmen.

'What was that about?' one of them panted.

'Two Romans came out of the waste drain there,' Galdus breathed hard. 'One of them is dead. As for the other, he could be anywhere by now.'

'They must have found that gay,' another man laughed sheathing his sword, 'stuck in the waste pipe for over a day. If that's all they had to drink the one that got away will catch the gastric fever for sure.'

A while later Galdus and Keara were sitting around a fire drying their wet clothes on the bank of the river. Galdus leant towards Keara. 'Why did you hesitate?'

'Hesitate?'

'Yes, in the river. You could have killed that Roman, but you hesitated. That Roman might have killed you then.'

'But he didn't,' she replied.

'Why did you hesitate?' Galdus persisted.

'I thought I recognised him.' There was a moment of silence and then Keara shrugged. 'The two men were the ones from Venta Icenorum.'

At the tone of her voice, Galdus looked up sharply. '*The* two men, the ones who...'

'Yes.'

'And which was which? No, you don't need to answer,' Galdus broke off. 'I can guess. At least we can tell Caitlyn that her body's enemy is dead.'

Keara stirred the fire with her sword. 'It is a shame we have no head to show her though.'

'How could you be so sure that the sewage pipes would be wide enough for you?' Zia's anger was tempered with relief as he listened to his master's account.

'I couldn't but as they were the main pipes that joined the water works from all over the city they had to be the biggest,' Titus answered wiping his face.

'And why is he still alive?' Zia grumbled indicating the mass of crumpled blankets on the rush bed.

'I have no idea, but he comes from an influential family in Rome.'

'I know exactly why he's still alive.' Zia shook his head at Titus. 'You probably saved his life again. I wish you would stop doing that.' Zia tutted. 'It's because of your medical training.

Not that you're a doctor or anything but because of your uncle's household.'

Titus had left his uncle's house when he was still a child and had been sent to Rome as a hostage in order to be educated there. He had known nothing but the army ever since, but had never forgotten the rudiments of his early medical training.

'It must have been pretty disgusting this time though,' Zia continued. 'Cleaning out the man's mouth, full of shit.'

'I didn't mind hitting him on the back so much,' Titus rejoined.

At this Marius stirred again and raised his head in the dim light of the roundhouse. He was looking at Zia. 'Give me some water.'

Zia pretended not to hear him and stomped out of the hut. A few moments later, he was joined by Titus. 'We must be off now Zia.' Titus was frowning. 'Where are my horses?'

'Your horses are in the stables round here. We have the other horses in the fields.'

'Just open the gate for them.' Titus nodded his head towards the field. 'We can't take all of them with us.'

'Your stallion, Cabrel found his way back here,' Zia continued, 'as he had already learnt the way. I'm keeping my mare though. You'll have to let that Roman arsehole have your other stallion – if the horse will let him on his back.' Zia pursed his lips and turned off to the stables. 'And you'll have to harness your own horses,' he added over his shoulder.

'What insolence!' Marius screeched, as he came out of the hut. 'I'll have his hide for this.'

Titus held him back. 'Now is not the time. We must saddle the horses and be off to Londinium as soon as possible. But you may have to ride with Zia for my stallions do not like strangers.'

'I *will* ride your second war horse,' Marius cried. 'I'll ride with no slave.'

Riding into Londinium, Titus rode the first horse into the city. He led his second stallion on its harness, followed by his dappled, pack-horse which was carrying two men: Zia and Marius.

V

Ynys Môn

O N Ynys Môn crows were already pecking at the dead. The bodies of the Celtic tribes lay across the beaches and in amongst the trees where they had fallen. Some floated in the rising tide ebbing in against the green-clad stones. Their long, dark hair trailed out like seaweed around their heads and shoulders.

Trajanus, the senior tribune to Legion Twenty, stood on the beach. He called a soldier to him, 'Do we have any prisoners?'

'Not many, sir, as the general only wanted to keep a few to clean up after us. He told us to spare the men who looked fit and uninjured. The other prisoners have already been executed.'

'You mean the women and boys?'

The soldier looked a little uncomfortable for a moment. 'Yes, sir.'

'A real massacre then.' Trajanus spoke this half under his breath so he wouldn't be heard by the man. 'Where are the other tribunes?'

'They are with the legates in the ancient grove of the druids.'

A messenger came running up to Trajanus telling him to join his own legate, Bolanus in the druids' grove. Trajanus finished cleaning his sword and hands in the sea waters. He also washed the blood off his thickset arms and legs before cupping some seawater in his hands and throwing it over his face. He strode up the shore following a path inland. Many of the soldiers were resting or being tended to by the legionary doctors, but the Roman losses were few compared to those of the Britons. The surviving Britons had been immediately disarmed and had their ankles shackled together. They were being directed to clear the shoreline of the dead and load the bodies onto wagons.

'Where are they taking all the bodies?' Trajanus asked a centurion's second, an optio, who was supervising the work.

'For now, they are taking them to their own groves, sir, and will burn them there. May Mithras protect us.' The man stamped his foot on a rock to conjure the Roman god, evidently afraid of the anger of the druidic ones. Trajanus could understand his fear: all around him this sacred world of oak trees was being pulled down. There would certainly be enough wood for cremating the dead, Trajanus thought wryly, as he passed a team of mules pulling huge logs of freshly fallen oaks. At that moment there was a cry of pain as a prisoner was knocked to the ground by a legionary for refusing to cut down the holy trees. He refused again and was stabbed in the abdomen by his overseer. 'Let that be a lesson to the others!' the soldier cried spitting on the dying man at his feet.

Hurrying on, Trajanus soon arrived in a large and open glade. The failing sun still threw bright rays of light through the dappled leaves that edged the druids' holy grove, but on one side only. The eastern side had already been cut down and showed an ugly scar of white, boned stumps that swept away into the forest. Suetonius was sitting on one of the stumps and was speaking to the other two legates and their senior tribunes. Trajanus joined Bolanus who gave him a sign to choose a tree stool to sit on. Suetonius nodded at him and continued his résumé of their work so far.

'Just to quickly recap for you Trajanus, but you know much of it already, we are currently garrisoning the island despite the pockets of resistance our men are still meeting as they cross the forest and swamps. The prefects are supervising this last piece of work. All the druids have been crucified.' Here, Suetonius lifted an arm to indicate the line of crucifixes that ran from the grove along an ancient trackway inland. Trajanus turned his head to look. Most of the men and women who hung from the crosses were already dead. He listened, as Suetonius continued, 'The greatest glory of these last few days has to be the capture of their holy man, the lord Sacrovar, who is on that first crucifix. He died almost immediately, but the bard who tried to save his life is still clinging onto life, despite the wound he took to his shoulder in the fight.'

Trajanus could see an old man drooping dead on the first crucifix. Next to him a tall, redheaded man was also hanging unconscious. He had only moments still to live. The row of crosses continued into the shadows of the forest.

'As you can see the forests of sacred oaks are all being cut down. We must obliterate the last traces of this savage religion from these Roman isles. We must obliterate it from human memory. Their sacred altars have already been dismantled and their priests killed. They do not use the written word so druidism will soon be a bad memory only.'

Bolanus, the legate of the Twentieth Legion asked about the dead, 'Can we show any respect for their fallen?' His heavy brow creased even more as he looked squarely at Suetonius.

'We can always show respect for the dead,' Suetonius snorted. 'Our own dead will be given the proper ceremonies and their ashes will be buried in the ground. The legions' funeral fund will cover all expenses and manage the different rites. The bodies of our enemies will be burned too, but all together. Their bones and ashes will be interred in a hill they call, Brin-y-Beddau: the Hill of Graves.'

'What should our men do with the prisoners we have spared?' It was Gaius who spoke this time, the rugged, grey-haired legate of the Second Legion. He had left his legion on the river Exe under the command of its camp prefect to whom he had given clear orders to keep the Southwest calm and stable.

'Once they have finished clearing up they shall be executed. There can be no pity for these religious fanatics and political activists.'

Gaius stroked his chin and nodded in agreement just as a messenger arrived and entered the small council meeting of military leaders. He spoke to Suetonius and then withdrew.

'It appears that a small band of Carvetii tribesmen have participated in the defence of Ynys Môn.' The other men shook their heads in surprise.

'And have they found any trace of their leader, Venutius?' It was Bolanus who spoke.

'No, but he can't be far. I will send word to Cartimandua to be vigilant and to arrest him.'

'Can she be trusted?' Bolanus narrowed his eyes. 'She has not caught him yet, and we have been after him for years. His lands are within the Brigantian lands of Cartimandua.'

Suetonius threw up his hands, tired of the day's work. 'Of course she can be trusted. She has been a client queen of Rome for nearly twenty years.'

'But only an ex-wife of Venutius for four,' Bolanus interjected.

'She does not hate him completely, that is true, but she does prefer his armour-bearer in bed.' Suetonius raised an eyebrow and snorted as the men around him laughed. 'You all know that Cartimandua is loyal to Rome. Without Rome, she would have nothing. And as a woman she cannot be condemned entirely. They are not exactly trained for warfare.' Here a second messenger arrived, looking a little more anxious than the first, and a lot more tired and dirty.

'Voada has rebelled in the South,' the man panted. 'Camulodunum has fallen and the Ninth Legion was ambushed trying to reach the colony.'

By now, Suetonius had already risen to his feet, immediately followed by his legates and tribunes. 'What about Cerialis?' Suetonius cried in a loud and anxious voice.

'He managed to get back to Clac-nyn with his cavalry, but the legionaries were lost.'

'All of them?' Suetonius's voice dropped a tone.

'Half, sir: two thousand foot soldiers. Some are here with you, sir, some were on other missions, and one thousand remained at the fort of Lindum, further north.'

'Send a message back to Cerialis telling him to stay in his fort and keep the North under control. There is to be no rebellion in the North; some tribes will try to join the Iceni.' A secretary immediately wrote the order and passed it to Suetonius to sign. It was sealed, and a dispatch rider was immediately sent off to Clac-nyn. The original messenger was questioned further by Suetonius. 'Give me the full story of Camulodunum,' he commanded. 'Then you can drink and rest.'

When the man had finished, Suetonius clasped his hands together and was silent for a few moments. 'I will leave for Londinium immediately,' he exclaimed, raising his head. 'Bolanus, as legate of Legion Twenty you will stay and take command of the field here. You must finish off all the resistance and will keep one thousand foot soldiers, some cavalry and auxiliaries with you. Has any trace of Venutius been found?'

'No, sire,' Bolanus answered. 'I think not.'

Suetonius gritted his teeth. 'You must make sure his Carvetii tribe are not able to stir up more resistance here or in Brigantian territory. And find Venutius. He must not join Voada's forces.'

'Yes, it will be done.'

Suetonius nodded at Bolanus and turned to the other commanders. 'Legion Fourteen will be with me at full strength, along with the rest of Legion Twenty. An order must be sent to Legion Two to join us at Mandvessedum…'

'Legion Two is only under the command of Poenius Postumus, its prefect,' Gaius Marius interrupted. 'As its legate I left my base, along with Agricola, to join you in the field with many of our men. Poenius has orders to stay in the southwest and to keep the Dumnonii and the Durotriges under control. I'm not sure how he will manage under such pressure.'

Suetonius was impatient now. 'You will add your own seal to mine, but I am the Governor of Britannia and Poenius will obey his order to join us at Mandvessedum.'

'Why have you chosen Mandvessedum as the meeting point?' All heads turned to stare at Mark Anthony, the prefect of Legion Twenty. Trajanus answered him slowly, patiently, as though giving a lesson on military strategy to one of his students. 'Mandvessedum is at the crossroads of the two main roads from Londinium to Deva, and from Isca, on the river Exe, to Lindum in the Northeast. It would be the same journey time for all the legions and a good meeting point.'

'Of course, we don't know what Voada and her rabble plan to do next,' Suetonius added. 'Perhaps they plan to march to their Sacred Isle to save it, but it is too late for that. Or, they will march from Camulodunum to Londinium, a rich jewel indeed, and one which cuts off our supply routes to Gaul. I will leave immediately with a small detachment of cavalry for Londinium – if it is still free. We'll take ships from here to the Deva Estuary, thus reducing our land journey by a third, and then ride direct to Londinium, just a hundred and eighty miles. By changing horses at the fortresses along the road, we can reach the city within three to four days. The foot soldiers will follow at a slower pace, around twenty miles a day.' He was already leaving the circle of men and had begun to shout orders to prepare the horses and supplies.

Venutius lay on the ground beside another man. Covered in the clay earth and decomposing leaves his men hardly breathed as they looked out from the forest floor onto the track below, waiting for an order from Venutius. The Roman soldiers passed beneath them, but Venutius gave no sign to move. When all was clear, he rose cautiously from the ground and gave a clear whistle, that of the grey-headed wagtail. Immediately, several other figures rose from the sodden, rotting earth and crossed the now empty path following their leader to the coastline.

Far ahead on the track one of the Roman legionaries had heard the bird whistle and recognised the species as one that lived in wet meadows and not in woodland. He ran forward to the head of the line and told the centurion who then stopped his men and gave orders to spread out across the forest floor and search for the final remnants of the Britannic fighters. All over the island the Roman soldiers were working meticulously under Bolanus's orders, scouring the last forest land and coastline for any remaining resistance to the Roman occupation. Bolanus needed to be sure that the Carvetii leader was eliminated. When a messenger arrived saying that a small party of armed Britons had been spotted near the Northwest coast, he felt sure it was Venutius. Riding fast on a fresh horse

Bolanus followed a path along the eastern coastline towards the furthest point of the island. He had brought a hundred cavalry riders with him who soon reached the spot where the earlier scouting party was waiting for him.

He thundered up to the waiting centurion with fragments of grey stones skittering off the path on either side of his horse, and shouted, 'Well? Have you found him yet?'

'We have, sire.' The centurion stepped forward to take the reins of Bolanus's horse whilst the legate jumped off. Despite his middle years and thick build, Bolanus was an agile horseman.

'Where is he then? And how many are they?'

'They are there, in that creek.' The man pointed to a steep and narrow path that led directly down a granite slope which looked as sharp as a cliff. The grey, pebble beach at the bottom could not be seen from the top of the cliff but the foot of a dead man lay to one side, at the top. There was nothing attached to the sandaled foot. It had been a clean cut from below.

'They are about ten men, all armed,' the centurion continued.

'Is there any other way in or out of the creek?' Bolanus asked surveying the grass and ferns around them.

'Not as far as we know.'

'Then check,' Bolanus cried. He ordered some men to follow the path down to the creek and, despite the evident danger of such a task, he began the descent himself. It was soon clear, however, that the climb would be impossible with such heavy body armour and weapons. Two men died within seconds of leaving the cliff-top: the first man received an arrow through his throat and then slid a few metres down the path, making a second man lose his footing; he plunged to his unseen death below. Bolanus scrambled back up to the top with his men. Angry with his own misjudgement he pulled his helmet off and threw it to the ground. 'May Jupiter strike him down,' he shouted. Turning again to the centurion, he ordered the man to send a messenger back to the camp and for boats to be sent along this side of the coast. A soldier broke in though, indicating the danger of such a project: the coast here was too rocky for the Roman boats to follow; Bolanus abandoned the idea.

'Then we must find another way down,' Bolanus concluded, turning once again to the centurion. 'And how did they get this far in the first place?' he wanted to know.

'They know the land and were well-hidden from sight. It was only by chance that we found them at all and managed to follow them this far, but they have been cornered now and have no boat to escape.'

'The gods are on our side; Neptune will not help them here.' Bolanus snatched his helmet from the dry grass and turned again to the ocean; he looked over the swelling waters of the rising tide. 'In the gods we trust,' he murmured to himself, before asking his centurion how high the tide would rise.

'And so,' he calculated, 'Venutius, and his remaining men, will be completely cut off by nightfall and will have to climb this path back up to us or drown below. It sounds too easy for me, but we shall have to wait whilst the men find another access route.' He sat down on a fallen tree and gave orders for his men to spread out and guard the area.

Below in the creek, Venutius and his men waited quietly in a shallow cave. One man guarded the entrance whilst another stood further out with his bow aimed at the path. A sharp wind blew through the cave, for it was a small archway: a natural tunnel bored in the arm of rock, stretching into the sea. Hidden there in the darkness, the men were silent. Each man knew that all was lost on Ynys Môn. They had seen their priests strung up like chickens and their royal oaks torn down like twigs. Their holy places, their shrines and altars had been destroyed and their religion made a mockery of. Many good men had fallen in the last few days – those who had not sailed for Hibernia. Despite their desperate situation the men felt reassured by Venutius's side, and each man would follow him into the land of the dead if need be. Tall and lean Venutius squatted down on the pebbles with his back against the rock. His elbows on his knees, he rested his chin on his fists and waited.

It was night by the time the tide had fully risen, but the moon was not yet visible. Water scuffed across the stones and lapped the sides of the cliff, sucking the air out of the cracks and hollows of the rock. Venutius and his Carvetii men stood knee-deep in brine within the cave. Between them, they held the sides of a small sailing vessel and began to lift it and move forward, aided by the sea. They could hear men suddenly scrambling down the cliff, followed by some whispering outside of the cave and orders being given in Latin. Venutius's men were already moving towards the opposite opening. There was a flurry of movement and then the harsh clash of iron on iron at the mouth of the cave. The Carvetiis tried to move faster into the deepening water, but this became more difficult. However, they did have the advantage of the wind and, as soon as they left the back of the cave, Venutius managed to raise the tannic-black sail. His men pulled themselves into the vessel, and the boat gathered speed.

There was bewildered shouting on the beach as the Roman legionaries finally understood that the Carvetiis did have a plan of action and did have a means of escape. The legate's voice could be heard commanding his men to shoot at the boat. Two arrows fell into the water beside Venutius who ordered his men to crouch low below their shields. Two more arrows struck the side of the boat and one flew through the sail, but it was too difficult for the Roman archers to fire into the darkness against a moving black target. The wind picked up, and the sounds from the beach ebbed away with the coast. Venutius did not immediately set full sail for the open sea. He waited a few minutes until two pairs of arms grasped the sides of the rocking boat and the swimmers were pulled aboard. They looked like drowned otters in their dark clothes and streaming woad paint. Venutius clapped both men on the shoulders and gave orders to his helmsman, 'let's get home.' The stern of the sloop immediately turned up through the wind, and the Carvetii men left the Isle of Ynys Môn in the hands of the Romans.

VI

The roads to Londinium

THE TEMPLE OF CLAUDIUS LAY BURNING STILL. The city of Camulodunum had cascaded, smouldering, and all that had once been Roman lay in embers behind them. Voada and her daughters took to the road, following the Roman cobbles southeast, paving stones that lay over the ancient trackway to Londinium. The journey could have been done in less than two days, but, with so many men to move, it would take longer. What was more, Keara noted, the Trinovante tribesmen were less disciplined under their leader, Dubnov than the Iceni were under Voada and Rory. They only seemed to be interested in scouring the scattered farmsteads and villas in search of more spoil, and were then finding it difficult to carry all their pickings. Some men would disappear for hours, even a day, and would then reappear, lighter than before, having placed their treasure in a surer place.

The beauty of that spring morning was a sweet balm after the atrocities of the past few days. Keara closed her eyes and let her pony lead the way, following the line of Britons ever onwards. She breathed in the rich smell of grass and meadowsweet blossoms that pierced the fields. She let the warm rays of sunshine sink into her marbled skin and listened to the sounds around her: the clatter of hooves, the creak of wagons and wheels, the barking of dogs. *Where would this road take them?* She reflected.

Caitlyn's pony moved gently by Keara's side, its flank stroked her leg as the two riders rode together through a stretch of blackthorn trees lining the road. Creamy white blossom brushed their hair and shoulders, seemingly kissing their passage. Caitlyn looked tired and dirty.

'We are all tired,' Keara smiled at her sister, noting Caitlyn's flushed cheeks, 'but this war will not last long. Once we have Londinium, the Roman army will be cut off from the continent and its supplies will soon run out.'

'What about our own supplies? Many of our people have not planted their fields this spring. They hope to take our grain back from the Romans, and the last harvest was poor.'

'Caitlyn, I know you are queen and must think of our people, but do not think too much of the future. We will first reclaim our land, and our land will provide for us. Once the Romans have gone, we will have enough to trade with the Norsemen and the Germani once again.'

Caitlyn raised her head to look at her sister. 'Has our mother thought of everything? The Atrebates and the Regni both have treaty arrangements with the Romans and will stay loyal to Rome. What if they ride up from the south to attack us at Londinium?'

'They won't move.'

'How can you be so sure?'

'King Cogidubnus is too old to move now and won't risk anything unless he has a Roman legion with him. And the Atrebates are no longer warriors. They are only farmers and herdsmen.' Keara's voice held a slight edge of ironic contempt, and, despite her own doubts, she added, 'We will have a clear, quick victory in Londinium. Our goddess has predicted it, and she has named our mother the Boudica.'

Caitlyn nodded and gave Keara a weak smile, 'But we must find Catus too, before he escapes to Gaul.'

'We will find him.' Keara's expression suddenly hardened. 'He must pay for what he has done to us.'

'I sometimes feel that I will pay every day of my life for what happened to me.'

From her pony Keara leant towards her sister and tipped her head onto Caitlyn's shoulder. 'I will be here for you. Never forget that.'

'I know.'

Keara looked once again at the fields surrounding them. They did look beautiful, but they held no crops: only the rough, fragile beauty of wild flowers.

After a day's hard riding Suetonius and his small unit of cavalry riders had arrived in the late evening at the vexillation fortress of Mandvessedum. He had dispatched another rider southwest to Isca to make sure that Legion Two was on its way, and then he had rested a few hours in the private suite of the commanding officer. In the early light of the following morning, and on fresh horses, he continued to ride down the Londinium road. He was anxious to make good speed so had only taken a small force of a hundred riders with him, including Flavius, his senior tribune. He had left the legions under the command of Gaius Marius, legate of Legion Two, who would take many days to reach Mandvessedum.

Suetonius was also impatient to get news of Catus and Vettius. At the end of the following day, his cavalry reached the Catuvellauni town of Verulamium and stopped at the timber fort, but he stayed only long enough to change horses and to eat. The people were equally anxious to have news of the rebellion, but Suetonius simply told them to take their valuables and leave the town. Because many of the Catuvellauni had taken Roman citizenship they were hated by the surrounding tribes; Suetonius could only advise them to travel northwest and place themselves under the protection of the Roman army. By the time he was back in the saddle, a number of families were already leaving the Roman municipium. Within a few hours, the governor-general would reach Londinium.

LONDINIUM

'Where is he?' Suetonius repeated his question, believing he had misunderstood the tribune standing in front of him.

'He has, err, gone – that is, he has left Londinium for Gaul.' Marius gulped, feeling terrified under the fierce, almost wild, glare of Suetonius. He felt he needed to justify the absence of Catus. He gulped. 'The Iceni and Trinovante tribes will reach Londinium any hour and Catus felt he needed to oversee the evacuation of Nero's taxes and other valuable assets that the rebels would otherwise have taken – should they reach Londinium.' He was immediately relieved when the office door was flung open and Vettius entered.

'The bastard has fled!' Vettius walked up to Suetonius and embraced him. 'I am glad you are safe and that you have got here in time, for we have no more ships and the tide is low. Catus took the last ship this morning; said the Emperor had recalled him – what bullshit. He wouldn't wait for you to arrive. He said the rebels would be here before you. They will be here very shortly. So where are your men?'

There was a long moment of silence in the Procurator's

office. Catus may have left, but the luxury of his lifestyle could still be seen, Suetonius noted, casting his eyes over the marble-topped desk and chairs, the rich couch and cushions, the embroidered screens and elaborately decorated oil lamps that still remained. Suetonius brought his eyes back to his law officer. 'Vettius,' he began, biting his lip. 'I only have a small unit with me. It was the only way we could reach Londinium so quickly. I needed to appraise the situation and see what could be done. And as I see things, nothing can be done to save the city; we must abandon it. The rebels are already at the northeast gates.'

Vettius stepped back and, looking intently at Catus's richly painted office walls, he spread his hands. 'And abandon all this?' His question indicated the whole city of Londinium, which was still pulsing with life, and included the great Roman investments in business, buildings, warehouses, dockyards, brickyards, breweries, taverns and temples.

'Yes.' Suetonius looked darkly out of the window. 'As I came in the northwest gate, I saw a great number of people still working in the city. They cheered as we arrived, but they must leave now. Those who are able, may leave with us back up the Mandvessedum road – if they are able to keep up. And we could do with the extra manpower as our forces are so few.' Here, Suetonius turned back to Marius and told him to give the order to evacuate the city.

Walking across the stone-flagged floor Marius heard Flavius speak for the first time. Suetonius's senior tribune showed some small concern for the population, 'But, sire, if the people are still here it is because they don't want to leave, or they can't leave. They are mostly tradesmen and merchants who will lose their lifetime's investments if they abandon the city.'

'They will lose their lives if they stay,' Suetonius responded sourly, sinking exhausted into one of Catus's basket armchairs.

'Pour me some cumin wine, Vettius. I need five minutes' respite in the midst of war.' He had already pushed Marius out of his mind as the tribune left the office. He, Flavius and Vettius sat down to drink a farewell toast to a city that was already burning.

As Marius left the basilica and entered the forum, he was assailed by a number of citizens clamouring for help. These were the poorer ones, those who did not have the means to pay passage on a ship or even to travel south into the client kingdom of the Regni. He did not care for them or their poverty. He simply passed on Suetonius's orders to a centurion who began to organise the evacuation by speaking to the crowd. He had to pound the ground several times with his vine rod for quiet. The confusion was great though, as not everyone understood Latin, but the message was clear enough.

In the stables Marius began to prepare his horse for the exodus. There was a lot of activity in the military stables. Zia was busy brushing down Titus's horses and preparing their horse tack for the journey into the war zone once again. Titus was in the horse yard, giving orders and advice to the men in his cavalry squadron. He was not well-liked by his men, it seemed, but he was generally respected for his horsemanship and topographical knowledge of Britannia, which is one of the reasons why he had been sent to Camulodunum to help the colonists. His men were only too pleased that Catus had sent foot soldiers to the colony and not many cavalrymen for, as everyone knew, of the two hundred soldiers who had gone, only two had returned, not counting the slave Zia, and one of those men owed his life to Titus. Marius began packing his saddle bag and filled up a waterskin for the journey. All belongings had to be left behind. They could only take what their horse could carry on a long march.

Before leaving the yard, Marius noticed Titus taking food and water to a box stall and shook his head in disgust; he couldn't understand why the decurion was still feeding that animal. Titus unbolted the stall door and entered the box before being leapt upon by a massive fur creature. He just had time to lay down the bowls so that the animal would transfer its attention from the man to the food. Titus stroked the dog, running his hand along its back and down to its muzzle and then he left, closing the door behind him.

'Why did you buy that Iceni dog?' Marius asked him with faint curiosity, but he did not wait for an answer. Sighing lightly, he added, 'What a waste of your wages, and now to abandon it here.'

'She would be too much trouble on the road and would not always obey me.' Titus gave a shrewd smile to his man, Zia, who was waiting for him by the gate with their horses and supplies. Zia just threw his eyes up to the sky and shook his head with impatience.

Titus and Zia were amongst the last men to cross the timber bridge over the river. Very few of the civilians on horseback had decided to join Suetonius's march. Most, whether on foot, mule or horse, were continuing south into the safe lands of the Regni. Titus watched them take the southern road to Noviomagus, the capital of King Cogidubnus who was already building fortifications against the Britannic rebels. The refugees would be safe behind the earthen banks of the Regni, so Suetonius had no compunction in abandoning Londinium to the barbarians. Titus turned back to the timber piles and decking in order to oversee the destruction of the drawbridge in midstream. The Tamesis was wide here, but still deep, so that it would take a long time for an army to cross it with no bridge and no boats. The south bank included a series of low-lying islands, creeks and marshy lands on which the Roman engineers had laid timber piling, earthen causeways and, in some places, small timber bridges to continue the roads through the Tamesis Valley.

On the northern bank of the river, steep terraces descended from the two low-lying hills to the close-set warehouses on the water front. The terraces were already coated in the wild horsemen of the rebel clans. A number of warriors were prancing on their horses shouting war challenges across the river and thumping the sky with their swords and javelins. Moving slowly and methodically down the main road to the bridgehead Titus recognised the royal Iceni party. Voada and Rory rode at their head. Behind them Titus recognised Voada's two daughters and nephew. There was a druid with them too, it looked like Greer, and further back, there rode King Dubnov of the Trinovantes whose horse was jittering with its ears pinned back. *An angry beast*, Titus thought, *to go with its master*. Dubnov was already feasting on the wealth of Londinium and his men were running in and out of shops and villas looting, vandalising, burning.

The thick ropes of the drawbridge had finally been axed through, and the timber fragments were floating down river. Titus ordered his men to withdraw and to rejoin Suetonius's forces that were marching west along a secondary Roman road in order to return to the Verulamium highway before Voada's forces cut them off. He gave one last look to the fallen city; smoke rose in many places, and all over the urban and commercial plots there could be seen great showers of fire drops. The smell of burning wood, straw and textiles crossed the river, along with the smoke and cries of the victors and victims; some inhabitants of Londinium had refused to leave, and now they were paying the price for such stubborn pride. Some of the dead and mutilated were already being strung up for the Romans' viewing across the river. All those who had stayed behind: men, women, old and young, were being killed. There could be no mercy for the Roman merchants and their families. Titus stared across the empty gap of water between himself and the Iceni's Boudica. She looked exultant, proud and full of bitter hatred. Titus turned and strode back onto the southern bank where Zia was waiting for him. The dusk was beginning to fall, as were scattered flakes of fire, but the smothered sky over Londinium burned long into the next day.

'We must keep some prisoners as sacrifices to Andraste,' Voada spoke to Dubnov whose men were sparing no one in the city of Londinium.

The Trinovante leader wiped the wine off his lips with the back of his hand. 'Pffrr! What does it matter if we kill them here and now or keep some dainty pickings for my men's amusement?' Dubnov was a rough man who rarely showed any pity. His tribe had suffered many humiliations at the hands of their neighbours, the Catuvellauni, a tribe that had collaborated with the Romans, and had doubled the labours, the strife and the taxes of the Trinovantes, and then had also divided their lands.

'We will claim our wealth back, and exact full retribution. Then we shall march on the Catuvellauni centre of Verulamium and destroy it.' He spat into the unlit fire of the Roman villa's dining room and grinned.

'We must carry out the rites to Andraste and fulfil our promises to her first.' Voada stirred. 'She promised us victory and we must now thank her with the blood of our enemies.' Voada's voice rose a little here in order to impress this duty onto the minds of Dubnov and his gaggle of men; they looked volatile and ill-disciplined in such an elegant setting.

Behind Voada, Rory stood silent. Greer was present too, along with Keara and Caitlyn, who were all sitting in comfortable wicker chairs in the merchant's villa. They were not far from the burning forum and Keara knew that her own chair would soon be alight. She wriggled on her seat and listened to Greer; he had interrupted Voada and was evidently trying to wriggle out of making any human sacrifices. 'I am not a druid who is qualified to make human sacrifices; few druids are as it is considered an inhumane act, even in times of war. I am not an oracle either. I am a druid teacher and an old warrior. I support our fight for freedom, but Voada, is this really what Andraste has asked for?'

Voada curled her lip. 'Yes,' she snapped. 'I am certain of it, but, if you cannot do it, then Dubnov will find me a druid who can.'

Greer rubbed the back of his neck and closed his eyes. 'I'm sure he can,' he muttered.

'Aye,' Dubnov interjected, 'I have a man for you, but you are a prophetess, so you must lead the sacrifices.'

'Find me a grove outside of the city walls and we will go there tomorrow with the council and tribal leaders.' She spoke the order to Dubnov who then rose unsteadily to his feet and raised an empty beaker to his mouth.

'I will find you one tomorrow then, but first I must make my own sacrifice – to Bacchus.' Here he raised another arm holding a ceramic jug and poured more Roman wine into his cup. 'Would anyone else like some?' No Iceni answered, but his men roared in acquiescence. Dubnov threw back his drink and then staggered out of the room to call for more wine from the cellar below.

Keara felt almost as sick as Caitlyn over the next few days. Watching the sacrifices in the grove was more than she could bear and though she was meant to remain seated beside her sister she was able to disappear from time to time. Caitlyn was

queen and had to hold court with her mother who had ordered
the sacrifices. A druid priest from the Trinovantes had been
found to make the sacrifices to Andraste. It was Dubnov, Rory
and their men who seemed to take great pleasure in spiking
the heads on sticks and hanging them from the branches of
the surrounding oak trees. Galdus stayed with them whilst
Keara wandered off through the camp in the woods. She
was accompanied by her dog, Sapho, who had been found in
the wreckage of Londinium, barking furiously in the Roman
stables. The Britons had released a number of their own
ponies, dogs and other animals before burning the stables and
animal pounds.

Keara passed Greer seated before a fire where Caitlyn's
maid, Amena, was cutting up cep mushrooms for a casserole.
Beside them a slave girl was preparing small broad beans to
add to the cauldron. Greer was helping too. He held a wooden
board on his knees and was cutting up a bunch of herbs for
the stew: sorrel and wall pepper. He smiled at Keara as she
passed with Sapho, and said that he would catch up with her
soon.

'How are you feeling?' Greer was looking at her intently and,
though he said that his sight was becoming weaker with age,
Keara knew that his view of the world was just as clear.

'I am fed up with the killing, and anxious about spending
so much time in the Tamesis Valley. Shouldn't we be preparing
to meet the Suetonius?'

'Certainly not in the field,' Greer responded; 'we are no
match for the Romans in open battle, though our war leaders
believe we have might, right and the gods on our side. Despite
our recent victories, we must fight as Caratacus did in the
Western Mountains.'

'Yes, I agree that his skirmish tactics were successful, but he did lose his set battles, and he was finally captured and sent to Rome.' She picked a burr off her skirt and clutched the linen cloth as they waded through some thick ferns.

'Argh, we are no match for the legionaries in a field battle. We must avoid that at all costs and, as you know, Caratacus was only taken prisoner by the governor of that time because he was betrayed by Cartimandua. She must never be trusted Keara.'

'I know.' She frowned, darkly reflecting on Cartimanadua's groomed beauty at her father's funeral. The woman's manicured nails said everything about her: well-shaped, painted and sharp.

'How are you feeling? You haven't answered my question.'

Keara stopped in her tracks and turned to look at the old man beside her. She waited a moment, looking at Greer evenly. 'I am not pregnant.'

She looked so certain, so sure that Greer did not pursue the issue. Rather relieved, he changed the subject altogether and mentioned Diodorus, who had stayed behind in Saham Toney.

'I have had news from Diodorus, who tells me that everything is calm back home in the Iceni lands. He even sounds a little bored now that he doesn't have anyone to teach Greek to.'

'You can tell him that I do miss his classes. I loved his lessons on Sapho.'

'Yes, the tenth muse, as Plato called her.' He looked at Keara's dog as he said this. She was almost as tall as Keara as she plodded by her mistress's side, and both seemed happy to have found each other again. A most unexpected find.

'And as the only female poet, I love singing her songs.' Keara's voice sounded more animated now.

'You have a beautiful voice, although the eastern Greek tone is not always easy to follow. Perhaps you could sing something now.' Greer was obviously trying to distract her, and distracted she wanted to be. She began to hum one of Sapho's songs, one written by the poet for her lover. She then broke into the words themselves, but remained in a quiet voice, breathing deeply beneath the sunlit canopy of the forest roof. Keara's song was broken by a shout from the camp: a fight had broken out between some of the Trinovante men.

'The Greeks used the word *barbarian* to refer to someone outside of their known world. I think later generations will call us *barbarians* for having no education and no self-control.' Greer sighed, and he led Keara round to another side of the camp where it was a little calmer. He then continued speaking, 'Dubnov's men do not always obey their leader's orders, and with your mother as confederate leader of the armies I'm not sure they will follow her for long.'

'It's clear to me,' Keara knuckled her brow, 'that we must all attack Suetonius as quickly as possible. We should have stopped him from rejoining his main army when he left Londinium.'

'I agree,' Galdus sighed again, 'but it is too late now. The Trinovantes and some of the other clans do not want to leave Londinium until they have picked its bones clean. Let us hope that your uncle, King Corbreid is able to join us from Caledonia and, also, that the Roman Legion Two is kept pinned down in the southwest by the Dumnonii.'

'At least we have decimated Cerialis's Legion Nine. Cerialis has only his cavalry at Clac-nyn and only a few legionaries isolated at Lindum. He is going nowhere until we come to get him.' A sudden wave of planned action and cold anger crossed Keara's face. 'I should perhaps get back to the grove for the last of the sacrifices.'

'That, it is true, *is* one of our barbaric customs,' Greer smiled grimly at Keara.

The road to Mandvessedum

The confederation of Britannic tribes sidewinded out of the damp fields of the Tamesis Valley and snaked along the main road towards Verulamium. Many of the clansmen also spanned across the countryside ransacking outlying farmsteads which slowed down the onward march. At an abandoned signal station Voada and Rory stopped for a moment to water their horses.

'We need to go faster,' Voada spoke. 'Dubnov's men are savouring each moment of this victory by pocketing every coin that they find on the road, and they are slowing us down.'

'It is difficult for you to hold the clans together.' Rory weighed his words slowly. 'You are the elected leader and chosen Boudica, but you must please everyone or the different factions will split up.'

'We are currently riding on the crest of a wave, the wave of victory, but in order to consolidate that victory we must move quickly and defeat Suetonius.' Voada stared at the green undulating landscape that led to Verulamium before her: lush meadows, groves of trees and swathes of bluebells spread before them, basking in the warmth of the morning sun.

'These harebells are in full bloom,' Voada smiled suddenly, using the old name for Andraste's flower.

'Yes, her dead man's bells will toll for our dead today,' Rory grinned, noting this lucky sign from the goddess.

'Yet,' Voada added, turning back to Rory, 'I cannot help but worry. We all want different things, and I am not sure that it's possible to please every man. Look again at this land.' She nodded at the great tracts of arable fields before them. 'This is rich land, Catuvellauni land that Dubnov wants. He and his men want their wealth back. Our Iceni tribe want their lands back too, and their indentured men. I want revenge for my daughters and a kingdom back for Caitlyn.'

By then the horses had finished drinking and others were riding up to the waterlogged ditch at the deserted station. Voada and Rory led their horses back to the road. A scout was cantering towards them: an Iceni man who panted out, 'Verulamium is empty of men and goods; it has been abandoned by the Romans and by the Catuvellauni.'

Voada nodded at the man, glad for the tidings of the Catuvellauni retreat. She then sent him on to find Dubnov and heard Rory's, 'No dead today then.'

'At least Verulamium won't slow us down if there is nothing left to pillage or kill.' She clapped him on the shoulder.

'There is still something left to destroy,' Dubnov cried when he reached Voada and had listened to her orders to press on ahead. 'The Catuvellauni have humiliated my clan for generations, and now it is our turn to destroy their homes. I have already told my men to burn everything they come across. This road passes through the heart of Verulamium so I will savour every moment of their loss.' He did not wait for an objection from Voada but kicked his horse into movement. His men followed, driving on ahead with the Trinovante war host.

By the time Voada and her family passed through the *municipium* town of Verulamium, it was already wrapped in tongues of fire. In frenzied joy Dubnov's warriors were throwing burning torches, soaked in flammable pine resin, onto the thatched roofing of the buildings. The colonnaded walkways, shops and stone houses were grand and imposing. They took longer to burn than the wattle and daub buildings behind, but burn they did. However, not a single hoard of coins or of grain could be found: the Catuvellauni had had plenty of time to transport their goods and families into the Roman military zone and the town stood as empty as a graveyard. In their frustrated rage Dubnov's Trinovante warriors spent the next few hours and much of the night destroying the town.

'You slowed us down with your sacrifices in Londinium. Now you can give me the time to exact satisfaction from the destruction of my enemy's capital.' Dubnov furrowed his brows as he spoke to Voada across the fire on which a leg of lamb was burning on a spit. He took some bread from a serving woman and then cut himself another slice of meat from the spit.

Around the fire sat the council members who included the Iceni household, two other Trinovante leaders, a Corieltauvi leader and a dark-bearded Dumnonii prince introduced as Tremayn. Keara wondered how he had managed to cross the Roman militarised zone from the furthest southwestern tip of Britannia. He must have managed to sail into the mouth of the Severn. They sat in the open air under the starry night. The balmy breeze soothed the nerves and lulled the mind, or perhaps it was the wine and the beer, thought Keara dreamily. She was tired, weary of the disputes, the discord, the dragging of feet. They were working more slowly than the Roman administration and its paperwork, she thought.

'We must move quickly now and attack the legions as they march down this road, before they have time to rest.' It was Voada's voice. 'Before the Second Legion has time to reach Suetonius's forces.'

Another voice spoke, that of the Dumnonii prince, 'My tribe is holding the Second Legion in place at Isca which only has the prefect in command. Its legate and senior tribune are both with Suetonius's forces. The prefect, Poenius Postumus, has been ordered to march north and join Suetonius at Mandvessedum but my tribe is stirring up trouble and keeping the Second Legion busy. It is pinned down for the moment, but we can't hold it for long.'

Keara took in the man's appearance which seemed to be both feline and ursine at the same time. He wore a necklace of rich, twisted gold, but this was half-hidden beneath his long hair and amber tunic. Voada responded to Tremayn's words, 'Which means that we must move faster northwest to meet the Roman army.' Then, giving a direct order to the Dumnonii prince, she asked him to return to his tribe and to continue harrowing Legion Two in the southwest.

'Speed is not of the urgency,' Dubnov interjected: 'Suetonius's forces are running out of supplies; my informant tells me that they are now on rations.'

'That may be, but we don't want the Second Legion to reach them, and we don't want reinforcements to arrive through the Regni lands from across the Channel.' It was Rory, who spoke now, supporting Voada's wish for speed and a full-frontal attack on the legions.

'We are no match for the Romans in a pitched battle,' Keara could not hold back any longer. 'We must use surprise attacks and fight as an invisible army.'

'I am ashamed you should say that.' Voada glared fiercely at her daughter. 'This is our land, built from our own sweat and blood. You know that our cause is a just one, condoned by the gods. We have enjoyed success after success, and we will drive the Romans out of Britannia. We shall never be invisible again.'

Keara shuddered at her mother's fierce tone and narrowed eyes. Her face reddened.

Here, Greer threw in a grain of prudence, 'Remember that ten years ago Caratacus and the Cymru tribes were only successful against the Roman legions when they fought in surprise attacks against the occupying forces. They lost a lot of terrain, and Caratacus's family was taken when they finally met the Romans in a fixed battle. They had become overconfident, which goes to show that pride comes before a fall. We must be careful, and I agree with Keara's strategy.'

Keara felt grateful for Greer's support, but her relief was

tempered by fear of her mother's repudiation and by the next words that came from her cousin.

'I don't agree. My father will join us with his Caledonian men, and we far outnumber the Roman forces here already. They have only twelve thousand fighting men. We have over one hundred thousand.'

'But it will take weeks for him to reach us,' Keara put in, finding her voice again, 'and he is blocked in the north by Cartimandua's Brigantian tribes.'

'Venutius and his Carvetii tribe will clear the passage for the Caledonians through Brigantian territory, you know,' Galdus added.

Greer felt compelled to put in another point. They had already learnt of the fall of Ynys Môn. 'You know that Venutius lost a lot of men on Ynys Môn. I don't know if he can help us.'

'Let us hear what our queen has to say. What do you believe Caitlyn?' Voada looked intently at her daughter, sitting beside her.

Lifting her chin, Caitlyn regarded first her mother, then her sister. Her round cheeks glowed in the firelight, but her eyes seemed dull in the darkness. 'I agree with our mother. We should finish this now and return to our lands.'

Voada gave her daughter a smile of acknowledgement and continued, 'When we catch up with the Romans we will fight them full-frontal. These lands belong to us and the Britannic clans. We will nourish the earth with the Romans' blood, and the land will protect us. Then we can return to our homes and enjoy our freedom, our peace and our wealth. The ocean will guard Britannia against the Roman Empire, just as the Rhine River protects our Celtic cousins in Germania. Since they defeated the Romans, more than fifty years ago, the Germanians have remained a free people.'

Then Voada closed the war council, adding, 'History will

repeat itself for the Britons. We will leave in the next few days and challenge the Romans in open combat.'

There was general agreement at this decision, though Keara did not remind her mother and sister that the German tribes had defeated the three Roman legions in a forest ambush and not in an open battle. She and Greer exchanged looks of discontent, but there was nothing more they could do, or say, to influence the decision, both knowing that it had been based on impassioned leadership and not reason.

Keara and Caitlyn were sharing a Roman army tent. They had found it in one of the store rooms in an abandoned fortlet along the route. Amena was sleeping with them also, as was Keara's mastiff, but Amena was out for the moment. Voada had refused to use the Roman tent and was in her own Britannic one nearby. A tallow candle was burning beside Caitlyn's sleeping mat and the girl was lying on her back. She could no longer sleep in the darkness and always had to have a candle burning. The flame flickered a little, sending shadows shrinking and stretching across the leather roof of the tent. She closed her eyes and breathed deeply before speaking into the silence, 'You are lucky Keara. You have started bleeding today.'

Keara stopped what she was doing. She had been combing her, now, short, black hair. She put her bone comb down on the mat where she was sitting, and turned to look at Caitlyn lying motionless on her bed. Keara's heart sank, for she knew what was coming.

'I have had my blood cycle twice since Venta Icenorum.' She could not use other words to describe the attack for the memory was still too painful.

'I… have not. I have not,' said Caitlyn plaintively and she rolled onto her side with her back to her sister.

Keara crawled over to her sister's mat and shook her shoulder. 'Caitlyn, I will fetch Greer. He will know what to do.' Caitlyn did not answer. Keara stood up and threw a light shawl over her shoulders. Slipping on some wooden clogs, she ducked out of the tent flap and went to find Greer in the camp. There were guardsmen everywhere, but they let her pass. Within a few minutes, she had found Greer's tent and could see a light within. She called to him, 'Greer, are you awake still?'

'Mhm. Only pondering some verses. Come in Keara.'

'You need to come quickly to see Caitlyn. She is ...,' Keara faltered.

'Yes,' Greer sighed. 'I'm coming.' He snapped the clasp shut on his cloak and followed Keara outside. He strode across the beaten earth of the camp until he reached the sisters' tent. Once inside, he knelt down beside the young Iceni queen and called her name softly. Caitlyn was crying: heavy tears of despair, as she sobbed, 'A Roman child as heir to the Iceni kingdom is not possible.'

'I know, I know,' Greer whispered.

'Get rid of it for me,' Caitlyn implored. 'Please.'

'Caitlyn, listen to me now. You must be at three months. It would be too dangerous for you if I gave you something or if the wise woman treated you. Why have you waited so long to speak?'

'Because I could not face it, the truth, the shame. And I thought that our mother goddess would not allow it.' She began to cry again. 'Why would Modron create this life in me?'

'The goddess has her own reasons, but it is too early to know if the child will live. Be strong, for our mother goddess, Modron will look over you, as will the other gods.'

He asked Keara to pour her sister some water and then he added a few drops of valerian root oil and told Caitlyn to drink it.

'It will help you to sleep. Be brave little queen.'

Caitlyn raised her red-rimmed eyes to Greer and her sister, but she could not speak. Taking the wooden beaker from Keara's hands, her own hand shook. She swallowed the liquid and then lay back, seeking respite in the oblivion of sleep.

'You knew, didn't you?' Keara asked some moments later.

'I had spoken to Amena, yes.' Greer nodded sadly. Before Keara could pose her next question, Greer had already anticipated it. 'Your mother suspects as much too. We can do nothing about it now.' He stroked Caitlyn's forehead. 'Let her sleep.' Then he got up and left the tent.

The hedges were ripe with the dog rose. Its pale pink flowers were in full blossom, climbing high over the bushes along the road, whilst the fields beyond which were a dazzling, lustrous yellow from the riot of buttercups which were jostling for space amongst the grasses. In the bright sunshine, it was almost blinding to look out across the land. Voada held one hand to her eyes as she gazed at the distant horizon along the road. They had been travelling for almost three weeks since leaving Londinium, a long ride indeed with all the men, women, wagons and transportable goods to move.

Some faces had disappeared, mostly amongst the Trinovantes who had taken what they wanted from the dead and then vanished into the night with their gold and coins. However, new faces had appeared as news of the rebellion spread across Britannia and tales of Voada's victories inspired others to join her. There were now groups of men from all over the isles. Some had brought their whole families with them, displaced victims of the Roman expansion into Britannia, who wanted to watch their warriors win back the land of their ancestors.

A scout was galloping along the road towards Voada's

forces and stopped when it reached Rory's guard. 'Suetonius's army is waiting for us,' he panted.

'How many miles north?' Rory questioned.

'About five. They are not far from the vexillation fortress of Mandvessedum but have chosen an open field just off the road in which to meet us. The Romans have made camp in a forest with a narrow defile before them: it is an open plain without cover for us.'

'Can our warriors attack from behind or from the sides?' Voada wanted to know.

'The defile is like a steep-sided gorge and the Romans are protected at the top of a slope by the trees at their back. These are also protected by the auxiliary fort behind it in the militarised zone.'

Voada tipped her chin out to dismiss him. 'Should we attack them now in a pitched battle do you think?' she demurred to Rory, remembering the reservations of both Keara and Greer.

'We have won many victories and we now have over a hundred thousand warriors waiting for battle. The Romans are outnumbered ten to one. They are tired and are almost out of supplies. We should attack whilst the gods are with us.' Rory sounded so certain, so sure.

Voada called to Greer, who was resting on a bank by the side of the road. He had been listening to their words and, coming over to where Voada and Rory were standing, he looked solemn. 'You know already what I think. Suetonius's men are well trained and armed. They may be few in number, but they will obey orders and fight as one body. Our army has so many factions that are already fighting amongst themselves and breaking up.'

'All the more reason to attack Suetonius quickly. Our army will overwhelm the Romans in sheer numbers,' Rory responded.

'But our men wear no armour,' Greer countered. 'They have only the body paint of war to protect them. We should use the same tactics as the Cymru tribes in the west: ambushes, skirmishes, traps.'

'That is only the war of the weak,' Rory retorted pulling his shoulders back.

Voada reflected for a moment and then made her final and irrevocable decision: 'We will meet the Romans in a pitched battle and secure both our freedom and glory. We'll continue on this road and make camp for the night when we are closer to the Roman army.' Speaking more to herself, she murmured, 'Tomorrow will seal our fates.'

VII

Mandvessedum

IN THE FORT, SUETONIUS SAT AT A TABLE IN HIS headquarters. He was reading a number of dispatches and studying a map of Britannia rolled out before him on the desk; counters from a board game were being used to represent the movement of his men and those of his enemies. He looked at a counter representing Bolanus on the Isle of Ynys Môn, then at that of Cerialis held down at Clac-nyn. One legate was holding off resistance in the west, the other had been told to keep the north stable with Cartimandua's control of the Brigantian confederacy. He turned to the three men who were sitting further along the table: his senior tribune of Legion Fourteen, Flavius; the senior tribune of Legion Twenty, Trajanus; and the legate of Legion Two, Gaius. 'Gaius, have you heard any news from your prefect yet in the southwest?'

'No, sire, but we have received a message along the signal stations saying that the southwest is in revolt. The Durotriges have joined the Dumnonii in the Southwest Peninsula. I don't think that Poenius will be able to join us with Legion

Two, but his forces are strong enough to put down the small disturbance there.'

'It is taking him a long time to do so.' Suetonius frowned in annoyance. 'So that leaves us with Legion Fourteen, detachments of Legions Twenty and Two, and auxiliaries from the nearest forts: ten thousand men in all.'

Gaius smiled grimly back at Suetonius. Both were rugged and experienced soldiers with weathered faces and greying hair. As the only other legate in the field, Gaius was effectively second-in-command. If Suetonius fell, then he would have to take full command of the forces in Britannia. The four men had already deployed their men at the front, but still had to discuss the finer details. Suetonius pointed a finger at the layout of counters on the battle line.

'We will have the legionaries here.' He pointed to the middle ground on the map. 'The infantry auxiliaries will be on either side of the legions. They are lighter and more mobile. And we will have the cavalry on the wings.'

'Where shall we place the civilians who want to fight?' Trajanus spoke, looking up at Suetonius.

'They will stay here in the fort, along with the administration clerks. They will be more of a hindrance than a help. Our men know all the commands in the field whereas the civilians will get in the way. You can tell them that they are to defend the fort.'

Trajanus nodded back at his commander who then added, 'I want a double guard around the fort and the camp, continuously, and Trajanus...'

'Yes, sire?'

'I want all the tribunes and the prefects at the front with the men. Go tell them.'

'Yes, sire.' Trajanus nodded again and left the commander's building along with the other senior tribune.

Gaius leant back in his chair and rubbed a thumb along the stubble on his chin. 'Will the Britons meet us in the field do you think?'

'Voada will make the same mistake as Caratacus. And she cannot hold the Britons' war host together much longer. They all come from different clans and there are always intertribal conflicts at the best of times.'

'Mmm, but the Britons know that we are running low on food. They only have to wait and harry us from time to time.'

'They cannot wait,' Suetonius uttered. 'We just have to hope they take up the challenge and swarm openly onto the plane to fight us.'

'May Mars protect us,' Gaius murmured.

'Oh, he will,' promised Suetonius. 'I have a reputation to recover here. How will I explain the loss of three cities to the Emperor if I don't justify it with a great victory in the field!'

Later in the evening, Suetonius called Vettius to him. Vettius had been working in an adjacent office writing last wills and testaments for a number of the senior officers. Despite the help from two scriveners, he was bored with the paperwork and glad of the break.

Suetonius did not wait for Vettius to sit down. 'I want you to write a report for the Emperor, tonight. And tell me, who were the two men who violated the Iceni princesses?'

'An auxiliary cavalryman, a decurion, I believe, and the tribune, Marius, who had been based in Londinium with Catus.' Vettius rolled his eyes, evidently exasperated by the subject.

'You know it was the flame that started this rebellion?'

'Yes, I do, Suetonius, but I am a lawyer and, following Voada's refusal to respect the Iceni client agreement with the Emperor, I gave legal advice to Catus who then applied the law.' Vettius held out the palm of his hand to Suetonius as he added, 'He was well paid for it too. He seems to have disappeared into the mists of time with all the money. No news has been heard of Catus since he left Londinium.'

'That is no surprise: no news seems to be getting in or out of the province. Some messages are managing to pass through the Regni lands to the south but that is all. I want your report to reach Rome.'

'If I take it myself, then I can guarantee its personal safe-keeping. I am certainly keen to return home, but if you defeat the Britons tomorrow, then we retake Britannia and the frontiers are reopened anyway.'

Suetonius nodded and, anxious to return to an earlier subject, he announced, 'I have a piece of information from the Iceni camp. Apparently, one of the Iceni princesses is with child. Could you ask the decurion and the tribune to come to me now? I also need you to be present in order to discuss the legal implications of such a pregnancy.'

Vettius's ears pricked up at such news. He enjoyed listening to gossip, but, not wanting to sound too animated at such rumours, he drawled, 'Yes, of course. I will send an officer to find them.'

An hour later Marius and Titus entered the commander's office and gave a respectful bow to the Governor and to Vettius. Both officers remained standing as Suetonius did not invite them to sit. He questioned them regarding who had despoiled the eldest Iceni princess. Marius was ill-at-ease speaking to the Governor on such an intimate subject, but seeing Titus's raised eyebrow he felt obliged to break the silence. 'It was I,' he confessed at last. 'I was following the orders of your law official, Vettius.' He looked askance at Suetonius's law officer and, feeling confused by such a question, added, 'May I know why you are asking, sir?'

'No, you may not, but tomorrow Marius, you are to remain at the fort, along with Vettius, and help protect it.'

Before he could stop himself, Marius stepped forward and demanded, 'Why am I not to take part in the battle?'

Suetonius knuckled his brow at the impudence of the young tribune and, poking the man's shoulder harshly with his index finger, he barked, 'Because I promised your family to give you military experience in Britannia, but I also promised them to keep you alive – much to my regret.' Then, turning to Titus his tone remained cold as he contemplated the dark skin and thick build of this decurion. Suetonius recognised him as a man from Mauretania in North Africa and thought he should recognise him. And Titus knew Suetonius as an ex-governor of Mauretania, who had put down a revolt there. Titus knew him too, as the first Roman general to have crossed the Atlas Mountains. Suetonius had no time to reflect further on Titus's name and face though, for he had more pressing matters to discuss with Vettius. He told the decurion to be on the frontline the following morning with his cavalry riders. Then he dismissed both men.

Sapho gave a low grunt and then a growl. She stood up holding her tail low to the ground and nudged Keara, breathing heavily into her face.

'I'm awake, Sapho. I can hear it too.' She rolled off her mat and put her hands on her sword and shield.

'What is it?' Caitlyn asked from her own mat beside her sister.

'I think it's nothing,' Keara answered. 'I'll leave Sapho with you and Amena and take a look.'

Telling Sapho to stay in the tent Keara crept out. Towards the north of the camp, there were some rising noises. Torches were being lit and she was joined by her mother and by Greer.

'Rory and Galdus have gone to see what is happening,' Voada told her. 'The guards have reported some movement on the outskirts of the camp, but it is a dark night.'

Within moments a number of horses came cantering into the centre of the camp. Two men rode on the first, and upon its arrival in front of Voada the back rider jumped off. It was Galdus laughing, and, as the second man jumped off, Galdus disclaimed, 'May I introduce you to my youngest brother, Brekus of the Caledonians!'

Astonished, Keara stared at the young man by Galdus's side. He was a little taller than his brother, and just as lithe, though his hair was darker and wilder. Wearing plaid trousers and leather sandals, he wore nothing else but a copious amount of woad paintings on his chest, shoulders, arms and back: swirls, knotwork and a boar's head. Speaking only in Caledonian, he knelt at Voada's side and smiled up at his aunt, his cousin, and at Greer, professing his pleasure at meeting them. Other horsemen came to a halt, headed by a large, burly man who dismounted. His short, ginger beard twitched as he strode up to his sister and threw his great arms round her.

'Hello, Voada, my little sister, or should I now call you the Boudica?' he chuckled giving her a broad grin. 'I'm glad we made it in time for the final victory.'

'Oh, Corbreid,' Voada cried, joyful, almost light-hearted. 'How did you get to us?'

'I'll tell you everything, but first get someone to take our horses. And get me a drink!'

Voada led her brother into the makeshift council tent, followed by a great number of armed warriors. Other horsemen were dismounting behind, including Rory, his man, Varney, and some different clansmen. Greer recognised the Carvetti prince, Venutius and strode up to this man to greet him and ask for fuller news of Ynys Môn.

'Not good, I'm afraid,' Venutius spoke wearily. Leaving his horse with another warrior, he followed Greer to a tent. Once inside, he collapsed onto a rush mat and gave Greer a detailed account of happenings on the Sacred Isle.

'Ynys Môn is now in the hands of the Romans and they have already started destroying the sacred oaks and altars in our forests. Sacrovar and Taran have been crucified. A few of our holy men did get away to Hibernia, along with some of the island people, but most have been executed or enslaved. Some of my men and I managed to make it back to Carvetii and thus, were able to help Corbreid find a passage to you.'

Greer gave Venutius a grim smile and gripped him gently on the shoulder. 'You did what you could on the island, but Sacrovar and Taran are a sad loss. Thank you for joining us for the last fight.' He passed him a wooden cup of mead and then cut him some bread and cheese.

Breaking the bread in his hands Venutius asked, 'Why has Voada chosen to face Suetonius in a fixed battle?' He frowned before continuing, 'She knows the Romans are far superior to us in training and equipment.'

Greer poured a cup of warm mead for himself and sat down on a mat beside Venutius. 'She has been chosen by Andraste as the Boudica, who has promised us victory, but I'm not sure that victory is guaranteed in an open battle. Keara wanted to continue our rebellion with the same guerrilla tactics as Caratacus – as did I – but we were outnumbered by the council. Dubnov and Voada led the other tribal leaders in voting for a pitched battle. They feel that the gods are on our side despite their abandonment of our Sacred Isle.' Greer sighed. 'For many of us tonight I feel that this will be our last meal, so eat: you'll need your strength. Tomorrow we will do what we can for the Britons' freedom. You should talk to your men.' He raised the cup to his mouth and savoured the sweet flowered honey of the drink. 'Mmm!' he swallowed. Then placing his cup on a tray, he sighed again and added, 'I'll come with you, and then we can join the others.'

In the council tent Corbreid put down his own great tankard of mead and wiped his mouth on the back of his hand. He stared at his sister's back. 'Cover it up. I have seen it and will make the Romans pay for what they have done to my family. However, I could not get my whole army across Brigantian territory. Cartimandua has closed the roads through her lands. I managed to come this far with a small division of men thanks to Venutius who passed us through his Carvetti lands and then along the west coast. It was no easy feat crossing the southern border of Brigantian territory and passing through the militarised zone to reach you. Where is the man?' Corbreid looked around at the faces with him, but could not find Venutius.

'He is with Greer,' Voada answered, 'and will join us shortly, but you and your men must rest. Tomorrow we fight Suetonius.' A flicker of anxiety crossed her face. 'Who have you left in the north?'

'I have left my second son, Tulcane, with the Caledonian clans in the Highlands. He is a skilled warrior and will protect the northern lands from any Brigantian incursions.'

'Well, it is good to meet my third nephew, Brekus as a grown man.' Here, she smiled across the crowded tent of heads to where her two nephews and Keara were in animated talk.

Later that night Galdus could not sleep. Jumping up from his mat, he decided to go to the Iceni supply tent and fetch some more arrows. A couple of guards were on duty outside the tent. He entered and found Keara cross-legged on the floor in the process of sharpening a sword. There was a candle burning beside her.

'Oh, you can't sleep either,' she said, glancing up.

'No.'

'Is Brekus asleep?'

'Yes, I left my brother snoring away. He's exhausted after the long journey south but, if I remember rightly, he always sleeps like a pup no matter what wind is up.'

Galdus began to rummage through one of the ground quivers in the tent. From time to time, he would press the point of an arrow with his thumb to check its prick. Then he chose a few.

'Ouch!' he snapped, suddenly placing his thumb in his mouth.

'And *you're* suckling like a baby,' Keara gave a hollow laugh. 'You'll see more blood than that tomorrow.' Galdus came over to her and sat down. 'I only hope it's not yours,' he said, leaning forward with his clutch of arrows under his arm. 'There is something I must say to you, before tomorrow.' He hesitated, certain of what he felt, but unsure of what to say.

Keara's face was closed. She continued to rasp her sword with the sandstone, fixing her eyes on the sliding movement of the smooth rock on the metal blade. Such short, rhythmic strokes seemed to calm her nerves and stop her from thinking. After a moment she said, 'And I only hope it's not your blood tomorrow, or that of Caitlyn, or Brekus or my mother. My family is precious to me. And we *are* cousins Galdus, though we have grown up as brother and sister. We will fight side by side tomorrow and the gods will decide who lives and who dies. I cannot think beyond that.' She looked at him sadly, then rose from the ground and padded out of the tent with her sharpened sword by her side.

There could be no enemy, Suetonius knew, except at his front, where there was open country without cover for ambushes.

Suetonius had drawn up his legionaries in close order and, as planned with his staff officers, he had placed the light-armoured auxiliaries on the flanks with the cavalry on higher ground on the wings. The Roman blocks of silver and painted red armour stood out on the narrowed head of the flood plain. The soldiers' weapons of daggers, javelins and the double-edged swords glinted and winked in the rising sunlight of the morning air.

Surveying the Britons, Suetonius noted with some satisfaction that despite the seething mass of their numbers their apparent lack of order, training and equipment would work against them. In unprecedented hordes the Britons' bands of cavalry and infantry roamed over the open plain singing war songs and shouting taunts at the Romans. The chariot-mounted chieftains wore the fine helmets and decorated shields of their clans and, driven by their chariot riders, they were able to jump off the vehicle from time to time in order to exhort their men to fight for liberty and glory. In order to show their prowess some of them even walked along the chariot pole, stood on the yoke and then danced back into their chariot as fast and as nimble as a hare. Armed with the great swords of their ancestors, they were a class apart from their followers who could brandish only their knives, farming implements, hunting spears, slingshots and the occasional sword or javelin. Yet, the Britons' confidence was such that many had brought their families with them; women and children stood upon their wagons on the furthest outskirts of the plain, cheering their clansmen on, waiting for the battle.

Suetonius took the necessary time to address his military staff, telling them also, to relay his words to the other soldiers across the ranks. From where he stood on higher ground overlooking the terrain below, his speech was both clear and rousing. Trusting to his men's bravery, he offered encouragement and rewards.

'Disregard the clamour and fierce looks of our enemy. In their ranks there are more women than fighting men. They are mostly unarmed, more used to tilling the earth than fighting a war. Do not fear them because they have burned three cities for they did not capture them by force nor after a battle: one was betrayed to them and the others we abandoned in order for us to regroup and face them here. Do not fear them because of the atrocities they have committed; rather be filled with the desire to avenge those who have fallen. You have heard how they hung up naked the Roman men and women they captured alive, how they cut off the women's breasts, castrated the men and then sewed these to their mouths, in order to make the victims appear to be eating them. Afterwards, they impaled the victims on sharp skewers run lengthwise through the entire body. All this they did to the accompaniment of sacrifices, banquets and wanton behaviour, all in the name of their goddess, Andraste. But their goddess has abandoned them; we know because we have the gods on our side. They are our allies, for the gods almost always side with those who are wronged, and we have Mars Ultor fighting alongside us today.

'Also, do not forget that we are Romans. Courage is our heritage and we have triumphed over all mankind by our valour. Do not forget our prestige, for those with whom we are about to engage are not soldiers but our slaves, whom we have conquered even when they were free and independent. We have routed them so often in the past that they will break up immediately. They may be numerous, but each of you is worth at least ten of them. Just keep in close order, throw your javelins at the order, and then carry on: use shield bosses to fell them, swords to kill them. Do not think of plunder. When you have won, you will have everything: glory and gold.'

His words were enthusiastically received by his men,

particularly by the old battle-experienced soldiers who longed to avenge the deaths of their comrades at Camulodunum and those who had fallen on the road to that colony. Yet the men waited quietly for the battle signal to be given. They looked at the wide field before them and concentrated on the weapons in their hands and the barbarians before them.

Voada ordered her two daughters to stand in her chariot with her and then they drove across the great plain stopping at the different tribal bands in order to speak to each one in turn. Most of the fighters wore no body armour of any sort, only a pair of loose-fitting trousers and the traditional woad paintings of their clan. Voada and her daughters were an impressive sight in their light, wickerwork chariot and their tribal war dress. Voada had loosened and brushed her long, red hair so that it fell to her hips covering the handle of the long, ancestral sword at her side. She wore a brightly coloured tunic of chequered cloth which was fastened with the double-crescent moon of her tribe. At her throat she wore her badge of victory, the great golden torc, as did Caitlyn, Queen of the Iceni. Only Keara wore the loose trousers and close-fitting jacket of the Britannic warrior. She had decorated her arms and face with the woad paintings of her Iceni clan, an outbursting of wolves, horses and crescent moons. Her dark hair stood in short limed spikes, but she also carried a helmet to be worn into battle. Her back was covered by a light, wooden shield decorated with the same woad paintings as on her body. This contrasted greatly with the symbolic weaponry of her mother who carried a heavy, oblong shield made from polished bronze and red glass which sparkled in the morning sunlight. In Voada's other hand, she gripped a long, iron-headed spear that she held up to the warriors as she spoke.

'I am your Boudica. I and my daughters are descended

from the mighty families of this land, but now I am not fighting for our kingdoms and wealth, I am fighting for the gods, for Andraste and for you.' She stared from face to face before continuing, 'for our lost freedom, for our outraged daughters and our bruised bodies. Now, Roman greed does not even spare our bodies. Old people are killed, virgins are raped. But the gods will grant us the vengeance we deserve! The Romans know that they cannot win this day. The Roman division, which dared oppose us is annihilated. The others cower in their camps or watch for a chance to escape.'

Then, at Voada's command, the huge carnyx horn gave the signal for battle and like the bursting of a great dam the Britons exploded into a forward movement, racing ever faster towards the Romans' standing army in the distance.

At first, the Roman troops stood their ground in silence. In serried ranks they watched the Britons' approach: five hundred yards, four hundred yards, and the sweat began to run down their arms; three hundred yards, two hundred, and they could see the eyes of their enemies; one hundred yards and Suetonius finally hoisted the red flag and gave the signal for action. Wearing the emblematic wolf skin of Legion Fourteen the General's standard bearer stepped forward. With his face hidden by the dead face of the wolf's head, he gave a long, clear blast on the huge horn-trumpet that curved round itself and opened into a cacophony of sound. The other emblem bearers in the field below, followed suit: the standard-bearer for Legion Twenty wore the skin of a wild boar; that of Legion Nine the heavier skin and head of a dead bull; the trumpet blower for the small number of legionaries from Isca wore the skin and head of a lion.

Keeping to the defile as a natural defence, the Romans stepped forward and launched the first of their two javelins at the fast-approaching Britons. This initial volley of fire was deadly: travelling over one hundred feet the first seven thousand javelins rained down onto the mass of Britons racing up the sloping plain towards the narrowing defile. For those who carried shields and were able to raise them above their heads, the javelins bent on impact and could not be pulled out, so those warriors lucky enough to survive the first shower of javelins then had to discard their shields and were unprotected from the second volley.

Then, from a second blast of the horn from the four Roman standard bearers, followed by the waving of a signal baton and roar from each unit's centurion in the field, the Roman forces shunted forward in wedge formation, as did the auxiliary infantry on their sides. The legionaries met the Britons head-on, first battering at their bodies with their shields which drove great clefts into the broad waves of fighting men and women. Pulling out their short stabbing swords, the Romans began the murderous task of cutting down the oncoming hordes. The British tribesmen were at a disadvantage: out-of-breath from the long rush uphill, their longer and more cumbersome swords were ill-adapted for such compact fighting. They fell like corn in a summer field. And yet, they continued to pour ever onwards towards the Roman line. From time to time a group of hardened warriors would hack and hew its way through the Roman troops, but would then be surrounded, cut off from the rear, and pinched out like candles in the wind.

Suetonius followed the fighting closely from his position on high ground. The battle lasted the morning and much of the afternoon. At other calls from the standard-bearers, the Roman cavalry had swept down from the slopes on either side of the defile, glad to be freed at last from their immobile positions. The riders had been enduring painful thigh cramps from squeezing the flanks of the horses for so long to keep them still, and with their lances extended had eagerly descended on the fighting plain and had demolished all remaining resistance. The Britons' chariots were no match for the Roman cavalry. Having thrown out their now useless shields, the charioteers were open targets on the field for the Roman archers who made short work of picking them off.

It was turning into a bloodbath. Voada and Caitlyn watched from a high slope, on the opposite side to that of Suetonius, and could see their warriors being cut down in their thousands. Voada groaned as she saw the fall of King Dubnov below. He and his charioteer both received arrows to their bodies, and both fell to the ground, leaving the horse and chariot to skitter off amongst the Trinovantes creating havoc in its wake. On another side of the plain, Voada watched Keara fighting alongside her cousins, Galdus and Brekus. There was a mixture of Iceni, Carvetti and Caledonian warriors who were working together under King Corbreid and King Venutius. Keara was using her slingshot well, but soon ran out of space to swing her cord so pulled out her sword. She had a slight advantage over the others here for, being of a smaller build, she used a shorter sword which was wieldier in the tightened mass ahead of them.

Voada clenched her fists and prayed to Andraste to protect her daughter. There was a given moment of frozen time for Voada herself when a small group of highly trained auxiliaries approached from one side in a surprise attack and broke through Rory's guards. Rory reacted immediately by protecting Voada and the queen with his own body and engaging several Romans at once. He was quickly joined by Greer who used his staff as a baton, deftly beating back one opponent. Rory took a sword cut to his arm and another to his chest. He would have taken a third and final thrust to his heart, but from nowhere Sapho appeared. With a low and menacing growl, she sprang upon the group of Romans, creating panic in their group as she leapt at their armoured bodies and ripped them into broken pieces. Covered in the red and steaming blood of their enemies Sapho padded over to Voada and licked her outstretched hand.

'Thank you, Sapho.' She gave the mastiff a deft stroke before turning her attention to Rory's wounds. The warrior lay on the ground where he had fallen, hardly breathing now, but still conscious. Voada, Caitlyn and Greer knelt by his sides. Varney came running up the slope to them and with a few other men carried Rory over to the shade of a silver birch. As he was laid down on the soft earth and leaves, he opened his eyes. Upon recognising the tree above him, he smiled.

'Argh, the silver birch. It is found in the land of the dead, you know.'

Greer smiled softly down at the warrior and rejoined, 'It symbolises the return from the dead Rory, did you know that?'

'Can you save him, Greer?' Voada whispered to him.

'I'm not dead yet, my queen, so no need to whisper,' Rory gargled, as blood seeped from his mouth. Greer shook his head slowly and gripped Rory's arm.

'Go in peace, my friend, to the Blessed Isles, and rest for a while.'

Rory gave an imperceptible nod and looked at Voada.

'Thank you, my friend, for your life, your loyalty,' she cried.

'And my love,' he finished, and then his head sagged to one side and all expression slipped from his face.

Caitlyn took her mother's hand and after a brief moment she pulled Voada to her feet and spoke, 'We must return to the ledge, where our soldiers can see us. Come, Mother,' and she and Greer helped Voada walk back to the plain where all seemed now lost in Voada's heart. She watched and heard the sights and sounds of the battle field: all blood and screams, but she felt almost impassive to the story unfolding before her.

The Romans were so organised, so synchronised in their movements. It was like watching a macabre Greek mime where all the players are masked and dance in unison to a silent rhythm on the stage below. As each front line tired, they moved back as one body, obeying the trumpet call of their standard-bearers. As they did so they carried their dead and wounded comrades back with them and were immediately replaced by the rows of legionaries who had been covering their backs. These new men stepped forward to continue the fight. To the rear of the fighting legionaries, the medical orderlies ran across the field, seeing to the wounded. For those with cuts and dislocated limbs the orderlies tended them on site, putting bones back into joints and cleaning cuts with anaesthetics and a few stitches. For those with more serious wounds the orderlies stemmed the bleeding as far as possible, and then placed the men on stretchers. These wounded men were immediately picked up by the stretcher bearers and carried to the military hospital which stood in tents at the back of the field. Here, the surgeons operated on those who could be saved: extracting arrows and slingshots, sawing off limbs that were too damaged. For the dying men, the Roman priests sat by their sides and said prayers over their bodies whilst purifying their souls with libations of water.

For the Britons on the field, there was no such care as they were cut down by the advancing Roman lines. Late in the day the tide turned decisively against the Britons. Those Britons still standing turned and fled, but their escape was almost impossible because of the great ring of wagons which blocked the outlets. They were harried by the Roman cavalry and cut down from behind. Heads, arms, legs were sundered from their bodies. Torsos, limbs, bowels and writhing ponies lay scattered across the crimson plain. The Romans advanced ever forward stamping over the dead and the dying in their hard-hobnailed boots. They did not spare even the women or children. Caitlyn saw Amena below on a wagon. She was with her family watching events unravel towards her. And then she was gone; jumping from her wagon to escape the wave of running Britons, she was crushed beneath the flood that overtook her.

Baggage animals too, transfixed with weapons, added to the heaps of the dead. Caitlyn took her mother's hand and said a silent prayer for Amena, for Rory, and for the others who had now passed into the Otherworld. As the evening advanced, a number of Britons were taken alive, and only spared by the Romans in order to clear the field of the dead. A few Britons did make their escape, and scattered into the surrounding shrub land and woods in order to regroup.

Keara's group was amongst those able to get away. As they fought on the wings, they managed to make a rapid retreat to where their horses stood and were unencumbered by the blockade of wagons. An auxiliary wing of Moorish cavalrymen did try to stop them, but the skirmish was short. Led by a Mauritanian decurion the North African horsemen were light-armoured, nimble and excellent in the saddle. Distinguished by their dark skin and African braids they fought with short swords and small shields and seemed to be everywhere at once. They would have dispatched far more of the Britons if they had not been called off by their decurion in order to rescue a hard-pressed Cassius, the prefect to Suetonius's Legion Fourteen. Both Keara and Galdus had recognised the decurion.

VIII

'CAN I HAVE THE NUMBER OF DEAD?' SUETONIUS asked his prefect, Cassius, the next day.

'A thousand of our men fell,' Cassius answered, 'and another thousand are seriously wounded or injured. They are being tended here in the fort, but we don't have enough beds as this is only a small hospital in a vexillation fortress.'

'We shall have to make do. Do we have enough medical staff?'

Cassius nodded in the affirmative though he knew the medics were exhausted; some had been working all night.

'How many of the Britons were killed?' Suetonius then wanted to know.

'Around forty thousand, sire.'

'Good, good.' Suetonius nodded in satisfaction. 'Kill those who are wounded.'

'Yes, sire.' Cassius was about to leave the office but hesitated.

'Yes, what is it?' Suetonius cried a little irritated by the man's hesitation.

'I would like to add a man's name to the list of soldiers who are to receive awards for courage.'

'Whose name? And why?'

'That of the decurion, Titus, who saved my life yesterday. My men and I were almost surrounded when he and his cavalry broke into the fight to make way for us to get back to our lines.'

'I gave the order for his troop to come to your aid.'

'Yes, I know, but he and his men took a lot of risks in that fight. He lost a number of men and he, himself, took a blow to the shoulder when he pulled me up behind him on his horse.'

'I'll see what I can do.'

'Thank you, sire. Could he have the Civic Crown?'

Quite irritated with his prefect, he shook his head fiercely, 'There, you ask too much, Cassius. That is only for Roman citizens who save the life of a fellow citizen. Your auxiliary decurion is Mauretanian. I can grant Roman citizenship to the man and his cohort of thirty men, but no more.'

'Thank you, sire,' the man repeated, 'but he lost a number of men.'

'Then I will give them citizenship posthumously,' Suetonius breathed out exasperated.

Cassius nodded and left the office.

In the overcrowded hospital, Titus lay on a camp bed on the wooden floor. Zia was squatting by his side tending his shoulder which had a deep gash in it. He had stitched it up the night before and was changing the bandages and cleansing the wound with some acid vinegar.

Titus winced in pain. 'I hope you cleaned everything properly,' he growled.

Zia instinctively drew back from his master's anger. 'Of course,' he answered. 'I wouldn't want you to die, would I? That would make me a free man.'

Zia's sarcasm seemed to irritate Titus even further, but he had little strength in his left arm as he flung a pillow at his slave. Zia ducked this and went on with cleaning the gash.

'It's a good thing that axe was almost blunt and that your shoulder was protected.'

Titus grunted as his man rubbed lanolin onto the wound so that it would heal more quickly, but he said nothing more. The ward was noisy enough with the movement of orderlies, the groans of the wounded and the clatter of pans. Even the flies were busy, buzzing over drops of blood and sodden cloths.

Zia continued, 'You have been granted Roman citizenship for saving Cassius's life. It will be granted at the awards ceremony this afternoon on the parade ground.'

At this, Titus's eyes seemed to question Zia.

'How many men did I lose?' he asked at last.

'Five. But two more will probably die today. They had to wait to go into the operating theatre because the injured Roman citizens had priority.' Zia frowned at the injustice of this.

'Good men, all of them. I sometimes wonder if the end goal is worth the sacrifice. I'm getting out of here,' Titus spoke, clearly disgusted with the crowded wards and the groans around him. He began to rise from the bed, but felt too hazy.

'What the hell did you give me, Zia?'

'One of your own remedies to help you sleep. You can stay here for now, but I'll come and get you for the awards ceremony later.' Zia smiled in satisfaction. 'And here's some more opium for the pain if you need it.' He placed a glass of juice by Titus's bed and got up to leave.

'How is Cabrel?' Titus wanted to know before letting Zia leave the ward.

'Your horse is fine. He's in the pasture now, outside the fort. I've looked after him well, not that he looks after me,' Zia moaned. 'He's as vicious as usual.'

'Good,' said Titus. 'That's a good sign. Go take him some apples.'

'I already have. Now I'm going.' Zia left, smiling.

They were only a small number of warriors hiding within the ferns and brambles across the forest. Voada's group lay or sat on the leaves and miry earth which spread upon the forest floor. They did not light a fire for fear of attracting the Roman 'sweepers' who were clearing the land of any remaining vestiges of Britannic resistance. Their horses and ponies had been tethered to one side and cropped the shoots of grass. Voada looked at the faces around her: her daughters, her brother, the Carvetii prince, and her druid. Then she looked up at the starry night above her head and whispered to the Iceni goddess, *Andraste, where are you now?*

No one spoke for a while. They were all too shattered: tired, thirsty, hungry, defeated. A small noise could be heard, the snapping of a twig, the shuffle of leaves, and all heads were alert, but it was only Galdus and Brekus returning from a forest forage. They had found some wild duck eggs and a clutch of dry walnuts from the winter before. They had also filled some water bags and were careful to make Caitlyn eat and drink first. Keara gave some of the walnuts to Sapho and let her lick the egg shells. Then she lay down beside her dog to try and sleep. The warm snuffling air of Sapho on her cheeks reassured her and she stroked her paw in the darkness. She could hear her mother discussing their future with Greer and the others. Venutius was saying that he must head back to the north to join his tribe. He could try and prepare a safe passage for them across the Brigantian lands so they could reach Caledonia in secret. Her uncle thought this was a sound idea and the only possible one.

Corbreid was saying, 'The Romans will not forgive you for this uprising. Your warriors have killed too many Romans and destroyed too much for you to be forgiven. They have lost Camulodonum, Londinium and Verulamium. You must come back with us to my kingdom and continue the resistance from there. It is also your land. You were born in the north, you grew up there.'

'I understand all this, but I cannot abandon my people here. Caitlyn is Queen of the Iceni. We must go back to Saham Toney. Whilst I must face my own fate, Caitlyn must try to make peace with the Romans, for our people's sake, and for the sake of her child, my grandchild.'

'A Roman bastard,' Galdus whispered to his brother.

'Suetonius will take you, Voada.' It was Greer speaking here. 'He will take you in chains to Rome and parade you in his triumph before the Emperor, like he did Caratacus and Vercingétorix. He will also take your daughters.'

'He will never take me,' Voada snarled in anger, sounding a little incoherent after her earlier remarks. There was a moment's silence before she spoke again, 'Now, I will rest. I have lost too many good men and women today to think of the future, for I feel that I have none.'

Venutius spoke apart to Corbreid and Greer, 'I will leave in the morning and I'll send news to you if I can of how to travel north.'

'We need ships to take us from the Icenian coast to Caledonia,' Corbreid stated.

'We may have enough as we are so few now,' said Greer, 'but the North Sea is a dangerous place: the winds are harsh and so are Cartimandua's pirates!'

Iceni

In the early hours of the morning the Britons left the shelter of the woods to begin the horse trek directly east to Iceni territory. They followed some deer tracks out of the woods, and then Venutius left them to travel north.

'I'll send word as soon as I can,' he said, 'and will only use the Ogham code.'

'Safe journey,' called Greer.

'Don't fear for me.' Venutius half-smiled as his horse reared on its two hind legs. 'I'll join my men where we have meeting points along the way.' And he was gone, cantering off into the still penumbra of the early morning mists. Keara watched him go then followed her family.

Greer led the small Iceni group in silence across a tract of open land and towards the luminous horizon ahead of them. Turning to the others in his saddle, he told them that they would take the ancient trackway. 'To avoid being found,' he uttered, 'but we will travel one behind the other so that if the Roman scouts do find out tracks they will not know how many we are. This path will take us two to three days to reach Saham Toney, depending on how fast Caitlyn can keep up.' He paused for a moment before continuing, 'but we must move fast because the Roman fortress of Clac-nyn lies directly halfway between us and home. If Cerialis hears of the Roman victory before we pass, then his cavalry will be out hunting us down. He still has one thousand men with him.' He swivelled back round in his saddle and began to canter off along the Black Salt Way.

Reaching Clac-nyn the following night, they did not stop to rest until they had managed to bypass the vexillation fortress. Crossing Coritani territory south of the fortress, they noted with some satisfaction that the Roman defences had been reduced in size in a very hurried manner: obviously in response to the Iceni's ambush of Legion Nine. The fort had now been reduced to the size of an auxiliary fortress, just large enough to protect those cavalrymen who had reached Clac-nyn.

The Britons avoided the fen causeway which contained the Roman system of roads and canals from Clac-nyn into Iceni territory, and followed their own route past carved stones that marked the trackways or ford crossings through the softly undulating fenlands until they reached a river path leading to Fison Way. They did not stop here, though they did give the sad news to those still occupying the farmsteads. They continued on their way, taking the only crossing through the fenlands to Saham Toney, warning those left behind to hide and protect themselves or to leave the land altogether. Many did leave. Those that did so, followed the ancient track, the Icknield Way, to the limit of the Iceni territory on the northern coast and tried to find passage across the Wash in the fishing boats there.

Reaching Saham Toney, Greer and Keara were most pleased to find Diodorus safe and secure in the Iceni stronghold. He seemed immune to outside affairs, wrapped up as he was in his books and writings and farm animals. Corbreid and Brekus understood not a word of what he was saying, and Galdus had to translate from Greek into Caledonian for his father and brother until Diodorus switched to Celtic which everyone could follow.

'Nothing has been happening here,' he was saying. 'We have had absolutely no news from you, and life is much the same as it always has been. We have been trying to look after the fields, but we are not enough, so we have mainly concentrated on the livestock.'

'We are certainly not enough to man the defences against the Roman forces that will be arriving in a few days, a week at the most,' Voada said. She shook her head as she looked at

the small numbers of men and women. 'We must move on to
Venta Icenorum. As it is partly Roman, we will try to make
terms there.'

'Mother, how can we make terms there since we overran
the small detachment of Roman soldiers who had been based
there?' Keara asked in disbelief.

'We have no choice.' Voada sounded lost.

'Mother.' This time it was Caitlyn's plaintive voice. 'I cannot
travel any further. I am in too much pain and I have a little
bleeding.'

Shocked at the paleness of Caitlyn's face Greer strode to
her side, along with Keara, saying, 'She must lie down.'

They helped her into a round house to rest. Voada followed
them into the hut and sat down by Caitlyn's mat. Resigned
and cross-legged Voada looked at both her daughters and
smiled gently at the two of them. 'We will stay and wait for
the Romans to arrive here. We have time to strengthen our
defences as they will want to consolidate their forces in the
Middle Lands before coming to find us. Perhaps then, we will
be able to make a bargain with them.'

Keara responded with a frown, then left the dark hut to
find Rhonda. Rhonda was already running down the track
towards her, carrying her medicine basket. Seeing that she
wasn't needed anymore and that she would only be in the way
Keara joined her cousins who were stabling the horses. The
stable lad, Blair was also helping, only too eager to take part
in the war effort.

MANDVESSEDUM

The cohorts stood erect on the great plain outside their fort.
Their standard bearers stood before the men holding up each

legion's standard and Eagle. Despite its size the fort was too small to accommodate all the Romans for the military awards ceremony, especially since several bulls were needed for the religious rite of thanks to Jupiter and Mars Ultor. An altar to Mars had been carried onto the field and placed along the bank of the river. Then a bull was led up to the stone slab at the foot of the altar and sacrificed by a priest who cut out the bull's entrails as an offering to the Roman god of war. Several other bulls were also sacrificed and then cut up for the soldiers' banquet that evening.

Suetonius addressed the assembly of men, praising them in the light of the sun god for their courage, and thanking the war gods for their victory. He named a few soldiers for their acts of bravery and called out a list of names to receive awards and decorations. With each name a man stepped forward and the prefects and centurions presented the man under his command with a crown, a torc, an armband or a disc. It was Marius who presented Titus with a document granting him Roman citizenship, although Marius didn't seem too pleased with this act. Zia mentioned afterwards that it was probably because Marius should have told Suetonius that his own life had been saved by Titus in Camulodonum – but he probably hadn't wanted to outline the unheroic details of being covered in shit.

That evening under a clustered sky of brilliant stars the high-ranking staff and those men who had received awards were placed together at the same mess tables on the parade ground within the fort. Rationing had been laid aside for this evening since the Britannic war host had been broken. Great slabs of steak, coated in salt, pepper, cumin and anchovy sauce, had been laid on platters in the middle of the tables, along with huge bowls of lettuce and egg salad, and lentils with chestnuts, which were all served with baskets of bread and jugs of honeyed wine, followed up with cheeses, stuffed dates and sweet wine cakes. The rank and file had lesser things to eat and drink, but they still enjoyed their sour wine and beef steaks – and refreshing life.

Suetonius took this opportunity to make plans for the next few days ahead and to give his orders. He was particularly anxious to restore order to the province by putting down all remnants of the rebellion. He was sending the legate and senior tribune of Legion Two back to the southwest to put down the Dumnonii and Durotriges clans and to have the prefect, Poenius Postumus arrested for disobeying orders.

'The charge is serious,' Suetonius added, speaking to the legate, Gaius. 'He is to be executed.'

Gaius was more of a humane man who wanted details of the rebellion in the Southwest Peninsula. 'Poenius is a good soldier who has served Rome well for a number of years. He must have been held down at the Isca fortress.'

Suetonius looked for a long moment at Gaius and then conceded a little. 'You can give him the choice: execution in front of the men or his own stoic death.'

Gaius nodded, sadly shaking his head, but accepting Suetonius's words.

Next, Suetonius turned to Trajanus, the senior tribune to Legion Twenty. 'Your legate, Bolanus is to leave bases on Ynys Môn and at Caernarfon and Caerhun in order to reinforce our control of Cymru. I have already sent him word. Your prefect, Mark Anthony is to stay here in the Middle Lands. I am putting him in charge of the huge supply base which is to be built in order to manage my movement of reprisals and control.'

'Yes, sire,' Trajanus responded. 'And where am I to go?'

'You and the remaining soldiers of Legion Twenty will take my law officer, Vettius down the main road to Londinium.

You are to re-garrison the fortlets on your way and clean up Londinium. Take all the Britannic slaves you need to do the dirty work.' Then turning to Vettius he added, 'I need you in Londinium to wait for news from the Emperor and find out where in Hades Catus has got to.'

Vettius gave a smile of relief at this order. 'At last, I return to civilisation! They can't have burnt the whole city, so I will try and find myself a comfortable villa. As for Catus, you have no jurisdiction over him, but I will set up an enquiry to track him and his treasure down. Where are you off to?'

'My Legion Fourteen will march into what we can now term *enemy territory*. We must go east to Clac-nyn in order to relieve Cerialis's remaining Legion Nine and destroy all vestiges of the Trinovante and Iceni tribes.'

'When are we to set out?' It was Cassius who asked this question.

'In just a few days. Enough time for the men to rest and to pack what provisions we have.' Then, looking down the table he added to Cassius, 'I want the tribune, Marius to come with us, and the decurion, Titus. They are both to ride with my staff, but first tell Titus that I want him to attend on me tomorrow morning.'

'Yes, my lord. I will see them now.'

THE GYRUS

After they had crossed the Mandvessedum-Londinium road, they had marched for about ten miles south until they reached the River Sowe and were clearly in friendly territory: Catuvellauni lands. To be sure of this Suetonius had his men build a floating bridge so they could cross the river. Then they followed the river until their path rose onto a sharp plateau that was protected by a loop in the River Sowe below. On this escarpment Suetonius established camp. He had brought only one cohort with him, a detachment of just under five hundred able-bodied men who escorted a large number of war prisoners and Iceni horses: live pickings from the battle field. Once the general had taken refreshment, he called for Mark Anthony and Titus to accompany him on a walk. A number of bodyguards also followed in their footsteps.

Suetonius led the two men to an open field where the Iceni ponies and horses were tethered and were being fed grass and barley. The chained prisoners had been set to work sawing down trees, splitting the wood and erecting posts in the ground. Titus could clearly distinguish the circular outline of an arena. Other men were erecting tents and giving orders to slaves to dig ditches for barrack blocks, granaries and pipelines for water supplies and sewage clearance. Some engineers were also giving instructions to the Britannic slaves to dig ditches for defences around the future supply base.

Suetonius stopped in the middle of the circular ring and, facing Titus, he swept his arm over the site. 'This is to be our collecting point for Iceni horses.' Titus glanced at the wild or semi-wild animals that were clearly frightened by the noises of sawing, hammering and digging all around.

'Mark Anthony is now in charge here, responsible for the reception of provisions and the supply of our front lines. The logistics of this should keep you very busy.' Suetonius slapped the prefect roughly on the back, giving him a grin. 'Titus will help you in this over the next few days.'

'I do not understand, sire,' Titus said. 'I am not trained in such matters. Do you mean me to work with the horses?'

'Yes, I do.' Suetonius's reply was curt and sharp. 'You see all those wild animals over there, jittering and jerking on their ropes? They are to be broken in and trained in this *gyrus* and more will be arriving every day as we advance into Iceni territory. The Iceni clan have the greatest supply of horses and ponies in Britannia. That is why Iceni is often referred to as the Kingdom of the Horse.' Here, his voice had acquired an edge of sardonic derision. 'More pony than horse though. And you,' he looked Titus directly in the face, '*are* trained in such matters. You must decide which animals are to be selected for use by the cavalry, which ones are fast for our dispatch riders, which ones can be used for traction and as pack animals, and which ones will be good only for horse meat. The animals will be trained, or butchered, in consequence.'

Ignoring the barely concealed contempt in Suetonius's voice, and not knowing if it was for him or the Iceni horses, Titus protested, 'Sire, it might take only a few days to break in a horse, but it would take a month, at the very least, to train it.'

'You have three days. I need you to follow my army into Iceni territory because I need cavalry riders with me, and linguists. In those three days, you have the time to identify to which category each horse belongs. I have other horse trainers here, so you'll work with them until I call you up for the advance movement.'

Resigned, Titus bowed slightly. 'Yes, my lord.' He stared keenly at the skittish ponies and horses surrounding them. In his mind, he had already identified a number of fine cavalry horses, and even race horses, which were attached to posts on the edge of the field.

'You must start right away. Brutus!' Suetonius called to a stout, long-faced centurion already working with a horse. 'This decurion is to work with you and select the animals for the field. He will help you tame some of them and begin training with you.'

'Yes, sire.' Brutus signalled to Titus to follow him and Suetonius watched them go before addressing Mark Anthony.

'I am returning right away to the Mandvessedum fortress. You are to send the decurion back in three days before I begin the advance movement eastwards. You understand all my instructions about the supply base?'

'Yes, I do sire, and I will not let you down. Everything you send back from the front will be stocked here for our winter supplies: horses, grain, livestock. And I will make sure that all four legions across Britannia are fully provisioned.'

'Good man. Now I must leave you.' Suetonius turned and left the field with his bodyguard. Taking only one century with him, he left Mark Anthony to oversee the construction of the base.

From a side field enclosing a great number of horses, Titus stood by Brutus and watched the Governor leave. He was only half-listening to the Roman centurion who was giving orders to him about the new intake of horses, 'You understand what we have to do here. The influx of horses is enormous, so we have a big job on our hands. I want you to stay here and manage the horses in this field. Decide what to do with them and the legionaries will lead them off to different enclosures for training, or to the abattoir. You can do that with your arm?' Brutus indicated his bandaged shoulder. The man was clearly tired and sweat was pouring off him. Titus nodded a *yes* at him and the man plodded off to another enclosure of ponies.

Looking at the horses, Titus noted a war prisoner carrying a bucket of water in either hand. The man had tattoos of crescent moons on his back, along with a number of cuts and bruises. His ragged hair fell in tethers across his neck and shoulders, matching the thick muddy rope between his ankles. Titus recognised him as one of the Iceni guardsmen to the old queen. The man had also recognised Titus and spat on the ground as he shuffled past him. It was an audacious act for a man who risked a beating, but Titus chose to ignore it. Just then Zia arrived.

'Our horses are in the new stables down by the river. I've put our tent up within the base camp.' Zia rested his crossed arms and chest on the newly raised fence and watched the Iceni slave empty the buckets into the water trough for the horses and then whistle to the animals to come and drink. Some of them recognised the call and skittered over to the man who stroked and patted their necks, reassuring them with soft words.

'Do you want me to calm that man down?' Zia asked, indicating the Iceni slave with his chin.

'No, I don't, but he could be useful to us. He is certainly a fine warrior and an excellent horseman. He would be good in the horse races too. You can speak to him.'

'He won't collaborate with the Romans. He's too proud for that.'

'But he's still alive, isn't he! He won't listen to me though, so I need you to *speak* to him.'

Titus was not sure what Zia had said exactly to the man, but he found out his name was Varney and though the man was reticent about working with Titus, he did take good care of the horses over the next days, until the final day when he suddenly vanished, along with a horse. The centurion, Brutus, was furious at Titus's neglect and wanted to know how the man had escaped. Shards of rope had been found where the man had been 'tethered' along with the other prisoners at night. He stood standing on the beaten earth, staring down at the broken rope. He had Titus standing next to him.

'He clearly had a knife,' Brutus almost whimpered, fearing the prefect's anger. 'How in Hades did he get hold of a knife?'

'I am not responsible for the war prisoners at night,' Titus responded raising his eyebrows. 'And I could ask why the man had a rope and not chains like the others?'

'We had no more chains left, and the man was quiet enough and seemed to pose no risk.'

'There you were clearly wrong,' Titus rejoined, watching Zia pack their bags onto his horses and lead them over to them. 'But he won't get far. The rebellion is over, and he'll soon be netted again.'

'He could be anywhere by now. And what is worse is that he stole the fastest horse we had.' The centurion groaned.

'Ah. There you have a problem. And, don't forget he still has the knife.' Titus added, clicking his tongue. He jumped onto his own stallion's back and gave the man a mock look of support as he made himself comfortable in the padded saddle. Then, urging the horse into a rapid canter, he left Zia to make his excuses to the centurion. At a slower pace, Zia mounted his own mare with all the baggage and followed in Titus's wake back to the governor's fort north of the river.

IX

Clac-nyn

A FEW DAYS LATER AT CLAC-NYN, CERIALIS WAS relieved to see the Roman army on the road approaching his pinioned fort. Seeing that all the rebels had now fled, he ordered the gates to be opened and ran out with his men to welcome the arrival of the Fourteenth Legion.

'General,' he cried, as Suetonius dismounted, 'it is such a relief to see you and your men. We have been holed up here for weeks.'

'Did you get news from my dispatch rider?' Suetonius wanted to know.

'Only the one who arrived an hour ago. Otherwise, nothing. We have received no news here and have not had the manpower to leave the fort. You know that I only took half of my legion down to Camulodonum. The other half remained at Lindum guarding the north with Cartimandua.'

'Yes, I know.' Suetonius passed his reins to an orderly and walked with Cerialis into the fort, noting the impromptu defences and reduced number of men. 'We have put down the rebellion,' Suetonius told him, 'but now we must teach these rebels a lesson. We stop here for the night, and tomorrow I move down to Camulodonum with my men to restore order amongst the Trinovantes. The Catuvellauni warriors will help us as their intertribal hatred is legendary. You must stay here, and I'll leave four cohorts of my men with you. In four days you must move into the Iceni lands from the west. I'll be moving up to their lands from the south. And we will crush them in Hannibal's pincer movement. It will be a war of extermination. You will have your victory Cerialis.' He clapped the legate on the back and stepped before him into the commander's building.

'And what happened to the Britons' leaders?' Cerialis was eager to know.

'The leader of the Trinovantes is dead: killed on the battlefield. As for Voada she escaped with her family, but we don't know where she is. Perhaps with her brother's forces heading for Caledonia, in which case Cartimandua and our Roman troops in the north will find her. Our scouts have picked up tracks leading this way across the fens, so it could be her. I want her found and kept alive to be sent to Rome for public execution before the Emperor.'

'Do you know anything about her daughters?'

Here, Suetonius gave a cynical laugh. 'One of them is pregnant. Thanks to Catus's punitive measures at Venta Icenorum. It's what started the whole bloody rebellion!' He seemed to have forgotten the legal advice given to Catus by his own law officer advising such violence against Voada's royal household. 'I have the father here amongst my men,' he continued: 'a high-ranking tribune from one of the aristocratic families in Rome. He's here for his education. He's certainly had that if he goes back a father. And what progeny!'

Looking at Cerialis's questioning face, he added, 'It's the

eldest daughter, the *nominative* queen of the Iceni. I'm waiting to hear back from the Emperor for orders. But first I want to bathe, eat and sleep. I hope your bathhouse is still working.'

Cerialis smiled. 'I'll soon see to that. As we've been confined to the fort, we haven't been able to get down to it, so it's been strip-washes in the courtyard.' He called to an orderly, telling him to send men down to the bathhouse furnaces. 'And it will have to be a light supper for the men as we've been living on rations and all the fresh food has gone.'

'They're a hardy lot,' Suetonius grunted. 'They can manage on what we've got left. Just send some men out to forage for fresh foods.' Suetonius called for an orderly to take his body armour off. When the man had finished, Suetonius reclined on the very comfortable settle of the commander's salon and waited for the man to untie his greaves. Spying a board of backgammon on a wooden table in the corner of the room, he said, 'I see you've been keeping busy whilst confined to the fort.'

A little embarrassed by the relative calm of his situation over the past few weeks, the antithesis of that of Suetonius and his men, Cerialis spoke in spurts, 'Apart from weapons drill and err..., patrol duty and um... grinding corn we had nothing much else to do but play dice and backgammon.'

'Mmm, I'm not judging you there. After the beating you and the men took, it's not as if you had the manpower to take back Britannia. You had to keep the soldiers occupied. I could do with a game myself. Bring the board over here.'

Relieved, Cerialis carried the small table, with its board and counters, over to Suetonius and pulled up a stool opposite him. And they began to play.

The following morning Suetonius took to the roads again. Now with just six cohorts and his cavalry he had over three thousand men. Following the Londinium road south for twenty miles, he took the left fork off to Camulodonum and, with a great number of Catuvellauni warriors scouting the land around them and clearing the route ahead, the Roman legion met with very little resistance.

As though anticipating the retribution that was to come, the Trinovante families left the land, and those warriors who had escaped from the battle hid as well as they could in outhouses, hedgerows and marshes. Some were able to make it to the heathland on the coast and tried to find boats to leave, but most of them were found, enslaved or butchered. Their homes and crops were burnt, their animal stock killed. When Suetonius's men found the rotting corpses of their veterans in the colony of Camulodonum, they could feel no pity for the tribe who had caused such carnage. It was not so much the destruction of the Temple of Claudius that shocked them, but the lack of clemency for the women and children, and the lack of respect for the dead. Even the old Roman gravestones outside the city walls had been desecrated: pulled up, broken and overturned.

After two days, Suetonius left men there and gave them their orders: to continue the clean-up operation with their Catuvellauni collaborators and their Trinovante slaves. Sweeping north, he sent messages to Cerialis that he was on his way into Iceni territory and their wings would probably meet around Fison Way. He ordered Cerialis's troops to dismantle the Iceni religious centre and its defences. Any material there could be used to rebuild the Roman forts and buildings that had been destroyed in the uprising.

SAHAM TONEY

Voada walked down to the bulrushes that fringed the Great Lake and sat on some dry roots beneath an alder tree.

Dragonflies darted everywhere, and down on a clear grass verge some children were fishing. Voada breathed in the summer breeze and gazed at the beauty of the morning light. It was hard to imagine the bestialities of the war ever happening. Her eyes dropped to the roots at her feet where some purple flowers were growing; she looked with longing at their bell-shaped blossom which had opened, proffering the yet unripe green, sweet berries inside. Life's treasure was everywhere – and so was death's: it was time to harvest both.

Returning to the settlement Voada sought out Greer and entered his hut where she found him writing. She didn't wait for him to put down his quill. 'You know I have no choice about my future,' she began. 'When the Romans arrive here, they will kill all my people, including you because you are a druid. I and my daughters will be taken to Rome in chains. The only way to protect them a little is if I remove myself from the picture. I must take some dwale.'

Greer's face paled a little and he stared at her, searching her eyes for a shred of madness. He put his quill down slowly on his desk and tried to reason with her. 'You cannot do this. We can all escape if we follow the river to the sea.'

'But Caitlyn cannot be moved. If she stands she will lose the baby – which would be a good thing, but she may also bleed to death. She must stay in bed. My death will ease Suetonius's anger and lessen the retribution he will exact from my people. It must also be a sacrifice to our goddess Andraste. She has abandoned us, but may protect my daughters if I give my life to her.'

'Voada, you know that over the last few weeks I, too, have felt that the gods have abandoned us and, like Socrates, I have come to question them all. Your death will appease no one.'

'But I have made up my mind, Greer. I feel this is the only path for me; I want you to help me. This way, I will have time to say goodbye to my family before I close my eyes on this life.'

After a long silence, Greer understood that Voada had made her decision and there was no changing it. He acquiesced. Taking Voada's hand, he said that he would prepare something. Voada passed him the plant she had picked at the lake: the flowers and berries of the belladonna, and then she sat down watching Greer open his medicine trunk and pull out a mortar and pestle. With these he pounded the berries into a soft paste and, when he was satisfied with the texture, he added the opium and hemlock, and mixed the poison well before pouring it into a cup with a little water.

'This is what Cleopatra took,' Greer said in a soft, almost toneless voice as he passed the cup with a trembling hand to Voada.

'Then I will rank amongst the warrior queens of history.' Voada smiled grimly, raising the cup to her lips.

'Please,' Greer interceded, immediately regretting what he had done, 'you need time to think on this decision. Discuss it with your brother at least.' But she was already drinking the dark poison.

'How long do I have?'

'A few hours.' Greer gripped Voada's arm, stupefied by what had just happened. 'The belladonna will make you sleep. They are all deadly plants, but the opium will stop any pain. You will pass away in your sleep.'

'Help me to my hut will you, Greer? Then give me time with my family. No, take me first to see Caitlyn.' She seemed a little confused already, but perhaps that was the fear of death. Her eyes had begun to dilate, and she clutched Greer's hand to steady her nerves.

From the fens and brecklands around Saham Toney men and women had emerged as if by enchantment to line the shores and say farewell to their martial queen. Marked by their silence and their sorrow they stood on the lakeside to see Voada's passage into the Otherworld. Many of the Iceni had brought what offerings they could find to give to the goddess of the waters. Voada's body had been placed in the prow of a small boat attached to the wooden jetty at the settlement. She looked at peace in her ceremonial costume, her marriage torc and plaited hair. It had been Keara who had washed her mother's body and face, dressed her and brushed her hair, placing a dark, embroidered cushion behind her head. At her feet, Keara had put the brass and glass-gemmed shield. In her hands, she had placed the great sword of their ancestors, and on the shoulder of her dress she had attached Voada's brooch showing the double-backed crescent moons of their tribe. She had kissed her mother's eyes and let the Iceni warriors carry the body down to the bank of the lake where Greer was to carry out the funeral rites. Caitlyn, too, had been helped down to the waters.

Greer spoke first to the crowd before him and then to the goddess, Sulicenii, describing the victories of Voada, her fight for her people and their lands, for liberty and retribution. Keara stood between Caitlyn and Galdus. Next to Galdus there was his brother and father, and behind them others: Diodorus, the elders of the Iceni Council who had stayed at Saham Toney, their families, and then those who worked in the settlement and farmed the land. Iceni warriors were also present: those who had survived so far, including a new arrival, Varney, who had arrived only hours before, exhausted and emaciated, on a magnificent charger.

Keara thought back over her mother's words of the night before. 'My child,' Voada had spoken to her, and had even smiled faintly at her youngest daughter. 'Do not be afraid. My brother has promised to protect you and Caitlyn. He is King of Caledonia; don't ever forget that. Caledonia will never be conquered by the Romans. It is a free land. He and his sons will take you there to protect you, if need be.' But Keara would not listen to her mother; she was only angry that her mother was abandoning them.

'Why did you take the poison? Why? Why?' she had cried.

'To protect you and the land. To appease the gods.'

'But we still had time to leave altogether.'

'Caitlyn cannot be moved. And she cannot leave our people. Diodorus will be her spokesperson and will try and make good terms with the Romans for her in the Iceni Kingdom.'

'How can our uncle protect us and take us to Caledonia if Caitlyn cannot be moved?' Keara had riposted. But Voada was already losing the thread of her thoughts, becoming incoherent in her rationale. She had signed for Keara to go to the chest at the foot of her bed and open it. Raising the lid Keara had smelt the familiar resinous incense of sweet gale and wild thyme which was always used to keep away the mildew and moths. On top of some folded clothes, the symbols of Iceni power had been laid: the crown for sovereignty and the great golden torc for military leadership. Voada had made a hissing sound as she drew in her breath, finding it more and more difficult to speak.

'For Caitlyn and you,' she had gasped. 'You are the Boudica now. But they must not fall into Roman hands. Bury them. Hide them somewhere.'

There had been a moment of calm as Keara closed the chest and moved back to kneel beside her mother, and then Voada had begun to talk to other people, those who were already dead: her husband, Prasutagus; her dead son, Taranis; her close friend and guardsman, Rory. Voada could see them standing in the hut with her, standing beside the living who were still with her: Greer, Corbreid, Galdus, Brekus, Caitlyn and Keara. At the very end, Keara had hugged her mother closely and whispered in her ear. Voada had clasped Keara's hand very gently, reassured by her final words. Then she seemed to have another visitor, one she spoke to calmly, even smiling at him, before letting go on life and letting her spirit leave the body. 'What did she say?' Caitlyn had asked her sister, who had been the only one to hear Voada speak, and Keara had repeated those final words, 'Ah Death, my old friend.'

Keara returned to the land of the living, listening to Greer. 'Sulicenii.' Greer spoke in a low, clear voice addressing the lake's spirit in the morning light and his voice echoed across to the far shores. 'Voada returns to the land from where she came. We ask you to protect her on her journey to the Otherworld as she has protected us here on earth. May she one day return to us in a new life. We offer you our gifts and sacrifices, so that you may give us your blessing.'

Greer lowered his arms and then nodded at a warrior who was standing close to a wild boar attached to a post. The man picked up an axe, and swinging it high so that it glittered in the rising sun, he quickly dispatched the pig with one stroke to its head. The animal's blood spurted out in thick, crimson jets and soaked the earth around it in pools of blood. Greer placed a simple, clay cup under its throat and when this was full of blood, he carried it to a wooden table which stood at the end of the jetty. He and the warrior then carried a bronze cauldron along the wooden planking and placed it in the boat by Voada's side. The meat was cut on the lakeside altar, a large flat stone of weathered granite, and then Voada's family and followers each took a cut of pork to place in the boat.

First to pass the altar was Caitlyn and Keara. Keara helped her sister walk to the end of the jetty, and they both said a few words of farewell to their mother. They dipped a finger in the cup of blood and dabbed this on their foreheads. Then they unwrapped a long, heavy object that they had been carrying: the huge, carnyx horn of their tribe. They placed it by the side of Voada's body and left, followed in quick succession by all those who wanted to pay their respects to Voada and the gods. Galdus gave to Voada his beautiful leather harness with its finely enamelled terret rings. Others placed objects of value in the cauldron: coins, bracelets, brooches, bronze daggers.

Last to walk along the wharf was Greer. He placed a second sword by Voada's side, that which had belonged to Rory, and, looking across Voada's body lying in state in the gently rocking boat, he smiled sadly for a lost world, a world that would soon change beyond all recognition. Helped by two warriors, he lit the faggots that lined the bottom of the hull, and then he cut the ropes, pushing the boat out into deeper waters. Keara gazed at the delicate artwork of the wooden vessel as it moved forward on the dark, velvet ripples. Its prow was in the shape of a fine swan's head which slowly disappeared as the smoke-filled boat swam into, and merged with, the curling tendrils of mist. It did not take long for the flames to burn through the white-painted planks and for the timber to crack. Making the spitting noises of burning wood being soused with water the boat continued to float for a while before the mists and waters of the Great Lake swallowed it. As the air cleared, so did the shores of the lake: the people had gone.

Keara wanted to stay there and do nothing but gaze out across the world, a world that was rapidly disappearing, to be engulfed by time and empires, as she and Greer understood only too well, but she needed to help Caitlyn back to the hut. Other noises could now be heard too, coming from the further shores. Galdus shouted to Keara and Caitlyn to hurry back inside the settlement, 'I think Suetonius's forces have arrived.'

They walked quickly between the defensive lines of their royal seat and into the palisaded enclosure where the people who were left with them were trying to prepare for the Roman assault. Within an hour their settlement would be in a state of siege.

Suetonius's army had passed through Fison Way, arriving just after Cerialis's forces had already begun to dismantle the Iceni's religious and ceremonial centre. Suetonius left the Ninth Legion there to continue clean-up operations whilst he took the ford crossing northeast, to Saham Toney, destroying everything en route. He seemed to take a cruel pleasure in giving his orders to the men and in reading their reports: the number of farmsteads burnt, the crops burnt, the people taken, to be killed, deported for work in the imperial army or enslaved, which effectively decriminalised the acts of rape systematically carried out across the land. He sent his reports on to Vettius at Londinium for the Emperor in Rome.

Arriving close to the Great Lake he was first alerted to the closeness of Saham Toney by the plumes of smoke above the trees, but, arriving at the waters, there was nothing to be seen. He cantered on with his cavalry and laid out his forces, giving orders for the legionaries to surround the settlement and for the scorpions to be put into place. Men began to unpack the heavy wagons and to assemble the catapults, crossbows and battering rams which had slowed down their advance, but whose awkward and cumbersome bulks would be worth it now. Then Suetonius sent an envoy up to the wooden palisade to ask the settlement to open its doors and to surrender. Being met with silence, he gave the order for the defensive walls to be breached, and the scorpions began sending heavy bolts and thick burning arrows into the palisade and over the walls. It was not long before billows of smoke were rising from within the enclosure and the walls themselves were aflame.

Legionaries then approached the walls in the tortoise

formation protecting their heads and sides with their shields. In the middle of their formation they carried the battering ram, but, as they were preparing to fill the first of the outer ditches so that they could cross with their machines of war, the gates of the settlement were opened from within and a small crowd of Britons began to emerge, mostly elderly men and women with a few invalid warriors who had elected to remain at Saham Toney. Suetonius had his men push them all into the outer defence ditches as he entered the settlement, but there was no other life within, only the goats and chickens of the farmsteads. After questioning a few of the town's inhabitants, he told his men to fill in the ditches with earth from the banks and to bury them alive. A number of his men were horrified, but there was to be no stay of execution. The other legionaries thought of what their own countrymen had suffered at Camulodonum and Londinium. They thought only of the Britons as barbaric savages, as animals that deserved nothing less, and they looked with obdurate indifference upon the screaming, scrabbling mass of human flesh that coughed and spluttered out their last agonies of life. Then the soldiers were sent to flatten out the other defences. Once cleared of Iceni occupation, they began building a Roman fort on the site, bigger and more impressive than the Roman garrison that had been abandoned a few years before at the ford crossing.

Suetonius had already sent Titus and his cavalrymen out under the command of his prefect, Cassius to scour the countryside behind the settlement where they had found tracks leading to the River Wissey a mile and a half away. A number of horses had been abandoned there, including one Titus recognised as that stolen from the Roman *gyrus* just a few days earlier.

'Some people from Saham Toney have taken boats to join the river Ouse in order to escape across The Wash,' Titus said to Cassius. He wondered why the fugitives hadn't continued on their horses since the river twisted and turned so much it would be faster to cross the fens directly to the coast. Perhaps it was because the ground was too soft and wet for the horses. Cassius ordered Titus and the other horsemen to cut across land and to stop any boats. He had received information, apparently given by prisoners at Saham Toney, that Voada was dead, but the two royal sisters had escaped with a druid. His orders were to take the princesses alive; the Iceni priest was to be executed at the camp. Cassius dug his heels into the flanks of his stallion and galloped off with Titus and his men.

It was not long before Titus spied a movement on the river ahead. Some flat-bottomed boats were gliding slowly and quietly across the upper reaches of the river. They were being rowed by a number of warriors and sometimes dragged across the shallow waters of the wide stream. The Wissey was soon to flow into the more navigable lower reaches of the river where the waters were deeper and faster. Cassius told Titus to act quickly. He ordered one man to gallop ahead to a bend in the river, whilst Titus and a few others swam and waded across with their horses. Cassius had to wait on the bank as his own horse, snorting and champing on the bit, refused to step into the river. The Iceni group had heard the Romans' approach and were trying to make haste, but were too exposed. Titus could see the boat he wanted: it was the one with the two Iceni princesses in it and Diodorus was with them too. He shouted to his men to stop it, but not to harm the women or the druid, who was to be taken alive and crucified at the camp. He shouted the order again in Celtic.

In the boat Keara knelt by Caitlyn's head who was lying down, unable to move. She had Sapho, her great mastiff, with her, but she was whining unhappily with the dangerous rocking of the boat. A few of their bodyguards were felled with arrows from the shore and one hung onto the side being dragged along in the mire, slowing the boat down. The Iceni warriors could not hold up their shields and row at the same time. Varney was with them and was doing what he could to keep the boat moving.

Diodorus was trying to hold a shield before himself and the two girls and when he heard Titus's command to his men he understood that he had been mistaken for a druid and was not to be shot there. He looked ahead at the other boats that were a safe distance ahead, but which had deliberately slowed down. The closest one held King Corbreid and his sons, along with Greer. He felt a hand pulling his sleeve and turned to look at Keara who spoke quickly, 'Titus has told his men that you are the druid, which will protect you, but only for this moment.' *Titus must have said this in Celtic so that they would understand, but why?* Keara did not have time to wonder, adding, 'But Greer is in the other boat and if it stops he will be taken and executed, and my cousins killed. I must warn them.'

As the boat came to a halting stop against an outcropping of sand and reeds Keara stood up slowly and, turning her back to her enemies, she called out to her family and to Greer, 'Don't wait for us. Greer, you must escape with my uncle, and do not come back for us.' Then speaking in Caledonian, a language she knew Titus could understand just as well, she took a risk and continued, 'you know that they have orders to execute Greer at the settlement. Diodorus will be safe with us because he is a Roman citizen and will be freed once Suetonius is told this. My sister and I will be prisoners for the Roman triumph, but will not be killed. Save yourselves.'

Arrows were being fired at the other boats, but the Wissey waters had now met the lower reaches, where other streams were converging and the waters became a river, flowing quickly away from Keara's stricken boat. She saw Greer, Corbreid,

Galdus and Brekus lower their shields slightly in order to acknowledge her words and courage. 'We will come back for you.' These words from Galdus echoed across the waters as the Iceni boats were swept away by the currents.

Keara's boat was immediately gripped by a dozen hands, which pulled the dead warriors out of the hull and threw them into the reeds. Amongst them was Varney, who had taken an arrow to his shoulder and clutched at a reed briefly before sinking beneath the water. Keara stumbled on her feet and was forced to her knees again. The Mauretanian soldiers dragged the boat to the shore, whereupon Sapho clambered clumsily out of the vessel and padded up onto dry land to Titus's side. There was a look of surprise on both faces as Keara understood that it had been Titus, who had left Sapho in Londinium for her, and as Titus saw the pregnant state of Keara's sister.

'She cannot walk or ride.' Keara glared at the decurion who was staring at Caitlyn, frowning as though putting together the pieces of a puzzle. 'She is bleeding; and this only stops when she is lying down,' Keara added by way of explanation.

A soldier turned and spoke to Titus in Mauretanian, but Titus answered the question in Latin so that everyone could understand, 'No, Aelius, we do not have enough men to follow the other boats now, and we have what we were told to catch. We must return to Saham Toney and give the prisoners to the Governor, but the boat must be pulled back up the stream and across the marshes because this Iceni princess cannot walk.' He pointed at Caitlyn lying silently in the boat. Then he ordered Keara and Diodorus out and told them to walk ahead and to cross the river further up to where Cassius had been watching the whole scene. The auxiliaries attached the flat boat to their horses and pulled it behind them. Mounting his own horse, Titus walked at the back of the prisoners, letting Sapho step by Keara's side.

Stumbling into her home settlement Keara was shocked by the complete transformation: the palisade had already been taken down, the huts too. There were a few Icenians in chains who were clearing up the smoking embers and the ruins of their lives, but otherwise the place was eerily empty of townspeople. Those who were left stopped to drop their heads in a last gesture of respect, and farewell, as Keara walked passed them. Caitlyn was carried on a litter towards a large tent where Suetonius stood. The three prisoners were stopped outside. Titus's men laid Caitlyn on the ground and stood to attention.

Cold and hard, Suetonius turned his gaze on Voada's daughters and regarded them for a moment. Then he snorted with derision, 'What a fall! And what a rising!' Clearly indicating the rounded belly of Caitlyn and not the rebellion. 'Marius certainly hit the mark there. This has all the makings of a good fireside story back in Rome.' Next, he looked at Diodorus and, speaking more sombrely, he raised his voice, 'Druidism has been outlawed in the Empire by every emperor since Augustus and must be wiped out in these lands. It is a danger to Roman peace and prosperity and is a religion which serves only to stir up rebellion amongst savages. Its heinous rites are fit only for beasts and the games. This druid here,' he pointed his staff at Diodorus, 'can be crucified now at the entrance to the settlement for all to see.'

At these words, there was an outcry from both Keara and Diodorus, but Keara was silenced by one of Suetonius's guards, who struck her hard in the ribs so that the legate could listen only to Diodorus.

'I am not a druid,' cried Diodorus. 'I am the Greek tutor to the Iceni household.'

'Your Latin is perfect,' Suetonius said, raising his brows in surprise, 'but you *are* the Iceni druid, placed in the royal family to teach the princesses the ways of your gods. Why else would you be with them. Take him away.'

'I'm not a druid, only a teacher. My name is Diodorus. I'm a Roman citizen placed here by the Emperor himself to teach the girls Latin and Greek.'

'He speaks the truth,' Titus stepped forward before Keara tried to speak again. 'I know him now from Prasutagus's funeral where I met him last winter.'

'Then what did happen to the Iceni druid?' Suetonius shouted at Cassius, Titus and his men, but as he said this he was staring pointedly at Titus. 'How could you make such a mistake?' He then addressed one of Titus's men directly for more information, 'Were there others that got away?'

'Yes, my Lord.' It was the Mauretanian, Aelius. Not looking at his decurion, he added, 'There were other boats, but we were only ordered to take the princesses and the druid.' There was a pause in his words. 'But we did not have enough men to follow the other boats which had reached the lower reaches of the river.'

'Total incompetence,' Suetonius stormed. He looked at Diodorus again and asked, 'Then why were you travelling with the Iceni fugitives?'

'He was our hostage,' Keara burst out before Diodorus or Titus could answer. 'He was our only bargaining power whom we'd kept here in Saham Toney. He didn't take part in the rebellion.'

'Enough!' Suetonius shouted. 'I am satisfied that he is no druid. I certainly saw enough of them on Ynys Môn to know one when I see one.' Dismissing them all with a sweeping hand, he gave his final orders, 'Take the two women to the prison at the fort and clean them up. Free the druid – the Greek, the Roman, whatever.' He turned and strode back into his tent beckoning to Cassius to follow him.

X

'WHO'S THAT?' TITUS ASKED, NODDING HIS CHIN at the young boy whom Zia was holding by the collar of his tunic in the tack room.

'A prize of war for you, sire.'

Closing his eyes for a moment and frowning deeply, Titus sighed. 'Explain yourself, Zia.'

'When I brought your two other horses to the stables here, I found him.' They were standing in an isolated wooden building at the far end of a prairie.

Zia shook the boy. 'He was hiding in the straw above. I couldn't hand him over to the Romans as he would have been killed, along with all the others at the settlement. You weren't here so didn't see the butchery. You must claim him as your slave or he will be buried alive.'

'What has been happening?'

'Suetonius gave the order to kill everyone in the settlement by burying them alive.'

Titus hesitated as he untied the chin straps of his helmet and pulled it off. 'But the slave traders have been following the army on this campaign, ready to buy up any war prisoners.'

'Suetonius has only sold young, healthy men into slavery.

The old, sick, women and children were being thrown into the outer ditches in order to fill them in.'

Turning to the child, Titus asked, 'How old are you, boy?'

'He won't speak,' Zia answered. 'He hasn't said a word, but I reckon he knows his horses well and will make a fine stable lad. He'll have nowhere else to go to.'

'I will keep him.' Titus responded, punching his helmet into Zia's hands. He stepped past him, leaving the two slaves with his stallion to unsaddle. Then, at the stable door, he added, 'I have the princess's dog outside. The bitch must stay with you in the stables as I did buy her in Londinium, and they won't have her in the prison with the two women.'

As he let Sapho pad into the hut, there was the joyous cry of 'Sapho' from the boy who threw his arms round the great mountain of a dog.

'So, he can speak.' Titus gave the faintest of smiles before leaving them.

'It seems our postal system has been re-established.' Flavius smiled as he took two sealed rolls of parchment from the messenger who had journeyed up from Londinium. Suetonius's Senior Tribune strode over to the general and handed them to him.

Suetonius had established his headquarters at the old Claudian fort on the river crossing whilst his men continued building a new fort on the site of the demolished Iceni settlement. He had been sitting in his office rereading Julius Caesar's *The Conquest of Gaul* for its information on the Britons when Caesar had first invaded Britain, but it was over a century old now; still, his comments on the Britons' sexual arrangements were of interest, simply because they were so shocking. He had read the text aloud to Flavius: '*Wives are shared between groups of ten or twelve men, especially between brothers and between fathers and sons; but the offspring of these unions are counted as the children of the man with whom a particular woman cohabited first.*

'Such incestuous habits between the Britons would explain their inbred looks and mental deficiency,' Suetonius had snorted with derision. He then took the messages from his senior tribune and broke the wax seal on the first with a knife. It was a report from his legate at Isca.

'Gaius Marius tells us that Legion Two has re-established calm in the southwest. The prefect of Legion Two, Poenius Postumus has fallen on his own sword.' Resuming the report for Flavius, he further added, 'And the Prince of the Dumnonii was pretty effective in keeping that legion pinned down over the last few months. Poenius had been ordered to join us in the field.'

'He chose an honourable death for disobeying you,' Flavius remarked.

'Yes, and he denied his troops a share in the honour, glory and plunder of victory.' He raised an eyebrow to show his disapproval. 'It was a stoic's death for him; that, or face arrest, disgrace and execution.'

The second message had been sent from Vettius reporting on the administrative and legal situation in the province. Suetonius scanned the long page with interest. 'We have a new Procurator in Londinium,' he said, lifting his head to Flavius. 'The Emperor has nominated Gaius Julius Alpinus Classicianus to take over from Catus.'

'Isn't he a Gaulish man?'

'Yes, he is,' Suetonius answered; 'a wiry man, and only of equestrian rank. Why would Nero give him the position I wonder?'

'Perhaps because he is of Celtic origin and might have a better understanding of Britannia than Catus ever did,' Flavius speculated.

'But he is only Nero's financial minister in Britannia. I must ask Vettius and Trajanus to keep an eye on him in Londinium and make copies of the reports he's sending back to Nero.' Suetonius turned to the second page of Vettius' letter which concerned the proposals Suetonius had sent to the Emperor about Icenian and Trinovante tribes and lands, and one about the pregnant Icenian *queen*.'

'Nero has ordered the Trinovante lands to be redistributed to Roman veterans and private buyers. Icenian lands are to be taken over as imperial estates and the people are to be enslaved in order to work the land. Extra men, women and children are to be deported and sold as slaves or taken for military work abroad.'

'There won't be many of them left though,' Flavius broke in summarily, 'if we keep going at the rate we're going.'

'What do you mean there Flavius?'

'What I mean, sire, is that the population is being decimated by our forces who are exacting retribution for the destruction of Camulodonum and the loss of so many Roman lives. The Britons who are still standing have no crops or animals to eat, and so face a winter of famine.'

'Are you questioning the choices I have made Flavius?'

At such a direct question from the Governor, Flavius stepped back a pace, but kept eye contact with Suetonius as he answered, 'No, my lord. Your wise decisions in the field saved us our lives and the province. The Emperor must be proud of you.'

'He certainly should be. And he has agreed to the project that Vettius and I proposed. Send a man to find the tribune, Marius will you, and I want that Mauretanian horseman, Titus to join us too.'

Flavius nodded and went out onto the veranda to find a secretary.

Caitlyn lay on a straw mat in one of the barrack rooms. She had Keara with her. A Greek doctor had been sent to examine her and had given her some sort of concoction to drink. He had told Keara to attend to her and to keep her lying down. Then he had left. They had not had many visitors since, and the days were only broken up by the guards bringing meals or changing the piss pots.

Their room was small and had been unbearably hot for a number of weeks until the summer passed away and the temperature began to drop. They were being held in part of the centurion quarters, so it had another room attached which had once served as an office, though it now stood empty and bare. The building was built of wood and turf with a roof of straw thatching that was held up by posts of rough-hewn timber, but much of it had fallen in and the army was too busy elsewhere to repair the prison rooms. Occasionally, Diodorus was allowed to see them and he brought reading material with him: bound papyrus leaves of the Latin and Greek poets. A few times he also came with Keara's dog and a young boy, but Sapho was so excited to see Keara that she had to be kept in the outer room, away from Caitlyn, until she calmed down. Keara had recognised the boy as the son of a saddle maker from Saham Toney. He looked to be around ten years old.

'Blair, isn't it?'

'Yes, my lady,' he had answered, proud that she remembered his name.

'What are you doing here with Diodorus and Sapho?'

'One of the Roman slaves took me in.' He hesitated for a long moment and then mumbled, 'after the Romans killed my family.'

'How did you escape the … killings?' Keara asked in a gentle voice.

'I hid in the stables in the fields and he found me. He asked his master to take me, so I wouldn't be killed.'

'I remember your father and am sorry for his loss. He was a good man.' Curious to know what Sapho was doing with him, Keara had to ask, 'Who is your new master, Blair?'

'It's a decurion from Africa.'

'It's Titus,' Diodorus added, 'I'm sorry to say.'

'Yes, I know him.' Keara bit her lip. Then speaking again to Blair, she added, 'I am sorry to hear about your family. Do you know how your father died?'

The boy didn't answer her at first. Then he replied, 'No, but I saw the man who did it. It was a Roman officer.'

'How do you know it was an officer?'

'Because of his armour. It was heavily decorated, and he wore a crimson cloak. He is still here. I recognised him afterwards because of the scar on his lip.'

Keara and Diodorus looked at each other, both recognising the man as the Roman tribune, Marius.

'I thought he was dead,' Keara said in surprise.

'Apparently not,' Diodorus rejoined.

The boy continued, 'My father told me to run and hide. He couldn't run because of his bad leg. I didn't want to leave him, but I was frightened, and my father said the soldier would kill me if I was caught, and he wanted me to live.' He began stroking Sapho's mane.

Keara watched the boy, wondering what she could say to ease his sense of guilt. 'You obeyed your father. You were right to do so. You must not be hard on yourself. It means that you are alive and one day we will take our revenge, but you must be patient for the moment.' Changing the subject, she wanted to know if he was being treated well. 'Is the Roman soldier looking after you?'

'I have to work for him, m'lady, but I hardly ever see him.

He's out a lot with his men, and he sometimes takes Sapho with him. It's mostly his slave, Zia who tells me what to do.'

'And what do you do?'

'Zia asks me to look after the horses, which I like. He hates it because the two stallions Titus has are nasty animals – that is, to Zia I mean, but they don't kick or bite me. I have always worked with horses and ponies with my dad.' He fell silent a moment before adding, 'So I know them well.' The boy was suddenly distracted by Sapho who was tugging on his sleeve, so he began playing with her. Keara and Diodorus spoke together about news of the rebellion and of her family. They joined Caitlyn to keep her company and sat on the floor beside her.

'Do you have any news of Greer and of our uncle and cousins?' Caitlyn asked.

'No, nothing,' Diodorus responded. 'But no news is good news. I think they must have got away, along with the other boats and would have headed north to Caledonia. There is nothing more to be done here, and King Corbreid had to return to his kingdom. He will have his own frontiers to reinforce against any Brigantian and Roman incursions into his lands, and Greer will help him to protect their gods against our Roman idols.'

'They won't leave us here alone, will they?' There was a note of pleading in Caitlyn's voice as she asked this question.

'Caitlyn, it would be madness for our uncle to return for us. There are thousands of soldiers working for Suetonius in our territory alone. And if ever they caught our cousins, Galdus and Brekus would be taken as political hostages and Corbreid would have to hand over Caledonia to the Emperor.' Keara then turned her head closer to Diodorus and asked in a low voice, 'Do you know why they are keeping us alive and what they will do with us?'

Diodorus shook his head. 'Again, I don't know anything. The commander is waiting for a message from the Emperor in Rome, and a messenger arrived from Londinium today. I presume you are to be transported to Rome for Suetonius's triumphal entry into the city if the Roman Senate grants him one.'

'But why are they looking after us so well?' Caitlyn's voice broke into their remarks and she shook a little as she added, 'I mean, why do they care if I miscarry the baby? Why do they care if I live or die? Sometimes I would rather die than carry this baby to term. We have already lost everything, including our name and honour.' She looked pointedly at her sister as Diodorus answered, 'You are both political prisoners. You must remember that you are more valuable to Suetonius alive than dead. You give him bargaining power with the other clans and those rebels who are still active in the region, and you must live to protect them.'

'Such responsibility is beyond me,' Caitlyn cried, turning her back on both her sister and Diodorus.

'And are they looking after you well?' Keara asked her former tutor.

'Well enough,' Diodorus looked downcast, 'but I bury my head in my manuscripts, so I do not have to witness the misery around me. I share quarters with the Mauretanian man, Titus. It was he who asked the camp prefect, Cassius if I could visit you from time to time.'

'And he lets you?'

'Keara, they fear nothing from an old man like me. I am a man of letters not a warrior, and the region is now theirs not yours. What is more, even if we were plotting an escape for you, Caitlyn cannot be moved until the baby is born.'

'I cannot bear these four walls much longer,' Keara complained. 'When will this waiting end!'

'Be patient, my child. As Julius Caesar once said: *it is better courage to endure pain with patience than to volunteer to die.*'

'Very comforting words,' Keara rejoined in a mordant tone, 'but Caesar was never a man of fetters.'

'No, he was only a dead pretender to the throne.'

Both Marius and Titus were kept waiting for a long time. Marius sat in a wicker chair, but Titus remained standing. From time to time other visitors came and went: here to see members of Suetonius's staff, but they were never kept waiting for long. The waiting room had been swept clean of the autumn leaves that were now beginning to fall. Although there were no trees as such in the fort itself the lands around it were flat and open so that the winds were harsh, and fallen leaves and twigs seemed to accumulate in the fort's lanes and buildings. These buildings had been empty for the last two years and so were also overgrown with grasses and brambles. The fort was only large enough to house around eight hundred men and the second fort now being built on the site of the Saham Toney settlement would house the same number which meant that the majority of the soldiers were still living in their tents and would probably spend the winter under canvas, weeding out the last of the rebels.

Marius, who hardly ever addressed Titus, simply because they were not of the same social caste, was growing ever more impatient and could not help himself from asking, 'Do you know why we have been summoned?'

'No, I do not,' Titus answered, sounding quite unconcerned by Marius's impatience. 'You should know more than I as you dine with the commander and the other officers.'

'Well, a messenger arrived from Londinium this morning. Perhaps we are being recalled to Rome.'

Titus gave Marius a scathing glance before replying, 'I

doubt it. You have not completed your one-year term, and the rebellion here has not been completely put down.'

'And why has the commander been keeping me out of the fighting? He permitted me to fight at the beginning of the rebellion. He has even let me participate in the punitive measures here, but not in any direct fighting.'

Titus knew exactly what those punitive measures were and found it difficult to look at the man who continued to speak. 'And when we were stationed in Londinium the procurator sent me on several missions, including the one to Camulodonum where we nearly died.'

'Where you nearly died,' Titus corrected him. 'I can usually get myself out of most predicaments even if it means wading through gallons of human waste.' This was said quite sardonically as he wished that Marius would not pursue his line of questioning.

And perhaps, Titus mused to himself, *new pieces had been added to this game of strategy*. He had an inkling of an idea but did not know why this would include himself.

At length a secretary came and invited them to leave their belongings in the cloakroom before leading them up the staircase and along a corridor to the Governor's offices. Another secretary opened the door for them and led them up to Suetonius's desk. A brazier had been lit to warm the room a little and to dry out the dampness of the air. Suetonius sat at a large desk with a few other members of staff with him: his senior tribune, Flavius was seated by his side, a scrivener sat at another smaller desk behind Suetonius whilst an orderly was pouring some hot wine and honey into glasses which he then carried round the room on a silver tray. Marius and Titus were invited to sit down.

'Let us make a toast,' Suetonius smiled at everyone. 'To the end of hostilities and to the peaceful union between our peoples.'

At this Titus held his wine to his lips but did not drink. He heard the door being opened behind him and half-turned on his stool. He heard the rustling of skirts and cloth as two women were led into the room and seated on couches to one side of the room. It was the two Icenian princesses who had been cleaned up, brushed and clothed for the occasion. Caitlyn had been carried up the stairs on a litter chair and helped all the way to the couch. As Marius took in the size of her stomach, it was he who gulped his wine down.

'You have both met our Icenian princesses, I believe,' Suetonius said, addressing Marius and Titus. Neither man knew how to respond to their commander's caustic wit so both nodded at Suetonius.

'I have received advice from the Emperor regarding the problem of relations between us and them.' Here, he put his glass down and stood up. With his hands behind his back, he began to pad up and down the room, seemingly enjoying the moment. 'If we were able to forge some sort of an alliance between the Iceni and the Romans, we could improve relations.' He paused before continuing this idea, 'The Emperor Nero, being informed of the state of affairs in Britain,' he pointed to Caitlyn's stomach, 'believes that the Princess Caitlyn, as the eldest child to the late King Prasutagus, and as his heir, would be able to build bridges between our peoples if she married a Roman,' and, here, he pointed at Marius, 'and produced a Romano-Icenian son.'

Already, Keara was standing, telling her sister to stay seated as she shouted the clear refusal of herself and Caitlyn to make any such alliances. She was immediately silenced by a legionary officer who had drawn his sword at Keara's sudden movements.

Marius, too, felt alarmed at the very thought of marrying a barbarian. 'Sir, I cannot marry such a woman. She is not

Roman, she is not of the senatorial class, and my father would object.'

'On the contrary, Marius, she does have Roman citizenship. Her parents were granted that many years ago. And your father has already agreed to it. It is a great honour for your family to be allied to the Iceni royal blood. You will be nominated as head of the city magistracy at Venta Icenorum, and your son will be a great leader of this territory after you.'

'But sir,' Marius objected once more, 'I was simply following orders when I was sent to Venta Icenorum last winter. And my term of service is almost up. I am to return home shortly.'

'Now, you have been given a new order by Nero himself. You are to stay here and consolidate Rome's power in Britannia. By educating your children in Roman ways, it will bring long-lasting peace to this new province of Rome. It is a great honour for you.'

'But a great dishonour to me and my people,' Caitlyn cried from her couch. 'I would rather stab myself to death now than marry such a monster. Give me your sword.'

At these words the soldier before her quickly sheathed it and stood to one side as Suetonius approached the couch. Speaking in a slow, clear voice, Suetonius said, 'Quite the opposite, my lady Caitlyn for, with this marriage, you save not only your honour and your reputation but that of your unborn child. Marry this man and you save your name from falling into disrepute. What is more, this child will stand as an emblem of cooperation between our peoples, and will protect the Iceni interests, its lands and people, from further transgressions.' The word 'transgressions' was a little ambiguous here, for it was not clear whose transgressions he was referring to as he continued further, 'By marrying Marius you will help him *control* the Iceni territory. You can advise him and teach him your ways and manners, building cross-cultural bridges.'

'I cannot marry a man who has ... violated my body,' Caitlyn whispered.

'But if you marry him there is no question of violation. Your chastity is inviolate within marriage. Such a union already has a precedent in Roman history. Think of the rape of the Sabine women by the men of Romulus. Their later union protected their chastity and led to the founding of Rome.'

Sensing the weakness of her sister's resolve, Keara broke in, 'You cannot even consider it, Caitlyn. Think of our mother, of everything she lived and died for to protect us. Your rape by this man was a crime. It is a crime under any law.'

At this Caitlyn looked at her sister, and then closed her eyes before speaking, 'Our mother took her own life. She left us. Our father believed in the Roman future for our lands. I am the only queen they have left.' She let go of her sister's hand and opened her eyes again. Addressing Suetonius, she asked for a clear accord, 'I can consider this project only if you promise to protect my people from any more Roman killings and give them land to live on and food to eat. What is more, this child is to have an Iceni nurse, and a Greek tutor. Diodorus is to stay with us.'

Suetonius nodded, 'I agree to everything you say. As a tribune Marius is allowed to marry whilst still in military service so we will make arrangements within the week.'

'Within the week!' Marius cried.

'Yes, Marius. Do not forget that these are the orders of the Emperor. It is an enormous distinction he has made to you and your family. You will be married by the priest here in the garrison in a few days. Let us raise our glasses once again.' He returned to his seat and rang a small bell on his desk. Immediately two attendants entered carrying trays of dates, figs, almonds and olives.

'I reserved these delicacies for such an occasion as this.

We must celebrate the end of hostilities and the union of Iceni with Rome. Later on, you, Marius and your family, will move to Venta Icenorum where the Roman city will be rebuilt and you will be the chief magistrate of that city, and of the region.' Suetonius seemed to be taking great pleasure in this moment as he chewed on a date and licked his fingers. Then turning to Keara, who had remained standing by her sister's couch and had refused all the foods offered to her, he smiled unctuously, 'Of course, the same offer applies to you, my lady.'

'Never!' She spat on the floor. 'I would never agree to such terms, and I will never forgive my sister for accepting yours.'

'Tut, tut,' Suetonius pursed his lips, taking in Keara's fearsome defiance and Titus's wide-eyed astonishment. 'You are not in the same state as your sister and can be forgiven for your one-sided view of today's political landscape. However, I will give you the choice. You can agree to marry Titus, who is now a Roman citizen, but of a lower rank to that of Marius, which is also true of you since you are the second-born daughter or, you can refuse, in which case you will be deported to Rome and executed before the Emperor. Which ending do you prefer?'

'I would rather die a thousand deaths in Hades than marry a Roman.'

'Then, so be it.' He nodded at the two guards standing by the wall and they seized Keara by the arms.

'Wait,' Suetonius cried. 'Have you nothing to say, Titus?'

Titus turned his dark eyes on Keara. 'I would not force a free woman to marry me against her will.'

'Even one that you have already violated and who has lost her honour?' Suetonius's brow furrowed. He was obviously surprised by the incoherence of Titus's moral code.

Titus moved his weight on to his other leg before repeating

the words of Suetonius, 'Even one that I have already violated and who has lost her honour.'

Suetonius mused over this answer for a moment and then nodded at the guards to take Keara and Caitlyn back to their rooms. When everyone had left the room, he called one secretary, a Parthian slave, back to speak to him in private. 'What do you know about the decurion, Titus?'

'Only that he is from North Africa, the Mauritanian part of the Roman Empire, and that he was recruited into the army ten years ago as an auxiliary cavalryman.'

'Find out more about him, will you?'

'Yes, sire.'

For the past few days, Caitlyn had been housed with one of the tribunes' families. The tribune's wife had joined her husband for the winter in the fort, and they had their own apartment within the staff offices. The lady was to act as Caitlyn's chaperone and matron until the wedding ceremony. Caitlyn was to call her Sabina, and her husband Marcus, although she did not see Marcus. Both were members of senatorial families in Rome, and Marcus had been billeted in England for the last three years. They did not have children.

Caitlyn was in her bed chamber sitting on a stool whilst Sabina dressed her hair in the Roman style. This was a challenging process as Caitlyn's long hair had to be divided into numerous locks and fastened with fillets on the top of her head in a cone. Sabina had to ask help from one of the slaves. Caitlyn laid her hands in her lap and followed the lines on the fresco on the wall before her. It was a painting of an orchard, showing a number of Roman plants, flowers, trees and birds feeding on the ripe fruits. Caitlyn did not recognise all the plants, although a number of them had now been introduced into Britannia such as the fig tree, mulberry bush and sweet chestnut. A great number of other delicacies were imported through the ports on the south coast and along the estuaries leading inland.

Caitlyn did not say anything, even when a hair pin pricked her scalp. She seemed immune to everything around her and hardly spoke, although Sabina treated her kindly and seemed genuinely interested in local affairs. When Caitlyn's hair was finished, Sabina's slave held a mirror up to her face, but Caitlyn did not acknowledge the reflection of herself. In fact, she did not recognise the woman in the mirror. It belonged to another world. As she was dressed and given jewels to wear, she was impassive and indifferent. Like modelling clay she yielded to Sabina's every touch and acquiesced in everything she was told to do. The final touch was to pin the flame-coloured veil to her hair, which left her face uncovered. Then Sabina and the slave led Caitlyn to a litter to be carried downstairs to the courtyard. Diodorus came to meet her.

'I'll be with you, child, throughout the ceremony, so be reassured.'

'Where is Keara? I haven't seen her once,' Caitlyn fretted.

'She's been kept in her cell and has calmed down a little. I have tried to reason with her, and I know she'll come to understand your decision.'

'But can I see her?'

'She'll be there today.' Diodorus smiled at her, a little grimly, it seemed to Caitlyn.

Many people had already assembled for the bride's arrival. Marius stood nervously by Suetonius's side; he was acting as the groom's father. The other tribunes were there, as was Cassius and Titus, along with many senior members of staff. Marius's features were taut with anxiety, but he could not help smiling when he saw Caitlyn's Romanised beauty: her hair, her white muslin tunic and knotted girdle which carefully covered her rounded stomach. She was the very image of a high-ranking Roman maid. Caitlyn did not look at Marius as she was slowly led to the fountain in the middle of the courtyard. She scanned the faces in the crowd looking for her sister. She finally saw Keara standing between some of Sabina's household slaves, but she wore a veil and held her hands demurely behind her back, saying nothing.

Caitlyn's attention was drawn back to Sabina, who was addressing her and Marius, 'You must begin by making a sacrifice to the goddess of marriage.'

A stone altar to Juno had been placed before them, and a pig was led into the courtyard. It was the legions' priest who made the sacrifice by cutting the animal's throat and then opening its stomach in order to read its entrails. The auspices seemed good, for he then cut out the animal's heart, and whilst the slaves cleared the dead animal from the courtyard, leaving a trail of blood from the altar to the gateway the priest built up a small fire beside the altar on which to burn the animal's heart.

Caitlyn's nominated matron of honour, Sabina, told the bride to repeat the words, 'Where you are, Marius, there I am.' Caitlyn's throat was dry, and it was difficult to cough out such a verbal contract. She had to repeat the first syllable three or four times until she was finally able to speak the words. Sabina handed her a glass of water, which she drank from before Sabina took the glass from her hands and passed it to Marius to drink from too. Sabina then took their hands and joined them together with a libation of water.

'May Juno bless your union and bless you with many offspring.' Sabina then spoke quietly to Caitlyn, 'It is now time for the wedding breakfast. I will stay with you all day, as will Diodorus. Your sister will also join us shortly.' As she spoke these words, Caitlyn saw her sister in the corner of the courtyard being turned around by some guards. Keara's cloak and veil were being taken off in order to untie her hands and ungag her mouth. Caitlyn felt so sick she could not eat any of the wedding meal. Her sister had been led to the bridal table and did not touch a crumb of this feast.

The wedding banquet was a long affair in the hall of the headquarters' building. The stuccoed walls were decorated with fine scenes of warfare and Roman victories, and the floor had been tiled with red and white mosaics, mostly geometric in style, but the central design showed a gladiatorial combat in Rome. Someone was playing the flute, and a brazier had been lit in the centre of the hall to ward off the autumnal cold, but Caitlyn still shivered. She looked at the laden dishes of food and wine circling the room, but could not help observing the thin and underfed Iceni slaves who served it. Marius, on the other hand, had been taking full advantage of their wedding feast. His favourite dish was the roasted dormice stuffed with minced pork, and he was feeling quite stuffed himself, but that was probably due more to the copious amounts of the high-quality, and very expensive, Roman wine which he had been gratefully consuming all afternoon. As he approached Keara's seat in the late afternoon, he looked a little glassy-eyed. Leaning over her he slurred, 'Aren't you going to congratulate me on such a happy day?'

'You can go to Hades!' Keara responded, picking up a glass from the table.

'Don't even think it,' Marius said calculating Keara's next move with the glass. 'You wouldn't hurt your brother-in-law, would you?' Keara had to breathe in deeply in order to calm herself as Marius laughed at his own pleasantry and wandered off with another tribune. Slowly Keara put the glass down and looked at her sister. Caitlyn looked so miserable, so tired and lost that Keara could not find it in her heart to hate her for much longer. Caitlyn looked at her, pleading for help, and Keara gave her a faint, a very faint, smile of reassurance, but she was not permitted to stay any longer.

The meal had taken up much of the day and when Titus was ordered to escort Keara back to her cell, Caitlyn was placed in her litter in order to follow the traditional procession to her husband's lodgings. Torches were lit from the brazier and carried by some young soldiers to lead the cortege. Upon her arrival at her new rooms, Caitlyn found Marius already waiting for her. He lifted her from the litter, but whether it was from the wine or from Caitlyn's weight he stumbled a little and had to be helped over the threshold by both Diodorus and Sabina. It was Sabina, however, who led Caitlyn into her chamber which had been decorated with flowers, greenery and fruit.

'It was I and my servants who prepared this room for you,' Sabina uttered into the silence. She picked up a pomegranate, adding, 'These are traditional symbols of fertility,' but Caitlyn's stomach was such an obvious sign of fertility that Sabina quickly put it down again.

'We will say a prayer now to thank Juno for this day of plenty,' she said taking Caitlyn's hands. She held her own hands over those of Caitlyn's and said a few words of thanks to the Roman goddess. Still Caitlyn said nothing.

'I must undress you now and help you into bed.' Sabina took the jewels off Caitlyn and put them back into her own bag. She took Caitlyn's veil off and untied her hair, brushing it down her back in waves of golden corn. Finally, she pulled the wedding gown off over Caitlyn's head, but replaced the knotted girdle around her stomach.

'Your husband must untie the knot and take your girdle off when he comes to bed, so do not touch it yet.'

A short while later there was a loud knocking on the door

at which Sabina rose and left the room. Caitlyn pulled the blanket up to her chin as Marius entered their chamber.

'You don't have to play the prude with me, you know,' Marius chuckled. 'I've seen it all before.'

'They are running a security check on you.'

'Who are *they?*' Titus asked Keara, as he escorted her back to her prison cell.

'Suetonius.'

'How would you hear of this?'

'I may be in solitary confinement, but I still have my ears. I am at the end of the barrack block and I do hear the soldiers talking amongst themselves. One of them is to carry a message to Vettius in Londinium who is to check your file.'

'Why would you tell me this?' Titus raised one eyebrow questioning Keara's veracity.

'Why would I remain silent on a matter which helps Suetonius?'

Titus did not answer, and they walked in silence the rest of the way. When they arrived at her prison, Titus saw her into her rooms. He took a brief look at her Spartan quarters and left.

Later that evening Diodorus arrived. He carried a blanket with him and a cloak.

'Titus told me to carry these to you.'

'I do not want...'

'No fussing child. It is the autumn and it is getting colder. Take them.' He pushed them into her arms and sat on the one and only stool. Then he pulled a napkin out of his pocket and put it on her bed. 'And this is for you to eat. You have not eaten today.'

'I will not eat any of my sister's wedding foods.'

'That is why it is only bread that I have brought you.'

Keara opened the napkin and seeing that it was really only bread she began to eat it. 'How is Caitlyn?' she mumbled.

Diodorus was quiet for a moment, but could no longer hold his tongue. He blurted out, 'Her decision to marry Marius was a brave one.' He put his hand up to stop Keara speaking. 'It is Caitlyn, who is queen of the remaining Iceni, even if Rome does not recognise her position. It is Caitlyn, who is pregnant. In this new position, she must put up with the shame and humiliation of being married to the man who defiled her...'

'And who, now, can continue to do so.'

'But, in this position she can do something to protect her people and her unborn child. This child is half-Roman but do not forget that he is also half-Iceni. Caitlyn will do what she can to educate him in the ways of your people. I will remain with Caitlyn and when the child is old enough, I will educate him in Latin and Greek, but I will also teach him your myths, your lore and history.'

'And what about our gods?'

'I know that you think the same as Greer so do not pretend to be a druid. Your gods are cruel and hard sometimes. They may even demand human sacrifices, something that my Greek gods do not, but I will include them in my teachings as I will also include the Roman ones. Now try and sleep tonight because you are being taken to Londinium tomorrow.'

'For Rome?'

'Yes.'

'What about Caitlyn?'

'When the baby is due, she will be sent to Venta Icenorum to make her new home. It is the Roman capital of Iceni territory. I will stay with her and look after her and your nephew. Goodbye Keara. Knowing your courage and your fortitude, I know that the Emperor, Nero will pardon you in Rome just as Caratacus was pardoned by the Emperor Claudius before him. May the gods protect you.'

Keara took his hand. 'Thank you Diodorus. Can you ask Suetonius if I may see my sister before leaving?'

'I will see what I can do.'

XI

'HE SAID NO.'
Titus had come to collect Keara the following morning. She had nothing to take with her except the woollen cloak that Diodorus had brought her the night before. And she still had her ivory brooch of the owl which she had attached to her cloak. On hearing that the commander had refused to let her see her sister, she felt so wretched and lost, but she would not let Titus and his men see this. She put the cloak on and tied the cord at her throat.

'But he said nothing about not corresponding with her.'

Keara looked up quickly. 'Do I have time to write her a note?'

'I will be outside with the horses.' He placed a wax tablet and stylus on the table.

'Will it be read by anyone else?' Keara asked, suspicious.

'I will send Blair to your sister with your message. He cannot read, and he will tell your sister to wipe the message clear and to write back to you on the same tablet. Blair will give you her answer when he catches up with us on the road. I will give him orders to let no one else see it.'

'Blair is now your slave. Why would he obey you?'

'Because my orders are in your interests.' He left the room exasperated by Keara's questions.

LONDINIUM

Little sister, thank you for your words. I vow to do what I can for what is left of our kingdom. I am glad you have chosen not to marry that Roman, but I don't want you to die. I am praying that the Emperor will give you a pardon and your freedom. Yes: I cannot forgive the Procurator. If you find Catus, then, as Queen of the Iceni, I order you to exact revenge.

Caitlyn's words were written in the Ogham script. Keara held the wax tablet to her heart, then wiped the message clear with the spatula end of the wooden stylus and closed the box before returning it to Blair. After this, she had gone to sleep in the tent that Zia and Blair had put up for her. She had unrolled a sleeping mat and covered herself in her cloak. It felt good to be out of the Roman garrison.

On the road the day before they had passed by Fison Way. Suetonius had given Titus's cavalry escort orders to follow the same route that the Iceni and Trinovante rebels had taken when they had destroyed the Roman forts, villas and colony on their way to Londinium. She saw what the Romans had done to Fison Way: The Iceni stronghold and royal household had been completely dismantled and flattened out; Suetonius had not only wanted to destroy it, but to remove it from the land and from human memory. Not a trace of it remained. Only the stark earth stood testimony to what had been.

They had stopped one night in the garrison at Camulodonum. The clearance of debris and the reconstruction of the town had already started, but it was being done by Trinovante men. Many of them had been branded on the foreheads to mark them as military slaves working in the heavy labour industries such as road building, masonry, tiling and mining. They were chained together, and many had backs scarred from whips. Life was harder for them now than ever before. Their only consolation was that it would be short.

They spent another two nights in tents before reaching Londinium. Keara wondered why they were taking so long. They had no wagons with them, and they were all good riders. Maybe those were Suetonius's orders so that she would view with her own eyes the Britons' defeat and the full Roman conquest of Britannia – and she did: many rebels had been nailed up on crucifixes along the roads and, although they had been crucified weeks, even months before, their bodies stood as a warning to those still living not to defy the power of Rome. She suddenly felt broken. Bits of her heart were being chipped away with every step she took away from her tribal lands and, as her horse trod the Roman road, the tears ran down her cheeks. She pulled the hood up over her head and wept in silence.

They arrived at one of the eastern gates into Londinium the following morning and rode directly to a military compound. There were no longer any stables for the cavalry mounts, but canvas covers had been put up to shelter the horses from the rains. A number of wooden buildings had already been erected for the soldiers, and the garrison was protected by a double-ditched enclosure. Again, many prisoners of war had been enslaved and could be seen everywhere working in chains to resuscitate the fallen city. Nero had now declared Londinium a Roman municipium, to be the major administrative and trading centre of Britannia. As such, Londinium was being rebuilt as a planned Roman city: the centralised forum and basilica were being built in stone, as were the temples to the Emperor and to Mithras. Traders had begun opening shops next to the forum, and plans were underway to erect a timber amphitheatre which would eventually seat six thousand spectators. Work had also started on the bridge crossing the river Tamesis but for the moment the only way to cross to the south bank was by ferry boat.

A centurion came to meet Titus and to check his papers from the Governor. Keara was then told to follow him to the holding cells for prisoners. She was led off to a timber building where she was to await her deportation. Blair asked to stay with her, but Zia cuffed him on the ear for such stupidity, 'Do you want to end up a slave in Rome or as meat for the wild beasts in their games! Come, we have work to do with the horses: you must brush them down and clean their hooves.' He pulled Blair behind him to help untack the horses. Titus left Sapho with them and followed the centurion to the basilica to meet the new Procurator for Britannia.

Gaius Julius Alpinus Classicianus had been in Londinium for two months. A man in his fifties, he had arrived with his wife, Julia Pacata and they had settled immediately into the ruins of the Procurator's official residence, a villa close to the basilica. The villa's walls had been rapidly raised and temporary thatching added to the roofing for this first winter. Classicianus had brought with him a large staff made up mostly of slaves and freedmen, but he also had a number of guards assigned to him at the basilica for escort work, protection, control and policing of the civilian population. During this time, he had also got to know the Governor's jurist, Vettius, a man who seemed competent and composed, but who struck Classicianus as calculating and ambitious: a man in Suetonius's pocket. Suetonius's senior tribune to Legion Twenty, Trajanus was no longer with them: he had been recalled to his legionary fortress at Deva Victrix after the arrival of Classicianus and his staff.

When Classicianus first met Titus in his offices he smiled up at the man, before taking the two rolls of paper that Titus held out to him. He read the summary report addressed to him from Suetonius regarding the military state of affairs in Britannia, but he did not open the sealed, written report for the Emperor in Rome. He simply passed the second parchment to his secretary, telling him to add it to the imperial post. Putting the paper down at last, he looked at Titus and asked him for an oral account of affairs in Britannia. He told his secretary to take down notes. Classicianus seemed particularly interested in the lands lying to the east of the province and was very much concerned about the loss of revenue from the Iceni and Trinovante territories.

When Titus finished there was a moment of silence, and then Classicianus said, 'Do you know that the Emperor Nero was about to give up this province?'

Titus was taken aback by such a confidence. 'No, I did not, my lord.'

'Do you know why he hasn't?'

Titus shook his head. 'No, my lord.'

'Because it would reflect badly on the memory of his adoptive father, the Emperor Claudius who first incorporated this province into the Empire. That is why he has sent for reinforcements from Germania: two thousand regular troops, which should bring the Ninth Legion up to full strength. They will be arriving in Londinium in the next few days, along with eight auxiliary infantry battalions and a thousand cavalry men. They are to make up the losses sustained here and to help the General consolidate our hold on the province.

'However,' Classicianus stopped for a moment in order to gather his words for his next point, 'the punitive policies of Suetonius Paulinus are not exactly inductive to peace. In fact, they seem to be provoking further uprisings across the province. Small as these may be, I am anxious because our revenues are drying up. Should they do so we may be obliged, for financial reasons, to give up this province altogether, which is not what the Emperor wants. Yet, this province is costing the Emperor more to maintain in men than it promises to return in future revenue. We have no more taxes coming in at the moment for the simple reason that the population is either dead or dying. Soon there will be no one left to work the land or the mines. As it currently stands, nothing is being added to the Roman economy. Nothing is being exported to the continent, and any imports there may be, can only be sold in the south of Britannia for the simple reason that there are no other civilian consumers left!'

Quite exasperated, Classicianus leant back in his chair and knocked back a glass of water. 'My job in Britannia is that of financial manager for the Emperor. I am in charge of the grain supply, the mint and the mines – there is no grain, there is no gold and there are no miners! I am to report on financial matters here to the Emperor and will be sending him a report in the morning. I need to speak to the Iceni prisoner you have just brought in. Could you send her to me this evening? She will be leaving in the next few days for Gaul and you and your men are to escort her to Rome. The Emperor will have my report before you arrive as the imperial post will travel faster. Thank you. That is all.'

Titus nodded and left the Procurator's office.

That evening Keara was led to the forum by the centurion who had first met them at the garrison. Her wrists had been chained together and already her skin chafed where the iron rubbed against it. She felt anxious about meeting the new Procurator, the man sent to replace Catus. Waiting in the vestibule, she could hear voices coming from behind the further door. She suddenly shivered as she recognised one of the voices barking out, 'I insist on being present since I am the legal representative of the Governor, and this Iceni princess is a military prisoner under Suetonius's responsibility.'

Another voice rejoined, 'But don't you think you are being a little insensitive? You gave the legal advice to Catus and ordered the aggression on her family. You were a witness to it all.'

'I did not see it, but I did interpret the law for Catus and I simply passed on Catus's instructions to the men. Sir, once again, as Suetonius's legal administrator in Britannia I must insist on staying. I do not see what this has to do with you and if I had known about the arrival of the princess's escort sooner I would have been here for your meeting with the decurion.'

'This has everything to do with me as I must evaluate the current economic situation in this province and send a report to the Emperor. This Iceni princess can give me financial information about affairs in Britannia. You must stay then, Vettius, but you are to remain silent. You are not in court now, you know.'

Nothing further was said until the door was opened from the inside and a secretary beckoned to Keara to enter. She was pulled up by two legionaries who took her into the Financial Minister's offices.

'I am Classicianus, the new Procurator for this province. Please have a seat.' A seat was brought forward for Keara to sit on in the middle of the room. 'You must be tired after your journey. I am sorry for your current accommodation: nothing like what you were used to I'm sure.' He smiled in a friendly but awkward way, making polite conversation, trying to put her at ease. He offered her a glass of water, which she refused. She could not help looking sideways at the man seated on the couch against the wall. She had only met him once before, at the reading of her father's will in Londinium, and she had only seen him at Venta Icenorum from a distance, when she had heard his loud voice giving orders to the Roman slaves and soldiers to ransack their lands and their bodies. His presence made her feel sick, and she asked for a bowl to retch in.

'I am sorry for your discomfort,' Classicianus continued, 'but I need to ask you a few questions about the situation of your people in Iceni.'

'I will not speak in front of that man.' She raised her shackled hands in order to point at Vettius.

'He is only here to observe and listen. He will not speak.'

'I will not speak in front of that man,' she repeated.

Exasperated, Vettius flung his hands up and could not help throwing in, 'Then make her speak. You know that most of it will be colourful lies and exaggerated stories. The only way to have the truth is under torture.'

'Go ahead, torture me. What could be worse than what you have already done to my family! I will not give you any information about my people.'

Becoming exasperated himself, Classicianus made a decision and addressed Vettius, 'I must ask you to leave my office, Vettius. I am the appointed Procurator here and I am answerable only to the Emperor. I will speak to the prisoner with only *my* attendants present. My secretary will give you a copy of the interview tomorrow morning.'

Vettius, fuming, rose from the couch and, snatching his cloak from an attendant, he marched out of Classicianus's office. He did not even have the satisfaction of slamming the door after him as this was being held by another attendant who could not help but smile at the jurist's discomfort.

Classicianus sighed deeply and pressed his lips together, 'Well, that's one thorn out of my side, or one more enemy added. Anyway, he is gone now, and I do not want any information from you that I do not already know. I just need you to confirm the current situation in Britannia so that I can assess the economic climate for the Emperor Nero and the

Senate House in Rome. For example, I have heard reports that the General of our military forces here, that is Gaius Suetonius Paulinus, is being too harsh on the tribes who took part in the recent uprisings; so harsh, in fact, that many have been executed or are dying from starvation, and that, in some places, the lands stand empty. Is this true?'

Taken aback by the Procurator's change of tack and his very direct approach Keara did not at first know what to answer, but in this case, it seemed an opportune moment to adhere to the truth. 'Yes,' she said.

On the morning of Keara's deportation to Rome, Titus and his men took her down to the quayside where a mixed number of merchant and naval vessels were moored to the wharf. This was the furthest point of the tide, which made Londinium an ideal trading port for the province: the river was deep enough for heavy ships and was an excellent point for communication with, and transport to, the military frontiers within Britannia. However, despite the calm forecast for the winds, the rain was pouring down in great torrents and the sky was slated with heavy clouds. It was only the oiled wool in Keara's cloak that kept her dry. Beside a number of warehouses and fish shops on the waterfront, the riders dismounted and began to lead their mounts towards the military wharf. They passed a poorly dressed figure standing beside some large amphorae jars and barrels that were waiting to be carried inside a storage depot. It was an old Briton taking shelter under the awnings of the doorway. He looked thin and bedraggled with black teeth from the birch bark he was chewing. Keara wasn't actually paying much attention to him until Zia limped passed and angrily told the man to get out of their way. In turn the Briton cursed Zia, spitting his gum onto the ground and raising a ragged arm in a spasm of discontent which knocked the mare's reins from Zia's hands. Swearing at the man's clumsiness, Zia bent down to retrieve his reins and when he stood up the old man had already headed off towards a cargo ship.

At several berths ships were still being loaded with slaves, ponies, dogs and, in some cases, Celtic weaponry for private collectors in Rome. The sounds were deafening as sailors ran back and forth carrying crates, bags and ropes onto the vessels. Some were slipping on the sodden wooden planking of the wharf and shouting out for help with fallen loads. Others were blasting out orders to hurry up before the tide turned and they were marooned in this godforsaken land.

A fast, light galley lay alongside one of the military berths and was taking on board the imperial post. Next to this, a larger galley was being loaded with prisoners and slaves for Rome. Keara was led down into the hold of this ship and attached to other prisoners with leg irons. The wooden hatch above her head was closed, letting in only filtered rays of light. Despite the coldness of the season and the heavy smell of pine resin on the ship's wood, the air was oppressive and rank. Squatting down in the darkness Keara wrapped her arms around her shins and lay her head on her knees. In the second hold next to hers, she could hear the horses' hooves clatter as they entered the hull, passing directly through an open door that descended onto the wharf from the ship's stern. About twenty horses were loaded into the stalls, some of which were whinnying in alarm. She could even hear the bark of a dog and the reassuring words of a boy, at which she raised her head and smiled, recognising them at once as the voices of Sapho and Blair.

Within a very short time, the ships were unmoored and were all leaving the quayside on the outgoing tide. At the estuary mouth, many ships raised their sails and with a number of oarsmen, the faster vessels sped ahead to reach the open channel and cross to the Roman port of Boulogne in Gaul. They were heading there too, but would take far longer with such a heavy cargo. Many of the merchant ships sailed close to the naval squadron for security reasons, but, despite such a precaution, Keara's own ship soon found itself to be the last but one in the convoy of vessels heading south. There was another merchant ship lagging further behind them. The weather worsened, and the wind began to pick up. *Where had the port authorities got their weather forecast from?* Keara wondered. Her thoughts were suddenly interrupted by a question.

'And what's a nice lady like you doing in a place like this?'

This question, spoken in Celtic by her attached neighbour, startled her. The man knelt across her and Keara instinctively drew back from his bare and dirty shoulders, but not before noting his lank and smelly hair. The man gave her a mischievous grin and put a finger to his lips: 'Shush.' He tapped gently on the planks of wood separating the two holds and a flat blade was pushed through the joining walls. He began to pick at the iron lock holding the chains to the ring bolt on the floor.

'Not easy in the dark,' the man muttered. 'I'm Tremayn. We met at the council meeting after Verulamium.'

Keara remembered him then. 'Prince Tremayn of the Dumnonii?'

'That's right. I'm a political prisoner now, just like you, being sent to Rome for their gladiatorial games. My tribe has been *displaced* by the Roman legion in the southwest. Our hillforts were no defence against their siege engines, and when their legate returned, he finished us off. He only spared my life because I am a prince and will amuse the Emperor in his fighting games, but my guards were all killed.'

'What happened to the rest of your family?' Keara realised what a clumsy question this must be and quickly added, 'I'm sorry. I...'

'No, it's alright. My wife and child managed to escape to Hibernia. I got them to the coast in time.' In the darkness Keara could hear him sigh in relief.

'And who is helping you on this ship?'

'You'll see.' There was a sharp click as the padlock opened and Tremayn slowly and quietly pulled the chain from the ring. But the prisoners were still attached to each other. He started to unpick the lock on his ankle shackles. He undid those of Keara and passed the small blade on to the next prisoner beside him.

'This is my brother, Zethar.' In the penumbra they nodded at one another.

Listening to the noises above, Keara said, 'They can't hear us from the deck now. There's too much going on.'

'Good,' responded Tremayn. 'Not too soon, but we must be ready to climb the steps when the hatch opens.'

'From your helper?' she intoned.

'Yes.'

OCEANUS BRITANNICUS

The galley's captain had seen a ship approaching from the north. It was a Roman trireme he was relieved to see, but it was unusual to see a Roman vessel travelling alone. He noted with some surprise that the trireme was carrying a great number of men. He thought soldiers were being transferred to Britannia, not taken from it. He was not reassured by the worsening weather either: the Roman squadron was being scattered by the winds as it tried to cross the channel. The only other ship in sight was the cargo ship behind them, obviously struggling with a heavy load. What was more, the trireme was now using both its sails and oarsmen to pick up speed. It seemed to be travelling at more than eight knots, a speed which could only be kept up by rowers for short bursts and – the realisation hit him like thunder – it was only ever used to ram another vessel! He began to ring the alarm bell calling his men to arms as he understood the danger they were in.

'Pirates,' he shouted at his officers. 'They are going to ram one of the ships. We must pick up speed.' The sailor calling time on deck increased the drumbeats so that the oarsmen on the benches would row faster whilst the soldiers on board quickly buckled on their armour, greaves and helmets, and gathered their shields and swords. The captain ordered Titus and his cavalrymen to clear the decks and descend below in order to keep the horses calm. The animals were already beginning to buck and rear in agitation.

'And hoist the purple flag so that merchant ship knows we are facing a hostile enemy,' he cried to the flagman standing at the main mast.

He couldn't understand why the cargo ship was not taking any defensive action, even after he had warned it. It took him a while to understand that the other vessel was not the choice of target: *they* were. What was worse, was the new position the other vessel had now taken for it had veered away from the stern of his ship and was coming in fast along the port side. From the bridge, he could see the bronze ram attached to the keel of the pirate's trireme just below the water line, and as the two ships danced on the rising waves the elongated anvil of the ram waved dangerously at him. The other ship then closed in; it raised all its oars on the starboard as it sheered along the side of his galley with its ram snapping off the heads of his oars. The enemy had already lowered its sails, and the two boat hulls were now knocking sides. Grappling hooks were thrown across his decks and their iron claws dug into the timber planking of the galley, irrevocably coupling the two ships together. One of the rowers was too slow moving out of the way and was caught by a grappling hook which dragged him across the deck before digging itself into the man's thigh, crushing the leg as it came to rest against the bulwark. The man's screams of agony were immediately drowned out by the drop of the boarding bridge. The heavy, iron spike of the narrow platform embedded itself in the deck and a swarm of armed men passed across the dying man and onto the Roman galley.

At the signal from their officer, the Roman soldiers coupled their shields together presenting the enemy with a thick wall of leather-clad wood and gleaming bosses. They then began to push the pirates back. The Romans' studded boots gripped the planking and for a moment it seemed that they were gaining ground, pushing the pirates back towards the boarding bridge, but other boarding bridges were being dropped onto the galley and all the rowers, Egyptian freedmen, had fled to the stern and could barely defend themselves, much less fight the attacking pirates. The Roman marines fought hard: well trained and disciplined they were able to hold off the boarding pirates for a time, but they found it too difficult to keep their footing on a rocking, and blood-washed deck, as well as fight on all sides. Many were picked off by archers from the trireme and then killed on board after a heavy and bloody skirmish.

For those who were wounded but still alive, they were knocked overboard along with the dead. The captain would not surrender his ship to pirates and so was finally felled by the slash of a sword to his throat. For those soldiers and freedmen who had been pressed into service, and who spoke out in Celtic, laying down their arms, their lives were spared, and they were placed in the aft of the ship. Then the hatch to the prisoners' hold was opened and Tremayn sprang out with the other prisoners.

'What! Is the fight already over?' he laughed, grasping the outstretched hand of Corbreid. Keara ran into the open arms of Galdus.

'You came for me!'

'Of course, I did,' Galdus cried. 'I would never leave you.' He hugged her again. 'Now let us open the second hatch and see what fish we have caught.'

After climbing up from the hold, Titus was disarmed and had his arms pinioned roughly behind his back. He was then dragged and kicked across the bloody, rain-washed deck. Galdus and Brekus threw clenched fists into his face and stomach. Fresh blood fell from Titus's eye, and he spat out some blood. Keara screamed for them to stop, and hung on to Galdus's arm, holding him back, but her cousins would not be calmed. Galdus gave the decurion another punch to his face, and a kick to the stomach before having him bound to the mast. Titus's men were equally disarmed, but kept below with Zia and the horses. Only Blair was allowed to leave the hold and was given a shake of the hand by Tremayn – clearly the Britons' key helper on board.

'Why would you want to defend a man who abused you?' Galdus scowled at Keara angrily, and then remembered the fight in the river at Camulodonum. 'You let him go, didn't you, that day when you could have killed him?'

She gulped before replying, 'I can't kill him. I can't. There are things you don't know.'

'Like him buying your dog in Londinium!' Galdus turned away from her, angry and uncomprehending.

The winds had dropped a little and the large cargo ship, which had been following in their wake, had now caught up with them. On board Keara could see the long-bearded face of Greer. She recognised him now as the bedraggled figure from the quayside at Londinium. He was standing next to another man whom she also recognised: it was Varney, still alive and kicking, but with one arm hanging useless by his side. He raised a hand at her, but Greer had clearly not seen her.

'Do you have Keara with you?' he called across the waters.

She waved at him and saw his face crease into a smile. 'Then we must make headway, but Varney and I have to board first with the replacement oars.'

New oars were passed from the cargo ship to be fitted onto the disabled galley and the three ships set off west by south. Stepping on board, Greer gave Keara a firm hug and then, seeing Titus tied to the main mast, he told the men that the prisoner was not to be touched.

'He is the cavalry officer who is guilty of crimes against my niece and against our peoples in this war,' Corbreid roared, raising a fist. 'He must pay for his crimes and shall be sacrificed to Andraste in order to satisfy my sister's anger and need for revenge.'

'Exactly; that would be revenge, not justice,' Greer answered.

'Everything is just in times of war,' Corbreid scowled.

'My lord, he is our enemy, but I will speak first to his slave before you execute him. There is information he can give us about the Roman forces in Britannia.'

Corbreid could understand the sense of this argument but did not like it. Growling in acquiescence, he lowered his arm and told his men not to approach the prisoner. He forbade Keara from going near the man. Then he sent one of his warriors to the hold to fetch Zia.

Keara turned to Varney, staring at his withered arm. 'Don't feel any pity for me,' he snorted. 'That's all I need.'

'No, I was going to ask how you survived – twice? You

were hit in the shoulder at Saham Toney and then I saw you drown in the river.' Keara touched his arm gently.

'Yes, I'm real.' Varney twitched his shoulder. 'The arrow put me out of action, but I was able to breathe underwater. I used a reed. I was no longer any help to you, so the goddess Breckia carried me in the Wissey waters and I joined up with Galdus later.' He suddenly saw Titus and squinted. 'I actually survived three times. Don't forget I escaped from Roman enslavement after the last battle... but I had a little help.'

Keara was curious to know more and had opened her mouth to pose other questions, but Greer was calling to her from beneath the bridge. She closed her mouth and nodded to Varney, noting the inquisitive look on his face as he stared at her and then at Titus. She turned and stumbled over the rocking deck into the shelter of the spacious officers' quarters where Greer led her into the captain's cabin. They fell into the wicker chairs at the captain's table and laughed at each other, both relieved to find the other safe. Then Greer asked her for news of Caitlyn and Diodorus.

'Thank you, Zia, for your information in Londinium.'

'You are very welcome Greer.' Zia made a theatrical bow. 'But a lot of it was thanks to a dog!'

Zia was seated at the large oval table in the captain's cabin along with Greer, Keara and Corbreid who had left his two sons on deck to manage the ship with Tremayn. They were comfortably seated on the richly embroidered cushions on the chairs and bench, which also served as a bunk, and were eating bread, cheese and cold meats. Corbreid was already on his third tankard of barley beer, which Zia found difficult to keep up with. Corbreid scoffed at the others sipping their cups of rosemary tisane with honey.

'Call yourselves Celts. You can't even drink beer!'

'Did you know that rosemary improves your memory, Corbreid?' Greer asked him over the top of his steaming mug, 'Which is more than beer does for you.'

Corbreid gave a raucous laugh as he slammed his iron tankard on the table and watched the beer slop wildly in the cup. 'Ha! I didn't sign up to be a wise druid like you, and I certainly wasn't chosen to be the leader of the Caledonian confederacy because of my memory! Now tell me, Zia, how did a dog work in your intelligence services?'

'Keara's dog, Sapho, carried messages between us whenever Blair took him out in Venta Icenorum, Camulodonum and Londinium. Everyone sees a dog, but nobody frisks it.' He explained that messages had been carried in tiny cylinders placed inside one of Sapho's ears, but at the port he had had to pass a message himself to Greer to confirm their rescue plan.

'We also have other information to pass on to you,' Zia addressed all three of them. They stared at him expectantly as he, in turn, looked at them one by one, 'We know where Catus is.'

'We?' Keara asked.

XII

Venta Icenorum

In the Roman villa lying just outside Venta Icenorum, Caitlyn lay on a couch in her chamber. The room was small but seemed to be enlarged by the *trompe l'oeil* of the wall frescoes showing windows and doors opening onto a garden balcony overlooking ripening fruits, singing birds and rich, overarching flowers. In the centre of this garden scene, an ornamental fountain invited the viewer to follow his eye and to seat himself on its marble rim next to a statue of the Greek god, Priapus whose huge erection was feeding water into the basin, thus ensuring the fertility of the bedroom's occupants. Fertility was certainly the subject of the moment since Caitlyn's contractions were increasing, along with the pain.

They had left Saham Toney just a few days before. Suetonius had ordered their move to Venta Icenorum in order to re-establish a garrison there, to reopen the marketplace and begin work on building a more permanent forum and basilica. He had also wanted to oversee the shipbuilding programme in the estuary of Breydon Water, and flush out further members of the resistance – a small group of them had destroyed some Roman galleys that had been lying at anchor in the estuary, thus reducing Rome's naval forces in the Northern Sea. The sudden move of her household, and of the Fourteenth Legion, had not been welcomed by Caitlyn. She had not wanted her child to be born in the very place of her rape. Marius had taken great pleasure in telling her that she was to be carried by boat to the Roman settlement where he was to take up his new role as head magistrate of the city's council.

Pantheia, a young Greek midwife had arrived, sent by Sabina to help with Caitlyn's labour. She was a competent woman who had laid out the things needed: sea sponges, wool bandages, strong-smelling herbs, knives and needles, in case of a Caesarean birth, and she had asked another slave to warm up some olive oil and to bring her a large bowl of water. Between Caitlyn's shrieks of pain Pantheia clipped back her short, black hair and washed her hands in the water. She then applied hot compresses to Caitlyn's sides. She lay cloths soaked in the warm olive oil across Caitlyn's stomach and told a slave to gently massage the stomach whilst she opened Caitlyn's legs and dabbed some more olive oil onto her vulva.

At last, Caitlyn was moved onto the birthing stool and the midwife, who had wrapped her hands in woollen cloths, knelt before her whilst two female aides held Caitlyn's arms and shoulders. Caitlyn was encouraged by Pantheia who kept reassuring her that everything was going well, but Caitlyn did not feel reassured: the pain was atrocious – and was getting worse. With each contraction Pantheia would say, 'Now,' and Caitlyn would push. The delivery was taking a long time and Caitlyn was beginning to weaken and faint when she heard a woman scream somewhere far off. Suddenly, she regained her senses and realised that the screaming woman was herself. She could smell the repugnant odour of the herbs that an aide had waved under her nose, and she heard Pantheia's voice again, 'I can see its head. One final push my lady.' Caitlyn made a last effort and suddenly felt eased as the baby slipped out of her body into the waiting hands of Pantheia.

'It's a boy,' she said, smiling at Caitlyn's sweat-besmeared face. 'Well-done.' She held up the baby until it took its first gasp of life and then she laid the child in Caitlyn's arms.

'You need to make one more effort, and push.'

Once the placenta was out Pantheia clamped the umbilical cord before cutting and knotting it. She told the slaves to clear up the blood whilst she herself wiped Caitlyn's thighs. A few stitches were needed and then the midwife placed some lint and honey on the stitches to help the skin heal quickly and cleanly. Pantheia took the boy from Caitlyn's arms, bathed it and placed it on Caitlyn's breast to start it feeding. Caitlyn hadn't smiled yet. She was too exhausted and full of mixed emotions. She didn't want this child, a child which had decided her whole life for her. She had never wanted it – but then this child had never asked for anything either.

Seeing her reluctance, and knowing the full story of Caitlyn's circumstances, Pantheia whispered in her ear, 'Breastfeeding is also a natural contraceptive.'

The child had its lips pursed as it suckled the air, instinctively searching for its feed. Caitlyn hesitated a moment and then slowly placed a nipple in the baby's mouth. The small boy gripped the teat hungrily between its gums. Here, Caitlyn could not help but smile at her tiny, innocent and vulnerable newborn son. She did not notice the midwife leave the room or the slaves clearing things away. She fell asleep, along with her child. She was startled awake by the arrival of her husband who strode into the chamber and looked down at the small bundle of life by Caitlyn's side.

Marius seemed to have adapted well to his new life

of provincial politics and administration, but with such magisterial authority came a new sense of responsibility and power. And with his sedentary lifestyle he had begun to put on a little weight, but perhaps this was more from the fine foods, wines and other pleasures of the flesh that he liked to dabble in. Obviously irritated by this brief interruption in his daily routine he stood there inspecting the child with his arms crossed, and not a little contempt.

'At least it's a boy,' he said at last. Without looking at Caitlyn he added, 'but who's to say it's mine. You may have had other men.'

An exhausted Caitlyn could only whisper, 'He is your son – much to my regret.'

'Well, he is now my heir. Let's hope you don't regret the others.' He laughed, looking directly at his wife with such cruel intentions in his eye that Caitlyn turned her head away, too empty to say anything.

A few days later Diodorus came to visit the young mother and her son. He lived in a different wing of the villa and was mostly kept apart from Marius's private life.

'How are you feeling?' he asked, laying down a bowl of dried figs. 'I've brought you some nourishing food – from Greece.'

'Thank you, Diodorus.'

Caitlyn was now up, moving around, and able to help in the running of her household. Dressed in the Roman stola, a long-sleeved unbleached woollen dress, she wore her hair quite simply: it was parted in the middle and held in a bun at the back of her neck. She wore no ornaments. She had been folding up a number of woollen cloths on a changing mat when Diodorus arrived, but she rose to greet him.

'What a handsome boy,' exclaimed Diodorus, admiring

the baby sleeping in its wattle crib. 'And what name have you chosen for him?'

'Marius has decided upon Ovidius Marius Maximus, but I shall call him Aprastus, after my father.'

'To which god are you making an offering?' Diodorus asked, curious.

'I have sacrificed some clothing to Artemis to thank her for Pantheia's help, and I have also made a libation to our Britannic goddess of childbirth, Damara.' Her voice sounded tired and subdued, but she was pleased to see her old tutor. Leaving the child's room, Caitlyn led her old tutor into the salon and called for refreshments for him and herself.

'What news from the city council?' she asked him.

'Vettius has arrived from Londinium. He arrived last night, along with the imperial post with letters from Classicianus and from the Emperor, and is staying at the fort.'

Caitlyn grimaced at the mention of Vettius's name. 'Do you know what those messages say?'

'No. All I know is that Suetonius and Classicianus do not get on. I'm sure we'll learn soon enough what the messages are.' Diodorus helped himself to a glass of wine which a slave boy had brought in. The boy then added more wood to the fireplace in the wall and left the room. They did have central heating in this room and the hypocausts were very efficient in heating the mosaic floor, but the day was cold and damp. In some places it had even started to snow.

'Do you think we are to stay permanently in Venta Icenorum?' Diodorus asked.

'Marius says this is the Roman capital for the Iceni territory, although he does not say *Iceni territory*, of course. He uses the word *region* for the Roman province. So this means that we are now living here. My son will grow up here, as my sister and I did, and if the Britons do not regain control of our lands he will probably be sent to Rome for part of his education and one day he will be sent to do his military service somewhere else in the Empire.'

'That time has not yet come,' Diodorus said, placing a hand on Caitlyn's. 'And remember that I will be the child's tutor and you have a number of Icenians with you.'

'All slaves,' Caitlyn winced.

Vettius went straight to the Roman garrison in Venta Icenorum and was admitted into the Governor's apartments as soon as he had dismissed his escort. Suetonius rose from his desk and came to meet the jurist, extending his hand for the messages. 'What is the latest from Classicianus then?' he asked, sounding terse.

'The usual: he's trying to play Sir Nice, and has been interviewing many of your men, and even some of the rebel leaders.'

'Such as whom?'

'He interviewed Trajanus, before he was transferred back to his legion, and the decurion, Titus, before he left for Rome with the political prisoners, whom he also interviewed.'

'What is the man up to?'

'I'm sure he'll tell you himself in his letter.' Vettius eased himself into a soft armchair and watched Suetonius return to his desk. Suetonius broke Classicianus's seal on the vellum roll and began to read aloud:

G. Julius Alpinus Classicianus to G. Suetonius Paulinus, greetings.

My wife and I are now settling in well in Londinium, despite the ruins of the city. My new posting as Procurator of Britannia is certainly a challenge. After evaluating the damage done to the three cities of Londinium, Camulodonum and Verulamium, and to the outlying farmsteads, estates, and to the Roman garrisons themselves, the costs in repair work and renovations are phenomenal. What is more, the Roman state has lost a huge amount of revenue from this province, due to a loss of taxes, rent money and other income.

Here, Suetonius broke off and cried out, 'Then make the natives pay for the reconstruction work, just as they paid to construct the Temple of Claudius in the first place.' He began reading again:

Britannia has not been able to export any grain, livestock or other foods necessary to maintain the healthy state of our Empire. No minerals have been mined, no salt harvested. I understand that most production works came to a halt during the very recent rebellion of the Britons under the Icenian leader, Voada. However, with the very high loss in indigenous manpower I am finding it difficult to redirect the country towards economic recovery. Around eighty thousand Britons died in the revolt, and our reprisals have probably removed another fifty thousand, mainly in the Iceni and Trinovante regions, which will take decades to recover, as very few have been taken as slaves.

Urban renewal in Londinium is also very slow as the merchants, and the civilian population lack confidence in a safe and secure future. I have sent a report to the Emperor Nero and he is sending his imperial secretary, Polyclitus, to make an independent enquiry into the situation and to carry out an audit.

Suetonius finished the letter and then exploded with, 'Polyclitus! That Greek slave.'

'Freedman,' Vettius corrected.

'He spent his life as a slave first. The army will never take him seriously, and nor will the Britons.'

'But this time, our emperor has intervened personally in selecting Polyclitus for the job.'

'When does he arrive?' Suetonius barked out angrily.

'I don't know.' Vettius shrugged his shoulders. 'It depends on the winter roads and the channel crossing, but it will take him some time as he is crossing Italy and Gaul with a very large retinue.'

Suetonius threw the letter onto his desk. 'Does Classicianus have any idea of what it takes to lead an army in the field and to pacify a province in revolt?'

Vettius did not answer this rhetorical question. Suetonius opened the Emperor's letter and read it before addressing Vettius once again, 'The Emperor's secretary tells me the same thing: Polyclitus should be arriving in a fortnight, and I am to receive him at Camulodonum. It basically means that I am not to return to the frontier zone in the west, and not to carry on subduing the natives here. I will send my prefect and senior tribune, Cassius and Flavius back to our fort at Mandvessedum. The frontiers and interior should be covered with the extra garrisons and men here in Iceni. I will leave Venta Icenorum as soon as possible in order to oversee the reconstruction work at Camulodonum and make sure we have satisfactory accommodation for the Emperor's representative. Will he be sailing directly to us along the River Colne, do you know?'

'No, Classicianus also received a letter from the Emperor ordering him to receive Polyclitus in Londinium first.' Vettius stretched his bottom lip as he speculated on the adverse political significance of such a move.

'That means he hopes Classicianus will brief Polyclitus before the man takes the road to join us in Camulodonum.' Suetonius shared the same thoughts as Vettius. 'Then let us prepare ourselves. Julius!' he called to an orderly, 'Fetch us some wine and food. We will eat in my salon here.'

The salon had just been freshly redecorated for the legate. The mosaic flooring had been laid out in a simple geometric pattern, but the frescoes on the walls depicted many detailed scenes from Roman and Greek mythology: a wolf feeding Romulus and Remus, the rage of Achilles pulling a sword on Agamemnon, of Achilles killing the Trojan captives. The damp painting on the wall could still be smelt. Suetonius led Vettius to a couch and when the meal was laid out for them on a low table – oysters, whelks, cockles and mussels – Suetonius asked for more information about Titus, 'What did you find out about the man?'

'An intriguing background which should interest you.'

Suetonius took a sip of dry wine. 'Go on,' he said, looking into the depths of his glass, 'intrigue me.'

'You know he is of Mauretanian origin. In fact, he was heir to the Baquate tribe in the Middle Atlas Mountains until the death of his father when the tribe was taken over by his uncle.'

'Do you mean Sabalus was his father?'

'Yes.'

Sabalus had been the chief of the Baquates. Suetonius and another general, Gnaes Geta, had defeated the Mauretanian rebels under Aedemon and Sabalus after a four-year war in North Africa, seventeen years before. Geta and Suetonius had led the Roman campaign in the second half of the war in order to pacify the region after the death of its king, Ptolemy II and to prepare Mauretania for its annexation into the Roman Empire. Ptolemy had only had a client agreement with Rome, just as Prasutagus had had in Britannia, and many Mauretanians had not wanted to be integrated into the Roman Empire. There were suspicions that Ptolemy had been assassinated by the Emperor Caligula and this had provoked his freedman, Aedemon, to rage a rebellion against Rome.

Suetonius took up the thread of Rome's imperial history

in Africa, 'So when Aedemon and Sabalus were defeated and we held the peace talks in the Roman city of Volubilis, Titus was handed over as a political hostage in order to ensure the good behaviour of the Baquates.'

'Yes, that's it,' Vettius said, laughing at the irony of history.

'I should have recognised him. I thought he looked familiar.' Suetonius tutted at himself.

'You could not have recognised him because he was a child when the peace negotiations took place. He must have been only ten or eleven. He was then sent to Rome to be educated in our ways and manners.'

'Why did he not return to Mauretania?' Suetonius pursued.

'In my view, it is because it would have been dangerous for him. His uncle was the new elected leader of the Baquate clan. His father was dead. And it seems that Titus was angry with his father for *giving* him away. When he had finished his education, he had to do his military service in the Roman army, and because of the reputation of the Mauretanians as excellent and highly mobile cavalrymen he was chosen to be the decurion in one of our auxiliary units.' Vettius stopped here to help himself to another oyster which he poured into his mouth. Suetonius watched the white oyster slip smoothly off the shell into Vettius's waiting mouth. When Vettius had swallowed this plump morsel, he reopened his wet lips in order to finish what he had been saying. 'The Mauretanians are well-known for their fighting skills on horseback. It's not for nothing that Nero has chosen Mauretanian horsemen as part of his horse guard, although they do spend more of their time killing bears in the circus than defending the Emperor in the Forum.'

'Vettius, you can be so cynical at times.' Suetonius rose and began to pace back and forth. 'Do you think he can be trusted?'

'I don't know. He obeys orders: he did violate the princess Keara when I told him to, but I cannot really gouge his moral code of honour. He saved Cassius's life on the field of battle, and it is also rumoured that he saved Marius's life in Camulodonum, a fact that Marius denies.'

'Yes, he probably would. I see no moral code in Marius, apart from that of protecting his family's honour, which is good enough for me. Please, continue.' Suetonius waved a flaccid hand at Vettius.

'Titus is currently escorting Keara and other political prisoners to Rome, as you commanded, but I do not know what he recounted to Classicianus when he was interviewed in Londinium. He would not tell me, neither would his slave. And in light of your defeat of, and *sanctions* against, his tribe when he was a child, I am worried that he might identify with the plight of the Britons.'

'I do like your euphemisms, Vettius. I find them quite charming. And yet, you are always able to read between the lines.'

'Titus may well dislike the fact that you are the first Roman general to have crossed the Atlas Mountains with an army.'

'You flatter me there, Vettius. Geta and I had been ordered to pursue the fleeing enemy into their mountainous nooks. The enemy included the Baquates, the Macenites and the Bavares. It was also an expedition of exploration and intimidation. It was Geta who finally caught up with Sabalus and the Baquates in the desert beyond the mountain range and dragged him back to Volubilis for peace talks. It was a feat which almost cost him his life as his legion had virtually no water left. However, Geta and his legion were then transferred to Gaul by the Emperor Claudius for the conquest of Britannia. I stayed in Mauretania to oversee its division into Mauretania Tingitana and Mauretania Caesariensis.'

'So maybe Titus does hold a grudge against you,' Vettius conceded. 'It was you who oversaw the peace talks with his father at Volubilis. He may have been a child then, but he would have witnessed your harsh methods – to be blunt, this time, and he would have seen the defeat of his tribe in the mountains and the desert.'

'Enough of politics Vettius. Pour me another drink and let's be merry, for once.'

OCEANUS BRITANNICUS

'We?' Keara asked again.

'Yes: Titus, myself and our men,' Zia gave them a sly smile. 'We are part of the resistance movement in northwest Africa.'

'Ph-phew!' Corbreid spluttered, almost choking on his beer on hearing this. 'I didn't know there was one.'

Zia did not deign to respond to this, but smiled graciously at Keara's words: 'I didn't think he and his men got on very well.'

'You can never be too careful, and the best disguise for us is discord. This must not be known.'

They all nodded.

'Titus was sent to Rome as a political hostage and for a Roman education, but he always remained a free man at heart. Did you know that the Mauretanian highlanders are known as the Free Men, just like your people in Caledonia?' Zia raised one eyebrow as he addressed Corbreid.

'No, I didn't. And what about yourself?' Corbreid asked, feeling more respect towards his prisoners in the hold. 'You're Dacian, not Mauretanian.'

'Well, I was actually rescued by Titus when I was about to be thrown into the gladiatorial games in Rome. I had been arrested on false charges of banditry in the Carpathian Mountains in Dacia and sent to Rome for the Emperor's entertainment, but I was innocent, really, I was. I was just an out-of-work thespian.' Here, Greer snorted in derision.

'Yes, well, I was never very talented at it. It certainly didn't get me out of jail. It was Titus who did that. He took pity on me because he saw my limp and knew that I didn't have a chance in the amphitheatre. He offered to buy me. Being given the choice of the armed maniacs in the ring or Titus and his own wild horses, I chose Titus. He bought me, too, because he needed a servant, one that could read and write Latin and Greek. He also wanted me to teach him Dacian. He is a very talented linguist that one, which is why he was chosen for Catus's guard in Londinium – where all the languages of the known world are spoken.'

'Well, let's return to more immediate matters,' Greer said, clearing his throat; 'Where is Catus?'

'Oddly enough, he has fled to Mauretania Tingitana, on the western coast.'

Greer leant back in astonishment. 'Why would he go there?'

'Because he has stolen the Emperor's tax revenues from Britannia and thinks he will be safe in a frontier zone far from Rome, and Britannia. Whilst there is mayhem in Britannia, he is getting himself comfortably ensconced in the sands of Mauretania.'

'How do we know this information can be trusted?' Keara asked.

'Because of our own intelligence services. Oddly enough, we do have to communicate with Titus's Baquate tribe from time to time.' Zia fluttered his eyes. 'Information came to us of Iceni gold and silver, identified by the coins of your father – before you ask – being melted down in a workshop in the Atlantic coastal town of Lixus. Now, can we release my master?'

The cabin filled with a heavy silence which Zia did not at first understand.

'No, of course, he cannot be released. He may be a great freedom fighter for the Baquates but he has still fought on the side of our enemies, and, what is worse, he is responsible for the disgrace done to my niece,' Corbreid growled.

Zia looked at Keara, surprised by Greer's and Corbreid's ignorance. 'Have you not told them?' Both men turned their heads to Keara, questioning her silence.

'I have not had a chance, yet,' Keara protested, 'and it's not the sort of thing you bandy around. What is more, Titus told me not to tell anyone or it would happen to me for real because Roman law would have to be applied. As it is, I do not like to remember that day. It was awful being with him in that tent and listening to the screams of my sister, and the silence of my mother. He said he could do nothing for them. He could only spare me the rape if I never spoke of it. To me he was only an enemy with a conscience.'

'But, as I was told, Titus showed your blood to the soldiers, and you were later examined,' Greer said, and then he understood. 'He cut your hymen.'

Keara was red with shame and embarrassment.

On deck Titus stood against the mast with his head slumped on his chest. His cuts had stopped bleeding, but he found it difficult to open one eye and to keep his footing. The Britannic warriors found great pleasure in laughing at his discomfort, but they did no more than this. The storm passed over the heavens and the seas became calmer, which is more than could be said for Titus's rage. He saw Zia pass into the officers' rooms – and spend a long time there. Blair passed him too, went down

SAM F. HUTCHINS

to the hold with water for his men and came back up with Sapho. He let Sapho pad over to Titus and lick his hands and arms. Blair brought water to Titus but this was refused. Blair and Sapho then sat down on either side of him, which made Galdus laugh, 'What a bodyguard: a dog and a boy!'

Tremayn called down from the bridge, 'Leave him be. He helped Blair in our escape.'

'That's enough, Galdus,' Corbreid bellowed, coming out of the cabins. 'I need to speak to you and to your brother.'

The rain had stopped falling and some seagulls had taken to the skies again, despite the menacing dark clouds that were still hovering above. Corbreid took his sons to one side, letting Greer, Zia and Keara approach the prisoner. Sapho rose laboriously to her feet and placed her wet muzzle in Keara's hand, asking Keara to stroke her head. Keara tickled her gently whilst Greer addressed Titus, 'Zia has told us the truth about your background and your role in the intelligence service which helped us take this ship and free Keara and the other political prisoners. Keara has told us how you protected her at Venta Icenorum, not to mention Blair. However, you were still part of the Roman forces that helped Suetonius put down our armies in the final battle. Thus, we have a dilemma: we have to thank you for your help, and we do, in fact, have the same enemy, and yet, you also worked with Rome. We also know that your small cavalry unit could have done nothing against Rome's legions.

'May I suggest a compromise? A temporary truce, if you like? If we let you and your men go, will you take us to Mauretania Tingitana and help us avenge Voada? You and your men can *disappear* since Suetonius will believe that your ship and lives were lost at sea, and you can continue your own resistance in the Atlas Mountains whilst we continue our own in the Caledonian Mountains. In this way, we can also work together. If we keep our lines of communication open, we can time our uprisings together in the frontier zones.'

'How are we to travel?' Titus asked, spitting out some blood.

'You will take the other Roman galley.'

'And what about our horses?'

'They will travel back to Caledonia with King Corbreid and his sons on this ship.' Noting the refusal on Titus's face, he quickly continued, 'Such a gift would be a mark of your good faith. You know as well as I do that the sea journey to North Africa would be too long for the horses. Caledonia is much closer.'

Titus conceded a little here, accepting the wisdom of Greer's words, but was still sceptical. 'I'm not sure my men will agree to be separated from their horses.'

'You must reason with them. They will not like it, but it is the only way.'

Titus nodded. 'And what about the other ship?'

'The cargo ship will be given to Prince Tremayn who, after a few modifications to the vessel, plans a new career in the private sector.'

Despite Titus's anger, which had been slowly seeping away, he could not help but smile at Greer's choice of words. 'Yes, I have been watching him at work on this vessel. He is an excellent sailor and would make a good pirate, but I am cold, wet and hungry. Release me first.'

'Will you help us?'

Titus stared at the three faces before him: Greer, Zia and Keara. 'Only if that Iceni boy apologises to me.' He indicated Galdus with the tip of his chin.

'Mmm,' Greer mused, looking at Galdus. 'Galdus, after what you have learnt, will you apologise to Titus so that we can pursue our course?'

Galdus, having listened to his father, had been following their conversation. He threw out a *Never!*

Titus laughed. 'Just what I would have said. Despite his reticence, and his punch, I agree.'

'You must swear.'

'I swear on the spirits of my forefathers.'

'Then you are a free man, as are your men,' said Greer. 'You can untie him Blair.'

But Titus was already shaking his hands loose in front of him. 'I have been a free man all my life,' he retorted throwing the ropes down at Zia's fit of laughter before striding off to the hold to see his riders and horses. Despite his show of pride, he still had to clutch his stomach to keep up his stride.

Galdus pulled Keara to the side of the ship whilst everyone returned to working the sails and the oars. They were soon to be in mid-channel where they would meet the ocean crossroads to the four winds and the three ships would go their separate ways. Being the end of the autumn there were few ships on the sea roads, but they knew that Roman reinforcements would be crossing from Lower Germania to Britannia in the coming days.

'My father has told me about you and Titus,' Galdus burst out. 'I'm so relieved for you, but you could have told me. Didn't you trust me? And didn't you tell anyone else at all?'

Keara reddened and wiped the salty brine off her cheeks as though trying to hide behind her hands. She looked at her feet, afraid to meet his eyes. 'Of course I trust you, but I was too ashamed to speak to anyone, especially after what my sister was going through. Then it just became harder to tell anyone, and Titus had made me swear on our goddess of horses and of the Underworld not to tell another living soul. I told my mother just before she died; it made the going easier for her.'

'So you broke a sacred vow to Rhiannon?'

Keara looked up at her cousin and, half-choking as she chose her words carefully, she said, 'Not exactly. My mother was already on her way… to the Otherworld… when I told her.'

Galdus stared at the ship's prow slicing through the water below. Waves and frothy bubbles rippled out from the portside in tiny folds that faded away in their wake. The salty air stung his cheeks and eyes, but the ocean itself was deep and unfathomable.

'You know that I will be returning to Caledonia with my brother and father on this ship.' Galdus took a deep breath of the cold, hard wind. 'I would like you to come with us.'

They turned to rest their arms on the gunwale and look across the sea to Britannia: it was slowly receding into the background. Leaning over the banister with their hands hanging overboard Galdus slid one wrist over to Keara's hand and took her fingers in his own. 'Marry me,' he murmured.

Keara did not respond to this. She was too far away on the horizon to even consider such a proposal. Galdus continued, 'I am heir to the Caledonian throne. One day I will be king. You'll be my queen, and we will work together against the Roman invasion of our lands. They will never conquer the north. You know I have always loved you. I love you now and will love you forever.'

At length, Keara tore her eyes away from the distant skyline and turned her face towards Galdus. Her dark green eyes were like the ocean depths, he thought, and seemed to hold just as much mystery within. She withdrew her fingers from his hand and placed these on his arm as she spoke, 'You are my cousin, Galdus, but I love you like a brother. We have grown up together and shared the same roof. We have learnt the same things, played, hunted and fought together and I would not lose that for the world but…,' she hesitated and closed her eyes against the wet wind before continuing, 'I do not love you like a wife should love a husband.'

Galdus dropped his head for a moment. 'You need time to think about this Keara, I know, but we do not have much time.'

'I am not going to marry. I saw my sister marry that monster, Marius in Saham Toney and I will not ever make that mistake. She has sacrificed herself, I understand, in order to protect what is left of our people in Iceni but *I* will avenge those who are dead: our father, our mother, Rory, our people.

'I am going to travel to Mauretania Tingitana in order to seek out Catus and make him suffer for what he has done to us. He ordered the rape of my family and of our lands. He then fled like the rat that he is, with our gold. He deserves a coward's death.'

Galdus wanted to continue his suit, but stopped. The determination in Keara's voice and face was unwavering, so Galdus conceded. 'If you are never going to marry, then that must be my consolation. You'll change your mind one day, and when you do, I'll be waiting.'

'You can't *not* marry because of me, Galdus.' Keara smiled at him, but there was a sadness in her voice. 'You have to marry. Your father will make you marry.'

'But I can't lose you,' Galdus moaned.

'You won't, I promise. I will return to Caledonia once I have killed Catus. I shall be with Greer, and we have an excellent guide and warriors with us. Once our mission is finished, we shall return to Britannia. We have the Romans to fight, and I will defend our island with you and the clans. You know I have to come back to Caledonia because I am leaving Sapho with you. She hates travelling by water anyway and the journey to

Mauretania would be too long for her, and too hot. Caledonia is by far the better choice, but promise me one thing.'

'Yes?'

'When you sail along the Iceni coastline see if you don't get a chance to send a message to Caitlyn and see if she needs help. I know she has Diodorus with her, but Marius will not treat her well. Her baby must have been born by now... I wonder if it is a boy or a girl. Tell her I will stop on my way back if I can.'

'We will. I think my father has his own plans when we sail through Iceni waters. Thank you, Keara, for your answer, and may Rhiannon speed you on your way.'

He pushed himself away from the bulwark and staggered towards his father on the swaying deck. Corbreid and Brekus were waiting for him in the bow. Tremayn had come down from the bridge in order to bid everyone farewell. He, too, was leaving them in order to rejoin his own tribe, or the remnants of it, in the southwest of Britannia. Everyone was on deck to part ways. Tremayn lumbered across to Keara with a broad smile. 'I'll remember our sojourn together on the ocean, and our prison escape.' He winked at her, then descended into the small rowing boat which had been lowered into the choppy waters. He was quickly followed by his brother and some of the other men who had been prisoners with him in the hold. A few of the Celtic freedmen had volunteered to join his ship too, as he needed extra hands on deck. He pushed the boat off from the sides of the galley and one of his men rowed them the short distance to the waiting cargo ship. Once they were aboard, he waved from afar as one of his men turned the tiller to change direction.

Keara found herself standing next to Greer. He held her elbow, seemingly to keep his balance and whispered loudly in her ear, 'We must be on our own way now. It is time to change ships. This way, Keara.'

He guided her to the bow where their own rowing boat was waiting for them. Some of Titus's men had already crossed to the other Roman galley. All were reluctant to leave their horses, but Titus said that the Iceni warrior, Varney would take good care of them, and that despite having a lame arm he was still the best horse carer he had ever seen. His men were not that appeased, but they were certainly pleased to be alive and to be returning home. Keara made her farewells to her uncle and cousins, and to Titus's freed Iceni slave, Blair. Then she threw the folds of her cloak over her shoulders and climbed down the ladder into the waiting boat. Greer, Titus and Zia followed. Looking up at the bulwarks, Keara could see the front paws of Sapho and the huge head of her dog looking down at her. Sapho began to bark and wouldn't stop until Blair wrapped his arms around her thick neck and hugged her.

'Take good care of Sapho,' Keara shouted.

'I will,' Blair promised, but he was stopped from saying more because Sapho had suddenly pulled out of his arms and leapt over the side of the ship. There was an enormous splurge of water as the giant dog half-fell, half-rolled into the dangerous sea. Sapho swam the few yards next to Keara's boat and was finally, and with great difficulty, pulled aboard the other galley; the galley had to lower the boarding ramp in its hull in order to help the huge animal get aboard. Keara gave Sapho a long, wet hug for such fidelity and then waved back at the other ship. Sapho barked farewell to Blair.

The ships parted company in mid-channel: Corbreid's Roman galley tacked against the wind into the Northern Sea whilst the second galley followed Tremayn's cargo vessel into the Channel. Once they had passed between the straits of Dubris, Titus gave orders for their galley to take the southern highway to the Atlanticus Ocean.

XIII

The Northern Sea

THE WINDS WERE HARSHER IN THE NORTHERN Sea and it was a foolish captain who tempted its anger in the colder months of the year. Those who lived along its coasts knew it as the Morimaru, the Dead Sea because it could be perilous at times; the winter storms were so furious they could send mountains of water crashing onto fragile ships, splitting their hulls open like a broken biscuit, and sending voyagers to their graves. It took a good sailor, or a madman, to sail this sea in the winter.

That afternoon the waves were choppy and heavy, the wind was cold and sharp and the skies dark. Galdus stood next to his brother who was holding the tiller, and Galdus had to hold on to Brekus in order to keep his footing. It was raining heavily as they passed the Trinovante coastline which they kept in sight, more for reasons of navigation than for security – not that it mattered much as they were in a Roman ship. From afar, they could make out a small island: the entry point to the Colne Estuary. This part of the ocean was known as the Shining Sea because of its extensive cultivation of oysters. The beds of oysters filled the estuary here and provided a sure and reliable supply of oysters for the province. However, the rare pearls to be found were quite insignificant when compared to those found in the much warmer climes of the Roman Empire.

It was not shining very much today, Galdus thought, as he eyed the grey slates of rain that skirted the coast. At least this meant a closed port. Even at the best of times only lighter Roman galleys could enter since the estuary was not deep enough to receive heavy cargo vessels. This meant that the legionaries being transferred from Germania to Britannia could only be landed at Londinium or at the port of Dubris which they had already passed. Their ship continued tacking north and Galdus hoped they could be set down for a moment in Iceni territory.

Dusk had fallen when their ship dropped anchor just south of the Gariannum Flood Plain. They had chosen a place close to the beach which was protected from the rougher ocean by an arm of red crag that stretched its hand out dangerously under the water. The flat shoreline was still visible as Corbreid's men lowered the loading ramp from the hull into the water. Then Brekus and Galdus led the first of the horses out. This was a difficult and dangerous task as the horses were unfamiliar with their new masters and could not see the bed beneath the waves. It was not until Blair settled himself on Titus's mad stallion, Cabrel, and managed to coerce him into taking the first leap into the waters that the others began to follow. Cabrel swam for a few yards until his forelegs touched sand and then he jerked himself onto the sliding grit of hard land before trotting springily onto the beach and shaking himself off. Blair leant forward and fed him a slice of apple. 'Good boy,' he whispered, stroking his cheek.

He was joined by Galdus who was as wet as an otter and

complaining aloud, 'I can't believe how that horse let you sit on its back whilst it swam to the shore! Titus's horses are famous for being ferocious, untamed beasts. I'm on his second stallion and had to swim by its side: no easy feat in such cold weather.'

'That's because I'm the one who's been looking after him,' Blair laughed. 'I'm surprised his second stallion let you swim next to him.'

'Maybe he was just following Cabrel,' Galdus rejoined, leading his horse past Blair on the beach. As the horse trotted ahead, Galdus grasped the pommel of its saddle and pulled himself up onto the horse's back, commanding it to climb onto the coastal path. He was swiftly followed by his brother and his father's men, one of whom dragged a float behind him and then threw bundles of dry clothing and weapons to everyone. In the darkness they drew on their clothes and then knotted handkerchiefs of linen to their horses' hooves. They were only a dozen riders, but the warriors Corbreid had picked to accompany his sons were all members of his royal guard and the best fighters in Caledonia. Corbreid and his ship were already returning to deeper waters.

Galdus led his scouting party across the wetlands and, despite the black night, he was always sure of his footing. They had to be fast, but silent. The night was their cover, but the waterlogged land was not inductive to speed or silence. They passed a lone poacher whose presence was betrayed by the sounds of some babbling pink-footed geese taking flight on the mudflats. He immediately disappeared, but Galdus called out to him, 'We are Iceni friends.' The man did not return though. After three hours they had travelled over fifteen miles and reached the outskirts of Venta Icenorum.

The town was asleep, apart from the guardsmen at the gates and in the towers of the defence walls of the *civitas*. Watchmen also manned the bridge and turrets overlooking the river crossing to the western gate. The town's high-walled fencing demarcated the newly laid out grid system of the Roman roads. Empty plots of land had been put aside for the market and for the future constructions of a forum and temples. A number of wattle and daub houses lined the streets, some of which had once belonged to the dispossessed Iceni townspeople, but these were not enough to house the entire civilian population, most of whom were the women and children of the soldiers now serving in Iceni territory.

From the sprawling slums, which had sprung up outside the southern road and gate to the town, a number of late-night drinkers could be heard at the newly built, and thriving, tavern. Galdus stopped his men before they reached the Roman road.

'I'm not sure how to find Caitlyn here,' he whispered to his brother.

'We need to find a Briton,' Brekus suggested, 'one who is friendly to our movement. Can't we send Blair in? He's an Iceni.'

'He's never lived here, though. He only knows Saham Toney; and he's only a child.'

'Then why did you bring him?' Brekus asked.

'He didn't,' Blair piped up, 'but I'm the only one who can ride Cabrel, the fastest horse in Britannia, and we wouldn't be left behind. Brekus is right: I am the only Iceni here. I'll pretend to be a slave... well, no pretending there as I was one. I'll go into the tavern and say I've come looking for my master because my mistress wants him home.'

Galdus was still reluctant. 'How will you get the information we need?'

'No worries there,' Blair smiled. 'They're all drunk from the singing going on. It'll be easy: I'll say that my master is a freedman of Marius.'

'Everyone knows Marius as the chief magistrate of the

town. The chances are that someone will know his slaves and freedmen, so you'll be found out immediately,' Galdus calculated.

'Then I'll say I'm a slave of Diodorus. He must be in Venta Icenorum with Caitlyn as he's going to be tutor to her child.'

'Alright,' Galdus nodded. 'We'll wait here, but you must be quick.'

As he approached the door to the tavern, Blair looked at the graffiti cut into the plaster of the wall. It was written in Latin: *I saw, I fucked, I came*. He couldn't read, so was ill-prepared for the spectacle that met him when he entered the building: warm, lurid lights; soft music from a lyre player; the odorous scent of body sweat, burning oil and heavy perfumes; and a noisy crowd of semi-clad men and women reclining on couches. A number of girls circulated between the low tables refilling glasses when requested and serving food. There was frequent movement between the couches and the cubicles in the walls when the slaves of the *lupanar* changed partners. On entering the cubicle, the male or female slave would turn the wooden sign above the curtain to read *occupied*; prostitution was a thriving business in the Roman world – and a legal one. In fact, it was sometimes seen as morally necessary, especially in the militarised frontier zones of the Empire, and it was not uncommon for the poverty-stricken freedmen or women to look for work in the *lupanars*.

Ignorant of this, Blair was arrested by the artwork on the walls and stood to absorb what his eyes could clearly see: the different frescoes showed a man copulating with a goat, a naked woman sitting astride a man on a couch, a man performing cunnilingus on a woman, and another showed one man penetrating another. All plans and ideas that Blair had formed suddenly went out of his head.

'Are you looking for work?' a man asked, indicating the nature of that work by pointing at the frescoes. The man who had spoken was of middle years and was standing at a desk beside the door. He held a stylus in one hand and spoke in Celtic for Blair, but he was clearly Roman, judging from his prominent nose and the current fashion for sideburns. He also had a number of scars on his face, and the arm that was visible from beneath his toga had been reset badly after a broken bone. Perhaps he was a retired veteran, Blair thought. He was clearly the owner and was keeping tabs on all the cubicles and drinks consumed.

'No, I'm... I'm not looking for work, sir. I've been sent by my mistress to look for my master. She wants him home now.'

'I'm sure he's a better judge of when to return home. This brothel is particularly attractive with all the fresh young slaves from the region. If your master ever wants to sell you, tell him I'd be interested in buying. What's his name?'

'Diodorus.'

'The Greek teacher. I didn't know he was married. I can't say I've seen him this evening, though he does come in from time to time. I'll ask his favourite if she has seen him. Rhonda,' he called across the room. A tall, plump woman raised her head from a couch and walked over to them. Her tunic was almost transparent and every curve of her body rippled softly as she moved. She looked at Blair, perplexed.

'You're too young to be visiting a place like this. What are you doing here?'

'He says he's looking for his master, Diodorus. Have you seen him this evening?'

A sharp look of curiosity crossed the woman's face, but was quickly veiled; her owner had not noticed her surprise. 'He hasn't been here tonight,' she answered, pouting sourly. 'Perhaps he's with that other hussy down the road. Try Selene's house.' She turned and went off towards one of the washing cubicles. Blair said *thank you* to the man and had no choice but to leave the brothel. Returning outside, he was hit by the cold, night air and pulled his hood over his head, but, as he stepped into the road, he heard a soft tread from a side alley and a *Psst!* Approaching the dark, stinking alley with caution, he saw the prostitute from the brothel.

'Diodorus does not have a slave like you. Who are you?'

'I'm a friend of Diodorus and I have been sent to find Queen Caitlyn. I've been told to find Diodorus first, but I do not know Venta Icenorum and don't know where to look.'

'I cannot speak long or I will be missed, but I will do anything to help our royal family. Diodorus is with our queen in a villa just outside Venta Icenorum. He is a kind man and always treats me with respect. I know what I do is wrong, but I am a slave now and have no choice. Whom do you have with you?'

'Galdus is waiting for any information.'

'Galdus is alive! He knows me, as I was one of the druidesses here. I worked with Greer.'

'He is alive too, but is no longer in Britannia.'

'Dear Greer! Never tell him that you have seen me. If he only knew what I have become! I am so ashamed. I must go now, but tell Galdus that Caitlyn is living in the Roman villa that Prasutagus once used as a hunting lodge. He will know where it is.'

'Thank you,' Blair whispered to her as she turned to re-enter the *lupanar*, more for its warmth than its company.

'Caitlyn and Diodorus are in Prasutagus's old hunting lodge outside of the town. The woman I spoke to at the …,' here, Blair hesitated, 'at the tavern told me this. She is Icenian and used to be a druidess, so I think we can trust her.'

'A druidess in a Roman tavern!' Brekus was incredulous.

'She's a slave now, so has no choice,' Blair spoke in her defence. 'She also said that Galdus knew her as Rhonda.'

'Rhonda? Yes, I knew her. Was she tall?'

'Yes.'

'We can trust her,' Galdus said decisively. 'Let's be on our way.' He quickly remounted and guided his horse round the eastern fence of the town towards some fields of tall sedge and reeds, keeping out of the visual range of the watchtowers. They had soon reached the Roman villa where the chief magistrate lived. It was late into the night and all that could be heard in the outlying fields was the occasional *who-o-o, who-o-o* of a tawny owl and the distant barking of a farmhouse dog. They tethered their horses on the bank of the Tas River and spread out through the apple orchard approaching the villa from behind. Galdus told his men to stay where they were and to keep an eye on the stables and the handful of guardsmen walking the grounds whilst he crept up to the winged house.

Dim candlelight and hot steam could be seen through a low cellar window where the baths were kept in one wing, and Galdus thought he could hear the clinking of wine glasses and the laughter of a man. He crouched low to the ground as he moved around to the front of the villa and climbed over the balustrade onto the veranda. From the balcony above his head, he could hear a baby crying and then light footsteps.

'Aprastus, shh,' a woman's voice whispered into the night.

He recognised it immediately as the voice of his cousin and was so relieved. And by the name of the child it was a boy. He was about to climb up the vines to the window when he heard another woman's voice. 'I'm sorry, mistress, I must have fallen asleep. I'll look after him now. You can go back to your bedchamber.'

He heard the door close and the receding sound of

footsteps, but whose were they: Caitlyn's or the nurse's? He had to find Diodorus first. He could only be in the other wing of the villa. An instinct told him to try the library which had once served as Diodorus's office and living quarters. He entered the ground floor and crept along the stone-flagged corridor. The slaves and freedmen were all asleep. No one stirred as he stepped past a number of open doors in order to reach the large, oaken frame at the end of the hall. He tried to enter the room as silently as possible but the hinges on the door needed oiling and he could not prevent the sound of creaking.

'Who's there?' called a frightened voice.

'Ssh, Diodorus, it is me, Galdus.' He pushed the door closed behind him as Diodorus trembled to light an oil lamp.

'My boy, Galdus,' the old man cried, climbing out of bed. 'It is too dangerous for you here. Why have you come back?'

'I have come back for Caitlyn,' he answered, 'and for her son. I promised Keara and Greer that I would stop for her on our way back to Caledonia.'

'Oh, I must have their news.'

'They are well but are no longer in Britannia. I must be brief as I have men waiting below.'

'Then be brief, and tell me everything,' Diodorus requested, hugging Galdus before seating himself on his feather mattress and pulling a blanket over his legs.

Galdus quickly gave him an outline of events, including his knowledge of Rhonda and her help. Diodorus showed no abashment at Galdus's mention of his visits to the brothel. He simply said, 'I do what I can for her, but she belongs to that Roman veteran now and must service a lot of his comrades-in-arms. I also have my needs, as a man, and she is a beautiful and intelligent woman. As soon as I have enough savings, I will buy her from her master and she will come and live with me.' After another moment of reflection, Diodorus grasped

Galdus's arm and continued, 'I don't think Caitlyn will follow you.'

'Why not?'

'For the same reasons that she gave her sister: she can only help her people from within. She can raise her son as future leader of the Iceni, but he must grow up here amongst his people. They are enslaved now, but she hopes the day will come when she is able to free them.'

'But she cannot stay with that man who calls himself her husband.'

'He may call himself her husband, but she has other names for him,' Diodorus chuckled. 'He spends most of his free hours in the bathhouse with the female slaves of the household.'

'Diodorus, take me to her now. She is alone, I think, as it must have been Marius I heard drinking in the baths.'

'I will tell her to go to the baby's room where the nurse is. The nurse is Iceni and will be discreet.'

The old man stood up and drew on a long, woollen gown before indicating to Galdus to follow him. 'But I must warn you: Caitlyn has changed.' He left the Caledonian prince with the nurse and soon returned with Caitlyn. Despite the low light from the lamp, Galdus was taken aback by the physical changes in his cousin: not only had she lost a lot of weight but the fatigue had left her eyes dark and sunken. Galdus was shocked to see a number of dark bruises on her neck and wrists. She ran into Galdus's arms and ran her fingers down the bristles on his cheek and chin. 'I cannot believe it is you,' she half-cried. 'What are you doing here? How did you get in?'

'I will tell you later, but first tell me what does that man do to you?' He held her at arm's length staring at the marks of abuse on her. 'I will kill him for this, I swear. You and your son are coming with me,' Galdus cried, finding it difficult to keep his voice low.

'No, no,' Caitlyn answered, pulling him back from the door. 'If you lay hands on him, all our slaves will be executed under Roman law. They are my Iceni people. There is nothing to be done.'

'I will find a way,' Galdus vowed, 'and I will find a way this night. Will you come with us? My father's ship is waiting for us north of The Wash.'

'I cannot leave my people. I am the only protection they have left. If I take Marius's anger, then he is less severe on them.'

'Then we will take your household with us,' Galdus decided. 'There are only a few guardsmen in this villa. My men will deal with them. Pack your things. We are leaving for the north.' Seeing Caitlyn hesitate still, he added, 'What do you prize more: freedom for you and your son or a nebulous show of power? Here, you have neither. In Caledonia you will have freedom… and hope. Greer and Keara will join us there.' He told Diodorus to wake the slaves and asked the nurse to prepare the child for the cold journey north. Then he disappeared into the garden.

He found some of his men crouched behind the trees where he had left them and told them of his plans. They flitted off like night bats in the direction of the stables and villa grounds whilst Galdus took Brekus and Blair with him to the villa's bathhouse. He remembered how to get into the cellar via the furnace room outside.

Marius had also changed. In just a few weeks his languid and gratifying way of life had added fat to his frame. He particularly enjoyed his moments of relaxation and thoughtful reflection in the bathhouse, where the warmth and humid, sensual pleasures reminded him of home. Work in the administrative offices of the region, currently carried out in the fortress, was tiring he found, and of little interest. Since the departure of Suetonius, a few days earlier, Marius had been enjoying the liberties of his little fiefdom. He particularly enjoyed the favours of his slave, Sugwenn who was quite adroit at underwater fellatio whilst he tried to drink his Tuscan wine. He had already drunk enough to drown an elephant and great red droplets kept slurping from his glass and discolouring the pool every time he trembled with pleasure. The sounds were hushed in the warm bathroom of the villa, and the scents of oils and perfumes were rich and inviting. Added to this, the richness of the mosaic floors, the wall frescoes of dolphins and fish, and the stone pillars covered in painted green creepers gave the bathhouse the welcoming allure of an underwater grotto.

Galdus had already taken in the lack of attendants and the Latin rhyme on the wall,

Do not ridicule the small,
Little things can charm us all.
Eros was not big at all.

He stepped out silently from between the pillars and stared at Marius. Sugwenn gave a startled cry when she resurfaced and saw the three Britons standing by the pool. Marius had not moved: too drunk to react and too sure of his social position.

'H-h-hello P-P-Prince G-g-aldus,' he slurred. 'S-s-still a-live?' he giggled and took another gulp of wine.

Blair went to help Sugwenn climb out of the pool. Brekus quickly wrapped a dry towel round her body and told her to sit on the stone bench.

'I have come to collect Caitlyn and her son. I am taking them home with me to Caledonia.' Galdus spoke quietly trying to control his rage. 'I have seen what you have done to her: she, who is Queen of the Iceni. I have seen how you have abused her and mistreated her, and I want nothing from you but your death.'

Marius laughed again and, speaking more soberly, he rejoined, 'Y-you c-cannot touch m-me. If I d-die m-my h-household s-slaves die too.' He tried to pull himself out of the bath, but Galdus stepped on his hand. The pain seemed to bring some sense into the Roman for he reacted immediately by stabbing Galdus in the leg with his glass. As Galdus instinctively lifted his foot with the pain, Marius pulled his hand free and began to wade to the other side. He was met by Brekus who barred the way.

'Sugwenn, call the guards,' he shouted to the slave.

She stared at him, remaining silent and motionless, watching his growing panic as Galdus walked slowly down the steps into the bathwater. Blood from Galdus's wound mixed with the red wine already spilt in the water. He had pulled a dagger from his belt and approached Marius with slow steps. Marius raised his fists and, as he had learnt in his boxing classes in Rome, he managed to block the first thrust that Galdus made, knocking the blade from Galdus's hand. Brekus threw his brother a second knife which he caught in midair. Marius kept calling to the guards to come.

'No one will answer your calls,' Galdus reposted, despite the low sounds of fighting now coming from the grounds. Savouring the moment, he added, 'Revenge is sweet, but I have a boat to catch so must end it swiftly.' He made another thrust at Marius and stabbed him in the fist, but this time Marius was able to pull the knife back with his wounded hand and extract the blade from his knuckles.

'Now who has the weapon?' he hissed, approaching Galdus. The Caledonian prince slipped under the water and disappeared in the crimson waters. Marius moved from foot to foot, keeping one eye on Brekus and one eye on the eddying water. Suddenly from behind him Galdus burst from the water and held the first knife blade to Marius's throat.

'The only thing you have in common with Eros is a small prick,' he whispered. He slit the man's throat from ear to ear and pushed the body forward into the water.

'Let's go,' he shouted to the others, as he hitched himself out of the bath; 'Two dunkings in one night are enough for me.'

Stalking into the main house Galdus quickly changed into some dry clothes that Diodorus found for him and then led everyone down to the horses at the river, being joined en route by all the Caledonian guards. The slaves showed no reticence in following the band of warriors: they knew only too well the sanction that awaited them if they stayed in the villa. They also had Caitlyn with them. Despite the short but fierce skirmish that had taken place around the villa, the townsmen seemed not to have heard. The group was ferried across the river whilst the horses swam. Galdus's men had taken more horses from the stables, but many of the Icenians and Caledonians still had to ride pillion to the north of Icenian territory. Caitlyn was behind Galdus with the baby Aprastus in her arms. They rode as fast as the wind, blowing deeply across the reeds on either side of the causeways, but time was against them.

Only Caitlyn knew where the new Roman garrisons had been built, and she had to constantly indicate to Galdus which new track to follow or avoid. The pale dawn light was beginning to glow against the deep purple sky in the east when they finally reached a small bay to the right of The Wash. One of Galdus's men jumped off his horse and lit a lantern. Soon, a second light could be seen down towards a jetty on the beach. The Britons rode down the track to the waiting Roman galley and clambered aboard the lowered boarding door. Corbreid gave orders for the bridge to be drawn up and the sails raised. Many hands pushed away from the jetty, and the oarsmen began rowing. The Icenian refugees clutched the sides of the galley and looked at the last dawn many of them would ever see rising over their lands.

XIV

Camulodunum

POLYCLITUS'S HUGE RETINUE HAD FINALLY arrived in Camulodonum but Polyclitus had not wanted to discuss affairs with Suetonius until he had been refreshed and well rested. Suetonius had placed him in a newly restored villa on the outskirts of the town: *not much better than one of the imperial posting stations across the Empire*, Polyclitus had thought glumly. It had taken over a month to travel from Rome to Londinium and travelling conditions had not been easy. The cold winter had left him quite impervious to the splendour of the different landscapes he had passed through in Italia, Gaul and Belgian, and he had taken quite a fright when the mules at the back of his train had been attacked by wolves in Gaul. What is more, the different town councils had complained that it was very difficult to accommodate and feed such a large escort but, feed them, they had, much to their cost – and would have to do so again on his return.

Nero's Greek secretary had met with Classicianus a few days earlier in Londinium and he had been impressed with the financial agent's pragmatic approach to running the city and opening it up to new business ventures. He had taken note of Classicianus's concerns about the drop in revenue, a particular worry of the Emperor himself, especially since the disappearance of Cato with Britannia's tax revenue. Polyclitus had looked at the books and economic forecast for the province and had been struck by the downturn in the market. And now, Suetonius would have to explain himself.

Polyclitus had the Governor wait in the reception room for over an hour whilst he reread Suetonius's reports. Then he called the Governor into his office. When Suetonius entered, Polyclitus folded his pocket mirror and put it away in his bag. He told Suetonius to take a seat at the table, asking another secretary to take notes. Suetonius was struck by the strangely effeminate appearance of Polyclitus. The Emperor's secretary was a tall man, clean-shaven and well dressed in a brown damask toga, but he was also heavily perfumed with a narrow, powdered face and plucked eyebrows. His personal barber had also used curling irons on his black hair so that a number of buoyant ringlets framed his face. He was apparently following the current fashions in Rome, set by the Emperor himself.

'You know that Nero has sent me here to make an independent assessment of the situation in Britannia,' Polyclitus began. In contrast to his appearance, his voice struck Suetonius as strangely firm and imposing. Polyclitus continued, 'He has been receiving quite critical reports from his financial agent about your mismanagement of military affairs here.'

'Mismanagement!' Suetonius growled. 'It was a bloody uprising I had to deal with. I saved the province and lost a number of valuable men in the process. It was because of *his* financial agent's total cock-up in the first place that we had a revolt on our hands.'

'He is well aware of Cato's poor managerial decisions following the death of Prasutagus, the king of our client kingdom, Iceni.'

'It was the man's callous greed that led to the uprising. Has he turned up yet?' Suetonius asked with such feral impatience that Polyclitus hesitated before responding, '... No, but our intelligence service is looking into the matter. Now, to return to your work. I need to know why you thought you could leave the hinterland so unprotected whilst you were campaigning on the frontier and leading an attack on Ynys Môn?' Polyclitus's scrivener picked up a stylus and began to write on his wax tablets. 'Do you mind,' Polyclitus asked, sounding both imperious and cordial, 'if my secretary takes notes?'

'No,' answered Suetonius in a loud, confident tone, 'but you already have my reports on that. I left the interior lands with protection from Legion Two at Isca ...'

'Under the command of Poenius Postumus, the prefect?' Polyclitus interrupted.

'Yes, I had its legate, senior tribune and half of the legion with me fighting the Cymru alliance of tribes in the west of Britannia. Poenius was a competent and experienced soldier, and the tribes in the southwest peninsular were calm...'

'At that moment,' Polyclitus interrupted again.

'Yes, we only had trouble in the southwest once the rebellion began in the east of Britannia.'

'I was sorry to hear about the death of Poenius. His family in Rome has been informed. They took the news quite well. Sorry, please continue.'

A little put out, Suetonius resumed his outline of the military dispositions he had put into place in the province. 'I left the full Ninth Legion in the northeast of Britannia under the command of its legate, Quintus Petillius Cerialis.'

'Yes, again, I was sorry to hear of the death of its prefect.'

'The legionary forces that Cerialis sent out to relieve Camulodonum were ambushed by the Iceni and Trinovante forces. Petro was killed then.'

'I did have time to look around the city this morning and was sorry to see such destruction. The Emperor was upset to hear about the loss of the Temple of Claudius and the disappearance of the great statue of his uncle, the divine Claudius. Has that been found yet?'

Suetonius breathed in slowly and deeply in order to remain calm before he spoke, 'No, it has not. The bronze statue was pulled down by the enemy and hacked to pieces. Some pieces have turned up. They were taken as war booty by the rebels that we have since caught, but most of it has been lost. You can inform the Emperor that those rebels found in possession of such sacred materials have suffered a traitor's death.'

'I will certainly do that. Speaking of which, have you managed to put down the rebellion because I hear that small pockets of resistance continue to fight across the province, and that the rebellion even continues at sea; you recently lost a number of naval vessels.'

'Yes, I did.' Suetonius had raised his voice again. 'But the province is stable you can tell the Emperor. We still have the client kingdoms of Cartimandua in the north, and Cogidubnus in the south. They have both remained loyal to Rome because they know that the rebels cannot win against us.'

Polyclitus was silent for a moment and placed his chin on his ringed fingers, leaning forward with his elbows resting uncomfortably on the desk. 'You know I am here, not only to negotiate reconciliation between you and Classicianus, but to negotiate peace talks between us and the rebels and to end the war. We need to pacify native rebelliousness and implement a new policy of appeasement.'

'What are you suggesting?' Suetonius cried, raising his

eyebrows. 'That we shake hands with the barbarians as we did in Mauretania?'

'I do not think you understand the full political and economic implications of this uprising.' The voice of Polyclitus sounded self-possessed, even a little condescending as he explained those implications to Britannia's Governor. 'We risk losing everything in Britannia because of the military and financial incompetence that I have seen here. You are being too harsh on the population. Your reprisals amount to nothing less than genocide, and the province is no longer a good financial investment. Nero wants, and needs, stability in the Empire, and for this we must make a fresh start in Britannia. In order to do this Classicianus has to write off a number of the Britons' financial arrears and you must end your scorched-earth policy. Your three-year term is almost up, and you can soon return to Rome. However, Nero cannot give you any triumphal honours when you enter the capitol but, if I tone things down in my report, your professional career will not be damaged. You will no longer work in the military, but you may pursue a political career in Rome. Who knows, perhaps you'll be consul one day.'

Suetonius was silent. He looked at Polyclitus across the table, sizing him up and realising that the man was not only a pretty face. He had clearly underestimated Nero's secretary, for here sat an intelligent, observant and ambitious Roman freedman – and a close confidant of the Emperor. Suetonius nodded, acquiescing in agreement. 'You are right, of course. I have been here too long.' He sat back in his chair and sighed. 'This forsaken wilderness has made me lose all bearings of the real world across the Channel. I do need to pass the reins to someone else and return home. Who is to replace me?'

'We thought Publius Petronius Turpilianus would be a good man for the job. He can be here in a few weeks.'

'Turpilianus!' Suetonius burst out before he could control himself, for he was quite astonished by the choice. 'But he is consul this year.'

'That is true, but when he saw this opening in Britannia he seemed quite keen on taking up this opportunity and is ready to lay down the consulship.'

'I can imagine! After all, he is the nephew of Aulus Plautius who conquered Britannia eighteen years ago and became its first Governor.'

'That is right. Turpilianus has heard a lot of glorious stories about the Roman triumphs in Britannia from his uncle. He is keen to make his own mark in history.' Polyclitus hesitated a moment. 'From what I have seen of the province so far though, I think he will be a disappointed man. It lacks the finery and comforts of Rome. It certainly lacks sunshine.' Polyclitus nodded to the scrivener to stop taking notes.

'Turpilianus also needs to be removed from Rome for a while. He is currently out of favour with Nero. Here, he can consolidate Nero's new era of imperial policies in Britannia: that of Romanising the wavering tribes so that their children can enjoy the full benefits of Roman civilisation. He also needs to lie low for a while whilst you ... you can enjoy an honourable retirement in Rome. I think it is the best ending to this story, don't you?' Polyclitus smiled as he stood up in order to indicate that their meeting was now at an end.

OCEANUS ATLANTICUS

Sapho had found her sea legs and was now finding great entertainment in catching the jumping fish that were pulled out of the ocean in nets each day. One of the men had even trained her to help on the ship by walking to the other side of the deck with a harness attached to her neck and body, pulling the fishing net out of the water; a job she particularly enjoyed as the rewards were so great.

The men spent a lot of their time repairing the hemp ropes and netting, maintaining the sails and masts, and plugging the wooden hull to keep the ship tight. They spent their spare time playing board games on deck, or in the cabins when it was too cold. Greer and Zia often played merels but Zia always had to concede defeat when he found himself reduced to only two counters each time. Between Greer and Titus, it seemed to be fifty-fifty as both men were equally skilled at strategy and knew how to place their counters on the dots. It was the same with backgammon, a game that Keira was good at. However, whilst she often defeated Zia and other members of the crew at backgammon and merels she never quite managed to win against Greer or Titus so she preferred to stick to draughts with them. And whilst Titus enjoyed these moments of détente he would grow impatient with Keara if she took too long to think about her next move.

'It's only a game,' he exhaled, in a great sigh of exasperation, 'so why don't you take all day!' Keara quickly picked up her counter and jumped over one of his ebony counters thus removing it from the board, but Titus responded by jumping over two of hers.

'Don't let me distract you,' he laughed. 'Next time, I'll take a wine break, so I don't break your concentration.'

'And why don't you stop breaking wind every time you speak?' Keara rejoined.

'Whoa!' Titus laughed again, holding up both hands in submission.

From a distance Zia and Greer watched them both play. 'I've never seen Titus laugh so much before,' Zia said.

'And I've never seen Keara so determined to win before,' Greer smiled, glancing at her animated face.

Lixus, Mauretania

A month passed without incident as their ship skirted the western coasts of the Roman Empire: Gaul, Hispania, North Africa. The further south they travelled, the milder the weather became, despite the winter season. The men were relieved to be returning home and gave a loud roar of joy upon spotting the first outlines of Mauretania Tingitana. Their ship followed the coast further south until reaching the mouth of the river Loukkos where a Roman patrol boat asked to see their papers. Titus handed over the required authorisation to the harbour control officer who nodded, returned the parchment to Titus and let their ship pass into the estuary.

'Excellent work.' Titus glanced at Zia. 'Your paperwork is always so convincing.' Then he returned to the helm of the galley and shouted at his men, 'Full ahead.' His men dipped their oars into the waters and rowed another two miles following the river across the marshes until they reached the port of Lixus on the right-hand bank of the river. They were once again asked for their travel pass. This time, though, Titus had to pay a small fee to the harbour master, but spoke lightly of it as he counted out the coins, 'The taxes for sea ports are forever rising. Now, even the military has to pay!'

Upon approaching the mooring docks, they were met by the most odious smells of fermented fish entrails. The imperial outpost of Lixus may have been swarming with life, movement and noise, but it was also swimming in fish guts and flies. 'Don't mind the smell,' Titus smiled grimly at Keara and Greer as he, himself, wrapped a linen handkerchief round his head and over his nose. 'Lixus is one of the biggest exporters of garum sauce in the Roman Empire. The fish paste is produced in the factories here. The city itself is further up the hill, but we are going to one of the smelting workshops further along the industrial zone so hold your noses.'

After leaving the ship, Keara, Sapho, Greer and Zia followed Titus and his man, Aelius, through a number of narrow alleys which were only wide enough for a mule and cart to pass. Mud-dried houses and rickety stalls lined the dusty routes until they eventually reached some workshops. Titus left them at a stand where they could buy refreshments whilst he entered one of the metal-smelting sheds and told them clearly not to bring attention to themselves. They sat in the shade behind the vine-clad trellis of the drinks stand. The heat was that of a Britannic summer and the cool wine was quite intoxicating. What with the dry land and the heady smells of olives, leather-tanning and fish sauce, Keara forgot what language she spoke to Greer in as she asked how much longer they would have to wait.

'Do not speak Celtic here,' he hissed back: 'we will be noticed.'

'I think it's a bit late for that,' she rejoined. 'One limping thespian, a long-bearded wizard, a woman dressed in old rags and a huge Britannic hound is not exactly discreet. The only one who blends in is Aelius.' Aelius bowed solemnly at her words acknowledging that he was, indeed, the only one who did blend in: his short, coiled hair and beard were black and streaked with grey, his brown face was dotted with small dark moles under his eyes, and his dress was that of the Roman army.

'Then you should have stayed on board,' Greer scolded Keara.

'I needed firm land and a bath, and I'm never leaving Sapho behind again.'

'Come,' Titus called, rejoining them a moment later and frowning deeply as he took in the disparate and indiscreet visibility of his group. 'A friend of mine will welcome us in his villa outside the city. My men will stay with the ship and take her further south. I have also paid the harbour master to let me know if the Roman authorities have any news of our visit.'

'Did you hear anything of Catus?' Keara asked.

'Yes. He is not here,' was the curt answer.

'What?'

'He left Lixus a month ago for another city, Volubilis, which is much further inland. It is on a ridge overlooking the great fertile plains at the foot of the Middle Atlas Mountains.'

Zia smiled at his master: 'Running from the smoke and ... into the fire.'

They hurried on, trying to keep up with Titus who would not let them ask any more questions until they reached the outskirts of the city. He then pushed them into a carriage for hire and told the driver to take them to the aforementioned villa where Keara was indeed relieved of her rags and fatigue. After being washed, scrubbed, plucked, brushed and dressed by the female attendants of the villa's owner, an apolitical, but influential member of the city's merchant board, Keara, accompanied by her faithful hound, joined the men in the salon and was introduced to Junius Septimus Flavius, their host. He specialised in exporting goat skins from the semi-nomadic tribe, the Baquates, to the Roman legions on the frontiers of the Roman Empire. There, the skins were then made into tents for the seasonal campaigns of the army.

'What a delightful creature she is,' Junius sighed, kissing Keara's hand in greeting whilst admiring the velvet coat of her dog so that no one was quite sure whether he meant Keara or her mastiff. Sapho gave Junius a low growl, but was immediately quiet when Keara told her to be silent and to lie down.

'Come,' Junius ordered, leading Keara towards a cushion whilst keeping one eye on the dog. 'We must eat.'

The others, too, had washed and changed, and were all sitting on large cushions on a beautiful mosaic floor arranged around the most ornate of low tables. Keara's eyes were drawn to the rich, colourful, but empty table. Her stomach felt very hollow.

'Yes, I see that you are admiring my beautiful table. It is made from citrus wood, a commodity in great demand in the Empire, but in short supply. Mauretania is famous for its production.' He waited awhile whilst drinks and platters of food were laid on the table by a number of slaves. When the attendants had withdrawn, Junius told his guests to eat. Then he turned to Titus to speak in Tamazight, their Berber tongue. Between mouthfuls of the hot and spicy foods Keara watched their host with some curiosity, for he seemed an oddly incongruous choice of friend for Titus. Older than Titus, he was also taller, with lighter skin and softer hair, but it wasn't this that struck Keara as strange, but the fact that he seemed to be playing a role in a public spectacle: that of the successful businessman and languid patrician, the antithesis of Titus. But as the dinner wore on, he let fall the curtain a little.

'Titus, my friend, it has been a long time since I last saw you in Rome, and you left there a number of years ago, but I have always kept up to date with your news and have enjoyed reading your letters. What brings you back to Lixus, travelling from Britannia in the winter?'

'We are following the ex-Procurator of Britannia, Catus Decianus who fled from Britannia many months ago after a number of crimes, including brutality, instigating rape and the despoliation of some of the Britannic tribes. The money he took did not find its way into Nero's coffers.'

Junius glanced at Keara beside him, and then at Greer beside her.

'What has this to do with you and our cause?' he asked, switching to Latin.

'Overtly, nothing,' Titus shrugged, 'but I am bound by a sacred oath to help them find Catus and recover some of the stolen wealth.'

'And to make him pay for what he did to my family,' Keara cried out.

'What passion from one so young,' Junius smiled in admiration.

'I have also made an agreement with the druid, Greer, and with the High King of Caledonia, Corbreid. We can help each other in our military strategies and the timings of our rebellions,' Titus continued.

'Have you considered the huge distance between Mauretania Tingitana and Britannia? Two thousand miles. It takes over a month for ships to sail such distances, unless you propose communicating through trance images and dream words.' Junius raised his eyebrows. 'Perhaps the druid can help you there.'

'You sound like a sophist,' Greer remarked, 'to deny the existence of the supernatural.'

'I am one, and, as our great statesman and dramatist, Seneca himself said, *Everyone prefers belief to the exercise of judgement*. I could expound for hours on the question of rational thought and the existence of the gods.'

'As I could, myself,' Greer said, smiling back in agreement. 'I am one of the few philosophers of the Britons still alive. We do not write down our lore and histories, so everything is locked in here.' He tapped his head. 'To be passed down in my teachings to the new generation of our people. If we do not continue the resistance movement against the Roman incursions into our lands then we risk losing our religious and cultural identity. Hibernia and Caledonia are the last pockets of Celtic resistance. Princess Keara has lost her family, her tribe and her lands. By finding Catus and the lost wealth of the Iceni tribe, we will be able to continue our fight in the north just as some of your tribes continue their resistance in the Middle Atlas Mountains here. As for communication and coordinating our attacks, we can always use the carrier pigeon.'

Junius could not help but laugh. 'The carrier pigeon can only cover one thousand miles at the most, but we do have our posts across the Empire,' he conceded. 'Now, what in Hades is Catus doing *here*? And what induced him to steal from the Emperor?'

'Greed, no doubt,' Titus took up the discourse. 'But he is no longer in Lixus. He smelted down the Iceni gold and silver here, but then he travelled onto Volubilis.'

'Ha! What an imbecile! Doesn't he know that Volubilis lies at the foot of the Atlas Mountains where the Baquates live?' Junius turned his eyes from Titus to Aelius.

Titus responded, 'He doesn't know that we are following him, and that I and my men are of the Baquates tribe. We believe that he has chosen the royal capital of Volubilis because it is on the very edge of the Roman Empire. He thinks he is safe, and probably has a safe house there.'

'He probably has half the Roman army after him now if he has stolen from Nero, so I don't know how safe he'll be. Mauretania also has about ten thousand Roman troops permanently based here trying to maintain order. Be that as it may, I can help you move on to Volubilis. My mother still lives there, in the Jewish quarter. I'll come with you as I need to collect a transport of goat skins from the city and I haven't seen my mother in a while. You'll also need my horses and escort to protect you from the wild animals, and from the road checks.'

'Do you mean *wild*, wild animals, or the Roman forces?' Keara sat up straight and pulled on a strand of her hair.

'He means exotic, wild animals.' Zia leant forward and frowned. 'Like the elephant, leopard and lion.'

'I've never seen any of those.' Keara's eyes were round with curiosity. 'Though the Emperor Claudius did arrive in Britannia on an elephant, but I was only a baby then. I'm sure Sapho will protect us, but I would like to see the animals.'

'Don't worry, Keara, I'm sure you'll get plenty of opportunity to view them on our caravan journey to Volubilis,' Zia said dipping his fingers into the bowl of olives.

VOLUBILIS

It took several days to travel by caravan to Volubilis. Camels, horses and mules plodded along, and wagons creaked their dry, wooden wheels over the black sand of the road crossing the plain from Lixus to the Roman colony of Babba. Babba sat on the river Lix, and from there the caravan took the road south, bringing its articles of Roman fabrication, as well as the imperial post, to the administrative and civic centre of Mauretania Tingitana. A military escort accompanied the journeymen in order to protect them from the wild beasts on the plains. The Roman auxiliaries were from Parthia and did not remark upon Junius's group of Berber tribesmen, although they could not help but notice the large hound from Britannia. Titus had to say that he had bought it at an animal auction in Londinium for the games in Volubilis. This did incite a lot of curiosity, but also kept an indelible line of defence between Junius's small group and the Roman soldiers.

Keara had been dressed in the elegant and fashionable clothes of a woman from the wealthy class of the province: long, blue silks covered her from head to foot, and she had been told not to speak. In the Roman patriarchal society women were not meant to be heard, and the identity papers that Junius had managed to obtain for her showed that she was the new wife of Titus. She had complained about such an absurdity, as she saw it, but, as Junius was already a married man and was well-known in the region, she could hardly be passed off as the wife of anyone else.

'Why can't I be Greer's daughter?'

'That,' Junius countered, 'might only draw the attention of unwanted admirers.'

She dropped the argument and decided to play her part, ready to pay any price to get revenge.

At night they would stop at the Roman outposts for reasons of security, and Keara had to stay in her room for fear that her poor manners, as Junius explained, might betray her lack of cultural understanding. In order to protect her false identity, Titus also had to be lodged with her. This was a situation that Keara found uncomfortable at first, but, since Titus seemed unfazed, even amused, by their relationship, Keara soon learnt to put up with his presence. They spent time playing ludus with counters and dice, or Titus would teach Keara to speak a few words of Tamazight, but often they were so tired after a day's travelling that they would just sleep and would not even think of the uncomfortable sleeping quarters of Greer and Zia lying with Sapho in the stables.

Finally arriving on the fertile plains below the ridge on which Volubilis stood, Keara was struck by the magnificence of the city and its landscape. The plain was bordered on either side by small rivers that quenched its thirst. Hundreds upon hundreds of olive trees were being cultivated, packed together in tight knots, and there were also many fields of emmer and wheat that had just been planted in order to benefit from the mild winter weather. Volubilis overlooked all this wealth, and the city itself, once the royal capital of the Berber kings, displayed its Romanised influence in its choice of architecture, art and urban layout. The public buildings, temples, forum and basilica, and the private town houses and boutiques, all announced the affluence of the city dwellers. An aqueduct ran from a spring in the hills behind the city and fed the houses, the public baths and fountains with fresh, running water.

The only blot on the landscape, to Keara's mind, was the circuit of walls that entwined the city. The walls were built of mud bricks, laid on a stone foundation which was skirted by a ditch and pocketed by over thirty towers. It held six gates, all of which were flanked by towers. These were intended to protect the population from the wild animals that roamed the plains at night, Zia had told her, but the huge range of mountains that dominated the horizon behind the city seemed more threatening and majestic. The distant mountain peaks were crowned in the winter snows and the dark flanks of the mountains imposed a stillness on the world that startled Keara. This landscape was a lifetime away from the flat wetlands of her own homeland. She turned to Greer in her saddle and posed a question, 'Are these defences really to keep the wild animals out?'

'I'm sure the inhabitants would say *yes* to your question since the wall is also a sign to the hostile tribes in the mountains to stay away. The wall is a barrier between the Romanised Berber people in the city and the *uncivilised barbarians* without. Titus's Berber tribe, the Baquates, lives in the mountains there. Some of the herdsmen come down in the winter in order to pasture their flocks of goats at the feet of the mountains and there are occasional tensions between the two sides. The Berber tribes in the mountains are becoming more powerful and hostile, and Volubilis stands in one of the most vulnerable positions in Mauretania as it lies on the southeastern edge of the province. That is why it also has a ring of five forts out on the plains. See.' Greer pointed them out to her. 'And, behind those forts you see those mountains?' Keara nodded back to him as she gazed in the direction of his arm. 'There lies the unknown.' Greer paused a moment before continuing, 'Suetonius did cross it once with his legion and discovered only the desert. It is a harsh lifestyle – to live in the mountains – but it is a free one.'

'Why would Catus choose to come here, do you think?' Keara asked, confused.

'Because it is on the edge of the known world, but has all the amenities, wealth and discretion that money can buy. Nobody would think to look here. Catus is not of the senatorial order. He is a mere equestrian with money and, since the city has a very mixed community, his presence would not raise an eyebrow.'

'Zia has told me that there are many different religious groups in this city. There is a strong Jewish community. There are Phoenicians, Berbers, and Romans with all their gods and temples. He also says that there is a new sect which has just started up here, run by the Christians, who have split away from the Jews and are being persecuted by Nero.'

'As we, the druids are. Yes, every culture has their gods. We have ours, which are very different to the others for we see our souls as part of the universal energy in which we are recycled and reborn in this world. But Keara, I'm sure you can visit the different temples if you are interested in learning more, and perhaps we'll find Catus in one of them. Now silence. No one must hear us speaking Celtic. Let us follow Titus to our lodgings.'

The lodgings that Junius held in the city were in a large town house in the Jewish quarter near the city wall. His mother was pleased to see her son, and to see Titus again after so many years but, despite her Romanised name of Livia, she only spoke pigeon Latin and so found it difficult to communicate with Keara and Greer. Junius asked her if there had been any new Roman arrivals in the city, but she did not know.

'You ask at the Chamber of Commerce when you renew your licence for the purchase of goat skins,' she said. 'But, it is Saturnalia Festival now, so we have many people in the city.'

'What happens during this festival?' Keara asked Titus.

'It is very similar to what you have already seen in Britannia amongst the Romanised citizens. The Saturnalia will last for a few days during which time it will be complete mayhem in the city. It is a civic holiday when a public sacrifice is made at the Temple of Saturn to mark the shortest day in the year and, as the winter begins, the people ask the deity to watch over the land and crops. This is then followed by a public banquet in the Forum and streets at which roles are reversed, people give each other gifts, and there is a lot of gambling, drinking and dancing. It will make it easier for us to pass incognito, but, with a population of over twenty thousand, it will also make it more difficult to find Catus.'

'Vine growers also make goat sacrifices in honour of Bacchus so it also means that the price of goat skins is very low at this time of the year: good business for me,' Junius laughed rubbing his hands together.

'What he is neglecting to say is that he has already bought herds of goats from my Baquate tribesmen, which he then sells to the olive farmers who don't have their own goats, before buying the skins back at a low cost after the solstice!' Titus added. 'He has a good head for business.'

'Somebody has to sponsor your activities,' Junius retorted indignantly.

In the days that followed Keara would be escorted by Livia to the various temples in the city in order to find any sight or sound of Catus, whilst Junius, Greer, Titus and Aelius visited the markets, taverns, auction house and public baths. Junius would not say it was to no avail since, in the time spent, he was able to conclude a lot of business, although no trace of Catus could be found until one morning Junius returned from the Chamber of Commerce with, what he called, a funny story. He had been paying for his new trading licence when he had overheard two clerks discussing a similar transaction that had taken place that week: a slave had come in to renew his master's licence for his limestone quarry on the edge of the southern plain and had paid in Roman denarii.

'What is so unusual about that?' Greer asked.

'Nothing. I'm only telling this story because the limestone quarry is owned by a private family, not the state, and that the owner, Crassus Africanus, is one of the two magistrates of the city. The Africanus family arrived here from Rome about ten years ago and is already one of the richest in the Province. The silver denarii in question seemed to be counterfeit, one of the clerks had said, because it was a little lighter than usual, and would explain the wealth of the family, which is nominally based on limestone, olives and the games that sometimes take place in the quarry. There is also rumour that Crassus is quite corrupt and accepts large sums of money in exchange for his influence.'

'Ahh!' Greer smiled. 'There is nothing new there, but was the money counterfeit?' he asked, keen for Junius to get to the point.

Here, Junius paused as he poured himself a glass of water and squirted a dash of lemon into it, asking the others if they would like some more. Keara was hot in the courtyard despite the shade from the fig trees and was only half-listening to Junius's story, but she was thirsty so held out her glass. Junius poured her the same as himself and then picked up where he had left off, 'No, the denarii were not counterfeit, but one of the clerks reported that its silver content was very low and all the coins were of the same weight and content. It's just a funny story because the Africanus family is so rich and powerful, and yet it's using the cheapest coins. I'm glad you're smiling Greer, and you, too, Keara.'

Leaning forward, Greer asked, 'And did you, by any chance, overhear the percentage of silver in the coins?'

'I think it was around half.' He scratched his head. 'Yes, that was it. One of the clerks mentioned forty-eight percent, I believe, but he was probably exaggerating.'

'No, he was not exaggerating, and we know where to look for Catus now,' Greer said, grinning.

'Why would my story about the Africanus's Roman denarii help you find Catus? Catus has nothing to do with their family.'

Junius, Titus and Zia were staring expectantly at the two Britons. Greer broke the silence, 'Because the Iceni tribe minted their own denarii in order to trade within the Roman Empire and to pay its taxes to Rome.'

'And such denarii are produced all over the Empire,' Junius added, quite lost.

'The Iceni only included forty-eight percent of silver in their Roman coins, which was the lowest of all the tribes in Britannia,' Keara concluded putting down her empty glass and standing up. 'How can we reach the Africanus estate?'

'It is only an hour's ride from the city,' Titus answered, 'but we are not going today.'

'Why not?' Keara questioned, ready to leave on the spot.

'Because it would look suspicious,' Titus responded. 'Tomorrow there are some animal games in the quarry. Perhaps Junius can get us tickets for that?'

'Better than that: I can get us invited as potential sellers of your Britannic dog?'

'I am not selling Sapho,' Keara retorted.

'We are not going to sell her,' Titus reassured her, 'but it is true that her presence has incited curiosity and interest. And we have already told those around us that I am thinking of selling her. Let us take her to the games with us tomorrow and put her on display.'

Greer shook his head, 'But she will bring undue attention to ourselves. We don't want Catus to hear of us.' He was not convinced by Titus's plans.

'That is a risk we have to take.' Titus nodded, though he was not that convinced himself. He pinched his lip with his thumb and knuckle, thinking things through. 'But Britannic dogs are exported all over the Empire for games so it is not the first time such an animal has been seen here.'

'We are celebrating the waxing of the light, tomorrow, at the games,' Junius told everyone when he returned alone that evening with invitations for four. 'You will stay at home with my mother,' he told Zia and Aelius, 'as only I, Greer, Titus and his *wife* have been invited.'

Keara raised her eyebrows. 'Are women allowed at the games?'

'Certainly,' Junius smiled sweetly. 'As long as they are only seen and not heard.'

'And have you heard anything of Catus?' Titus interposed before Keara could retort.

'No, I haven't.'

'Who gave you the tickets?'

'It was one of the Africanus brothers at the bathhouse. He had seen Keara walking the dog with you one evening and is keen to meet her.'

'Who? Keara or the dog?' Titus rebutted.

Junius raised his eyebrows quizzically. 'The dog, of course. He is not one for the ladies. We have been invited into the guests' stand at the quarry, but we shall have to leave Sapho in the animal cages below, where she will be well taken care of because Crassus Africanus is thinking of investing in her.'

XV

T HE QUARRY SLOUCHED ON A LOW HILL JUST A
few miles outside of Volubilis. It was hidden from view
within the thick vegetation growing in tight knots around its
hem, so visitors had to keep close to the track. Torches lit the
main entrance into the pit, and many archways and steps had
been carved into the grey-blue limestone. When the small
group arrived, a slave met them at the gate and led them to
the guests' balcony where Crassus welcomed them. He was a
hard-looking man, Keara thought, with a nose like a knife and
eyes like flints. There was also something strangely familiar
about his shape.

Speaking Latin, Crassus told Titus to take his dog off
to one of the cages lining the pit below. Titus bowed and
Sapho obediently followed. Crassus then led Keara off to a
seat beside him. She was not sure what they were going to
watch this evening and did not dare ask questions. Young
female slaves brought them drinks and honeyed delicacies
which Keara accepted with caution, miming Junius and Greer
in their manners. Greer, she knew, was a well-travelled man
since he had travelled all over the known world in his youth
and understood the basics of many different languages and
the lores of different cultures and religions.

'Is your brother joining us this evening?' Junius asked their host.

'No, no,' Crassus murmured. 'He was never one for violence... that is, he cannot watch it. He is on the estate with his olives and his cases, no doubt.'

'But it was you, at the bathhouse, who said that your brother was interested in investing in the Britannic dog.'

'But I can choose for the both of us. This is my quarry and these are my games,' Crassus answered, before falling silent as the lanterns were dimmed to announce the beginning of the games, and a libation was made to the three gods of Jupiter, Neptune and Mars. In the twilight, all that could be heard was the creaking of metal hinges as the gates were opened onto the pit below. This was followed by the clacking of hooves into the arena. There was a low battery of drums as the lights flared bright again to reveal the scene in the quarry: a large, black bull stood before a slab of rock in one corner of the arena where he was pawing the hard, dusty ground in evident bad temper. Three men had also been released into the enclosed space and were armed with weapons. One had a net and trident, another had several long spikes, whilst a third had ... nothing. He looked quite lost, wearing his leather headgear with just a small, bright copper shield and a short stick. He dropped both and started to run to the wall. The crowd was laughing and booing as the bull began to canter in the direction of the fleeing man who was so obviously overweight and overdressed.

The second man, who was far younger and more agile than the running clot, began to sprint in the direction of the monstrous bull and, just as the animal turned his head to meet its assailant, the man somersaulted over the back of the bull, planting one of his pikes into its flanks. Then running off, jumping between several rocks, the man turned to meet the bull head-on, a second time, in order to vault over its back again and leave a second spike in its side. Blood was streaming down the animal's flank, but the pain only made the brute fiercer and wilder as it turned to meet its third assailant.

'I have never seen this game before,' Keara whispered to Titus who had rejoined them. 'What is happening? And why is that other man just running and hiding all the time?'

'These games were introduced during the reign of Claudius because they were originally cheaper than the gladiatorial games, but they are thought to be just as entertaining because of the baiting and the acrobatics. The running clot is added in order to give the crowd some comic relief. He is also meant to distract the bull in case one of the two baiters is in danger, but, judging from his size and evident age, he wouldn't have much chance himself there.' Leaning across Keara to speak to Crassus, Titus asked, 'How are these men selected for your games?'

'They are mining slaves from the quarry who have chosen to fight in the arena in order to try and win their freedom.'

'Even the buffoon? He doesn't stand a chance.'

'But he is making the crowd laugh, is he not?' Crassus wheezed with laughter, as the clot stumbled on his long robe and tried to cry out, but evidently had no tongue to speak.

'What happened to his tongue?' Titus asked in a tone of apparent disinterest.

'One of the foremen of the quarry cut it out when he criticised the Emperor. As one of the city magistrates I had to make an example of him, so I ordered the punishment.'

Keara held her own tongue and suddenly pinched it with two fingers to make sure it was still there.

'You have a comic wife yourself, Titus,' Crassus laughed, 'but I wouldn't cut her tongue out for I am sure her voice is too sweet.'

Keara smiled demurely at their host and had to bite her

tongue this time in order to stop herself from speaking and betraying her Britannic accent. She returned her eyes to the fight below. The bull was tiring, but his temper was just as fierce as the two hunters circled him and he swung his head from one to the other. At the far end of the quarry the clot could be seen crouching on the top of a rock for safety. The bull had also seen him and suddenly began cantering in his direction, having identified him as the weakest link. In sudden panic the large man stood up, but in doing so he trod on a corner of his tunic, which made him lose his balance and fall backwards. Before he even had time to roll over and pull himself up, the bull had reached him and begun to headbutt him on the ground, stamping on his body with his hooves before flipping the man up in the air with his horns and crushing him against the hard rock. The other two fighters ran over to distract him and continue the fight whilst the poor, lifeless body was dragged from the quarry by other slaves.

The games continued. Suddenly, Titus stiffened as though struck by a thought or doubt. He put his arm around Keara's shoulders and spoke in a loud whisper, 'Keara, my dear. You should have told me that you don't feel well. Let me take you home.'

'I...,' Keara began to protest when she felt Titus pinch her. 'It is the morning sickness ... again ... but in the evening,' she exclaimed in a weak voice.

'I shall make our excuses to our host and escort you home.' Titus turned to Crassus in order to take their leave. 'I must apologise for this sudden disturbance. I know the games will continue for many hours and I will try to return once my wife is safely at home with our household in the city. Greer and Junius, you must stay here and enjoy the games and the prophetic readings with our host.'

Before Crassus had time to protest, Titus already had Keara standing and leaning on his shoulder. He thanked Crassus profusely and said that if he could not return later he would return another day in order for the city magistrate to view his Britannic dog.

'Yes,' Junius reassured Crassus, 'Titus and his wife are with me for a few more days yet. Let me have another glass of your spiced Mauretanian wine and we can enjoy the rest of the festivities to celebrate the waxing of the light.'

Descending the shallow steps in the rock Titus led Keara to the cages and released Sapho.

'We must find that clot of a man,' Titus said.

'Isn't he a little dead?' Keara pulled a face.

Titus looked into the caves where supplies, tools and weapons were being stored, and where other fighters were preparing for their stage appearances. One cave was being used as a makeshift infirmary and charnel house. Sapho seemed particularly keen on exploring that.

'Stay here with Sapho,' Titus ordered her. 'I need to find out who the man was.'

Keara had no intention of staying put, but it was clear that Sapho had to be kept away from the bones. She led the hound out of the caverns and through the quarry gates to where their horses were tethered. With the cloak of darkness upon her, and Sapho's warm fur coat beside her, Keara felt safe waiting outside the hollow hill despite the roars and screams coming from within. There was soon some other movement on the track leaving the theatre, as the gate was reopened to allow a low-sided cart through. The cart driver whipped the mule on so that it would trot a little faster away down the road. A moment later Titus joined Keara.

'That slave is driving to the Africanus estate. We have to follow him.'

'Did you find out who the clot is?' Keara asked as she pulled herself into her saddle to follow Titus.

'No. The physician had already cut the body up to feed the animals, but his head is in that wagon.'

'His head? Did you see it?'

'No. I saw its masked head placed in a bag and tossed to that slave who has been told to take it to the Africanus estate. I know this land well. We can follow the river. This way.' He pulled his reins tight and began to trot across a sanded ridge down to the river bank. Keara and Sapho followed, stepping behind Titus along the water's edge. They soon arrived at the feet of some clustered dark trees whose gnarled roots clawed at the dry earth and whose knuckled fingers could trip up the unwary horseman. Titus pulled some weapons from his saddle bags and passed a dagger to Keara. She pulled off her long, silk stola to reveal her under garments of trousers and tunic. She then rolled up her robe and placed it in the saddle bag, leaving her horse tethered to a tree. Titus scribbled out a message which he placed in his saddle bag before dispatching his own horse, hoping it would find its way back to Volubilis. With Sapho between them, they made their own way through the grizzled tongues of olive trees towards the Roman villa.

After watching the villa for some time, Titus still seemed uncertain. 'It is too quiet,' he whispered at last. 'Where are the watchmen and guards to protect the estate?'

'Would they be visible at night?' Keara asked.

'To me, yes.' Titus sounded irritated, and a little annoyed with himself for losing his finer senses. 'Ssh,' he pulled Keara to the ground as the cart could be heard rattling its great wooden wheels up the drive and round to the side of the villa where two large doors lay open onto the gardens. A faint, soft glow came from within but this was darkened as a silhouette came to the door and took the parcel that was held out to him by the carter. The silhouette withdrew and the carter turned the mule around in order to lead the wagon away.

Telling Sapho to stay and stand guard in the trees, Keara and Titus slipped up to the open doorway, half-crouching as they stayed within the shadows from the trees, and ran across the moist, freshly watered lawn. Standing on either side of the entrance, they peered into the orange-lit room. It was a richly decorated library with shelves upon shelves of parchments and ancient tomes lining the walls. Several candle lamps illuminated the comfort of the room with fine grey-blue mosaics laid out on the floor – limestone from the quarry. Rare citrus wood made up the shelves, and an ornate wooden desk stood with chairs before the fire at the end of the room. In the back wall, a white marble fireplace had been lit to add a delicate warmth and perfume to such a mild winter. The fire was fed with the compressed and dried remains from the production of olive derivatives on the estate, products which included oil for bathing, lighting, medicines and cooking, and no doubt accounted for the briny scent of fruity almonds on the air. To one side of the fireplace, a deep sofa and armchairs had been placed with soft embroidered cushions and wraps.

Titus looked at Keara. He held a finger to his lips and made a sign for them to enter together. As they crept into the room, Keara noted a large pile of papers on the desk along with some parchments and a marble paperweight in the form of Justitia, the Roman goddess of justice. Justitia held a pair of scales in one hand and a detachable paper-knife in the other. However, as Keara glanced up at the fireplace, she stopped dead in her tracks for there, on the mantelpiece, perched the visible remains of a decapitated head. Its headwear had been taken off and a tiny stream of blood still flowed from the neck and open mouth, running slowly down the marble column.

Titus had already recognised the head and frowned at her, indicating that she must go forward. It was only when they were halfway across the room that Keara noticed a bronze framed mirror placed above the fireplace, and within it the reflection of a seated man whose heavy eyes hung upon her. She breathed in sharply as the man stood up and slowly turned to face them.

'I have been viewing my latest oeuvre.' The man before them tore his eyes away from the dull, dead eyes and fat lips of a man Keara knew as a Roman dignitary from Britannia, that of Catus, the Procurator.

'Vettius,' she cried in startled horror. 'What are you doing here?'

The man moved around the table, picking up the paper-knife as he went, and he gave them a slow, caustic smile. 'I came to hunt him down, of course,' he responded, pointing at the head with the knife. 'As an agent of the Emperor I was sent to arrest him and find the tax money that he stole from Nero.' He paused. 'I might now ask you the same thing. Titus and you are dead, of course. Lost at sea, so Suetonius believes.'

'We were freed by my Caledonian family.' Keara lifted her chin. 'They destroyed a few Roman galleys and came for me so that I could find Catus, the man responsible for the loss of,' she breathed deeply, 'everything I have ever known.'

'Mmm,' Vettius hummed. 'With the loss of those Roman ships, Suetonius is now in Nero's bad books and has been recalled to Rome, on the recommendations of Nero's imperial secretary, Polyclitus; a pretext only, of course, since the Governor was only creating more problems in the province. His severe measures of control had caused all revenues to dry up, and peace could not be maintained. Polyclitus understood this, so recommended his removal.' He breathed in deeply, evidently enjoying this moment of centre stage, before resuming his descant.

'Polyclitus is a man who has done well for himself: once a slave and now a freedman and close confidant of the Emperor himself. I know what it feels like to play second fiddle, just as you must, Keara, being only the second child of Prasutagus and Voada.' Vettius's voice sounded bitter now and even a little impassioned, but he was interrupted by Titus's voice, 'The Roman traitor has no tongue and was sent into the games to die and be fed to the animals. Why such a silent and anonymous death if you were meant to arrest him?'

'Arrest him?' Vettius placed a hand on his heart in dramatic astonishment. 'Such was not my intention. You see all this wealth and these lands? They belong to my older brother, Crassus. He was adopted by the rich and influential senator in Rome, Africanus, who had no issue. He was educated as the man's son and head of his *gens*, in order to maintain the Africanus's family cult. What did I have to inherit? Nothing but the law and my wits.' He pressed his lips together falling into melancholy silence.

Clarity showed in Titus's next question, 'This was *your* plan all along? You and Catus worked together, and he came here, *safe* on your brother's estate and under his protection, shortly joined by you.'

'Certainly,' Vettius responded, 'but I did not expect to be joined by you, Titus or you, Keara – until tonight that is.'

'Why tonight?' Keara asked, still confused by the turn of events.

'The Britannic hound gave you away. My brother told me that Junius had the dog and some unknown guests staying with him in Volubilis and that you were going to the games this evening for the festivities. The carter gave me a message from Crassus saying that you had left the games *in precipitous*.

The rest is history... And it shall remain so. I prefer history to remember you both as lost at sea. Guards,' he called loudly, and suddenly a number of armed men moved into the library from a corner door and from the garden.

Titus looked at Keara indicating that she should follow his lead. Then he held his hands up in submission recognising the inequality of the fight, but wished to pose one final question, 'Why kill the Procurator if you were working together?'

'Isn't it obvious?' Vettius shrugged his shoulders. 'He was good at numbers and was a good finance man, so he had his part to play in this ambitious enterprise. But the man was a greedy and lascivious fool, and a highly conspicuous one, as you have noted with his trail of breadcrumbs from Londinium to Volubilis. With him out of the way, I keep everything.'

'Including his head,' Keara noted.

Vettius threw back his head and laughed. 'It is my own breadcrumb to a Briton like yourself. I knew you would follow such a trophy. Now,' he said, stepping back a little, 'if you will forgive me, I do not like bloodshed so I will leave you to your executioners.' He turned on his heels and left the library.

Keara and Titus moved towards the fireplace, putting the desk and sofa between themselves and their attackers. Titus pulled the brass mirror from the wall and pressed it into Keara's hand so that she could wrap her fingers around the rope on its back. Then they stepped closer together, back-to-back, and raised their weapons – two short daggers – as their assailants moved in. The first metal struck upon metal, and Titus and Keara were hard-pressed to keep the sword thrusts off, but Titus was a more experienced soldier. Picking up the fire poker, he quickly disarmed the first guard. Moving in closely, he passed the man's sword to Keara. Only too glad to exchange a dagger for a sword she began a more equal fight.

'Thank you,' she shouted over her shoulder, 'and thank you for protecting me in Britannia.'

Astonished that Keara should choose such a moment to thank him for his gesture in Britannia he half-turned to look at her face. He took a nick to his left shoulder. As he bent down, clutching his arm, Keara rolled over his back and stabbed a guardsman in the stomach. In doing so, however, Catus's head began to rock on the mantelpiece and then took a plunge to the floor. Titus kicked it into the fire.

'Keep an eye on your back,' Keara cried, taunting him. 'Wherever did you learn to fight?'

Titus was snarling now. Piqued by Keara's words and wild fighting, he redoubled his attack and the two worked themselves around the table making for the garden. Many guardsmen fell: from knife wounds, broken necks and skulls. One had even taken a rabbit punch to the throat and was dead before he hit the floor. Yet, it was too much for Keara. She was breathing heavily and they were being pushed back hard against the desk. The desk toppled over and many of the manuscripts rolled into the fire. The papers turned yellow, orange, red, burning alongside Catus's head of hair. The attack continued, but Keara was visibly tiring. She was struck in the side by a blade and began to bleed.

'And we've only been married a few days,' she panted. 'Where are we going for our nuptial idyll? The River Styx?'

'Neither of us is dying today.'

'Leave me Titus and save yourself.'

Suddenly, Keara was struck from his side and took another sword wound – to the leg. Falling to the ground, she rolled onto her back and held up her girded arms to ward off the falling blades.

'I will never leave you,' Titus screamed fending off the blows. His snarl was suddenly joined by another, fiercer snarl:

that of Sapho who had finally disobeyed Keara's command to stay put, and had come crashing into the room. The animal's sheer size and brute animosity put the very fear of the gods into the guardsmen. Those who turned their weapons onto the dog were immediately disarmed, literally, and were finished off by Sapho's clawed paws and blood-drenched jaws. The few that were left tried to leave, but were prevented by the renewed attack from Titus and Keara.

'Good girl,' Keara called, stroking Sapho's blood-spattered mane of fur. 'Now we must find Vettius and the Iceni gold.' Keara nodded to Titus as they took the door that Vettius had left by, but not before Titus had had a quick look at Keara's stomach wound and injured leg.

'It's alright,' he breathed, relieved. 'Both are superficial: you'll live.' He quickly tied a strip of linen around Keara's leg and pressed a swab of cloth onto her stomach. 'Now let's find Vettius,' he said, gripping her shoulder.

In the darkly lit corridors, it was difficult to make out the plan of the villa. Keara re-entered the library which was being consumed in flames. She picked up a scarf from the back of an overturned chair and returned to the hallway where she told Sapho to sniff it and find the owner. The ominous huntress began snuffling loudly as she shuffled across the floor swinging her snout from side to side. It was evident that the scent was everywhere and from time to time Titus and Keara came across one or two Africanus slaves who were not at the games, but they would scuttle away, running out of the villa and away from the flames. At last, Sapho led them into a small, stone-flagged chamber, which evidently served as the family sanctuary to the Roman gods of Jupiter, Juno and Minerva. Sapho scampered up to the altar and jumped onto the slab of stone. She then jumped off it, dropping her head to the floor

once again as she moved rapidly to the back of the altar. She
started to bark, scratching at one large marble flagstone.

'This is their safety box,' Titus breathed, taking in the size
and shadows of the room.

'How do you know?'

'It is the place where all senatorial and equestrian families
have a cellar where they may keep the valuables they don't
want to keep in a bank.'

'Does it mean that the gold and silver of my tribe are there?'

'It means that Vettius is there.' Titus's mouth drew into a
harsh line as he leant down and pressed a dagger into the crack
of the stone but the stone was difficult to lift. The floor showed
some signs of rub where the stone had been pulled over the
floor and slid into the opening. There was a sudden commotion
behind, but Sapho did not growl. She simply strolled over to the
new entrants and almost purred with delight.

'Zia and Aelius,' Titus exclaimed. 'I'm glad you got my
message and were able to find us.'

'With the roof of the villa in flames I imagine that the
whole of the provincial military will be able to find you.'
Despite the lightness of Zia's words, he was anxious. 'We must
leave now.'

'No!' cried Keara. 'We cannot leave until we have Vettius.
He's in that hole. Help us lift the stone.'

Zia and Aelius moved forward and added their daggers to
that of Titus's. They were able to heave the stone up and reveal
a dark, square entrance. Stone steps descended into a pit.
Glancing at Keara with a nod, Titus took a burning brand from
the wall and descended into the hole, immediately followed by
Keara, Sapho and the other two. They found themselves in a
low and narrow passageway that sloped downwards towards
the river. They had to crouch as they followed the passage
towards the faint sound of running water.

'I thought you said this was a safety box,' Keara spoke, as she followed Titus's dark back.

'It is.' Titus stood upright as they came into a small cave. Sparkling in the light of the torch, blocks of gold and silver lay stacked on the ledges of rock surrounding them. Keara and the men stared in wonder at all this wealth.

'This is more than just the Iceni gold.' Keara picked up a bar with unknown symbols on it.

'It is Baquate gold,' Titus said with interest, looking at the bar in her hands. 'It has the stamp of my tribe on it. This must be bribe money that Crassus has been accepting in exchange for free range of the lowlands in winter. As city magistrate, he was certainly in a good position for backhanders.'

'Why do the Baquates have to descend into the Lowlands in winter?' Keara was puzzled.

'Not all the tribe does, but some have to come down in order to graze their goats.' Titus raised his torch high scanning the cave for any movement but there was only a damp stillness to the air. 'There is tension between the herdsmen of my tribe and the sedentary settlers of the plains. It is the job of the magistrates to keep the peace.' He paused. Then he spoke quietly to Zia and Aelius sending them back up the passageway to the villa. 'This way,' Titus said to Keara turning the brand towards another opening where the sudden sound of grating rock could be heard and a draught of warmer air almost extinguished the flame. He stepped across the uneven face of rock and held the light to the opening.

'It leads down to the river.'

'Where have you sent Zia and Aelius?'

'They have another mission, and if Vettius returns to the villa they are to meet him and kill him.'

They continued a short distance in silence and immediately came face to face with a wall of rock. They could hear the river on the other side, but there was no apparent way out until Sapho began scrabbling at the wall to one side. Titus held the torch up as Keara probed the cracks in it with her fingers. 'There seems to be some sort of round rock here,' she gasped, trying to move it.

'Here, you hold the light whilst I try.' Titus pushed the brand into Keara's hand and tried to shift the large stone. It trembled a little in its socket and then began to roll quite easily to one side.

'It's like a sliding door,' Titus breathed as the rock stopped against the trunk of an olive tree outside. Titus stooped to pass through the opening and he stepped immediately onto the bed of the river, ankle-deep in fresh, mountain water.

'Pass me the torch so you can follow,' Titus said. As Keara passed him the brand, there was a sudden movement from above and a rock fell from the embankment, hitting Titus on the head and knocking the torch out of his hand. The light was immediately extinguished in the waters, and Titus fell unconscious into the river. Keara scampered out of the cave and passed between the split trunk of an old olive tree. She was met by the well-built and well-kept form of Vettius who had jumped down from his hiding place in the embanked branches of the tree and glowered in the translucent light of the crescent moon. He held the paper-knife in his hand and had an irritated smile on his face.

'By the gods, you're a hard one to kill off,' he complained. He raised his arm and the knife sparkled a moment against the night sky.

Keara blocked his arm thrust with her sword, saying, 'Do you think your sword of justice can harm me now?' She looked at the animal standing by her side and in a slow, quiet voice she gave the command, 'Sapho, attack!'

Vettius had not seen the animal until now and taken by

surprise could only register a mild expression of discontent as he opened his mouth to speak, but instead of words only rapid sprays of blood came out between his teeth. The hound was already at his throat tearing the man's jaw and jugular vein. Such fountains of dark ink rapidly spread and discoloured the pure waters of the river. Vettius's small dagger, the sword of justice, dropped useless from his fingers before the man fell to his knees and clutched his throat trying to stem the flow of blood. Calling off Sapho, Keara approached the condemned man and watched his desperate struggle to hold on to life. She weighed her sword in her hands as though it were a precious bolt of Zeus's vengeful lightning. Then she plunged it into his stomach.

'That is for my mother, for my sister, and for my people. I shall take back what is ours and you shall die an anonymous death out here, alone, just food for the carrion.' Withdrawing her sword, she kicked the man into the deeper streams calling, 'May the gods have mercy on you in the Underworld.'

The man was convulsing in death, but this sight inspired no pity in Keara's heart: she had seen enough of death's many faces over the last year, and this one man deserved many deaths. Vettius's eyes bulged in pain and fear until the man inside the waxen frame disappeared and the eyes became vacant counters of listless ebony. There was sudden silence. The body would be carried by the currents out across the plains where the wild, hungry beasts roamed at night. By morning there would be nothing left of it. Sheathing her sword Keara ran back to Titus. Sapho was already licking his face. Face-up in the water, he was still breathing and the dog's fierce breath seemed to be reviving the man. He stirred slightly, then sat up clutching his aching head.

'What in Hades just happened? Are you alright, Keara?'

Keara dropped to her knees in the water and threw her arms around him so tightly that he could hardly breathe.

'Easy, easy,' he complained, 'or you'll have my head off –
again.'

The wheels of a cart could be heard descending the
embankment and splashing into water. Then a man jumped
off whilst another brought the mule to a halt. It was Zia and
Aelius. Zia limped over to them and helped Titus to his feet.
'Sire, what just happened to you? Did the lady knock you
over?' His white teeth could be seen clearly as he gave Keara a
broad grin.

'You'll have to ask the lady that,' Titus whistled. 'I was out
cold, and don't remember much of the evening; everything
seems to be a jumble of sounds and images.'

'Do not accuse me of anything,' she cried, more dismayed
by Titus's loss of memory than any light accusation. 'I and
Sapho just saved your life. It was Vettius who hit you with a
rock.'

'And where is that Roman bastard?' Titus cried. 'Did you
let him go?'

'Yes, I let his body go, his dead body that is. Sapho cut his
throat, and I got his gut.'

Titus looked at the excited and bedraggled animal
scampering back and forth in the water beside them, before
turning to Keara.

'How long was I out for?'

'Not very long: one or two minutes only.'

'Well now, we have work to do.' He looked anxiously at
the crimson light to be seen on the other side of the olive
grove. The villa was all ablaze now and too far from Volubilis
for the city's firemen to be of any assistance. He turned to
the mouth of the cave and gave orders to Zia and Aelius to
help him load the cart. 'We are going to take the Africanus
wealth and return it to its rightful owners, but we'll have
to work fast. Crassus must have seen the flames from the

quarry and will be on his way. You did send a message to Greer and Junius, eh Zia?'

'Yes, I did. If they get my message, they'll be waiting for us in the mountains.'

Titus tapped Zia on the shoulder, then bent down and disappeared into the mouth of the cave. They all followed him. Within a short time, the cart was loaded. Titus and Aelius rolled the rock back into place, hidden behind the branches of the olive tree, and then went to fetch Keara's horse, still tethered further along the river. Zia led the mule and cart over the river crossing, followed by the three riders and Sapho. A fourth horse had been tethered behind the cart and trotted along with the small group.

'Where does this route go?' Keara asked Titus, riding beside her.

'It follows the river up into the mountains. Once we are through those trees, on the edge of this low plateau, we will begin climbing into the Baquate highlands. Already, by crossing the river, we have passed into the Free Lands of the Baquates. The river marks the frontier zone.'

'Won't Crassus come after us once he has found the treasure gone?'

Titus smiled, then winced at the pain in his head. 'He wouldn't dare. He will stay on Roman land. And besides, the fire will blaze for hours before he is able to enter the villa.'

'What about the back entrance to the altar room? Won't he try that?'

'He will check it, but it only opens from the inside and we have blocked it. We jammed it, so again, it will take hours to clear.' He looked at her with incredulity. 'Do you think me incapable of dealing with any crisis?'

XVI

The Middle Atlas Mountains

A LITTLE LATER, A JAGGED LINE OF PEAKS AND valleys could be distinguished against the faint glow of light in the East. The welcome sun rose quickly, warming their chilled bones. Looking into the distance Keara admired the beauty of the silent dawn. Snow-clad mountains began to enfold them and when they reached the valley of the first outlying mountain they could hear horses on the path far behind them. Titus made a sign for them to leave the cart and to withdraw from the road. With arrows fixed on the approaching horsemen, they only lowered their bows once the riders had reached them: it was Junius and Greer. Titus and the others stepped from the rocks back onto the track and welcomed the two men.

'What has been happening in our absence?' Titus asked Junius, as Greer gave Keara a relieved embrace.

'Crassus is still fighting the flames at his villa. He seemed more anxious about the destruction of his sacred altar room than the loss of his brother in the fire.'

'I will tell you everything,' Titus said as he saw Junius's eyes upon the cart, 'but first, how did you manage to get away?'

'We simply said that we could do no more to help and would return to the city. We thanked him for a most enjoyable evening and left.'

'Ha!' scoffed Titus. 'As though he would let you go so easily.'

'You are right,' Junius sighed. 'We simply absconded. I left a message with one of the slaves, saying that we had returned to my mother's household.'

'And will she be safe?'

'Yes. I sent a message telling her to stay with a neighbour until it is calmer. Now, what has been happening to you?' He was looking with rounded eyes at the wagon load of gold and silver that Greer had just uncovered.

'This includes all the Iceni wealth and the Baquate gold that Crassus and Vettius had *acquired*. We are taking it back to its rightful owners.' With these words, Titus jumped into his saddle and pulled on the reins. 'Let us continue.' He scowled for a moment. 'We don't know if Crassus would dare send men after us. Only mercenaries would be fool enough, but we have a day's ride ahead and the cart is not fast.'

'No,' murmured Zia, 'it's the slowest cart this side of the Roman Empire, and I'm not sure its wheels will hold out.' He cracked the whip, jerk-starting the mule into a very slow plod. 'I'm not sure my nerves will hold out at this rate either,' he added.

Climbing higher into the mountains, the river they had been retracing became a stream and then disappeared altogether. They stopped to rest the horses for a moment and check the cuts Titus and Keara had taken in the villa. The wounds were clean, but Keara needed a few stitches to her side and leg. Greer tended her this time whilst Titus rested his bruised head against a rock. Next to him, Zia began looking through his bags until he found a small pouch which he passed to Titus. Titus opened his eyes and carefully unfolded the cloth. Then he stared respectfully at its precious contents: two skilfully crafted ornaments. He placed the first one on his left shoulder: a highly visible and decorated amulet of the Baquate people. It was a silver brooch depicting an open right hand with an eye in the middle, which would protect the wearer from the evil eye, but it was the second amulet, with the triple dotted crescent moon, that marked him as a nobleman. He attached this to the front of his jerkin.

As they continued on their way, the temperature dropped. Here and there, goats would scamper off the track and a lone herdsman would bow in respect as Titus passed, recognising him as a Baquate prince. The day passed, and the sun was beginning to sink in the west when they found themselves passing isolated low-built stone houses. As they travelled further into the mountain pass the number of buildings increased, bustling together on the terraces of snow-speckled scree. At last, they had to abandon the wagon and animals in the dry, stone shelters by the wayside, where a number of Baquate guards were on duty. They continued the rest of the way on foot. The road became a narrow path and many people started to appear on the way, welcoming Titus and Aelius back into their village. The presence of Greer, Zia, and Keara with a huge dog at her side incited curiosity, along with discreet and fearful glances.

At length, a man of middle years came to join the crowd. He emerged from a stone building, shadowed by two other men, and descended the steps where he embraced Titus and Aelius after him. 'It is good to see you, my nephew,' he breathed softly, smiling at Titus. 'After all these years you return to the fold. Come, follow me with your friends. Even the great hound is welcome in my home. You must eat, drink, rest and tell me your stories.'

With one arm round Titus's shoulders, he led his nephew back up the steps to his house. The others followed, as did a number of children, curious to know more about the strangers.

'You are a welcome sight for sore eyes, my uncle,' Titus began. 'Our journey has been long, but it is not over yet. Have you heard from my men on the ship I left on the Atlantic Coast?'

'Yes, they are all here with their families in the different hamlets in the mountains. Your ship has been left in one of my ports, just beyond the Roman border: a nice Roman galley, by all accounts.'

Watching them from behind Keara marvelled at the resemblance between the two men: broad shoulders, a heavy brow and keen, sharp eyes. Keara had not yet been introduced, but it was clear that Titus's uncle was the tribe's chieftain, judging by his richly embroidered kaftan of dark blue silk. He also wore a pair of loose trousers and a long, sleeveless jacket made from goat skin and hair. The small group followed the two men through the low entrance into one large open room. Titus's uncle immediately gave orders for food to be prepared whilst he, himself, poured out glasses of warm spicy wine. He told them to be seated on the cushions and rugs spread out over the floor before he gave a libation of wine, thanking the gods for their safe arrival.

Sitting beside Titus he said, 'My nephew, are you not going to introduce us?'

The mouth of Titus twitched as he began, 'This is Tuccuda, my uncle, and King of the Baquates. My father was king before him and now Tuccuda is the elected leader. Tuccuda, my lord, this is the Princess Keara of the Iceni clan in Britannia where I have been working for the past few years. This is Greer, the druid priest of her people. They have escaped from the destruction of their people by the Roman army, following the death of their king, Keara's father. This is Zia, a Dacian slave and my manservant.' Here, Zia gave a gruff cough at which Titus glared at him and Zia responded with, 'If only looks could kill!'

Titus picked up where he had left off, 'This is Sapho, Keara's Britannic hound and guard dog.'

'And of us two,' Zia grumbled, 'which one do you think is the dogsbody.'

Keara laughed quietly, as Titus finished with, 'Junius you know, of course.'

Tuccuda looked keenly at the small group. 'Your men from the galley have told me a lot of your story, but what has been happening in Volubilis?'

Titus gave him a detailed account and, when he had finished, Tuccuda conferred a warm smile on them. 'The return of Baquate gold is much appreciated and will help us continue the resistance movement against Roman incursions into our land. Your return is also much appreciated as, too, is that of your men. I understand from your papers that you and the Princess Keara are now man and wife. Is that correct?'

'No, no,' Titus and Keara protested together. 'That was our disguise for Volubilis.'

'And a very convincing one,' Junius and Zia threw in. Titus frowned at them both, avoiding Keara's eye for the moment.

'Well, since we have our own priest, and the Princess Keara has hers, there is no reason why we cannot formalise the ties with a Baquate and Iceni marriage,' Tuccuda said, at which Titus stood up, glaring at his uncle.

'The Princess Keara and I will not be part of any political union, and I will only marry a woman of her own free will. What is more, Keara is returning to Caledonia with her people's wealth in order for them to continue their own movement against the Romans.'

'Sit down, Titus,' Tuccuda laughed. 'Let us enjoy this moment first: one of reunions, a homecoming, and a gathering of friends and family.'

Dishes of hot food were brought in and placed on the floor before the chieftain and his guests. Steaming plates of lamb and fig stew scented with spices attracted the eyes and noses of everyone present and for a few moments there was no more talk of politics, violence, death and marriage.

Later that evening, in the darkness and cold that fell early, Keara excused herself in order to take the air and walk with Sapho on the mountain slopes. Leaving the hut, one of Tuccuda's guards gave her a fur wrap to wear. Tuccuda also indicated to Titus to shadow her, to which Keara replied, 'I have my own protection,' and she stroked Sapho's muzzle and mane. Keara followed her dearest beast up the stony path to the top of a mountain crest. Sapho snuffled her way up. Keara thought she, herself, must be equally noisy, as she panted the last stretch across a flat ridge. There, she found a low stone wall which barred the way and stopped the sheep and goats from plunging down a sheer escarpment. Keara sat on the wall and looked below into the depths of blackness. Above, she looked up at the brightness of the celestial vault: winking stars studded the heavens and she thought back to the comet of the year before which had crossed the skies announcing the death of an Iceni king and the storm that was to follow. All had come to pass. Suddenly she saw a single light above which threaded its way across the sky until it disappeared in a profusion of tiny sparks.

'You must make a wish now,' a voice spoke from behind her.

'I have,' Keara answered, 'for a shooting star is rare to see, and it only gives one wish upon its death.'

Titus stepped up to the wall and sat down beside her.

Sapho wandered off and lay down outside a small mountain cot.

'Why did you protect me?' Keara asked.

There was silence for a long moment. Then Titus answered, 'I was there only to feed back information to my uncle and my people about Roman manoeuvres, their military strengths and weak points. I was to gain their trust and work my way up the military ladder. I was not to interfere or to intervene in affairs that did not concern my tribe. I was meant only to obey the Roman orders in foreign lands.' He paused. 'But as a man, there are some things I cannot do. I did not know this about myself until I met you. When I saw your terror, your hate, your pride, and courage too, I hesitated. When you held a knife to your own throat and said you would rather die, I knew it was true. You would have slit your own throat rather than suffer the humiliation and annihilation of rape. It was then that I fell in love with you. And I have not stopped loving you since. You are everything to me and I would willingly obey my uncle in marrying you... but I will never force you to do something that is against your will.' He placed his hand over her hand and gathered it up, pressing his warm lips against her fingers. Keara was silent, thinking back to her refusal of her cousin's proposal and her promise never to marry.

'Your fingers are cold, and we are both very tired. We should go back.' Titus suddenly sounded a little curt. Taking her silence for a refusal, he placed her hand back on the wall.

Keara turned her eyes on him and then rolled her hand over so that their palms were joined, and she felt the warmth of his hand press through her. 'Tell me first: how did you know how to trick the Roman medic who examined me afterwards?'

'Here in Mauretania, one of my uncles was a doctor. I lived with him for a while, and helped him sometimes, until I was sent to Rome. There were some things I was not meant to learn whilst I was with him, but I read a lot of his books.'

'About female anatomy?'

'Well,' Titus remarked, smiling playfully, 'I was a curious young boy.'

Keara tapped her shoulder against him as though to admonish him. 'And where is your uncle now?'

'He is no more, but his death was a natural one: old age and drink. And can I ask you one thing? Why did you trust me with your knife?'

'I don't know,' Keara smiled faintly. 'I really don't know.'

Titus rose and pulled Keara up too.

'No,' Keara protested. 'I don't want to go back to the village. Just for one moment I would like to be away from everything and everyone. Can't we stay here?'

'Yes, we can.' Titus smiled at her inclusion of himself and tugged her over to the mud-brick cot. 'But we must stay within these walls and protect ourselves from the mountain winds and cold night dew.'

Inside the tiny cot a man could not stand up straight, but one corner contained a small chimney for a fire. There were also some wraps folded on a shelf.

'What is this place?' Keara asked.

'I'm sure you have the same in Caledonia. There are many of these cots over the mountains and they are mostly for the shepherds who guard the goats in winter. Sometimes, even the goats take shelter here, although it would become a bit squashed as it's really only meant for one man. Here, take these.' He passed her the fur wraps to lay on the floor. 'I'll get some wood for the fire.'

He was not gone for long. When he returned he came back in with Sapho. In his arms he carried a pile of logs and some smaller branches for the fire and he immediately knelt down to light it. The fireplace had not been used for some time, so it took a moment to get the blaze going, but once the fire was steady the cot warmed up quickly. It was too warm for Sapho who left them alone in front of the flames.

'It's good to be on the same side of the fire for once,' Titus joked.

Keara smiled sadly remembering the burning flames of her mother's crusade. She clutched Titus's arm and rested her head on his shoulder. He stroked her crop of hair, which was beginning to grow back thick and lush. He inhaled its soft perfume of thyme oil, which now mixed with the scent of oak from the smoke. 'You should never have cut your hair,' he scolded. 'You had such beautiful hair.'

'But no good for fighting. I was angry and didn't want to be beautiful.'

'You are still beautiful, and will always be beautiful.' He bent his head down and kissed the threads of her hair between his fingers. He could not resist raising her face to his and kissing her. Then he lay down on the floor and drew her down to him.

In the vague dimness of the early hours, Titus rose naked from the fur wraps of their bed and stoked up the fire. Then, he woke Keara, who lay warm and snug in the land of dreams, and he whispered in her ear, 'There is something we must watch together before we go back to the village.'

She wanted to argue, to stay there forever, but knew that she could not. Wrapped in nothing but their blankets Titus led Keara outside to the stone wall and made her sit down beside him. Enveloped in the warm furs, and shortly joined by Sapho, they waited in the darkness. Very soon the distant sky in the east began to reveal itself: pale colour threaded over the skyline. Light shades of orange, yellow and pink softly pierced the horizon as the top rim of the morning sun rose over the edge of the world. There was a rapid change as the sun sent bright shafts of light over the tops of mountains, the branches of trees and onto the flat plateaux, and began to warm the land.

Keara could not speak as she gazed upon this new world of beauty and promise. Birds started to chirrup and take to the skies, leaving the safe haven of the cedar branches. The goats emerged from the conifers and began to munch on the shrubs and on the dark green leaves of the abundant bushes of rock cress. Down in the valleys the water sparkled like glass reflecting the pink-blue of the sky above and then Titus broke the silence: 'I will leave all this and follow you to the ends of the earth. I would walk one thousand miles just to be with you, and I will. We are going back to Caledonia together.'

'You don't have to walk. We have a ship,' Keara chuckled, 'but, how can you leave all this? This is your land and your people.'

'My uncle is king here. His son will be elected king after him. I do not want such a world and have been away for too long. I would rather live alone in these mountains, or yours – with you.'

'We cannot live alone for the moment because we both have a responsibility towards our people. We must free them from the Roman yoke.'

Titus breathed deeply of the cold, fresh air. 'The Baquates are a free people and will always be so. The Romans cannot control the mountain regions here because they know nothing of mountain warfare. I will return to Caledonia with you and fight alongside your uncle and your family. My uncle's plan is a good one. Our two peoples can try and coordinate our movements of resistance, if possible. We will leave in a few days. But first, we have our wedding to plan.'

'Our wedding! But you haven't asked me yet!'

With this protest of discontent, Titus threw off his wrap. Bare and raw, he dropped to his knees and took Keara's hand. 'Will you kindly consider being my wife?' Titus uttered, trembling with the cold, 'but make it quick before my heart stops beating from the cold.'

Laughing, Keara threw her arms round Titus and wrapped them both in her blanket as they rolled over onto his back. Sapho gave them a doleful look and lay down, looking quite bored with the whole scene.

Acknowledgements

Thank you to my husband, Eric for his moral and technical support over the years, which include his maps. Thank you to my proofreaders for their invaluable feedback, ideas and editorial skills, and to those who have encouraged me: Miruna Craciunescu, Christine Lewis, Chantal Lévy, Willy Maley, Rosie Hutchins, Stevie Hardman, Beastie Hucklesby, Irina Hale, Ruth Reitmeier and Hugh J Keenan.

Thank you to Emmanuelle Burfin for her photographic support. Thank you, also, to Morgane Frénée for her design input and for her invaluable promotional and marketing efforts. A final thank you to Florence Monteil for her enthusiastic ideas and suggestions.

Maps©Eric Frénée

 Matador